POISONED PALMS

THE MURDER OF MRS. JANE LATHROP STANFORD

Dorothea N. Buckingham

ISLAND HERITAGE™
PUBLISHING

ISLAND HERITAGE™
P U B L I S H I N G
A DIVISION OF THE MADDEN CORPORATION

94-411 KŌʻAKI STREET, WAIPAHU, HAWAIʻI 96797
Orders: (800) 468-2800 • Information: (808) 564-8800
Fax: (808) 564-8877 • **islandheritage.com**

ISBN NO. 0-93154-813-6

Second Edition, First Printing — 2005
©2004 Island Heritage Publishing

for
Jack and Robert

⁕ PROLOGUE ⁕

Stanford University
March 24, 1905

At precisely one o'clock, the great university bell tolled. Eight student athletes approached the casket and draped it with the Stanford University ensign.

The students braced the casket against their shoulders and shuffled their feet to align their step and, in a slow, deliberate cadence, carried Mrs. Stanford's body to the waiting hearse.

Solemnly, they slid the casket into the hearse. Wood grated on steel.

The carriage master brushed the rim of his top hat. The students stepped back, and an honor guard of professors flanked the carriage. The sleeves of their robes billowed in the rain-misted wind.

The horses, shrouded in black hoods, shivered their heads and jingled their reins. The carriage master snapped his whip and the cortege began. It wound down the south valley toward Memorial Church.

Hundreds of mourners took up the somber walk. As they walked, the university bell tolled one deep stroke for each minute of their one-hour journey. Over six thousand bade her farewell—students, servants, clergy and politicians, captains of industry and impoverished faculty. They crammed the chapel and spilled into the quadrangle. Some huddled in grief, some sobbed openly. Few of them dared ask, "Who could have done such a thing?"

But the statement of the Stanford University Board of Trustees was firm: "Jane Lathrop Stanford, our Founder and Mother, died of natural causes."

Murder would not be considered.

❧ CHAPTER ONE ❧

Waikīkī
February 14, 1905

Hattie Lehua pulled a manila folder from a cubbyhole in her desk. It was labeled "Assistant to the Head of Housekeeping." She slid the position description out of the folder and reread the first requirement to apply. "Five years' experience in bookkeeping." She underlined the words twice.

She tore a sheet from a ledger and listed her experience yet one more time. No matter how hard she tried, it totaled three and a half years. She circled the numbers, bearing down on the pencil so hard she snapped the point.

Hattie had outstanding references. Her business teacher from Kamehameha School for Girls said she was "intelligent and loyal." Headmistress Brown wrote that she was "a girl of high moral standard, reliable, with unlimited potential."

What she needed was a letter from an accountant. But the only accountant she knew was her Uncle Makia, and he was an officer in the court of the deposed Queen Liliʻuokalani. Hattie was afraid to admit knowing him because Mr. St. Clair might suspect she was a Royalist sympathizer.

Mr. William St. Clair, The Palms Hotel manager, had arrived in Hawaiʻi during "the troubled times."

He was at 'Iolani Palace when the kingdom's flag was lowered and the Stars and Stripes were raised—the day the Hawaiians wept and U.S. Marines stood guard.

The night of "the Uprising," St. Clair was having dinner at a friend's home near Thomas Square. He was close enough to hear the gunshots, and he watched from the window as the wounded were carried away.

Mr. St. Clair believed everything the Annexation Committee told him, including the rumor that Queen Lili'uokalani had ordered all traitors to be beheaded. They warned him about Royalist spies infiltrating hotels; they suggested he sleep with a loaded pistol.

No, Hattie thought, she couldn't list her uncle as a reference. She was scribbling "Who else?" when Mrs. Martin knocked on the door.

"Hattie?" Mrs. Martin was the head of housekeeping. St. Clair had hired her from the St. Francis Hotel in San Francisco.

Hattie quickly shoved the folder back in a cubby. "Yes, ma'am."

Mrs. Martin cradled account ledgers in her arms. "I've been going over these entries all morning." She set the ledgers on Hattie's desk. "We spent eight dollars for new towels last month. It must be the laundry workers. They must be stealing them."

Hattie offered no defense. First of all, she knew it was useless, and secondly, she knew it could be true. Laundry workers were the lowest paid of all hotel employees.

"We had an average of twenty-six guests per day last month, and we bought sixteen towels." She jabbed at the number. "They've got to be stealing."

Hattie began, "We lost ten . . ."

Mrs. Martin held up her hand. "Please, not that story again."

Hattie had already told Mrs. Martin that Elijah Benning and his O'ahu College friends stole ten towels and two surfboards from the cabanas last month. But, they were O'ahu College boys, and the Bennings were regulars at The Palms for dinner.

"I'll speak to the laundry mistress," Hattie said.

"Mr. St. Clair wants the December books closed—today of all days. We have eleven guests from the Steamship *Korea*, and, so far, Mr. Heuish wants to be moved to a corner room, Miss Moore is suffering from seasickness, and the Stanford party hasn't arrived yet. We'll be burning the night oil tonight, Hattie."

On Boat Days, Mrs. Martin and Hattie worked long into the night.

"Bring your accounts to the front verandah. We'll work out there while we wait for Mrs. Stanford." Mrs. Martin paused at the door. Her voice softened. "You're my best girl, Hattie. I hope you know that. You'd make a fine assistant if Mr. St. Clair can be convinced of performance over experience. But it won't be easy to persuade him." Her voice warned Hattie against hope.

"Yes, ma'am."

"But we can try."

Hattie never believed she had a chance at the position, even though, at twenty years old, she was the youngest bookkeeper The Palms Hotel had ever appointed. Mrs. Martin hired her as a clerk one week after her graduation in June of 1902. Within a year, she was promoted to bookkeeper.

"I'll be on the verandah shortly."

Hattie collected the ledgers and grabbed a few extra pencils. On her way out, she checked herself in the mirror and smiled. "Hattie Lehua, assistant to the head of housekeeping."

Hattie had a wide smile, her lips were full, her nose slightly flared. Her eyes were keenly black, and her ears had a cup to them that her mother said was "to capture the sounds of the ocean." Hattie's mother was full Hawaiian, descended from the Pahanui line. Her father was German. He was an engineer who had worked in Lahaina for three years then returned to his wife and children in Europe.

Hattie locked her office door and made her way through the lobby. On Boat Days, the lobby was crisscrossed with bellboys wheeling dollies stacked with trunks. Maids scurried to deliver welcome baskets of mango and papaya, and newly registered guests sipped pineapple tea from crystal tumblers. As she walked through the lobby, Hattie caught snatches of their conversations. A gentleman in a blue blazer discussed the war in Manchuria. As he spoke, the woman on the settee across from him questioned why the United States should become involved in foreign matters.

"I've told you repeatedly." His voice was forceful. "The Japanese attacked Port Arthur. It was a sneak attack. There was no honor in it at all!"

The woman took a long draw of her cigarette. Her emerald ring caught the sunlight. "I still don't think it's any of our concern." She flicked cigarette ashes into the brass tray.

Hattie studied how the woman moved only

from her waist, how she crossed her legs at her ankles, how she looked directly at the gentleman.

The woman caught Hattie's eye. She lifted her empty glass and shook it. The ice cubes clinked. "More tea would be wonderful."

Hattie forced a smile and told the woman she would get a hostess, but the woman shoved the glass into Hattie's hand. "A bit more sugar this time."

Hattie juggled the ledgers, took the tumbler, and headed to the dining room where she spotted her cousin Koa. He was leaning against a column; his arms were crossed.

Koa Lyons was the desk clerk in charge of safe-deposit boxes. On Boat Days, he wore a white shirt and white trousers with a red cummerbund tied at the waist. Koa was grinning. "A bit more sugar this time," he whispered as Hattie came closer.

"Do me a favor, Koa, would you get the tea?"

"And what do I get for doing it for you?"

Hattie had no patience with Koa's nonsense. "Never mind." She started to walk away.

"Just kidding, cousin." He took the tumbler from her. "And I'll make sure it's extra sweet." He winked.

Hattie went out to the front verandah and set out the ledgers on a white wicker table. She settled in and looked over at the guests in their rocking chairs.

The Palms Hotel opened in 1901. It was dubbed the Grand Lady of Waikīkī and quickly became the resort of choice for European royalty and new-money Americans. The building was painted all white—the front verandah, the ocean-side *lānai*, the rooftop garden, even the cupola from where the American flag flew. Only the ceiling of the front verandah was light blue due to the stubbornness of

Hawaiian painters who claimed blue would discourage bees from making nests.

The architect raged. "The ceiling must be white to reflect light into the crevices of the columns."

The painters painted it blue.

There were ten columns at the entrance of The Palms—Corinthian columns carved by Portuguese craftsmen and erected by Japanese laborers. There were six columns on the front verandah, and four flanked the porte cochere.

Mrs. Martin arrived on the porch with Koa following right after her. "Make sure you do everything precisely according to hotel policy. I want you to reserve three safe-deposit boxes for Mrs. Stanford. And, Hattie . . ." Mrs. Martin pointed at her. "I need you to make a copy of Mrs. Stanford's safe-deposit inventory. Schedule a clerk from First National Bank to witness an inventory match and have a second hotel employee present."

Koa said, "We didn't do this much for Miss Roosevelt."

"Miss Roosevelt didn't travel with $75,000 worth of jewelry. According to Mr. St. Clair, Mrs. Stanford wears thousands of dollars of jewels each day, and she changes her jewelry daily. So, you can expect her secretary will be requesting access to the safe-deposit boxes often." Mrs. Martin sighed. "If it were up to me, I'd lock all her valuables in the bank."

Seventy-five thousand dollars was an inconceivable amount to Hattie. She knew that The Palms Hotel had cost $140,000 to build and that a home in Nu'uanu was $3,000, but they were amounts she couldn't fathom. A plantation worker made $30 a month—that she could understand.

"And Koa," Mrs. Martin added. "Check to see if there's a message from the Stanford party."

Koa gave a slight bow. "It will be my absolute pleasure."

Mrs. Martin smiled. "Someday that charm of yours will be your undoing."

Koa was *hapa haole,* like Hattie—half-white, half-Hawaiian. His mother was Hawaiian; his father had been an American stevedore who died of mosquito fever.

"Now back to the books." Mrs. Martin swiveled the ledgers toward herself and began the accounts reconciliation. Mrs. Martin called out a date and Hattie called out the expenditures and occupancy.

Hattie's accounts were precise. Her books always balanced. The December records reconciled. It took almost an hour with all the interruptions from maids, messages from Mr. St. Clair, and Koa's report that the hotel had not heard from the Stanford party.

The two women continued to work. The trade winds died down and the air was still—unusual for a winter day. Sweat crept down Hattie's spine. Perspiration prickled her face. She looked over at Mrs. Martin. Despite the fact that Mrs. Martin was wearing a gray cotton dress, high collared and long sleeved, she showed no sign of discomfort. Her face wasn't flushed. Hattie thought it was a plain face, like the portraits of early missionaries' wives.

"The only conclusion to this inventory discrepancy is that the laundry workers are stealing." Mrs. Martin sat back.

Hattie didn't protest.

Mrs. Martin unclasped her watch brooch and pulled it out to check the time. It was two o'clock. "Mrs. Stanford should have been here hours ago."

On February 21, 1905, the SS *Korea* limped into Honolulu Harbor after having been battered by southwest gales for seven days. Her rails were bent and her hull splintered, and she sat heavy with munitions of war. Weighted down by seventy cannons, three hundred rifles, and two hundred pounds of nitrate, she ran aground in the harbor and was marooned on the Honolulu Lighthouse shoal.

From the beginning, it was a difficult crossing. The steamship's departure was delayed for two days by San Francisco's fog. Her captain was replaced, her engineer fell ill, and on her first night in open water a bale of wire broke loose and shattered a dining salon window.

On board the *Korea* were Lieutenant General and Mrs. Douglas MacArthur, Captain and Mrs. "Black Jack" Pershing, and Mrs. Jane Lathrop Stanford. The army officers were off to observe the Russian-Japanese war in Manchuria. Senator Stanford's widow was en route to Japan for an extended vacation.

The captain ordered the *Korea*'s propellers reversed. Her engines whined, water churned, and passengers lined the deck. They watched as each attempt failed to free the ship.

Mrs. Stanford gripped the rail, white knuckled. She turned to her companion, Miss Benson. "This is a sign of things to come."

Miss Benson didn't respond. She stared at the foaming ocean.

"The trip was ill advised."

"It will be a fine trip." Miss Benson's voice was flat.

"I should have never left San Francisco."

The ship jolted and Mrs. Stanford staggered. But before Miss Benson could assist her mistress, Mrs. Stanford regained her balance.

At seventy-six years old, Mrs. Stanford was an imposing woman in both size and demeanor. Her voice had the resonance of an Episcopal bishop, and her carriage was commanding. She was a tall woman at five feet six, and she weighed at least 250 pounds, although she listed herself on the passenger manifest at a mere 160.

"This evening we will be at The Palms dining under the stars." Benson patted the matron's hand.

Mrs. Stanford withdrew her hand. Her face was set, her jaw tight. "This was never meant to be."

"Come, let's go for a stroll." Miss Benson reached for Mrs. Stanford's parasol, which was leaning against the rail. It was black silk with a mahogany handle that thickened toward the spokes since it was not a parasol at all, but a well-disguised cane. "Come." She put her arm around Mrs. Stanford.

"I'm afraid." Mrs. Stanford's breathing became rapid.

"It's all right."

"It's a sign." Mrs. Stanford's hands trembled. "Leland Jr. told me he was going to send me a sign. He visited me last night."

"It was just a dream."

"I should be with him."

"He's with his father," she soothed.

Mrs. Stanford's mouth was drawn downward. Miss Benson gently tucked a strand of Mrs. Stanford's hair back into her upsweep.

Mrs. Stanford's dreams of her late husband and son were becoming more frequent. And it was Miss Benson whom she called out to in the middle of the night, and it was Miss Benson who went to her mistress' room, wiped her forehead with cool towels, and sat with her until she returned to sleep. Recently, the dreams were becoming more grisly. There were recurring nightmares about Leland Jr. being swept away in a mob of thieves; in another, he was a crucified Christ.

Leland Stanford Jr. was the only child of Senator and Mrs. Stanford. He died of typhoid fever in Florence, Italy, at fifteen, tended to by his mother and the Sisters of the Holy Spirit. Nine years later, in 1893, Mrs. Stanford buried her husband. He, too, was reaching to her from beyond the grave. In her dreams, the senator screamed out her name as he was being burned in a circle of fire, or grasped for her hand as he was drowned. But the most horrific of her visions was about herself—a fantasy in which a butler served her own grilled heart to her, thinly sliced on a silver platter.

And each time Mrs. Stanford called for Miss Benson in the middle of the night, Benson's control over the old woman tightened, and Mrs. Stanford's dependency on Benson deepened.

Gertrude Benson joined Mrs. Stanford in 1882, first as a bookkeeper, then as a companion. She sat next to Mrs. Stanford during Leland Jr.'s wake; she rode with her on the train when Senator Stanford's body was taken across the country. She accompanied her to university meetings, was privy to the Stanford finances, and traveled with her to Europe, Egypt, India, and Australia. The house servants, the university board of trustees, attorneys, art dealers, and every dress shop owner who had ever fashioned a gown for Mrs. Stanford recognized Benson's power.

"Think of all the Stanford men and women who are waiting to see you. It will be a grand alumni dinner . . . and dear Dr. Townsend will be delighted to see you."

The ship pitched forward. Benson put her arm around Mrs. Stanford's waist. There was a grinding of gears and smoke spewed from the stern. There was a second jolt, and the *Korea* was free. The ship's captain announced that they would dock in fifteen minutes.

The *Korea* made her way through the harbor, threading through steamers, sampans, whalers, and fishing boats of every condition. It was noon when she finally docked at Alakea Wharf. Over the loudspeaker, the captain welcomed his passengers to Hawai'i. The dock was jammed with waiting family, police, press, and a gaggle of military officers. The Royal Hawaiian Band played "My Waikīkī Home." *Lei* sellers, with garlands of jasmine and plumeria hanging from their arms, lifted their hands to passengers who threw pennies in the harbor to halfnaked native boys, who dove to retrieve the coins.

Miss Benson turned to Mae McCauley, Mrs. Stanford's personal maid. "Get the day bag," she ordered.

Mae McCauley was sitting at the edge of a rattan deck chair. She was folded forward with her head in her lap. Her red hair closed around her like a curtain. Mae looked up. "Yes, ma'am." Her freckled complexion was tinged green.

For seven of the eight days at sea, Mae had been curled in her bed, clutching a chamber pot to her chest. As Mae got up, Mrs. Stanford said, "No. Not yet." Mrs. Stanford stood fast. "Not until every one of them is gone."

Miss Benson motioned Mae to sit down.

Mrs. Stanford stayed at the rail. She watched as Charles Dole, Mr. and Mrs. Andrade, Jenny Cooke, and Edward Rice disembarked. She cringed when the reporters pressed forward and aimed their cameras at Hawai'i's returning elite.

When Lieutenant General and Mrs. Douglas MacArthur appeared on the Korea's deck, the army officers let out a cheer and a chorus of "On, Brave Army Team." They drowned out the Royal Hawaiian Band. Reporters broke through the line; they surged the gangway. The police couldn't keep order.

"Look at them," Mrs. Stanford clucked.

Then Captain and Mrs. Pershing descended and a second cheer went up, and the officers let loose a rendition of "Here Comes the Bride" that was more spirited than on key.

"The press is making fools of them," Mrs. Stanford sniped.

"The Pershings seem to be enjoying it," Miss Benson said.

"They're being made into an amusement."

"We can all use a bit of amusement these days."

"The press will never have its day with me. Never."

The first-class passengers were followed by those in mid-class, then those in steerage. The docks cleared. The press had dispersed, the *lei* sellers had long gone, and the band packed up its instruments. Only the drayers were left—the drayers, the stevedores, and the waiting Thompson carriage sent by The Palms Hotel.

"Now," Mrs. Stanford ordered, and she took one grand step that set both Miss Benson and Mae McCauley in motion.

Captain Evans took Mrs. Stanford's hand and slightly bowed. "It was our pleasure to serve you, madam."

Mrs. Stanford acknowledged him with a nod of her head.

The captain snapped his fingers at a steward, who presented Mrs. Stanford with a bouquet of white roses. It was the bouquet given to her by Mrs. Gloss in San Francisco.

Miss Benson accepted the flowers, nestling them against her burgundy dress.

Mrs. Stanford was first down the gangway. She leaned heavily on her parasol, limping, but undaunted. She was wearing a navy cutaway suit that fell broadly across her hips and shoulders. The collar and cuffs were satin, and the skirt was sewn in nine gored panels.

Mrs. Stanford took her first steps on the dock. Miss Benson followed behind her. Last was Mae McCauley burdened down with the day bags and a brocade satchel.

At the corner of the wharf, a young blonde man, looking no more than eighteen, stood with one foot resting on a piling. He leaned forward with his elbow on his knee. A Brownie camera dangled from his wrist. He watched the Stanford party make their way down the gangway and across the dock toward the waiting Thompson carriage. He seemed to be measuring their gait, as if he were calculating an attack.

"Mrs. Stanford." The young man stepped directly in her path. "I've heard you've come to Hawai'i under duress."

She was taken aback.

"It's been said you were poisoned . . ."

Mrs. Stanford reached behind for her companion. "Benson!"

"Get away!" Benson shoved him.

". . . in San Francisco," the reporter persisted.

"I do not speak to the press!" Mrs. Stanford shook.

He slid his camera off his wrist and aimed it at her. Mrs. Stanford covered her face. Then, from behind the reporter, a man swatted the camera from his hand—it crashed on the dock.

The man grabbed the reporter's lapels and twisted them around his fists. "There is no story here."

"There is a story." He sounded like a recalcitrant child. "And I'm going to get it." Then he wriggled himself free from the man's grasp.

The reporter looked frail in comparison to the man.

"Not while I'm around," said the man.

The reporter bent down to get his camera. As he stood up, he snapped a photo of Mrs. Stanford and ran.

The man ran after him. The reporter got to his bike, straddled it, and pedaled across the dock.

The man ran after him. "Stop him!"

The stevedores barely took notice.

"Stop him!"

The reporter was riding off his seat, hunched over his handlebars. He was just to the street when the bike hit a patch of oil. The bike crashed, and the reporter was pinned underneath it.

The man caught up; he reached down and slid the camera off the handlebars.

"That's my camera!" The reporter scrambled to his feet.

The man opened the back of the camera and ripped the film from its barrel.

"You can't do that." The reporter's hands were scraped. His trousers were ripped.

"I just did." The man pushed the camera into the reporter's chest. "No picture and no story. Not while I'm around. Got it?"

The reporter didn't answer.

"Got it?" he repeated, louder.

"Got it." The reporter grunted and righted his bike, muttering, "But you can't be with her all the time."

As the reporter pedaled off, the man yelled out, "What's your name?"

"Charlie Banks." He rode away with his jacket tails flapping in the breeze.

The man shook his head. "Feisty kid." He banged the dirt off his straw skimmer and dusted off his trousers as he walked back to Mrs. Stanford.

He extended his hand. "Allow me to introduce myself. My name is Ted Cutler. I'm an accounts manager for Western Pacific Lumber. I was on the *Korea* with you."

"I am in your debt, Mr. Cutler." Mrs. Stanford turned. "May I introduce my secretary, Miss Benson."

Cutler took Miss Benson's hand. "Pleased to meet you." He held his eyes to hers a moment longer than a gentleman should.

"Mr. Cutler." She nodded as if he were an inferior.

He returned her disdain with a smile.

Gertrude Benson was an attractive woman. She had a slim figure, her features were finely chiseled, and, despite the fact she fervently denied wearing any powder, her cheeks were always dusted with the slightest blush of rouge.

A uniformed agent from the Department of Agriculture interrupted. "Excuse me, ma'am." He made a feeble attempt at tipping his hat. "Those flowers aren't allowed into the territory." He jutted his chin toward the bouquet of roses.

Miss Benson raised her eyebrows.

"I've got to take them." The agent reached for the bouquet; Miss Benson tightened her grip.

"It's illegal to take roses into the territory." He sounded apologetic.

"The flowers belong to Mrs. Stanford." Miss Benson cocked her head. "Do you know who Mrs. Stanford is?"

"I do," he said. "She's been in the papers all week. But the roses are still illegal."

Once again, Mr. Cutler stepped forward. He put his arm around the agent and turned away from Miss Benson. The two men talked as they walked toward the Department of Agriculture buggy. They exchanged words, patted each other on the back, and glanced back at Miss Benson. The agent smirked. Mr. Cutler nodded. Then they both chuckled, and Mr. Cutler dug deep into his pocket. He pulled out his money clip and then shook the agent's hand.

The agent turned to Miss Benson, tipped his cap, then laid the bouquet in the front seat of his rig rather than tossing it on the pile of confiscated fruit and flowers.

When Ted Cutler returned to the Stanford party, he took Mrs. Stanford's arm and escorted her toward the waiting Thompson carriage. "My dear lady, I wouldn't be surprised if those roses were delivered to you before dinner."

"I am again in your debt."

Miss Benson bristled as Mr. Cutler assisted Mrs. Stanford into the buggy. And when he offered his arm to Benson, she summarily refused, taking the steps of the carriage briskly.

"I think you missed your call in life, Mr. Cutler," Mrs. Stanford remarked.

"How is that, madam?"

"I think you would make a brilliant bodyguard."

"Perhaps." Then he extended his hand to Mae McCauley, who feigned a smile and tottered into the backseat and hugged her belly.

"Mr. Cutler, may I offer you a ride for your efforts?" Mrs. Stanford asked.

He answered that he was staying at The Palms.

"As am I."

Mr. Cutler hopped in the back with Mae.

"We shall be stopping at the cable office en route," Mrs. Stanford announced.

"Now?" Miss Benson asked.

"Now, Miss Benson." At times Mrs. Stanford could be as formidable as she was frail.

"To what purpose?" Benson's eyebrows furrowed.

"To cable Dr. Ambrose." Mrs. Stanford smoothed the folds of her skirt.

"I'm sure Dr. Ambrose assumes we have arrived safely."

Mrs. Stanford took in a deep breath. Her nose flared slightly. She lifted her chin and faced forward.

She was not an attractive woman when she was angry. At her best, her features were blunt, her eyes protruded, and her mouth all but disappeared into a wrinkled, taut line.

"To the telegraph office," Mrs. Stanford ordered the driver.

Gertrude Benson straightened her back. She tugged on her gloves—handmade, French-ribbed silk gloves. She pushed each digit deep into the fabric, then made a fist of each hand.

A few minutes later, Mrs. Stanford commented to no one in particular, "I read Dr. Ambrose's report on faculty salaries during our crossing." She still faced forward, not directing herself to Miss Benson. "I need to cable my remarks to him." Statements like these were the closest she ever came to offering explanations to Miss Benson, or anyone else.

Mr. Cutler perked up. "President Ambrose of Stanford University?"

"The same," Mrs. Stanford answered.

"I'm a great fan of Stanford's football club." Mr. Cutler scooted forward on his seat. When he did, Mae McCauley pulled her skirt away from him.

Mrs. Stanford's smile dropped. "Yes, football was Dr. Ambrose's venture." Her disapproval was audible.

"My cousin hoped to win an athletic scholarship to the university," Mr. Cutler said.

"All of our students are on scholarship—for academic merit." Mrs. Stanford's tone sharpened. "The senator and I have not, nor will we ever, impose tuition on our students."

Mr. Cutler slid back in his seat. He seemed bewildered. Senator Stanford died in 1893.

Mr. Cutler was quiet for the rest of the trip to the cable office. And while Mrs. Stanford and Miss Benson were in the office, Mr. Cutler and Mae McCauley waited in the carriage. Cutler pivoted his head, reconnoitering the area, as watchful as a soldier in battle. And when Mrs. Stanford emerged, her dark mood was broken. She asked Mr. Cutler if this was his first trip to the islands.

"It is. But, unfortunately, it's just a stop off for me. I'm on my way to Japan for business."

"I believe we were meant to make an acquaintance, sir, since we, too, are going to Japan."

Miss Benson huffed. "How fortunate for us."

Mrs. Stanford glared at her and all conversation ceased.

CHAPTER TWO

A Palms bellboy stood in the middle of Waikiki Road. He blocked the sun with his hand and leaned back and forth, looking down the street. "Mrs. Stanford's carriage is coming," he shouted.

"Finally!" Mrs. Martin stood up and pressed the front of her bodice with her hands. "Hattie, tell Mr. St. Clair that Mrs. Stanford is here. And get rid of all these ledgers." She brushed off her sleeves and tugged on her cuffs.

When Hattie returned with Mr. St. Clair, Mrs. Stanford's carriage was turning up the semicircular driveway into the hotel's portico.

St. Clair staged himself to assist Mrs. Stanford as she negotiated getting out of the carriage. She swiveled her hips and pivoted as she took each step with a definite placement of her foot. As she did, she leaned heavily on her black silk parasol.

Behind Mrs. Stanford was Miss Benson, who again refused any assistance.

When Mrs. Stanford and Miss Benson were on the verandah, Mr. St. Clair introduced Mrs. Martin to Mrs. Stanford. Hattie watched as they spoke. Mrs. Martin nodded and looked toward the carriage, where Mae McCauley and Mr. Cutler still sat.

Hattie studied Mae—her ringlets of ginger hair, the cameo at her neck, the laced hem of her skirt, and the covered buttons on her shoes.

Mrs. Martin pointed across the street in the direction of the employees' cottages. Mrs. Stanford nodded. Then Mr. St. Clair escorted Mrs. Stanford and Miss Benson into the hotel lobby.

Mrs. Martin approached Hattie. She told Hattie that Mrs. Stanford's maid, Mae McCauley, was ill, and she had arranged for her to stay in Hattie's cottage until she recovered.

Hattie glanced back at Mae. This time she noticed dark circles under her eyes, how pale her complexion was, and her lack of spirit. "How ill is she?" Hattie wanted no part of influenza.

"She's seasick."

"How long will she stay with me?"

"A day. Two days at most."

It had taken Hattie two years to have a cottage of her own. It was a luxury she knew would end when The Palms hired the next single woman.

"Until Miss McCauley is well, Mrs. Stanford will need an assistant," Mrs. Martin said.

Hattie's eyes were on the carriage. She wondered who the handsome *haole* man was. She guessed him to be in his early thirties. He smiled at Hattie and tipped his hat.

"Hattie, I suggested to Mr. St. Clair that you assist Mrs. Stanford."

Hattie's interest shifted.

"If you make a good impression, perhaps a good word from Mrs. Stanford will sway Mr. St. Clair to consider you for the assistant position." She nudged Hattie toward the carriage. "Now, go. Give the driver directions to the cottages then get up to room 120 to introduce yourself to Mrs. Stanford."

"A street-side room?" Hattie wondered why she wouldn't choose to face the ocean.

"Maybe she likes to hear the trolleys," Mrs. Martin said. "It may remind her of the cable cars at home."

Hattie couldn't understand why anyone would choose the clang of trolleys over the roll of the ocean.

After Hattie gave the Thompson driver directions to the cottage, she walked back into the hotel. Suddenly, she realized the impact of what the next two days meant to her. She was rigid with self-doubt. What if Mrs. Stanford didn't like her? What if she made a mistake? An unintentional slight? An omission? An ignorance? A breach of trust? She wished she had worn her hair in a bun not braids, that she had pressed her collar more crisply, polished her shoes brighter, spoke better English, walked straighter, sat straighter. Should she curtsy or bow? Address Mrs. Stanford or wait to be spoken to? There were too many ways to fail.

But she told herself she could do this. She was intelligent, polite, and no one worked harder. They were words she half believed. Hattie walked down the corridor with her shoulders pulled back. She lifted her chin and mimicked the walk of The Palms' guests. For years she had studied how the women walked. She scrutinized how they held their forks, how they spoke to the staff and made their requests. But she never spoke to one—nothing beyond a courteous greeting or giving them directions to the beach. And she never spoke to someone as important as Mrs. Stanford.

She softened her footsteps as she got closer to room 120. She padded lightly down the Irish wool carpet. The corridor seemed cavernous—the beaded white walls, the gleaming brass sconces, the crystal chandeliers. This was foreign territory for Hattie. The guests' quarters were to be entered only when they were vacant.

Hattie stood at the open door of room 120 and knocked.

Miss Benson was rearranging the doilies on the bureau dresser. "Don't just stand there. Come in."

Hattie stepped across the threshold.

"I assume you are Hattie," Miss Benson said.

Hattie was struck by her beauty. She thought Miss Benson looked like the woman on the Pear's Soap wrapper. "Yes, ma'am."

"This is Mrs. Stanford." Benson motioned toward the window, where Mrs. Stanford was sitting in the overstuffed chair.

Mrs. Stanford held back the lace curtain with her hand. Her hand was bloated and blotched with purple bruises. Barely turning in Hattie's direction, Mrs. Stanford offered a "Good afternoon." Her face was speckled with light brown spots.

Hattie tried not to stare at her jewelry—a three-strand pearl necklace, a portrait brooch, diamond earrings, a filigreed silver bracelet, and too many rings to count. Hattie pulled out her skirt and curtsied to Mrs. Stanford.

She didn't know why she curtsied. She was sure she looked stupid.

"Do you have a notebook?" Miss Benson asked.

"No, ma'am."

Miss Benson didn't respond. She was opening a large woven basket; she took out a bottle of Women's Helper Tonic.

Hattie started to leave the room to get a notebook.

"Where are you going?" Miss Benson demanded.

"To get a notebook." Hattie could hear the nervousness in her own voice.

"Have you ever been in service, Hattie?"

Hattie felt as though Benson was scrutinizing her. "What kind of service?" As soon as she said it she knew that question was her first error.

"Domestic service." Miss Benson turned to Mrs. Stanford. "This is not going to be easy." She rifled through the writing desk for a pencil and stationery. "Make a list." She handed the pencil and paper to Hattie. Miss Benson smelled of vanilla. "I want three spoons to be delivered to the room each day for Mrs. Stanford's tonics."

"Yes, ma'am."

"And red and blue ink." Miss Benson pointed to the crystal ink bottle on the desk. "This writing set has only black ink."

"Yes, ma'am." Hattie scribbled, "Get blue and red ink."

Then Miss Benson picked up the curved ink blotter, exposing lines of writing. "I have no interest in reading what a previous guest wrote."

"Yes, ma'am."

"Replace it."

"Yes, ma'am." Hattie glanced over at Mrs. Stanford. She seemed oblivious to what was going on. She just sat, looking out the window.

"And this . . ." Miss Benson moved to the bedside table. She lifted the ceramic pitcher. ". . . is cracked."

"Yes, ma'am." Hattie wanted to ask if the bowl under it was cracked too, but decided against it. She stood poised to take the next order. But there was none. "Is that all?" Hattie asked.

"For now."

"May I leave?" Hattie thought she saw Miss Benson roll her eyes before she dismissed her with a flick of her wrist.

Hattie walked down the corridor, debating with herself if she should ask Mrs. Martin to relieve her from service. A complaint from Mrs. Stanford was just as likely as a compliment. Her confidence waned.

In room 120, Mrs. Stanford opened a box of Lowney & Huyler Chocolates. The chocolates were a welcome gift from her longtime friend Lallah Upton. "You seemed a bit harsh on the girl, Miss Benson."

"I was firm, not harsh." Miss Benson stepped to the bureau dresser mirror and pulled the pins out of her hat. It was a Milan straw hat trimmed at the crown with a burgundy satin band. That particular hat, along with many others, was an unknowing gift from Mrs. Stanford to Miss Benson—a "commission" given her by the shopkeeper of Bettina's Millinery, to thank Miss Benson for bringing her Mrs. Stanford's business.

"She's a lovely looking girl." Mrs. Stanford opened the gold foil box.

"Don't you think chocolate will spoil your appetite, Mrs. Stanford?" Miss Benson tossed her hat on the bed.

"No, Miss Benson, I do not."

Miss Benson glared directly at the candy. "What about your sugar level?"

Mrs. Stanford didn't answer. She poked at one, then another, before selecting a white chocolate piece. She took a bite. "Miss Benson, can't you allow an old woman one day's pleasure?"

"It's a daily pleasure, Mrs. Stanford."

Mrs. Stanford took another bite, almost flaunting her rebellion. "You didn't answer me, Miss Benson, I said that maid is a lovely girl. Don't you agree?"

"I thought we were discussing chocolates."

"I was discussing the girl."

"Her features are too blunt for my liking."

Mrs. Stanford licked the chocolate from her fingers. On her right hand, she wore seven rings, two of them platinum—one encrusted with rubies, the other with diamonds. She also wore an emerald-cut aquamarine, an opal, a topaz, a star sapphire, and multiple bands of diamonds. "My dear, not all of us are blessed with your beauty," she told Benson.

"I find this mixing of races unsettling."

Mrs. Stanford looked over her choices and selected a chocolate-covered cherry. "I understand it's our men who are doing the mixing."

"It's my opinion that the Christian men of this island . . ." Miss Benson was interrupted by a knock at the door.

"*Aloha* and welcome to The Palms." Koa greeted the women with a slight bow.

"You're finally here." Miss Benson pointed to Mrs. Stanford's bed. "To begin with, Mrs. Stanford's bed is to be moved closer to the door."

"Excuse me," Koa said.

"And she has no need of a second chair. Remove it."

Koa interrupted, "Madam, I have the signature cards for the safe-deposit boxes."

Miss Benson looked at Koa as if it were he who was in error. "Leave them." She motioned toward the desk.

"They need to be witnessed," Koa said.

"We shall sign them and have a boy deliver them." Miss Benson's voice was both singsong and arrogant.

"I am sorry, ma'am," Koa insisted softly. "I have to watch you sign the cards."

"Give them to me," Mrs. Stanford directed, and she signed all three cards then ordered Miss Benson to do the same. "Have you given him a copy of the inventory?"

Miss Benson leafed through a leather portfolio.

"And instruct him as to how the inventory is to be handled," Mrs. Stanford said.

Just as Benson began her explanation, a stream of bellboys arrived wheeling in steamer trunks, a fortnighter, two leather footlockers, and a stack of hatboxes on a rolling caddy.

Mrs. Stanford, apparently uncomfortable with disorder, told Benson that she would be on the ocean-side verandah waiting for her friend Mrs. Upton's visit. When she left, Koa slipped out behind her.

———⋅•⋅•⋅———

Mrs. Stanford settled on the verandah in a fanned wicker chair. From where she sat, she could see Diamond Head in the distance; it was a blue-gray silhouette against the winter sky.

The afternoon sun cast long shadows of carved spindles on the polished maple floor; mock orange blossoms scented the breeze.

A hostess in a high-collared coral dress asked Mrs. Stanford if she would like a refreshment.

Mrs. Stanford answered, "A pot of tea and two

cups . . ." Mrs. Stanford touched her arm. "And perhaps a tray of pastries."

Then Mrs. Stanford rested her head on the back of the chair. The sun exaggerated the bags under her eyes and the bluntness of her nose. It highlighted the lines across her forehead.

When the hostess returned, Mrs. Stanford requested stationery so she could write to her dear friend Dora Perkins.

She dated the letter, "February 21, 1905."

My dearest Dora,

Only a few words to you, to let you know I have arrived safely in Honolulu. I have wanted to see you since New Year's, but, first due to illness, and later due to an unspeakable event, I could not bring myself to burden you with my troubled heart.

I cannot tell you now what you will hear about my misfortune, but I am sure you will be informed in a few short weeks. The newspapers will make great folly of me, and it is to my benefit that I am not in California.

I am more sorry than you can imagine that I was not able to bid you farewell before my departure. I left quite unwillingly for this journey. Under the counsel of my brother Harrison and President Ambrose, I have fled my beloved San Francisco and am retreating to Japan.

I want your kind thoughts and I need to be blessed by them, especially now, when I am old and my heart is broken. I have never known such loneliness, and I pray that God will nourish me with his strength.

God bless you and keep you.
                    Your faithful friend,
                    Jane L. Stanford

Mrs. Stanford's handwriting, once graceful, was now jagged. Her vision was poor, her hand jerked. She slid the letter in an envelope, gave it to the hostess. She closed her eyes, her jaw went slack, her mouth opened and she began to snore.

When Mrs. Noah Upton arrived at The Palms she was escorted to the verandah. Mrs. Upton watched her friend for several moments before she approached. It had been three years since they last saw each other. In those three years, Mrs. Stanford had aged rapidly.

"Mrs. Stanford." Mrs. Upton gingerly touched her shoulder.

Mrs. Stanford was slow to respond.

"Mrs. Stanford." Mrs. Upton shook her shoulder more firmly.

Slowly Mrs. Stanford opened her eyes, and upon seeing Mrs. Upton, she smiled. "How lovely it is to see you, my friend." Her voice was still raspy from sleep.

"As you," Mrs. Upton replied.

Mrs. Upton had been a year junior to Mrs. Stanford at the Albany School for Girls. She was the more attractive of the two, a fine-boned, blue-eyed blonde with an even ivory complexion. Sixty years later, her hair was silver, her eyes were gray, and her fine bones were hidden under a well-nourished body.

Mrs. Stanford grabbed the arms of her chair and pulled herself erect. "It's been too long between visits. Has it been since Jennie Clarke's wedding? When was that? Ten years ago?"

"It was three years ago, Jane, when you were here in '02."

"That's right." Mrs. Stanford nodded. "It was delightful."

Mrs. Upton laid her purse on her lap. "You're looking quite well, Jane."

"You've always been a poor liar, Lallah." Mrs. Stanford poured her friend a cup of tea.

Mrs. Upton put two cubes of sugar in her tea. "Then, you look well for your age."

"I'm sure the same thing will be said of me when I'm in my coffin."

"Don't be morbid, Jane." Mrs. Upton stirred her tea.

"Lallah, at our age, death is overdue."

"I won't have you speak like this. It causes melancholy. You should cultivate happy thoughts. Music and poetry. It keeps the soul young—it's a fact, you know."

"Lallah, it's my body that's decaying, not my soul."

"I insist you only tell me good news. How is your brother?"

"Poor Harrison, he's as henpecked as ever." Mrs. Stanford put a lemon petit four on her plate.

"What about his businesses?"

"They go very well. The publishing company is expanding, but it's the shipping company that's his success." Mrs. Stanford added some spiced nuts to her plate. "He's even established an office here."

"Yes. Noah and I were hoping Harrison would be here for its opening."

"His wife keeps him on a short tether."

"He was such a nuisance when we were young," Mrs. Upton recalled. "He called me 'Lallah Blay-lah.' Do you remember?"

Mrs. Stanford laughed. "'Lallah Blay-lah. Stinkweeds made ya.' I haven't heard that in years. It's miraculous I can remember."

"But it was better than what Peter Lawton's gang called you." Mrs. Upton sang, "Plain Jane never been kissed, gone for months and never been missed."

Their laughter could be heard from across the porch, and if they were unseen, they could have been mistaken for giggling schoolgirls.

"If that were the worst people would say about me now," Mrs. Stanford said.

"What ever happened to Peter?" Mrs. Upton asked.

"He's dead." Mrs. Stanford said matter-of-factly. "So is Edwin Winthrop and Alexander Markham."

"Caleb Wharton is still alive," Mrs. Upton said. "He's fat as a bull and wearing loose-made vests to hide his belly."

"We have all put on a bit of weight." Mrs. Stanford glanced down at herself.

"It's better for our health, Jane."

"My doctor suggests I practice the Bruckmeyer Diet." Mrs. Stanford chose a meringue twist. "Hot water with lemon for breakfast followed by a brisk walk, and the same at midday." She bit into the meringue.

"Is he concerned about you?" Mrs. Upton asked.

"At my age, he's always concerned."

"I had heard you weren't well, Jane." Mrs. Upton hedged her comment.

Mrs. Stanford's mood shifted. "You've heard gossip?"

Mrs. Upton shrugged.

Rumors of Mrs. Stanford's deteriorating health spread in delicately phrased letters and subtle remarks. In parlors in Washington, D.C., drawing rooms in Chicago, and boardrooms in San Francisco, there were allusions to her frequent bouts with the grippe and her constant head pain. But the more sinister rumors were those about her failed memory and her obsession with contacting the dead.

Mrs. Upton glanced toward the surf canoe riders. "I heard that you were fatigued . . . often."

"It's true, I've been under doctor's care." Then Mrs. Stanford repeated a detailed account of her visits to Dr. Wainwright for minor ailments. Finally she said, "But last month there was an attempt on my life."

"Your humor is in poor taste, Jane."

"It's true. Someone tried to kill me."

Mrs. Upton put down her cup. "Surely, no one would want to do you any harm."

"I was poisoned and someone in the Nob Hill house is the culprit."

"Perhaps you were ill . . . perhaps displayed some symptoms." Mrs. Upton prattled. "It's an easy mistake. My Noah says . . ."

"There was no mistake. The chemist calculated enough strychnine in my Poland water to kill twenty men."

"Chemists can be mistaken. I've read about such cases."

Mrs. Stanford opened her mouth wide to relieve a stiffness in her jaw. "The detectives suspect it was a domestic in service."

The Palms hostess stopped at the ladies' table. She bent forward and drew a breath as if she were going to say something, but Mrs. Upton dismissed her with a "not now," and the hostess left.

"Jane, this is difficult to believe. No one could plot your death."

"I'm not afraid to die, Lallah. In truth, I'd welcome being with Leland and Leland Jr. But I'm distraught beyond reason that I could have injured a human being so mortally that he would want to do me such harm."

"Jane, are you certain?" Mrs. Upton rested her hand over Mrs. Stanford's.

She nodded.

"Have the police any suspects?"

"No police. I didn't want any publicity for me or for the university. President Ambrose and Harrison engaged the Morse Detective Agency. The Morse detectives also advised me to leave San Francisco, so I went to San Jose." Mrs. Stanford let go of her friend's hand to massage her jaw. "And when Harrison visited me there, he suggested I take an extended trip to be safe."

"Jane, no one could wish you harm."

"Someone has."

Mrs. Upton looked around before she asked, "How many of your servants are foreigners?"

"Almost all. Mostly Chinese and Irish, a few British."

"The culprit's one of them." She came in tighter. "Are you acquainted with the Damon family?"

"Casually," Mrs. Stanford answered. "They're friends of Dr. Townsend."

"Last August, their son Ned was coming home from a sail at Pearl Harbor, and he saw one of his Puerto Ricans stealing a road lantern." Mrs. Upton continued, "Ned ordered him to return the lantern to its place. The Puerto Rican, named Miranda or Marcos or some such, responded by stabbing Ned with a common file. The poor boy died the next day."

Mrs. Stanford lowered her eyes. "His parents must be devastated."

"Their only justice was that the murderer was hanged that same night."

"Ned was to be married, as I recall," Mrs. Stanford said.

"In November. Instead of a bride, the poor girl is a widow at heart."

Mrs. Stanford's body sagged.

"And, despite this kind of crime, we continue to let these indolent people into our territory. They are threats to our safety, especially the Chinese. My Noah has said this for years."

"Lallah, most of my Chinese have been with me since we moved to San Francisco."

"Noah says they can't be trusted."

"Your husband speaks his mind often."

Mrs. Upton blotted the crumbs from her lips. "Noah says it's the Chinese who keep Hawai'i from becoming a county of California."

"You mean from becoming a state?"

"No," Mrs. Upton corrected. "I'm sure Dr. Ambrose spoke to you when he returned from his visit here last year."

Mrs. Stanford looked puzzled.

Mrs. Upton stroked Mrs. Stanford's hand. "How silly of me to talk politics when you're distressed."

"Refresh me, Lallah. The facts escape me."

Mrs. Upton continued. Her manner was frivolous, as if making light of Mrs. Stanford's poor memory. "Noah says that Dr. Ambrose will be instrumental in Hawai'i becoming part of California, either its own county or a part of San Francisco's—but no more of this." Mrs. Upton perked up in her chair. "We need to think of pleasant thoughts—nothing dire." She stood up. "Come, a walk will do us well."

"Lallah, I am tired."

"A walk will lift your spirits."

"And who's going to lift my bones?"

"Come." Mrs. Upton helped her friend to her feet. "We shall pretend we are promenading down the Champs-Elysées." She handed Mrs. Stanford her parasol, and the two friends walked arm in arm through the lobby and down Waikiki Road.

Waikiki Road was a wide dirt street that ran from downtown Honolulu to Kapi'olani Park. It was lined with expansive monkeypod trees and summer homes belonging to former royalty.

Many women of Hawaiian royalty had married *haole* entrepreneurs, wedding foreign financial power with historic political power. Their grand estates rose from the valleys, the beaches, and the city proper. Princess Ka'iulani's estate, across the street from The Palms, was still occupied by her father, Archibald Cleghorn, and the Ward family maintained a three-story Victorian "cottage" just Diamond Head of that.

As Mrs. Stanford and Mrs. Upton strolled down Waikiki Road, Mrs. Upton replayed the previous week's party given by the Dillards. But when Mrs. Stanford displayed no interest, she then recited lines of poetry and reminded her of the legions of angels who were watching over her and how Senator Stanford and Leland Jr. were probably smiling down from the heavens, watching them as they strolled.

Mrs. Stanford's spirits seemed to lighten.

Mrs. Upton invited Mrs. Stanford for a picnic at Diamond Head to spy whales off the coast. But Mrs. Stanford declined. Then Mrs. Upton invited her friend for a buggy ride through the arboretum, but Mrs. Stanford expressed no interest.

Mrs. Upton made one last attempt. "Oh, Jane, we must visit the aquarium!"

Her suggestion soured Mrs. Stanford's disposition. "I have seen it."

"We can take a carriage right now. It's less than a mile away."

"I have no interest in seeing it."

"Jane, we are all in Dr. Ambrose's debt," Mrs. Upton blithered. "His last trip was most advantageous. When he announced that the university would send two professors to conduct research at the aquarium, he received a standing ovation. It is a magnanimous gift."

Mrs. Stanford pursed her lips.

"President Ambrose established such goodwill for the university." Mrs. Upton beamed.

"The university establishes its own goodwill, Lallah."

"My Noah says that President Ambrose is single-handedly responsible for enticing talented youth to attend Stanford University."

"Your Noah makes many claims."

Mrs. Upton bubbled with enthusiasm. "Let's go to the aquarium. Shall we?"

"I prefer we return to the hotel."

Mrs. Upton continued her chatter seemingly oblivious of Mrs. Stanford's panting breath and her clipped remarks about President Ambrose. "So many people were disappointed that you didn't come for the aquarium dedication. But Dr. Ambrose served you well."

"Dr. Ambrose serves himself best," Mrs. Stanford muttered to herself, but to Mrs. Upton, she said, "He has been a good president."

Senator Stanford appointed Simon Ambrose as president of the university on February 4, 1893. He was the first candidate to receive the full support of the board of trustees. Ambrose had received a doctorate in letters from Oxford, and, at thirty-one years old, he was appointed a chancellor at Harvard College. When he was thirty-six, he became the fourth president of Stanford University. During the university's first three years, there were as many presidents. One of Ambrose's predecessors lasted less than a month. All of them were dismissed for veering from the Senator and Mrs. Stanford's rigid vision for the school.

Almost five months after Ambrose's appointment, Senator Stanford died in his sleep, on June 21, 1893, and Mrs. Stanford was forced to take the helm.

"Dr. Ambrose is quite adept with the press," Mrs. Upton continued.

"It's a fitting match." Mrs. Stanford leaned heavier on her parasol.

"Shall we rest, Jane?" Mrs. Upton motioned to the sheltered trolley stop with three empty wrought iron benches. No one was waiting; few trolleys ran on the Aquarium Line during mid-afternoon.

"Let's press on."

"My Noah says if it weren't for President Ambrose, the university would have collapsed after Leland died."

Mrs. Stanford smiled as she allowed her mind to slip back to the turbulent years that followed Senator Stanford's death. The same newspapers that had reported his death were quick to ring a death knell for the university. No one expected the sixty-four-year-old widow to understand the financial intricacies of running a university. Up until that time, Mrs. Stanford had remained in her husband's shadows. She was seen as the "mother of the boys and girls of Stanford University." She never made a public statement nor gave an interview. Several of the senator's business colleagues advised her to liquidate the assets of the school. They suggested she tour the world or involve herself in charity work to ease her grief.

The advice was not off the mark. In 1893 the United States was in financial panic; bankruptcies were becoming the norm. However, what the senator's colleagues overlooked was Mrs. Stanford's zealous dedication to the university as a memorial to her dearly departed son, Leland Jr.

During her two-week mourning period for the senator, when she should have been in seclusion, Mrs. Stanford requested that President Ambrose meet with her at the Nob Hill mansion. Her dictates were clear. The university would survive. Expenses must be cut. Faculty would work with only a promise of payment, new appointments were to be postponed and construction halted. And when the probate court allotted her $10,000 per month to maintain all the Stanford estates, the university, and her personal needs, Mrs. Stanford cut her household staff from 276 to 28, and she lived on $350 a month— the equivalent of the salary of a Stanford professor. She sold the senator's horses, ceased the vineyard operations, and refused to hire a carriage. At first she walked the hills of San Francisco to social calls among the elite, until she took her first trolley ride. Then the illustrious Mrs. Stanford became a routine passenger on the Powell Street cable car.

As she walked by the Honolulu trolley stop, Mrs. Stanford smiled.

❧ Chapter Three ❧

While Miss Benson was in Mrs. Martin's office arranging Mrs. Stanford's day trips, Hattie was in Mrs. Stanford's room unpacking the trunks.

She unpacked steamer trunks crammed with dresses of linen, silk, and batiste—travel tunics, tea dresses, evening gowns, shawls, and veils. There were nightgowns more luxurious than wedding gowns, and corsets edged in lace.

Hattie held a white tea dress to herself in front of the mirror. She ran her fingers over the smocking. She twirled around, the silk floated, and Hattie pretended to be dancing on The Palms verandah.

Next she unpacked a leather traveling case brimming with petticoats, bows, collars, jabots, and cuffs. Hattie laid them flat in the oak serpentine dresser, pressing them with her hand. In between each undergarment, she tucked lavender sachets just as Miss Benson had directed. The scent of lavender wafted through the room, stirred by the whirl of the ceiling fan.

There were dozens of hatboxes. Hattie opened one. Inside was a plum chiffon turban anchored with a sequined buckle. Hattie was sure it came from Paris. She opened a second box. In it was a yellow taffeta hat, edged with a shirred vermilion ribbon.

She told herself she'd open just one more box. She chose the one that was almost three feet wide. The box was covered with marbled paper and tied with a black silk cord. It took two hands to pry the top off. The hat was covered with a spray of velvet roses edged in scarlet. Among the roses were clusters of forget-me-nots and violets. On the brim, a black velvet ribbon drew itself into an Alsatian bow. Slowly, almost reverently, Hattie lowered the hat on her head.

She raised her chin and cocked her head. She smiled into the mirror coyly and offered her hand to an imaginary suitor.

"How do you do?" she said demurely.

The suitor she imagined was a Prussian army officer in formal dress—a tall man of strong bearing, hazel eyes, square jaw, and fair skin, like the man she imagined her father to be.

"I would be delighted to dance." She held out her hands and let her suitor lead. The whole time she giggled at his sharp wit.

"A walk?" She put her hand to her chest. "Perhaps." Then she reached for the ivory parasol. But when she tried to lift it, it was heavy, and when she went to open it, she couldn't. She thought it was meant to be some kind of prop. Maybe something the rich brought to patio parties, never intending to block the sun.

"Hattie?" There was a knock on the door. "Hattie, you in here?"

Hattie put down the parasol and took off the hat.

"Hattie?" It was Koa.

"I'm in the wardrobe room." She put the hat back in the box.

Koa walked in and set a vase of roses on the dresser, then he plunked down in the stuffed chair next to the window and proceeded to help himself to a piece of chocolate.

Hattie walked into the bedroom smoothing down her skirt. "What are you doing?"

"Looking for a vanilla crème." He lifted a second confection over his head and gave the bottom of the candy a slight poke.

"Don't!"

"They should tell you what kind is in the box." Koa flipped the lid over. "Lowney & Huyler." He raised his eyebrows. "Good stuff."

Hattie grabbed the box from him. The gift card fell on the rug.

Koa picked it up and read, "From your dear friend, Mrs. Upton."

Hattie put the lid on the box and set it on the nightstand, away from Koa.

"Mrs. Noah Upton?" Koa asked.

"I guess so." Hattie noticed the vase on the bureau. "Did you just deliver those?"

He nodded.

"Where's the card?"

"No card. They're from the Department of Agriculture." Koa walked over to the nightstand and helped himself to another chocolate.

"Stop it, Koa! Not one more!"

"She'll never notice."

"It's stealing."

"Stealing from Upton?"

Noah Upton was one of the Fathers of the Annexation—the annexation that had removed the queen, kept her under house arrest, and declared

Hawai'i as part of the United States.

"Koa, I'm not interested."

"You have to be."

"What's done is done."

"We still have a chance."

"It's over, Koa." But she knew that however impossible it seemed, Koa still believed that the queen would be returned to power.

"Four days ago John Nahulu got a cable from Congressman Blount. He invited Nahulu to Washington, D.C., to speak for the Hawaiians."

"All John Nahulu wants is to be the next governor." Hattie kept her back to him as she picked the brown-tinged petals from the roses.

"He speaks for Hawaiians."

"Not this Hawaiian." Hattie centered the vase on the bureau dresser.

"He's trying to get the kingdom back."

"Koa, I don't care what he wants. All I want is to be the best bookkeeper I can be."

"Like a good hotel lady?"

"If that's what you call it."

"Like a good *haole*," Koa mocked.

"*Hapa haole*, like you, cousin."

Koa looked more Caucasian than Hattie did. He drew from his father's side. His nose was slender, his eyes narrow, and his hair was tinged with red. Only the brown of his skin and the build of his body reflected his Hawaiian blood.

"Koa, I'm just trying to make something of myself."

"You already have," he said.

At seven thirty that night Miss Benson knocked on Mrs. Stanford's door.

"Enter." Mrs. Stanford was sitting at the window.

Miss Benson reached down for the dinner menu that had been slid under the door. "I see your roses have arrived." She aimed the menu at the bouquet on the dresser.

"They have."

"And they seem no worse for the wear." She lifted a blossom to her nose.

"In your opinion."

Miss Benson handed the menu to her mistress. "Portuguese beef and potatoes au gratin. And look. Peach Melba for dessert." Her voice was light. Her dress was pale—a mint-colored batiste with billowing sleeves.

"I'm not very hungry." Mrs. Stanford set the menu down on the table.

"They offer a clear consommé."

"I've ordered our dinner to be brought to the room."

"Not on such a lovely night."

"I'm fatigued."

"The conversation will invigorate you." Miss Benson extended her hand to her mistress, but Mrs. Stanford did not accept it.

"Mrs. Upton exhausted my limit for conversation."

"I take it Mrs. Upton chatted a bit?" Miss Benson stepped behind Mrs. Stanford and began to massage her shoulders.

Mrs. Stanford tilted her head to the left, allowing Miss Benson to work the muscles in her neck. "She spoke incessantly."

"Did she grace you with her opinions?" Miss Benson rotated her thumbs in slow circles.

"Lallah Upton hasn't had an opinion of her own since she married that pompous fool Noah." Mrs. Stanford bent her head back. "The man is an ambitious ox."

Miss Benson unhooked the buttons on Mrs. Stanford's collar. She pressed her fingers at the base of her skull. "What are the judge's current ambitions?"

Mrs. Stanford rolled her head. "He's been appointed attorney general of the territory. A fact that slipped my memory. Now he expects a Supreme Court seat. He believes it's his destiny."

"Do you think it will happen?"

"According to Lallah, Governor Nichols promised him the nomination, but the governor is reneging because he feels compelled to name a native Hawaiian."

"So are we to have a brown-skinned justice?" Miss Benson arched her eyebrow.

"I leave politics to the men. They've been able to foul it up quite successfully on their own."

"Your suffragette friends would not be pleased to hear you say so." Miss Benson lightened her touch.

"My suffragette friends are only pleased when I fund them."

Miss Benson fluttered her fingers over Mrs. Stanford's neck and shoulders and buttoned the back of her dress. "Are you feeling better now?"

Mrs. Stanford nodded.

"Shall we go to dinner?" Miss Benson encouraged.

Mrs. Stanford fussed with the lace at the back of her collar then folded her hands in her lap. "I prefer to eat here."

"You are brooding, Mrs. Stanford, and I shall not allow you to brood." And once more, she offered her arm to the matron, and once more, Mrs. Stanford declined. "We shall stay here."

"Fine, then we shall dine at the window." Miss Benson dragged the desk chair next to the table. "We shall have a table for two, watching the stars. And the only conversation will be ours."

But that night was starless. The only light came from Princess Ka'iulani's estate, across the street. Electric lampposts lined the driveway and clusters of tiki torches could be seen in the side garden, where the princess once played croquet and rode her pony.

"You are so patient with me, my dear." Mrs. Stanford's voice was subdued.

"Nonsense."

"Without you, Miss Benson, my life wouldn't be bearable." Mrs. Stanford's eyes filled with tears. "Promise me that you won't die before me."

During the recent months, Mrs. Stanford's mood swung more frequently from rage to remorse.

"I won't have such talk."

"Promise me." Her voice was desperate.

"I promise."

The two women ate dinner in Mrs. Stanford's room, then Miss Benson prepared the matron for bed. She brushed her hair, massaged lotion on her hands, and offered to read to her from the Book of Ruth. But Mrs. Stanford declined, and Miss Benson left her reading the Bible to herself in bed.

When the Central Union Church bells tolled ten,

Mrs. Stanford was still awake. She reached over for the portrait of Leland Jr. on the bedside table and cradled it to her chest.

When Hattie heard the Central Union Church bells toll ten, she was just finishing up her accounts. She rolled the top of her desk down, turned off the light, and locked the door. Then she checked the lock a second time.

The hotel was quiet. The only sounds were of men in the game room; their cigar smoke drifted into the lobby.

Hattie walked down Waikiki Road toward Diamond Head, turned left onto Kukui Street and left again into the hedge-lined alley to the employees' cottages. The wind through the palms sounded like rain, and in the distance, she heard the strumming of 'ukulele.

The employees' compound had six women's cottages and four dormitories for bachelors. It housed sixty-two of The Palms' two hundred employees. Married couples lived farther up Kukui Street; managers lived at an inn on the beach.

Hattie took off her shoes and edged the screen door of her cottage open. When she stepped inside, Mae McCauley tossed in her bed. Hattie stopped. Mae settled. Quietly Hattie reached over Mae's bed and unhooked the mosquito netting from the wall. She looked down at Mae, curled like an infant with her fist resting under her chin, her wavy red hair flowing over the pillow.

Mae's eyes flickered. "My thanks, Hattie." She had a thick Irish brogue. Mae closed her eyes and went back to sleep.

The next morning it was not a rooster that woke

the two young women but the screech of a peacock from Princess Ka'iulani's estate.

Mae leaned on her elbow and yanked the mosquito netting back. "What in the name of Mary is that?"

"Peacocks," Hattie answered.

"They sound like wailing children."

"They're in mourning." Hattie referred to the belief of some Hawaiians that the peacocks of the 'Āinahau estate mourned Princess Ka'iulani, who died at age twenty-three.

"Then someone put them out of their misery." Mae flopped on her back and covered her head with a pillow.

"They'll stop soon."

Mae lifted the pillow. "First the mosquitoes, now peacocks."

The night before, Hattie had thought Mae's brogue was lilting; this morning, she thought Mae sounded like a fishmonger's wife.

"The netting is for the mosquitoes." Hattie got up and put on her robe.

"They're the size of bats."

"No, the bats live outside in the trees." Hattie had never seen a bat in Waikīkī. She picked up her toiletry basket, heading toward the baths.

"Jesus, Mary, and Joseph. I'm in the bloody missions."

Hattie stopped at the door, tightened the belt of her robe, and in a calm, slow voice said, "How fortunate that you don't live here." Then she let the screen door slam behind her. Mae said something inaudible to Hattie as she walked down the path.

When Hattie returned, Mae was sitting on the

porch rocker wrapped in an ivory satin robe. As Hattie came up the steps, Mae asked, "What is that smell?"

"It's either the jasmine or mock orange." Hattie pointed to the white-blooming plants. "Why? Are they offensive, too?"

"It's heavenly," Mae answered with a smirk.

Hattie went inside and dressed for work, while Mae rocked on the porch.

"This is a poor woman's dream." Mae said from the rocker.

Except for the mosquitoes and the peacocks, Hattie thought.

"When are the meals served?" Mae leaned toward the window.

"They're not. There's an employee kitchen in the basement of the hotel." Hattie put her hair up in a bun. She thought it made her look more professional than braids. She snapped a new linen collar on her dress and inspected it closely in the mirror for wrinkles.

"Can you have breakfast delivered to me?" Mae asked.

Hattie ignored her.

"Can you have breakfast delivered?" Mae repeated.

"It's not done," Hattie answered.

"I'd like steaming oatmeal and some bananas, if you please."

Hattie came out to the porch. "I thought you were too sick to eat."

Mae stretched out her arms overhead and yawned. "I've regained my appetite. I haven't eaten in days, you know."

"No, I didn't." Nor did she care.

"On the sail over, the ship pitched so badly, the cooks lashed down their pots to the stove and I lashed my head to a chamber pot. But now, I'm ready to eat."

"If you're feeling better then you'll be going back to work today."

Mae lifted her hair off her neck and draped it over the back of the rocker. "No, today I will be putting my feet in the ocean. And maybe tomorrow I'll go back into service."

Hattie started down the steps. "I have to go."

"Take my warning, my dear, if Mrs. Stanford shows a liking for you, she'll make your life a living hell."

"I'm only doing this today," Hattie said, never breaking her stride. "You will be back to work tomorrow."

"Oh, Jesus!" Mae doubled over.

Hattie turned around.

"I think I feel a bout of the grippe and my stomach . . ." She doubled over. "It must be something I ate . . . a native food. Poor, dear Hattie, you may be in service a week."

Hattie resumed her pace.

"Just mind your manners," Mae called. "And keep your place."

Hattie's lack of confidence in serving Mrs. Stanford was dispelled by her opinion of Mae. She thought if Mae could do it, then certainly she could.

When she arrived in her office, Hattie found a schedule of Mrs. Stanford's events for the day. In the morning Mrs. Stanford would shop. At one o'clock

Mrs. Stanford was having lunch at the Townsend compound.

Mrs. Martin had written a note at the bottom of the schedule telling Hattie to be on the front verandah at 9:00 a.m. Before she could read her duties for the day, Koa barged into her office. "I heard Mrs. Stanford is going to Townsend's house."

"She is."

Koa paced in front of Hattie's desk. "Townsend wants to annex Hawai'i to California. Him and his annexation brigade."

Hattie ignored him and began typing a memo on her Remington.

"They're going to make Hawai'i part of San Francisco County."

Hattie kept typing.

"If they do, we'll never get the queen back. They've got to be stopped."

She banged on the typewriter's keys. "This scheme about California—it's just one more rumor."

"It's not a rumor." Koa leaned on her desk. "Seth Kiakona saw a letter. It had a map, like a butcher's diagram, dividing up the islands. He sent copies to Congressman Blount."

"And?"

"Blount wants more proof."

"So do I."

He banged his fist on her desk. "That's exactly what I'm asking you for!"

"You want me to spy for a bunch of Royalist dreamers!"

"We need you, Hattie."

"No."

"You have nothing to lose."

"My job?"

"Better than your country."

"It's over, Koa. Whether the congressman comes or not. It doesn't matter—no matter how many petitions you sign. No matter how many letters you write. Go ahead. Roam the streets. Smash a few windows. Nothing is going to change what's done."

"Will you do it?" he asked.

She didn't answer.

"Answer me, cousin!"

"I can't."

"You don't want to."

"Out." She wanted him gone.

"We need you, Hattie," he said.

"Please, Koa, no more."

"Then if you won't help us, at least don't betray us."

Hattie went back to her typing, without looking up. Koa reluctantly left the room.

Betray us? How dare he! Koa, the red-haired revolutionary. She could feel her pulse in her neck. Koa and his drunken Royalist friends. She slammed the file drawer shut.

Where was he on Annexation Day? she thought. While I was at 'Iolani Palace singing the American anthem—all of Kamehameha School forced to sing, standing in white *mu'umu'u*, watching as the Hawaiian flag was taken down.

Betray us? I was the one with an *Aloha 'Āina* band under the black band of my hat. I watched the flag come down, not him.

"I *am* Hawaiian." She snatched her straw skimmer off its hook. She stood in front of the mirror and stabbed the hairpins into her hat. *"I am Hawaiian."*

She stared at the face in the mirror then she left, locked the door, and walked through the lobby greeting each guest with the hotel's required "*Aloha*." All *haole* guests. All covered from neck to toe, hiding themselves from the sun.

As she walked toward the verandah, Hattie could already hear Miss Benson complaining to Mrs. Martin. Benson's breakfast scones were overly sweet, her tea was tepid. The morning newspaper wasn't delivered, her window rattled, her bed creaked. Just then, the Thompson carriage pulled up to the hotel and Hattie braced for Benson's rage.

The Thompson carriage was splattered with mud, the gilt letters on the door were peeling.

"This is unacceptable," Miss Benson ranted.

The brown-toothed driver made no response. He just continued to chew on his tobacco.

Miss Benson demanded a more suitable buggy, and Mrs. Martin called Mr. Thompson and asked him to send his best surrey.

Through all of this, Mr. Cutler sat on the verandah reading the *Pacific Commercial Advertiser*. The headlines read: "Soldiers Refuse to Follow Orders after Russia's Bloody Sunday."

When Miss Benson threatened Mrs. Martin, saying that Mrs. Stanford would never stay at The Palms again, Cutler tipped the corner of his newspaper down. Cutler caught Hattie's eye and he winked. She immediately cast her eyes down.

Mrs. Stanford arrived on the verandah and sat next to Mr. Cutler. When she saw Hattie, she asked her to bring her some stationery.

Mr. Cutler slid his chair closer to Mrs. Stanford's. "I've been reading about Stanford's football team," he said. "I was at the Rose Tournament cheering the Cardinal on."

"It wasn't much of a contest," Mrs. Stanford replied.

"Stanford gave it a valiant try."

"The board of trustees convinced me it would be a morale builder for the students. It was a fiasco."

"But Michigan had four professional coaches. After the tournament, I hoped Stanford would hire professional coaches."

"Student coaches are sufficient."

"Today's paper said there won't be a separate gymnasium for the athletes."

"May I see the paper?" Mrs. Stanford asked. In the article there were quotes from President Ambrose. It was an interview that Ambrose did not receive Mrs. Stanford's permission to give.

After reading it, Mrs. Stanford said, "President Ambrose presented the university's policy quite accurately, Mr. Cutler."

"Even the University of California hired professional coaches for next season." Mr. Cutler made his case.

"The University of California also hires anarchist professors."

Hattie returned with the stationery as Mrs. Stanford handed the paper back to Mr. Cutler.

Mrs. Stanford began drafting a cable to Simon Ambrose regarding his interview: "When you speak of athletics or the gymnasium you must always state that the mission of Stanford University is to develop men and women of conviction, not brawn for its own sake. And in the future, as you have been advised so often in the past, you will not grant any interviews, make any remarks to the press, nor will you assume to speak for me unless specifically told to do so." She signed her name with great flourish. Then she instructed Hattie to have her memo sent to the Honolulu cable office.

Hattie gave the memo to Koa for him to arrange it to get to the office.

By the time the second Thompson carriage pulled up, Hattie was convinced she should have never accepted the temporary position. She was convinced there was no way to please Miss Benson, and began to believe Mrs. Stanford was beyond pleasing.

The second carriage was a gleaming hunter green buggy with maroon stripes and gold leaf curlicue letters. Its canopy was trimmed in cotton braid, the seats were upholstered in tufted horsehair, and the driver had all his teeth.

The Stanford party boarded the buggy and the driver made a slow turn to the road. The carriage rumbled over the trolley tracks, rocking Mrs. Stanford.

"Got one more tracks," the driver said as he eased the buggy over the last set of trolley rails. He introduced himself as Clinton Akana.

Hattie sat with her hands folded in her lap. She noticed a smudge of ink on the heel of her hand and rubbed it off with her finger. She looked down at the buttons on her shoes—they were threadbare. She didn't own a watch and her dress seemed shabby and haphazard. In fact, at that moment, all of Honolulu seemed haphazard to her. She noticed the lopsided tilt of the electric poles, the half-paved streets, and the walkways littered with *kamani* and *wiliwili* seed.

When a Hackfield's Department Store delivery boy rode by on his bicycle, Hattie imagined San Francisco to be a city where delivery boys wore brass-buttoned uniforms instead of cambric shirts and rolled-up trousers.

Honolulu was a maze of bamboo-scaffold construction. Streets were constantly being torn up, electric lines needed repair, and water pipes burst. In the outlying neighborhoods, clusters of New England-style homes mimicked the cities their owners had come from. There were Georgian, Cape Cod, and saltbox houses with manicured yards and white picket fences. Homes that were built in a style to keep out the cold and keep in the heat were duplicated right down to the nine-over-nine pane windows and working fireplaces.

Mr. Akana turned down Mililani Alley, at the corner of the Opera House, then past 'Iolani Palace. After the annexation, the palace was renamed the Territory of Hawaii Executive Building and the grand ballroom was divided up into offices. On the wrought iron gate, where the crest of the kingdom used to be, there was a jagged gap. From the flagpole on its turret, the Stars and Stripes flew.

As the party rode through the business district, Mrs. Stanford remarked on the new shops that had been built since her last visit. "Chan's Exotic Shop," she read out loud. "And look." She pointed to a shop protected with iron bars. "Best Pearls of the Orient." She asked Miss Benson to remember the shop, and Miss Benson, in turn, ordered Hattie to copy down the shop's name and address in her notebook.

Two doors down from Best Pearls was the Fortune Jade Store. By the time the driver pulled up in front of Marshall's Dress Shop, Hattie had written down the names and addresses of six jewelry stores.

Mrs. Marshall welcomed Mrs. Stanford and escorted her inside. Mrs. Stanford and Miss Benson sat at a silk settee. On the coffee table in front of them was a silver service of tea and chocolate pots, china cups, shortbread, sliced apples, and spiced nuts.

Hattie had never been in Mrs. Marshall's. For years she walked past the shop and looked in the windows. Mrs. Marshall's gowns were frequently mentioned in the social column. Mrs. David Brewton and Mrs. Noah Upton wore only Marshall's fashions.

It was a narrow store with high tin ceilings and low fans. Its walls were crammed shelves of Chinese silk, French linen, and Italian wool. There were hats on wire forms—straw hats, turbans, and wide-brimmed chiffons topped with great plumes of feathers.

Hattie stood behind the settee with her back to the window. The store smelled of hot chocolate, tea, and talcum-powdered salesclerks. Behind the glass counters and in between the aisles were seamstresses at the ready with yellow tape measures dangling from their necks and red tomato pincushions tied on their wrists. Each was poised to assist Mrs. Stanford. Mrs. Marshall had closed the shop to the public.

"Miss, could you move over."

Hattie admired a case of shawls.

"Miss." The voice was louder.

"Hattie." Miss Benson turned and motioned Hattie to the left.

The seamstress said, "You're blocking the sun on the fabric."

Hattie stepped to the side. Her back was almost against the window. The sun burned her neck.

Mrs. Marshall sat next to Mrs. Stanford, turning pages of a Paris pattern book and suggesting styles that would suit her. As she did, a parade of seamstresses displayed bolts of fabric.

Mrs. Stanford nodded between bites of shortbread; she tapped the sketch of a ball gown. Some shortbread crumbs stained the page with butter.

"Perhaps a flared skirt would complement your figure." Mrs. Marshall turned the page as she spoke. "The gored panels create such elegant movement."

One of the clerks held up yellow chiffon fabric.

"More light," Mrs. Marshall ordered, and a seamstress scampered to the window and drew back the drapes.

Hattie had a clear view outside. Across the street was a young man leaning against the Williams' Mortuary window. He was a *haole* man, about Hattie's age. There was something in his hand. Hattie squinted to make out what it was, but only when he held it to his face could she recognize it as a Brownie camera.

Mrs. Marshall layered a slip of lavender chiffon over the yellow, and an ivory silk under it. When she held it to the light, the effect was shimmering.

"Do you think it too vibrant to be worn in Japan?" Mrs. Stanford asked Miss Benson.

"Perhaps." Benson fingered the chiffon. "But it would be exquisite at the Founder's Day Ball."

Each April, in honor of the founding of Stanford University, Mrs. Stanford hosted a grand ball for the university community and the society of California.

"It would be most appropriate for the ball," Mrs. Stanford agreed.

Hattie watched the man with the camera cross the street. He was talking to Mr. Akana; he pointed to the horse. Mr. Akana nodded, smiled, and posed for a photograph next to his carriage, then the two men continued their conversation.

Mrs. Stanford ordered a ball gown, as well as an English rep suit and a wool travel cape.

As the sun rose higher, Hattie felt more heat through the window. Her collar was damp. By the wall clock, it was quarter to one. Hattie knew that Mrs. Stanford was scheduled to have lunch at the Townsend compound at one o'clock. She knew Miss Benson was aware of the appointment, but wondered if she had forgotten.

Mrs. Marshall opened a polished wooden box lined with red velvet. On the velvet were French kid gloves in white, ivory, and black. Miss Benson ran her fingers over the white pair. She turned the glove inside out and examined the workmanship. "Quite lovely," she remarked.

Hattie was sure that Miss Benson was distracted. She cleared her throat, but no one took notice of her. She cleared it again. "Excuse me." She tried to imitate Mrs. Martin's voice and posture. "It is quarter to one."

Every woman in the shop faced her. Not one of them spoke. Mrs. Stanford looked at Miss Benson—Hattie knew she had overstepped.

"Mrs. Stanford has an appointment." Hattie tried to recover.

"Wait in the carriage," Miss Benson said.

Hattie waited, sure she had offended Mrs. Stanford, certain Miss Benson would complain to

Mrs. Martin about her. She played out the worst of scenarios. By the time Mrs. Stanford boarded the carriage, Hattie was sure she would be fired. When Mrs. Stanford addressed her, she held her breath.

"Hattie," she said. "Confirm with Miss Benson what time she will call on me for dinner." She shooed her off with her hand, and Hattie gladly went in the shop.

Miss Benson was at the cash register with Mrs. Marshall. Hattie stood a short distance behind her. She didn't want to intrude while Benson was settling Mrs. Stanford's account. But Miss Benson was trying on the ivory French kid gloves.

"Add them to the account," she instructed Mrs. Marshall. "And there will be the service commission, of course."

Mrs. Marshall appeared to understand.

"Ten percent. To be paid directly to me."

Mrs. Marshall nodded without question.

Hattie watched, uncertain.

"Excuse me, Miss Benson. Mrs. Stanford wants to know what time you will be calling on her for dinner."

Benson barely acknowledged Hattie's presence.

"By the time I finish with her errands, it may be five o'clock." Benson sighed and shook her head, looking at Mrs. Marshall. "Tell her I'll be in her room at seven o'clock."

❧ CHAPTER FOUR ❧

The driveway of the Townsend compound was lined with royal palms. The Thompson carriage's wheels creaked over the gravel path as it wound past the children's homes, Dr. Townsend's office, and the aviary before stopping at the main house. The two-story white clapboard house had black shutters and a railed porch that wrapped around three sides. The front entrance of double doors was painted red. On each side of the entrance were flagpoles, where the American and Hawaiian flags flew in an uneasy peace.

Dr. Townsend greeted Mrs. Stanford. He was slightly stooped by his eighty years, but he still carried himself with the dominant spirit of his generation. He took Mrs. Stanford's arm.

The two walked together comfortably. A widower and a widow, they had met in Washington, D.C., when Townsend was President Grant's physician and Leland Stanford was a senator from California. On weekends they picnicked together on the banks of the Potomac, where they taught their young sons to swim. Both the couples were older in starting a family, both men were embroiled in Washington politics, and neither Mrs. Stanford nor Mrs. Townsend had an interest in the intrigue of government.

The "Washington years," as Mrs. Stanford referred to them, were a whirlwind of soirées, European holidays, and dinners with President and Mrs. Grant. There were monthly séances at the White House, which for the most part were giddy entertainment. But one March night, when winter still held Washington in its grip, an unlikely Greek baker was invited to share his vision of the future. He had no crystal ball nor smoke screen props; he spoke hesitantly in an immigrant's accent. According to the baker, the futures of the Townsends and the Stanfords would again be shared. He predicted both would bury their only sons. It was a prediction that came to pass and a grief that bonded the two couples for the rest of their days.

Dr. Townsend escorted Mrs. Stanford through the drawing room. Hattie followed at a respectable distance behind. She was glad Benson didn't join them. Benson seemed to keep everyone around them on edge.

The Townsend drawing room was paneled in ebony, the floors were covered with Chinese rugs, the chairs upholstered in damask, and the side tables draped with brocade. Hattie cautiously sidestepped a spindled gilt easel that held a portrait of a woman riding a horse.

"How is Catherine?" Mrs. Stanford asked Dr. Townsend about his daughter, a Stanford alumna.

"She spends her days scrambling after her two boys." Townsend was a soft-spoken man, and like Senator Stanford, his speech was slow; his critics called it "plodding."

"And things with you, Mrs. Stanford. How do you fare?"

"I'm well, Isaiah." She left it at that.

As they walked through the library, a butler instructed Hattie to wait there while the doctor and Mrs. Stanford lunched in the gazebo. The library was darkened by heavy drapes. The walls were crammed with ornately framed mirrors, oil paintings, and certificates of huge proportions. Hattie sat in a straight-backed chair. At first she was afraid to move. The gazebo was a Victorian glasshouse just outside. It was close enough for Mrs. Stanford to see her. Hattie scanned the room; she wasn't alone. A tabby cat, licking its tail, was curled on the bench of the baby grand piano.

Dr. Townsend stepped back to allow Mrs. Stanford to enter the gazebo. His attention to her was unfaltering. He appeared so kindly that it was hard for Hattie to reconcile the fact that this grandfatherly figure was the "Architect of the Annexation." It was this same understated demeanor that disarmed Townsend's political friends and foes. He lulled them into a false trust and caused them to expose their vulnerabilities. "Jane, do you remember trudging in the snow in Washington this time of year?"

"I remember snow in April, Isaiah."

As she entered the gazebo, the two men who were seated at the dining table stood. The older man greeted Mrs. Stanford first. She called him Judge Upton.

Before that day, Hattie had only seen photos of Judge Upton in the newspapers; usually he was in the company of John Natling or Ellison Huntford. To Hattie, one of those men was the same as the other.

Upton introduced the young man to Mrs.

Stanford. His name was Dr. Bernard Speckerd. Upton referred to him as a "recent medical school graduate who was interested in the future of Hawai'i."

From where Hattie sat, she caught snatches of their conversation. She had no intention of spying for Koa's Royalist cause; she listened more out of curiosity. The guests exchanged pleasantries about their families and details of the Stanford Alumni Dinner. It was to be held March 1 at the Alexander Hotel. The guest list had grown beyond twenty-five.

Judge Upton sat across from Mrs. Stanford. "Senator Stanford would have been pleased at such a turnout." Upton was a roundheaded man, rigid in posture. His collar was starched, his moustache was waxed into a curl, and his spectacles were clipped on the bridge of his nose. Hattie thought the doctor's moustache made him look like a walrus. It was as white as the hair on his head.

Hattie moved to the piano bench. From that vantage point, not only could she hear better, but she could amuse herself by petting the cat, despite the blanket of hair it was shedding on her skirt. But when Dr. Speckerd mentioned Mrs. Marshall's Dress Shop, Hattie's interest sharpened.

"Corsets and cannons," Speckerd snickered. He had the face of a spoiled child. "To Marshall's munitions." He raised his glass in a toast and slammed down his drink.

Mrs. Stanford looked at Dr. Townsend.

Dr. Townsend explained, "Mrs. Marshall smuggled ammunition for the Annexation Committee during the overthrow."

"We shipped rifles in crates addressed to her shop," Judge Upton added.

"If your brother, Harrison, had his shipping line then, we would have used it to deliver the freight." Dr. Speckerd addressed Mrs. Stanford directly. "Then he could have enjoyed some of the profits."

"Speckerd!" Upton admonished.

Once again, Dr. Speckerd addressed Mrs. Stanford. "Mrs. Marshall was a supporter of the provisional government from the beginning. She was one of our first spies."

Speckerd had been in medical school in New York City during the annexation years. He was a latecomer to the American takeover who enjoyed the resulting economic benefits, but who took no personal risk. As the son of a liquor purveyor, Speckerd didn't descend from money and felt the path to success was in education. However, as brilliant a medical student as he was, he failed to learn the social graces necessary to be bequeathed full membership into the gentry.

Speckerd was known as a dandy among Honolulu's families of means. He was notorious for womanizing and attracting less than the best class of women with his propensity for gambling, drinking, and Chinatown's brothels. But what made him stand out more than the opinions of others was his dress. At staid *haole* gatherings, he could be easily spotted in his garish velvet jackets and narrowly cut trousers. He didn't wear a beard, as was the style for men of the time, but let his moustache go wild, and his sideburns flared from under his ears to halfway down his jaw in unkempt auburn wisps.

"A spy in a dressmaker's shop?" Mrs. Stanford asked.

"She was dressmaker to the queen, and she still

has her ladies as customers," Upton said.

Hattie cocked her ear toward the gazebo and kept perfectly still to hear better.

"There are still pockets of Royalist rebels who believe they can bring back the past. But nothing of any concern," Dr. Townsend assured her.

"And when they do rise up," added Speckerd, "we have thugs who patrol the streets. Montague Peterson commands the Thomas Square Four." He toyed with his moustache as he spoke. "Mrs. Stanford, I believe you know Montague's sister, Cynthia. She's a Stanford alumna."

"What do you make of these uprisings?" Mrs. Stanford directed her question to Judge Upton.

"We make fools of them." Speckerd offered his unsolicited opinion.

Hattie scooted her bench closer to the gazebo.

Mrs. Stanford asked, "Dr. Speckerd, how is it that a young physician is so keen on politics?"

"I am more an entrepreneur than a physician," he boasted, "as I am sure Dr. Ambrose told you."

"Dr. Ambrose and I do not discuss persons of inconsequence," she answered.

Hattie shoved the cat in the direction of the gazebo. Then she appeared to chase after it. She crouched down in the ti leaf plants next to the gazebo, pretending to look for the tabby. Her shoes were sinking in a puddle, and the hem of her skirt was muddied.

Townsend explained, "When Dr. Ambrose was here for the dedication of the aquarium, he discussed the mutual benefit of the annexation of Hawai'i as a county, perhaps initially brought in under San Francisco County."

Koa was right, Hattie thought.

"What are the benefits of this annexation?" Mrs. Stanford fingered the brooch of Senator Stanford's portrait at her neck.

Judge Upton unclipped the spectacles from the bridge of his nose and set them down on the table. Hattie watched as all three men leaned forward, as if converging on Mrs. Stanford.

Upton said, "If the Board of Trustees of Stanford University supported our efforts for annexation, the facilities of the aquarium and agricultural stations would be available for Stanford research. Aquatic and tropical studies would be limitless."

Speckerd ungracefully added, "Mrs. Stanford, the financial potential from the research into rubber tree cultivation alone could benefit the university more than the railroad did in the past. With the increased production of automobiles, the demand for rubber will swell."

While the butler was pouring tea for the men, he spotted Hattie.

Mrs. Stanford asked Dr. Townsend, "Isaiah, are you in agreement with this?"

"There are benefits to the plan, Jane. With its annexation to San Francisco County, Hawai'i would lose its representation in Congress and the Californians could overwhelm the native vote. Then we can get on with civilizing this place and begin business on a large scale."

The butler walked toward the door. The whole time he kept his eye on Hattie.

"This sounds like a plan that eradicates the natives." Mrs. Stanford's tone was sharp.

"Protects them, Mrs. Stanford," Judge Upton argued. "Left alone, these people will stagnate. It's inherent for them to be content. The island's resources would otherwise be left untapped, and children five generations from now would be living as they do now."

The butler walked toward Hattie. She snatched up the cat. "He got loose," she whispered. She tried to focus on what Dr. Townsend was saying to Mrs. Stanford.

"Jane, before Ambrose left, he promised he would present the plan to you."

"He knew better."

Hattie strained to hear the conversation. Then Dr. Speckerd blurted, "Madam, if your husband were alive, he would be on the forefront of this design!"

There was silence.

Even the butler turned to see what would follow.

Dr. Townsend stood up and whispered something in Speckerd's ear, who got up and left.

The butler took the cat from Hattie and made a most definite suggestion that she wait inside the library.

Hattie walked back slowly to catch phrases of Judge Upton's remarks.

"Speckerd is young, Mrs. Stanford. It is a condition from which he will recover."

"Perhaps he will age, but I doubt wisdom will ever overcome him," she said.

Dr. Townsend added, "He's longsighted in matters of finance. And his view for Hawai'i is sound."

Then the butler closed the French doors, and Hattie could hear nothing more.

"We have support for the idea in Washington," remarked Judge Upton. "Most of the East Coast is with us. The southern plantation owners and the northern industrialists are behind us 100 percent. But there is still resistance among the Californians. However, if you were to give us support, we could rally the entire party."

Townsend lowered his voice to a whisper. "Jane, it is our destiny to expand into the Pacific."

Dr. Isaiah Townsend was the uncontested shadow power of government. Even during the brief restoration of Hawai'i as a sovereign entity, it was Townsend who selected Nichols to be Hawai'i's governor, and it was Townsend who sent Prince Kūhiō to Congress. With a simple raise of eyebrow, he could change the direction of history.

Mrs. Stanford became visibly agitated. "Gentlemen, it is the university that is my concern, not your battle cry of Manifest Destiny; it has nothing to do with that institution. Isaiah, you know my distaste for politics. I will not have the university involved." Her hands shook; her head had a slight tremor. "This is my university, mine and Leland's."

Townsend acquiesced. "As it always will be."

"Mixing education with politics is a deadly game." Mrs. Stanford placed her napkin on her plate. "I will never allow the university to become embroiled in political collusion." It was statements like those that proved Mrs. Stanford's ignorance of Senator Stanford's Washington influence and the entanglement of university and Central Pacific Railroad funds.

"This is a fair plan." Townsend made a last attempt to present his case.

"No more, Isaiah."

The conversation turned toward the alumni dinner, the weather, and the lightness of the berry meringue dessert.

At the end of lunch, Judge Upton then asked Mrs. Stanford if his wife could call on her the following morning.

Mrs. Stanford declined the offer.

"It would be her pleasure," said Upton.

"I am engaged tomorrow," she refused.

"Lallah could review the details of dinner with you."

"I will review the details of dinner with Dr. Townsend." She signaled the butler for her parasol, and Dr. Townsend took Mrs. Stanford's arm.

As they walked through the library, Hattie heard Dr. Townsend say, "The university must change with the world, Jane."

She didn't answer but walked more independent of his assistance and relied heavier on her parasol.

"We shall talk about this again, Jane. Just the two of us."

Mrs. Stanford did not respond.

He helped Mrs. Stanford into the buggy. "Consider it, Jane. Although it could have been better stated, Speckerd is right when he says that Leland would have recognized the merit of this plan. It would benefit us all."

"Good day, Isaiah."

Hattie sidled into the backseat of the carriage as unobtrusively as she could.

Hattie didn't go back to her office when they returned to The Palms. She knew Koa would be ready to pounce on her for information about Dr. Townsend, and she preferred to avoid his assault. She had another of her headaches that incapacitated her. Since Christmas they were becoming more frequent. She needed to go back to her cottage and rest.

"Welcome home, my dear." Mae held up a plate of éclairs and madeleines as Hattie climbed the steps to the cottage. "Have a pastry. Koa brought them by."

Hattie was suspicious of Koa's sudden generosity.

"How was your first day in service?" Mae was too cheery for Hattie's liking.

Hattie sat on the rocker on the opposite side of the porch. She rested her head on the back of the chair and closed her eyes. "I'm not sure."

"You look undone."

"I'm just tired."

"Could it be that you've been shopping with Mrs. Stanford?" Mae smiled. Her lips were full and undefined, like they were painted on her face with a too-broad brush.

"We shopped in the morning."

"Did she visit every shop in the city?" When Mae smiled, two deep dimples creased her cheeks.

"Just one dress shop. Then we had lunch at Dr. Townsend's." Even simple conversation caused Hattie's head to throb.

"Only one shop? She must have been brooding."

Hattie rubbed the back of her neck. "She was fine, honestly. I just have a headache."

"I have some Orangeine headache powder." Mae braced her hands on the arms of the chair to get up.

"I don't want any Orangeine. I'll be fine," Hattie said.

"Would a sweet bring you around?" Mae offered the pastries again.

Hattie was sure Koa had lifted the baked goods from that night's menu and not from last night's leftovers. "No, thank you." She wondered how Mae and Koa had become acquainted.

"How was my dear Miss Benson?"

"She left us after the dressmaker's shop."

"Did Benson pay the bill?"

Hattie nodded.

"And added her 10 percent?" Mae lifted her eyebrows.

"You know?"

"Don't be such an innocent, my girl. It's the least of what she does."

"But she dotes on Mrs. Stanford like a daughter."

"A daughter from hell." Mae ran her finger over the chocolate topping of the éclair and licked her finger. "She has total control over the woman. She knows her every want and fear, and she uses it to her advantage. We thought we were rid of her in January by pinning the poisoning on her."

Hattie rubbed her temples with her fingers. "What poisoning?"

"You really are an innocent." Mae smirked. "I thought you knew. Last month, at the Nob Hill mansion, Mrs. Stanford was poisoned—or not poisoned." Mae recited the account in the lilt of a bedtime story. "As she does most nights, she took her Poland water. About ten o'clock she yelled for Miss Dobbs, the upstairs maid. She asked Dobbs to taste the mineral water because she thought it was bitter. Dobbs, a great one for the royal drama, said it tasted like poison, and she forced the old woman to drink warm water to vomit. But Mrs. Stanford told her she had already thrown up." Mae remarked to Hattie as if it were an aside, "It's her common habit to vomit if she overeats. Or I should say, when she overeats."

"Is that common?"

"As a fat priest in a poor parish."

"Was the water poisoned?" Hattie rolled her head to the left, pressing her ear to her shoulder.

"I'll not have your headache ruin my stories." Mae got up and opened the screen door. "Once Dobbs was able to calm the mistress, Mrs. Stanford told her to fetch Benson. The rest of the story will have to wait." The screen door slammed, and she returned moments later with a glass of water and a packet of Orangeine headache powder.

She handed them both to Hattie and continued. "When Miss Benson came in the bedroom, Mrs. Stanford asked her to taste the water. Benson refused, claiming she had a raw cut on her lip from dry toast." Mae slid her finger across her bottom lip.

"All three women agreed they saw particles floating in the water, so Dobbs was instructed to take the bottle to Dumas's Pharmacy for analysis that very night." Mae quickened the rhythm of her rocking as she told the story. "The pharmacist's report stated there was strychnine in the water. It was an agricultural-grade strychnine—common rat poison. And there was enough to kill twenty grown men."

"What did the police do?" Hattie asked.

"No police." Mae shook her head. "Mrs. Stanford loathes publicity. She called her brother, Mr. Harrison Lathrop, and he hired the Morse Detective Agency to investigate. The detectives held the entire San Francisco staff hostage. No one could leave. That's when Mrs. Stanford, Miss Benson, and I moved to the Hotel Vendome in San Jose."

"Why you?"

"Because she trusts me. My parents work for Mrs. Stanford. I was born at Vina Ranch. So when Dobbs was fired, I was called into service."

"Dobbs was fired?" Hattie was confused. "If Dobbs drank the water that was supposed to be poisoned, why was she fired?"

"Now you're catching on." Mae smiled. "It was Miss Benson who wanted her fired. There was a time when Dobbs and Benson were cronies. The two of them would share a pint in Miss Benson's room and crow about the mistress. But they had a falling out, and Dobbs threatened to tell Mrs. Stanford about Benson's 'commissions.' But she never did. So when the water tested as poison, Benson told Mr. Lathrop she suspected Miss Dobbs, and she got the boot."

"Was Mrs. Stanford poisoned or not?"

"If you believe Inspector Whelan of the Morse agency, she was not. He said he would stake his right eye against a dollar that there was no poison in Mrs. Stanford's water."

"But you said the chemist found strychnine in the water."

"The inspector's theory is that it was put in the bottle *after* she drank it, on the way to the druggist, and that Dobbs put it there."

"Then Mrs. Stanford was never poisoned."

"Who's to say? It's all peculiar. Because after Dobbs was fired, then the suspicion was on Ah Nee."

"I think Mrs. Stanford mentioned his name. Does he supervise the house while she's away?"

"The same." Mae shooed away a mosquito. "Ah

Nee's been with the Stanfords from before the mister was the senator, from when he had a general store. The nights the senator was waked in the parlor, it was Ah Nee who slept on the floor next to the coffin. But even then, Benson accused him of wanting to steal the gold from the senator's teeth."

Hattie squinted and lowered her head.

"Didn't the Orangeine work?" Mae asked.

"Sometimes nothing works but laudanum—but go on with your story."

"Benson told the detectives she believed the poison was meant for her, not for Mrs. Stanford. She told them that Ah Nee had threatened to kill her—which is not wholly untrue." Mae paused dramatically. "Ah Nee did tell Benson he was going to plant rats in her bed—a bit crude, but effective."

Hattie dropped her chin to her chest and massaged the back of her neck. "So that's why Mrs. Stanford came to Hawai'i?"

"Just sit back and listen." Mae continued to spin her tale. "One might think we were here because of that, but according to the *San Francisco Herald*, Mrs. Stanford is taking an extended tour of the Orient to recover from a case of tonsillitis."

"Why?"

"Because Wilhelm Huber is the Stanford's acquaintance and he keeps the family's name out of the paper."

Hattie said, "There's a sugar plantation owner on Maui, Claus Huber."

"Brothers. And Claus's daughter, Lilly, is Mrs. Stanford's goddaughter."

"They all know each other? Stanford, Huber, Townsend."

"Townsend, Dole, Carnegie, Morgan—the rich are a colony of fleas. And they intermarry like gypsies," Mae went on. "Lilly Huber is to be married to one of the Vanderbilt boys. Mrs. Stanford was supposed to host a bridal luncheon next week."

Hattie felt ignorant and naïve.

"It's a handful of them that run the world."

All the rumors Hattie had dismissed as impossible lies were obvious facts to Mae.

"She may tell you about Lilly while you're dressing her tonight. She's quite fond of the girl."

"I didn't know I was dressing her."

"It's part of the job," Mae said, and she explained to Hattie what to do. "Are you sleeping in her room?"

"There's only one bed," Hattie answered.

"It's a good thing. Her nightmares are horrid. On the ship, she didn't have one night's peace. They're almost all about her husband and son these days. If you ask me, she's tired of living without them."

⚫━⚫⚫━⚫

When Miss Benson called on Mrs. Stanford for dinner that evening, Mrs. Stanford replayed the luncheon conversation at Dr. Townsend's. Her anger was aimed at President Ambrose.

"Simon Ambrose is a *servant* of the university. How *dare* he involve it in such scandal. He will explain this 'coalition' as they refer to it—eye to eye." She lifted an envelope addressed to Ambrose. "I've ordered him to Honolulu. He will be locking his heels at attention!"

Miss Benson waited until there was a lull in her

rage before she reached into her pocket for a cable from President Ambrose.

"He is already on his way," she said, "in response to your first cable." She handed it to Mrs. Stanford.

Mrs. Stanford read some of the cable aloud. "The SS *Mariposa* . . . yesterday . . . in Honolulu within a week." She crumpled it in her fist. "I am, and until the moment of my death, the Mother of Stanford University. But he is not deigned to remain president. I shall start a search for a new president immediately."

"There is more." Miss Benson was guarded.

"Speak."

"This afternoon Mrs. Upton telephoned my room. She called 'out of concern' for you." Miss Benson treaded lightly. "She questioned me about the poisoning attempt, stating that the only reason she doubted you is because she was aware of your worsening condition."

"What condition?" Mrs. Stanford demanded.

"Mrs. Upton has been corresponding with Dr. Ambrose."

"Get on with it!"

"President Ambrose suggested that you are suffering from dementia, and he asked her to watch over you while you are in the islands."

"I shall have his head! He will *feel* the wrath of a demented old woman!" Her breathing quickened. "He has taunted me enough!" She clutched at her chest. "I shall expose his political collusion." Mrs. Stanford gasped.

"Mrs. Stanford, please." Benson tried to calm her.

"He has gone beyond." Her voice was hoarse.

Miss Benson hurried to the wardrobe room, returning with a brown glass bottle. "Valerian," she said and poured one tablespoon for Mrs. Stanford; she took it. "I refuse to allow Simon Ambrose to affect my health. He will be dismissed."

Benson held up two fingers and Mrs. Stanford took a second dose, then said, "And God have mercy on him if he attempts to excuse his behavior."

———◆•◆•◆———

In The Palms' kitchen that evening, kitchen boys splashed buckets of scalding water over marble counters, chefs screamed orders in French and German, heads of ducks were whacked, and waiters gave silver a last polish. The menu included roast mallard duck, steamed asparagus, and éclairs and madeleines for dessert.

Mrs. Stanford and Miss Benson arrived an hour late for their seven o'clock reservation. Mr. Cutler, noticing the hostess seating Mrs. Stanford at a table near the kitchen, walked over and asked if she would like to join him and a Dr. Lowell for dinner. "Ocean side and under the stars."

It was Miss Benson who accepted their invitation. Mrs. Stanford was still agitated, and perhaps Benson's urging was self-serving or a means of breaking Mrs. Stanford's mood.

The evening of February 22 was cloudless. On the rooftop garden, the stars competed with the frosted white globe lights that hung from the white latticed walls.

Each table was lit with a candle under a hurricane glass, and the lapping of the ocean and the chatter of guests almost masked the music of the Vincent String Quartet.

When Mr. Cutler escorted Mrs. Stanford to his table, Dr. Ian Lowell stood. Dr. Lowell was a fine English gentleman, schooled in fine English manners.

"Ian Lowell," the doctor introduced himself. He was an older man, perhaps fifty, with keen eyes, a waxed moustache, and a surgeon's fine hands. His appearance was meticulous.

Dr. Ian Lowell was a resident at The Palms Hotel. He and his wife, Fiona, retained an ocean-view apartment. The doctor was known by the hotel staff to be aloof but gracious, and, despite offers to the contrary, he was ever faithful to his wife. Mrs. Lowell was known for being less than gracious. She was intolerant of all that was not British and bemoaned having to leave her beloved England. She spent half the year in London. The hotel staff wished she would stay longer.

From where she sat, Mrs. Stanford could watch the moon rise over Koko Head. An evening rainbow made a halo around it, and, in a passing remark, Mrs. Stanford recalled a similar moon she had seen in Egypt. When she did, Dr. Lowell mentioned his trip to Egypt, and the two of them calculated they were in Cairo a mere six weeks apart. Mrs. Stanford's mood lightened. She exchanged stories with the doctor about riding camels and posing for photographs in front of the pyramids of Giza.

Miss Benson, perhaps feeling neglected, interrupted their conversation with her announcement that there were no cables from San Francisco.

Mrs. Stanford ignored her and enthusiastically

catalogued her purchases of tomb vases while she was in Assouan.

Miss Benson interrupted again, advising Mrs. Stanford against overeating—comments the matron ignored.

It was Dr. Lowell who discovered that he and Mrs. Stanford shared the same art dealer, a Mr. Clayton Adams of San Francisco. Cutler's only contributions to the conversation were his repeated comments about Mrs. Stanford's bravado.

Mrs. Stanford's mood was gay, and when their waiter offered a dessert menu, she ordered a sampler.

"I thought the chocolates were today's indulgence," Miss Benson commented.

"Miss Benson, I am not long for this life." Then she addressed Dr. Lowell. "Doctor, don't you think I'm entitled to a few luxuries?"

He nodded graciously. "All things in moderation."

Benson next remarked that the cool evening air was not good for Mrs. Stanford's health.

"I'm comfortable," Mrs. Stanford answered.

"But even I feel chilled," Benson argued.

"Perhaps you should have the girl bring you a shawl."

Mrs. Stanford requested that the waiter call Hattie.

When Hattie entered the rooftop garden, Benson summoned her with a wag of her finger. She ordered her to get Mrs. Stanford a shawl.

Mrs. Stanford spoke, not to Benson, but directly to Hattie. "I am content, my dear. It is Miss Benson who is running a bit cold this evening."

"Get my white crocheted shawl," Benson said. "It's in the bottom left drawer of my bureau."

Hattie stood, waiting for more instruction.

"Don't dawdle, girl." Benson waved her off with neither a please nor a thank-you.

Hattie knew she had to go to the reception desk to get the key to Benson's room; she also knew that Koa would be working.

When she got there, Koa was soothing an irate guest. She leaned over and asked for the key. "Just wait," he told her. She paced as she waited; the guest finally left.

Koa took the key from its cubby and slid it across the counter. "What did you hear?"

"You were right. There is a plan to attach Hawai'i to California."

"What else?"

"Koa, I've got to go. Benson is waiting."

Koa flipped up the panel in the counter and followed Hattie through the lobby.

"They were trying to convince Mrs. Stanford to support it. But she didn't agree," Hattie said.

"Who was there?"

"Where are you going, Koa? You can't leave the desk unattended."

"I'll just walk you to the stairs. Who else was there?"

"Judge Upton and Dr. Speckerd."

Koa shook his head. "Never heard of Speckerd."

A potbellied man staggered out of the game room. He was chalking the end of a cue stick. He laid his hand on Koa's shoulder. "Boy, I need more chalk."

"Yes, sir." Koa nodded.

"And a round of brandy for five."

"Right away, sir," Koa said, and he continued up the stairs with Hattie. "What did Townsend say?"

"Koa, the desk is empty," Hattie said.

"Nothing important happens this late."

When they reached the top of the staircase, Hattie asked him, "Don't you have to get chalk and brandy?"

"That guy was too drunk to remember he even asked me." They walked down the corridor. "Was Dole there?" Koa asked.

"No, just Judge Upton and Dr. Speckerd."

They were at Benson's room. Hattie jammed the key in the lock. She fumbled to unlock the door. "Benson will be fuming. I'm taking so long."

"Let me." Koa opened it.

Hattie headed to the dresser, found the shawl and whipped it out of the drawer. When she did, a box flung to the floor spilling cream-colored powder on the rug.

"Oh, no." Hattie scooped up the powder with her fingers and sprinkled it back in the box. Most of it was still on the rug.

Koa grabbed the dinner menu off the dresser and scraped up fine bits of powder.

"Hurry." Hattie picked up a piece of paper that had fallen out of the box—it was written in Chinese, with numbers and calculations like a recipe.

Koa brushed what powder was left into the rug and Hattie forced the lid back on the box.

The door slammed open. "Thieves!" Gertrude Benson stood in the doorway.

"I was just getting your shawl," Hattie stammered.

"What are you doing with that box?" Benson asked.

"I picked up the shawl and it fell out."

"It just flew out of the drawer?"

"It's the truth," Koa said.

"What are you doing here?" Benson demanded.

"The door lock was stuck," Hattie stuttered. "I needed help to get it unlocked."

"And it took you all this time?"

"There was a guest at the reception desk and I had to wait for Koa."

"Mr. St. Clair will hear about this first thing in the morning!" Benson was enraged.

"I can tell him," Koa said. "No need for you to see him."

"You little heathen, why would I believe you'd tell him?"

"I don't lie." Koa tensed. He stood straighter.

"Out!" Benson yelled. "Both of you!"

Hattie ran down the hall in tears. She swung open the service stairway door and sat on the top step. She put her elbows to her knees and covered her face with her hands.

Koa sat next to her.

Hattie pulled her skirt down to her ankles. "Benson's probably telling Mrs. Stanford what happened right now."

"Maybe not." Koa soothed his cousin. "She seems to do her worst complaining when the old lady's not around."

"Then she'll tell Mr. St. Clair in the morning and we'll both be fired."

Koa brushed a strand of hair off her forehead. "At least one of us." He smiled, pointing to himself.

"But I'm the one who did it, Koa"

"Hattie, you did nothing. Neither did I."

"It doesn't matter, not when she talks to St. Clair."

"I told you, I'll talk to him. I'm going to tell him you were trying to keep me from stealing. He won't be able to fire you."

"I can't let you do that, Koa."

"Listen, Hattie, with all the Ka Leo people working in hotels, I can get a job anywhere. Don't worry about me. You just do your job, pretend nothing happened and find out what Townsend is planning."

Chapter Five

Gertrude Benson lifted the papier-mâché box. The top was painted cobalt blue, edged in quick strokes of orange flowers. A hunter was crouched behind the flowers; his crossbow was aimed at a leaping deer.

Benson put the box back in her dresser and checked to see if anything else had been disturbed.

"Heathens." She swirled the shawl around herself.

Miss Benson returned to the dining room with short, tight steps. Dr. Lowell stood when she took her place at the table. Mrs. Stanford made no note of her return and continued to exchange remarks with Mr. Cutler.

Benson sat listening, or half listening, to Dr. Lowell's exploits with the Royal Army Medical Corps Expeditionary Force while in India.

Benson brooded and pouted, and stared at couples dancing the newest waltzes; they swirled with their arms extended, their heads erect and their feet in time. Mr. Cutler asked Benson if she would like to dance. She declined feigning an ailing hip.

Dr. Lowell asked Mrs. Stanford if she would honor him with a waltz.

Mrs. Stanford beamed. "I would be delighted. But you see I am the true owner of that ailing hip."

Then Dr. Lowell suggested taking cordials at the beach "to continue the spirit of the evening."

"It's damp at the cabanas," Miss Benson warned.

"It is the ocean, Miss Benson" was Mrs. Stanford's reply.

"You'll catch a chill," Benson volleyed.

"I'm not the one cocooned in a shawl, Miss Benson."

"I advise against it."

"I heard you, my dear."

When Dr. Lowell stood to escort Mrs. Stanford to the beach, Miss Benson interrupted. "May I have a word with you, doctor?"

Mr. Cutler took the doctor's place and escorted Mrs. Stanford.

As soon as Mrs. Stanford was out of earshot, Benson snapped, "Doctor, Mrs. Stanford is an aged woman, just recovering from the grippe. I was hoping to enlist your support in her avoiding exposure to the damp."

"Miss Benson, Mrs. Stanford is not my patient." His voice was marked by condescension.

"But you can see that she's frail."

"Actually, madam, I cannot."

"If she were under your care, you wouldn't be so dismissive," Benson attacked.

"If Mrs. Stanford were under my care, I would suggest she continue all pleasure in moderation and avoid persons prone to bleak pessimism." He excused himself.

As Mr. Cutler and Mrs. Stanford ambled down the lava rock path, Cutler absentmindedly tapped his fingers on her arm.

"Morse code?" Mrs. Stanford jibbed.

"Excuse me, ma'am." But after a few more steps, he was tapping her arm again.

Mrs. Stanford stared down at her arm. "Mr. Cutler?"

"Mrs. Stanford, there's something I need to tell you." Cutler walked her to the bench under the banyan tree.

"Go on."

"Mrs. Stanford, I'm not with Western Pacific Lumber. I'm an investigator with the Morse Detective Agency. Mr. Lathrop and Dr. Ambrose contracted the agency for me to accompany you as a bodyguard. I was told not to disclose my identity unless I felt hampered in performing my duty." He confessed like a guilty child.

"And do you feel so hampered, Mr. Cutler?"

"No, ma'am. I prefer to be honest."

"An admirable trait in a bodyguard." Mrs. Stanford paused. "So my brother and Dr. Ambrose think I need to be protected?"

"They feel it is in your best interest."

Mrs. Stanford eyed Dr. Lowell's progress toward them. "Do you report to Dr. Ambrose?"

"To my agency."

"And what risk do you perceive in Hawai'i?"

"None that I am aware," Cutler answered.

"Well then, Mr. Cutler, unless you think I shall be in harm's way, I am about to risk some revelry on the beach."

They resumed walking; Dr. Lowell joined them. Miss Benson, unescorted, trailed behind.

The Palms cabanas were lavish tents of white and rose striped canvas. Each evening at dusk a cadre of Chinese hotel boys carried rattan chairs, bamboo tables, liquor chests, and a wicker chaise into each cabana.

The party filed into a cabana close to the water. Cutler stood at its entrance, surveying the area as hotel men lit the tiki torches that lined the board-walk. Other men, in black pajamas and with waist-length queues, went from tent to tent delivering folded cotton blankets for the guests and taking orders for refreshments.

Dr. Lowell ordered a round of the "Sultan's Cocktail." It was his own concoction of spices, fruits, and hundred-year-old Scotch, and was familiar to The Palms bartenders.

Mrs. Stanford lounged on the wicker chaise. "What an elegant theatre this is," she remarked as she watched the festivities.

On moonlit nights, Honolulu residents, both white and brown, took to the ocean, surfing in dou-ble-hulled canoes. Tourists strolled the boardwalk. Some ventured down the thirty-foot pier that extended into the ocean. At its end was an octagonal gazebo where, most nights, beachboys serenaded guests with songs.

Miss Benson unfurled a blanket and covered Mrs. Stanford's lap. Mrs. Stanford slid the blanket off her lap and let it drop on the sand.

"Listen." Mrs. Stanford cocked her ear toward the ocean.

"It's a song about Princess Ka'iulani. She was next in line to be queen," Dr. Lowell explained. "Her estate is across the street." He lifted his glass back, toward the mountains.

"I am aware of her." Mrs. Stanford nodded. "She, too, died young, like my Leland Jr."

"It all sounds like incessant wailing to me. Even their ballads sound like dirges." Miss Benson's comments struck a jarring note.

"Actually their singing reminds me of the night the senator and I were engaged," Mrs. Stanford said. "My father announced to the house servants that we were to be married, and Mr. Freeman and Mr. Younglove brought the news back to their quarters. Such a cheer went up!" She beamed. "There was dancing and singing—choruses of African harmony. They sang through dinner and continued during our parlor games."

The doctor sat on the chair next to Mrs. Stanford's; he put his feet up on a rattan trunk, crossed his ankles, and loosened his tie. Cutler, taking his cue from the doctor, removed his tie and detached his collar.

"The music would have lasted all night but my Leland was uncomfortable and he asked father to have it stopped." Mrs. Stanford paused. "We were married soon after in Albany."

"There's quite a community of New Yorkers in Hawai'i," Dr. Lowell noted.

"Yes, there seems to be a significant number of expatriates in general, especially in Honolulu," Mrs. Stanford remarked.

"We have our own hamlet of civilization, and except for the mosquitoes and an occasional uprisings of natives, Hawai'i is paradise."

"What do you make of these rebellions, doctor?" Mrs. Stanford's question sounded like casual curiosity.

"Not much; I have no taste for politics."

"But if you did?"

"If I were interested in politics, I would not be the gentleman that I am." He smiled most politely.

"Dr. Lowell, I am accustomed to forthright answers." Her manner threatened the mood of the evening.

"Mrs. Stanford, I am a physician. And, in truth, I am probably the best surgeon in the islands, and I have neither the time nor the inclination to be concerned with America's management of her colonies. I am a British citizen, and as a subject of the Crown, I am afraid that the Empire has shrunk too dismally for my opinion to have any authority."

Mrs. Stanford gazed outside. *Kukui* nut torches hung from fishermen's canoes, effecting a twinkle of fire on the water. "And what of the education in the islands?" she asked.

"There is none," Dr. Lowell quipped. "It is the sadness of my life that our children are in Cambridge for schooling. But if there should be established a university as fine as yours, perhaps our daughter could be educated here."

Cutler pulled the canvas entrance flap back even further and observed the beachside activities. He poured himself a second Scotch and returned to his post at the entrance.

"I hear that Stanford University is establishing a school of marine research at the aquarium. Is that the purpose of your visit?" Lowell said.

"I'm here on holiday," Mrs. Stanford answered.

"A well-equipped research laboratory would be an asset to the scientific community, even if it is for fish," he joked. "But the subject is intriguing. I hear they're investigating the medicinal effect of seaweed from Maui; the natives claim it shrinks tumors. The challenge is that if touched, it is a deadly poison that inflicts a torturous death." Dr. Lowell sipped his cocktail. "There seems to be growing support for a joint venture between Stanford University and the aquarium. Dr. Ambrose spoke brilliantly on the topic."

"It's a pity I never received a text of his remarks." Mrs. Stanford's words were pinched.

That night Koa reported himself to Mr. St. Clair, and, as expected, he was summarily dismissed.

Hattie waited for Mrs. Stanford in room 120. She wondered if she even should be there. She was sure Miss Benson had told Mrs. Stanford what happened and didn't know if she was still in service. Hattie played the scene over in her head—Benson's rage, her threats. She imagined herself being fired by Mr. St. Clair; she planned to resign. She mentally composed a letter to Mrs. Martin. She decided it was best to leave The Palms. Then what? She had no idea.

Hattie sat on the chair next to the window and looked out at 'Āinahau. Tears welled in her eyes. She thought of Princess Ka'iulani—a "daughter of double race."

Hattie forced herself up. She turned down Mrs. Stanford's bed and plumped the bed pillows. Each time Hattie heard the elevator gate open, she stood up and faced the door. Finally, about ten o'clock, Mrs. Stanford returned; Benson was right behind her.

"What are you doing here?" Benson demanded.

"I'm here to help Mrs. Stanford get ready for bed."

Benson pulled her skirt toward herself as she whirled by Hattie and headed into the wardrobe room. The scent of vanilla lingered.

"Do you need a bicarbonate?" Benson asked Mrs. Stanford from the wardrobe room.

"I do not." Mrs. Stanford sat at the dressing table.

"Do you need any Garfield tea?" Benson asked Mrs. Stanford.

"No."

Benson tramped from the wardrobe room to the bathroom and back to Mrs. Stanford. She doled out three pills to Mrs. Stanford and handed her a glass of water.

"Is there anything else?" she asked.

"The girl can tend to me."

Miss Benson put her hand on Mrs. Stanford's shoulder. "If you need me, I'll be next door." Miss Benson trained her eyes on Hattie.

"So you've made me aware." Then Mrs. Stanford assured Hattie, "Shall we proceed?"

Hattie approached Mrs. Stanford, not knowing what Benson had told her. She stood behind her. Cautiously she unbuttoned her blouse—each silk-covered button was pushed through its loop—forty buttons from her collar to her waist. She lifted the blouse over the matron's head. Next Hattie untied the matron's chemise. She recited Mae's instructions to herself. She unhooked the stays of her corset, unlaced ribbons through grommets, and peeled off the whalebone girdle. With her eyes averted, she draped Mrs. Stanford with a Chinese silk robe. Mrs. Stanford smelled of roses.

Hattie remembered Mae's directions, "Brush her hair next." Hattie reached her fingers deep into Mrs. Stanford's bun and removed the pins and the hair rat. As she did, Mrs. Stanford took off her sapphire ring—the stone was as large as a dove's egg. She eased off her topaz ring, and a band encrusted with rubies.

When Hattie loosened Mrs. Stanford's hair, it cascaded onto her shoulders as the skin on Mrs. Stanford's face sagged and the balding on the top of her head exposed a mottled scalp.

Hattie brushed Mrs. Stanford's hair with slow, deliberate strokes. The old woman winced and Hattie worked softer.

"Your name is Hattie?" Mrs. Stanford's hair smelled like lemon.

"Yes, ma'am." With each brushstroke, strands of hair fell to the floor.

"Are you a Christian, Hattie?"

"Yes, ma'am," she answered, even though she hadn't been inside a chapel since leaving Kamehameha School.

Mrs. Stanford motioned to a Bible on the table next to the window. "I enjoy having the Psalms read to me at night."

"Yes, ma'am."

"Are your parents Christian?"

"Yes," Hattie answered, never having met her father and unsure if Mrs. Stanford would accept her mother's eclectic worship.

After braiding Mrs. Stanford's hair, Hattie massaged almond crème on her elbows. Mrs. Stanford's skin felt like watered waxed paper. Hattie worked lightly. She rubbed rose oil on her face. She thought of Mrs. Stanford as a sensible woman who would disdain primping.

Hattie helped Mrs. Stanford into bed. She pulled the stuffed chair next to the bed and picked up the

Bible. It was a black leather Bible, with a gold embossed monogram that was barely legible, and the gold gilt on the edges was mostly worn away.

"The red ribbon," Mrs. Stanford told Hattie, who opened to the marked page.

Mrs. Stanford pulled her braid over the sheets, settled deep into the pillows, and folded her hands over her bosom. "Begin."

Hattie read, "Help me, Lord, for no one loyal remains; the faithful have vanished from the human race. Those who tell lies speak with deceiving lips and double the darkness in their heart."

As Hattie read Mrs. Stanford mumbled the words with Hattie.

"May the Lord cut off all deceiving lips, and every boastful tongue. Those who say, 'By our tongues we prevail; when our lips speak, who can lord it over us?' Because they rob the weak, and the needy groan. I will arise, says the Lord; I will grant safety to whoever longs for it. The promises of the Lord are sure, silver refined in a crucible, silver purified seven times."

Hattie continued, "Lord, protect us always. Preserve us from this generation. On every side the wicked strut, the shameless are extolled by all."

"That's enough, Hattie." Mrs. Stanford's order was abrupt.

It felt strange to have Mrs. Stanford call her by name.

When Hattie stood to leave, Mrs. Stanford told her to stay with her until she fell asleep, so Hattie sat down, straight backed, with her hands folded in her lap. Mrs. Stanford closed her eyes. Hattie stared at the old woman. Her breath was shallow and uneven, and periodically her body jerked.

Hattie intended to stay awake but accidentally fell asleep. The next thing she heard was Mrs. Stanford's scream.

"Gertrude!"

Hattie jolted awake.

"Gertrude!"

Hattie stood over her.

"Lord, spare me this pain." Mrs. Stanford was drenched with sweat. "Thank God for you, Gertrude." She clutched onto Hattie. Her grip was strong. "Spare me, Lord." Her voice rattled.

"It's all right," Hattie soothed her. "It's all right."

"Hattie." Mrs. Stanford recognized her.

"Yes, ma'am."

She took Hattie's hands into hers. "It was Leland Jr. He was standing in front of Memorial Church. He reached his arms out to me."

Hattie stroked her brow.

"But I didn't reach out," Mrs. Stanford continued. "I was afraid when I saw him."

"Does your son seem afraid?" Hattie spoke in a soft, rhythmic tone.

"No, he's calling to me."

Hattie risked addressing Mrs. Stanford. "My mother says the dead visit us because they miss us." She massaged Mrs. Stanford as she continued speaking in a soft, peaceful tone. "My mother might tell you that your son visits you so he can be with his mother again. She believes that the dead are comforted to see us again."

Mrs. Stanford seemed to be pleased by Hattie's explanation. "Leland Jr. was my only child."

"It must give him such comfort to be with you."

"Yes," Mrs. Stanford said. "It must be hard for a boy to be without his mother—even in heaven."

Hattie let go of Mrs. Stanford and stood up.

"Don't leave!" Mrs. Stanford grabbed her arm.

"I'm just getting a warm cloth."

Hattie returned from the bathroom with a face cloth doused with warm water. She wiped Mrs. Stanford's brow. She lifted her head and worked the towel under her neck. She felt Mrs. Stanford release the weight of her head into her hand. "Your son must love you very much."

"He was fifteen when he died."

Hattie wiped Mrs. Stanford's arms, still wet with sweat. "My mother says it's only when we sleep that the dead can call to us."

"As I call him during the day, and he comes so willingly. He doesn't resist." Her breathing became regular. Her body relaxed and her eyes closed again. "Dear son."

———————

At seven o'clock the next morning, Hattie's alarm clock rang. She resisted waking up. She curled her knees to her chest and kept her eyes closed.

"Good morning," Mae called.

Hattie heard the creak of Mae's iron bed and the drone of her yawn. The doves cooed, the peacocks screeched, and an early crew was leaving for work. Reluctantly, Hattie sat up.

Mae pulled the mosquito netting back. She was leaning on her elbow; her hair was draped over her eyelet nightdress. "I tried waiting up for you last night, but I finally went to bed about eleven." Mae sat up and coiled her hair into a makeshift braid. "I assumed Mrs. Stanford had a nightmare."

Hattie nodded.

"Her son or her husband?"

"Her son." Hattie sat up and pushed back the mosquito netting.

"Lately, most of them are about him."

Hattie put on her robe. "When did he die?"

"March 1884. It's coming up on twenty-one years. And she still keeps his rooms like shrines."

"How did it happen?"

"Fever—when he and the mistress were traveling in Italy." Mae put on her slippers. "She's still in such deep mourning that whenever the servants can't find her, they look in Leland Jr.'s room—no matter which house it is, she'll sit there and do nothing."

"She seemed so fierce at Dr. Townsend's."

"She's a scared old woman. And her enemies feed off it—her husband's old cronies are the worst, with Benson running a close second."

When Hattie heard Miss Benson's name, she remembered what happened. "Miss Benson will probably call you back into service today."

"I told you, I have a bad case of the grippe that only three days of ocean bathing will cure."

"It won't be my idea. I'm sure she's asked Mrs. Martin to replace me already," Hattie said.

"Nonsense. How much of a mess of things could you have made after one day?"

Hattie told her what happened. "If I'm not fired, I may resign."

Mae came over and put her arm around Hattie. "You're just suffering from the first slings of the Good Lady Benson." Mae rubbed Hattie's back. "I know the wench, and I can guarantee by this morning she's on to something else."

"I got Koa fired. I'm sure of it. And it was all my fault."

"It seems you think everything wrong with the world is your doing." Mae held Hattie's face in her hands. "It's not all your work, my dear. Leave some credit to the Lord."

"If I resign maybe Koa can get his job back."

"Listen to me." She raised Hattie's face until Hattie looked her in the eyes. "I'll wager that Mrs. Martin herself has suffered at least one tongue-lashing from Benson, and if she has half a brain in her head she'll know this accusation of thievery is just her ranting."

"I don't think so. Besides, Koa . . ." Hattie began.

Mae put her finger to Hattie's lips. "As for your Koa, from what I've seen he seems quite capable of getting the boot all on his own."

"But . . ."

"No more buts, Hattie, you're too lovely to be so monotonous."

"But . . ." Hattie protested.

"But nothing." Mae stood. "As for me, it was nice while it lasted, and Jesus knows I deserve a few days of leisure, but it's time for me to get back into service. I need to handle Benson myself."

As Hattie and Mae walked up the steps of the front verandah, Hattie spotted Ted Cutler reading the *Pacific Commercial Advertiser*. He was wearing his tan flannel trousers and blue blazer. His legs were crossed, and he sat back in a relaxed, confident manner.

"Look at her." Mae stopped at the lobby

entrance and jutted her chin toward Miss Benson at the birdcage elevator. "The cause of misery herself. If I had the chance, I would see to it she was the one getting the poisoned water," Mae huffed. "And I'd have ten servants standing next to me swearing I didn't do it."

Hattie turned to see if Cutler was listening. He appeared to be reading the paper.

"And as God as my witness, I'd be whistling while I planned the deed."

Hattie tried to hush her, but Mae went on. "If only I wouldn't burn in hell."

Hattie tugged on Mae's arm and motioned in Cutler's direction. "He might be listening."

"And just why should he give a bloody good damn?"

Cutler lowered his paper.

❈ CHAPTER SIX ❈

That morning Mr. Cutler greeted Mrs. Stanford on the front verandah. She sat next to him and scanned the newspaper headlines.

"I appreciate you allowing me to accompany you today," Cutler said.

"I'm quite pleased for your company. It's been a long time since I've picnicked with such a young man. My son would have been about your age now. Thirty-six?" she guessed.

"Twenty-eight, actually."

"You resemble him somewhat. He had fine features and fair hair. He looked more like the senator than me. Even his build was slender."

"Is that a portrait of him?" Mr. Cutler pointed to the brooch Mrs. Stanford wore.

"My husband." She clasped it. "It was taken the year we were married."

"He was a man of great vision," Mr. Cutler commented. "I was surprised that you've managed the university so well."

"Mr. Cutler, your gift is not diplomacy."

"I mean that after the senator died, I would have put money on the university collapsing. But you've pulled through."

"To the astonishment of many," she remarked.

"With the mind of a man."

"With my own mind, Mr. Cutler."

"Well taken." Cutler nodded.

The month after the senator's death, his estate was locked in probate. The courts allotted Mrs. Stanford piecemeal funds to cover her expenses. When the funds were released two years later, the federal government then attached a fifteen-million-dollar claim against the estate. It took six years of court battles for the claim to be dropped and the money to be released.

Mrs. Stanford made the announcement of the release in the Outer Quad of the university. Mr. Owen Coswell, Senator Stanford's partner in the Central Pacific Railroad, stood shoulder to shoulder with her. It was an odd gesture given that Coswell was the senator's chief accuser of using railroad capital to fund the "extravagance of grief," as he called the university.

Coswell told the Stanford students, "The future of this university hung by a single thread and that thread was the love of a good woman."

Mrs. Stanford always suspected Coswell as being an adversary, and when she voiced her opinion, she was accused of being paranoid. Later, when it was confirmed that Coswell was responsible for the federal government calling in the railroad loans, Mrs. Stanford's "paranoia" was never validated—neither by the press nor by her friends.

Cutler jolted Mrs. Stanford from her thoughts. "Your maid, Mae McCauley—how long has she been in service?"

"She was born in service."

"Is she a part of the Nob Hill staff?"

"Vina Ranch," Mrs. Stanford answered.

"Was she in San Francisco in January?" He pressed on.

"Mr. Cutler, what is your interest in Miss McCauley?"

"Curiosity."

"Or suspicion?"

"I am concerned," he replied.

"About Miss McCauley?"

Mr. Cutler brought the tips of his fingers together. "It may be a matter of a servant's grousing, but Miss McCauley may be a threat."

"Miss McCauley's parents have been with me since the senator started Vina Ranch."

"I'm sure she's loyal, but I have my concerns."

Mrs. Stanford looked straight ahead. At that early hour, few trolleys ran on the Aquarium Line, and the only women walking about were Japanese maids toting fair-skinned infants in blue cotton slings that hung from their shoulders to their hips.

"Mrs. Stanford, I'm suggesting that you don't return Miss McCauley to service."

The Japanese women's high platform wooden shoes clattered down the sidewalk.

"It's a precaution," Cutler said.

"I cannot imagine her doing me harm. Her mother is a devout Catholic—she attends church daily."

"It's for your protection."

Mrs. Stanford looked off. It was her habit not to face bad tidings, or the bearer of their words. "Mr. Cutler, this is a horrid path for a woman my age to endure."

"It is in your best interest."

"Decided by everyone except me." She turned to him.

Cutler said nothing.

"I will remove her from service, as you request. But it is temporary until your suspicions can be discredited."

Cutler agreed.

When Miss Benson arrived on the verandah, Mrs. Stanford informed her that Mae McCauley would be removed from service and Hattie would replace her during their stay in Hawai'i.

"It's not well thought," Benson protested, looking hard at Cutler.

"Miss McCauley is to be taken out of service," Mrs. Stanford repeated.

"For what cause?"

"Miss Lehua will replace Miss McCauley."

"Is this the doing of your bodyguard?" Benson's voice was sharp with sarcasm.

"It is my doing."

"That girl is not to be trusted," Miss Benson insisted.

"Miss Lehua will also share your room."

"I cannot allow it."

"*You* shall not allow it?" Mrs. Stanford bristled.

"She's a thief. Last night I caught her and a native boy ransacking my room."

"Did you report it to the hotel?" Cutler asked.

Miss Benson appeared annoyed that Cutler dare question her. "I was distracted last night, tending to Mrs. Stanford."

"Did you report it this morning?" Cutler asked.

"I have yet to see Mr. St. Clair, let alone Mrs. Martin. In fact, the entire hotel staff seems to avoid me."

"What did they steal?" Cutler asked.

"They had no time to steal! I caught them rummaging through my dresser."

"For your shawl?" Mrs. Stanford sniped.

"Through my belongings!"

"You asked the girl to bring you your shawl. Did you not?" Mrs. Stanford was firm.

"Did they take anything?" Cutler said.

"They took nothing because I foiled them!"

"And what valuables were they in the process of stealing?" Mrs. Stanford challenged.

Benson didn't answer.

"Well, Miss Benson?" Mrs. Stanford demanded.

"You are smitten with the half-caste," Benson accused.

"I guarantee I am not."

"You are blinded, but I tell you, the girl will steal you blind."

"It's been done by better than she, Miss Benson."

It was Mrs. Martin who told Mae that Hattie was replacing her. Mrs. Martin called both girls into her office. She told Mae that she was not allowed in the hotel except for the employees' kitchen.

Hattie and Mae exchanged glances.

"You are restricted to the employees' compound and may not have any contact with Mrs. Stanford." Mrs. Martin sounded like she was reading a sentence.

"This is Benson's doing," Mae said to Hattie.

"This request is from Mrs. Stanford," Mrs. Martin replied.

"My arse!"

Hattie reached for Mae's arm to calm her. Mae shrugged off Hattie's hold. "This has Benson's hand all over it. There's no way the old woman would dismiss me. None."

Mrs. Martin continued, "For now, Miss McCauley, you must remain in your cottage."

"And let Benson go free to manipulate the old woman."

"That's enough, Miss McCauley," Mrs. Martin warned.

"For how long has she put me out of service?" Mae asked.

"I don't know," Mrs. Martin answered.

"I wish she would fire me. Put me on a steamer back home. Then I'd tell Mr. Lathrop to his face. Benson is mad!"

"Miss McCauley!"

"My apology, Mrs. Martin," Mae said. "It's not your doing, I know." Mae lowered her eyes. "I'll be going back to the cottage until I hear otherwise."

Hattie wondered if Mae was truly giving in. Her response seemed suddenly passive. Soon as she left, Hattie asked Mrs. Martin if she could accompany Mae to the cottages. Mrs. Martin agreed.

Hattie caught up with Mae on Waikiki Road. "Mae!"

She didn't answer.

"Mae!" Hattie ran to catch up.

"What?"

"Are you going back to the cottage?" Hattie knew how foolish she sounded.

"Like a good queen condemned to the tower." Mae quickened her pace.

"Enough," Hattie said.

"You still have no idea how evil Benson is."

"You didn't help yourself with that show you put on for Mrs. Martin."

"I know Benson is behind this." Mae kept her pace brisk.

"You don't know that. Maybe it was Cutler, maybe he reported your ranting about killing Benson. She can't always be the villain."

"Is that so?" Mae spun on her heels. "What if I tell you one of the houseboys saw her in Chinatown—in an herb shop on Grant Street. He saw her buying rat poison. He swore it. But don't believe me—wait until she kills the mistress."

Hattie wasn't sure what to believe. She didn't trust Benson, but Mae saw every one of Benson's actions as proof that she was a murderer.

"Mae, please."

"She plans to do her in while we're in Japan."

"Just go back to the cottage," Hattie said.

"You'll see," Mae said as she walked away.

"Only the cottage!" Hattie didn't trust Mae to stay put.

There were few who escaped Benson's wrath that morning. Hattie could hear Benson's complaints from Waikiki Road as she headed back to the hotel.

A kitchen boy was unwrapping the food in the picnic hamper for Benson to inspect it.

"We shall never book here again." Benson sniffed and poked at the gingerbread. She split the cake open and thrust it at Mrs. Martin. "This is raw.

And these." She flung the finger sandwiches back in the basket. "It's all unfit!"

Mrs. Martin asked the kitchen boy to take the basket back and instructed him to ask the chef to please make the selections for Mrs. Stanford himself. "Hattie, go with him."

Hattie followed the boy. She never looked back at Benson; she remembered the fate of Lot's wife.

Benson's displeasure was not assuaged, not with the new basket of food, not with Mr. Akana's care of the hamper, nor with his gracious assistance as she boarded the carriage.

Benson commanded Hattie to sit in the front seat. "Speak clearly so Mrs. Stanford will be able to hear you narrate."

Narrate what? Hattie wondered.

Mr. Akana suggested that Hattie talk about the whales. "All the *haole* like stories about whales."

"And we are also interested in Hawaiian history and culture. Fables, flora, fauna," Miss Benson announced from the backseat.

Hattie didn't know what fauna meant.

Mrs. Stanford boarded the buggy with Mr. Cutler. She and Cutler had been talking with Mr. St. Clair.

When Mrs. Stanford sat next to her, Hattie's mind went blank. She couldn't remember a name, a date, or the succession of Kamehamehas.

Mr. Cutler got in the backseat and Mr. Akana turned toward Diamond Head. Hattie wondered if she should tell Mrs. Stanford about the rocks that the *haole* thought were diamonds. She pointed to the crater. "Hawaiians call Diamond Head Lae'ahi."

"We're aware of the myth of diamonds." Miss Benson's words were clipped.

Hattie pointed out the three-story white Federal-style home next to The Palms Hotel. "That is Mr. Pembroke's house. He owns The Palms Hotel."

"We are aware of that also," Miss Benson said.

Mr. Akana leaned back. "Tell her about Diamond Head Mel."

Mel Chow was the eighty-year-old lighthouse keeper at the Diamond Head Light. He wore a self-fashioned uniform of a white pith helmet and Bermuda shorts, and every afternoon at three o'clock, he piped "Amazing Grace" on his bagpipes.

"I don't know who he is," Hattie lied.

She then pointed out Mr. Castle's house. "Next to the Pembrokes is Mr. Castle's house." It was a grand birthday cake of a Victorian home. "It was one of the first American-style homes to be built on the beach." She waited for Miss Benson to say she was aware of that, but she didn't.

"And there, up a little"—she pointed up toward a masonry building with a red Chinese-style roof—"is the Honolulu Aquarium. It opened in 1903."

"1904," Benson corrected.

"1904," Hattie repeated.

"It's on the sign," Miss Benson informed her.

Hattie had never noticed the sign swinging from the red torii. It read: "Honolulu Aquarium, founded in 1904." The letters were painted in gold.

"Mr. Castle and Mr. Cooke helped to build the aquarium."

"Another startling revelation," Benson remarked.

Hattie looked over at Mrs. Stanford; she sat erect, facing forward, seemingly oblivious to Benson's barbs.

Hattie continued, "The Honolulu Aquarium is

open until 9:00 p.m. on Friday and Saturday nights. It's free on Thursday."

"Information that is critical to Mrs. Stanford," Miss Benson commented.

Hattie wanted to ask Miss Benson why she didn't give the tour herself.

Mrs. Stanford commented, "Frugality is a virtue, sometimes overlooked by those who need to practice it the most, Miss Benson."

Cutler scooted up. "Good tip about the aquarium. Thanks."

"Otherwise it's ten cents," Hattie added.

"Good at any price," Mr. Akana offered.

"So you enjoy the aquarium?" Mrs. Stanford inquired of the driver.

"They've got a fish with feet. It walks on sand." He held the reins with one hand and with the other, he gestured how the fish walked. "And a fish with three eyes. It's good for kids. They can learn."

"A show of ocean freaks," Benson huffed.

They turned up Makee Road, and Hattie pointed out Makee Island and mentioned that rowboats could be rented.

"We toured Kapi'olani Park when we were here three years ago," Benson said.

"But we never hired a rowboat," Mrs. Stanford replied.

"I could arrange it . . ." Hattie began.

"As can I," Benson cut her off.

"Actually, Miss Benson, I'd like to go to the aquarium," Mrs. Stanford said.

"The aquarium?" Benson was incredulous.

"But not a special tour. I want to see it as Mr. Akana's family would."

"I'll schedule it for next Tuesday." Miss Benson flashed her eyes at Hattie, as if arranging the tour was her victory.

Mrs. Stanford asked the driver if Mount Tantalus was much farther.

"Not far." Akana took a shortcut through the Mōʻiliʻili rice fields.

Chinamen and water buffalo were both shoulder deep in mud. Hattie blubbered about the ricebirds that stole rice grains from the farmer. Mr. Cutler waved to the children pulling each other in a crate wagon. The children giggled and tried to keep up with the buggy.

On the road up Mount Tantalus, Hattie pointed out the algaroba and ʻulu trees and told stories about the wallabies that lived in the palisades.

The higher up the road they climbed, the more wild ginger and ferns lined the path. Guava and lilikoʻi grew along the switchbacks. Hattie told Mrs. Stanford that the name of the road was Hog Back Road and that there were eighteen switchbacks. Then she told her the story of puaʻa heʻa, the blood-stained pig. She finished the tale when they were at the seventh switchback marker.

"What a rich mythology," Miss Benson sneered.

Mr. Akana spit.

Hattie continued unfettered. "That smoky blue cloud floating on the ocean is Molokaʻi and the gray patch behind it is Maui."

Mrs. Stanford craned her neck to get a better view.

Mr. Akana pulled over and Hattie got out of the carriage; she offered Mrs. Stanford her hand.

"You shouldn't expose yourself to the damp

winter wind," Benson advised and Hattie climbed back into the carriage.

When they reached the top of Mount Tantalus, Mr. Akana parked the carriage. Both Cutler and Akana helped Mrs. Stanford down, then the men carried out the food hamper. Miss Benson directed them where to spread the tarpaulin and the *lau hala* mats. Over the mats went a red *palaka* tablecloth.

Mrs. Stanford wandered toward a patch of long-stalked flowers. Hattie walked a half pace behind her.

"What are these?"

"Shampoo ginger." Hattie squeezed the tight clove of red flowers and a scented gel oozed from it. Mrs. Stanford smelled it.

"Lovely," she said and moved on. When she walked, she leaned heavily on her parasol.

"That's yellow ginger. You're supposed to pick it at night," Hattie told her.

Mrs. Stanford twirled a blossom between her fingers and the petals melted into a translucent sheet. "Is it a cultural practice to pick them at night?"

Hattie shook her head. "It's so the flower will live longer." Hattie risked going on. "A Hawaiian legend says that if you weave a *lei* of yellow ginger picked on the night of a full moon, it will protect you from any darkness in your life."

Mrs. Stanford smiled. "The ancient Greeks believed a necklace of violets was a protection against deception." Then she paused. "Do you know who the ancient Greeks are, Hattie?"

She nodded. "Mrs. Pope taught the classics at Kamehameha School. She taught us that violets sprung from Orpheus's lute."

"Quite right." Mrs. Stanford appeared surprised.

"Come," Miss Benson called, waving her hands over her head. "We're ready."

Cutler and Akana set up a makeshift table using the buggy's tool box, and Benson artfully arranged the platters of finger sandwiches, molded domed salads, gingerbread, stuffed eggs, pickles, celery, olives, canapés, and a pitcher of pineapple tea. There were two trays of desserts—one with chocolate crèmes and the other with sliced mango, pineapple, and banana.

With Akana and Cutler on either side of her, Mrs. Stanford lowered herself onto the ground. "I'll need all four of you to get me up. In fact, you may need a catapult." She huffed and rocked her hips back and forth. "I wish I could recline like these native women."

While Mrs. Stanford was getting settled, Hattie went back to the ginger patch. She made a basket by lifting the front of her skirt and filled it with blossoms, which she strew between the platters of food.

"How very kind of you, Hattie," Mrs. Stanford remarked.

Miss Benson scooped up the petals closest to Mrs. Stanford and tossed them away. "What if you're allergic to them, Mrs. Stanford? You risk your health too freely."

Hattie thought that Benson's face was frozen in a permanent look of displeasure.

Mrs. Stanford remarked that the ginger blossoms reminded her of the summer she was eleven years old. "That summer I visited my Aunt Maude and Uncle Ira at Sackets Harbor. My uncle filled a galvanized tub with scalding water for my bath. Then Aunt Maude came in the back door, holding up her apron, just like Hattie." There was a slow rhythm to Mrs. Stanford's words. "She had filled her apron with clover blossoms that she tossed in the tub. I can still remember the smell—like rain in April." Mrs. Stanford glanced over her audience. "My aunt picked hundreds of blossoms. The fragrance! It filled the kitchen, and I curled in the tub and steeped, and when the water cooled, my aunt sluiced my back with water. I can still picture her speckled enamel pitcher. It is one of my most cherished memories."

"What a marvelous story," Cutler commented.

"What about you, Mr. Cutler? Do you have a big family?" Mrs. Stanford asked.

"My mother lives in Sacramento, and I have a maiden aunt in Livermore."

"Is your aunt a career woman?" Miss Benson asked.

"She's a clerk for a magnesium mine company. She's been surrounded by eligible bachelors all her life, but she never married. She said she'd rather die a spinster than a mining widow with a houseful of kids. She spends what leisure time she has with my mother—her sister."

Miss Benson offered Mrs. Stanford the platter of fruit. She asked for the sweets instead.

"And your father?" Mrs. Stanford set three chocolate crèmes on her plate.

"He died in '02 and my mother is not over it yet."

"Mr. Cutler, you do not 'get over' someone's death. You carry them with you throughout your life. That's what remembering is about."

"Yes, ma'am." Cutler sounded like a corrected child.

"My friends ask me how I go on living my life alone. But I am never alone. I tell them I keep my husband or my son with me all the time." Mrs. Stanford stated it as a matter of fact. "It's a happiness that most people don't understand. You see I can feel their presence. This union is so very sweet, it's a wonder to me that more persons don't attempt to develop such a practice. But these are visits I choose. When they come at night, I am afraid. I have been haunted by nightmares." Mrs. Stanford looked at Hattie. "But it's been explained to me that in dreams it is the departed who are calling me to them."

"It must help to keep you from feeling alone," Cutler remarked.

"Mr. Cutler, I have tried to explain to you that I am *not* alone. I am with my husband each day. I never transact business or decide any important matter without consulting his advice."

"The senator's?" Cutler asked.

"I'm not daft, Mr. Cutler." She wiped a bit of chocolate from her lip. "The senator and I both studied communicating with the dead as early as our Washington years. It is a discipline that takes practice, but now, I can lie on my couch and summon my husband or son." Mrs. Stanford raised her empty glass. Hattie reached for the pitcher of tea, but Miss Benson got to it first.

"I am unfamiliar with spiritualism," Cutler said.

"I am not a spiritualist nor am I a religionist, although the newspapers are fond of reporting that I am. I am no different from you or from your mother or your maiden aunt. I believe if anyone has loved someone, deeply and wholeheartedly, she cannot help but summon his spirit."

"You must miss being with them very much," he remarked.

"You still miss my point, sir. I am with them."

"Are they calling you to join them?"

"If you are asking if I contemplate suicide, I do not. I intend to live every day God decides, and when he calls me, I shall go gladly."

"I understand," he said.

"I doubt you do."

"Are you familiar with the studies of philosophy or science?" Benson asked him.

Hattie watched. She knew Benson was aiming at Cutler's weakness.

"I am not."

"What about the arts? Do you have any interest in music?" Miss Benson pushed up the raglan sleeve of her blouse, and she reached for the tray of canapés.

"I've been told I'm a fair singer after a few shots of Scotch whiskey."

"I meant classics." She offered the platter to Mrs. Stanford, who took several pieces of smoked Gouda. "Art that is inspired by the muses."

"My education ended at eighth grade, and the only music I've been exposed to is popular tunes."

"Can you grace us with a song, sir?" Mrs. Stanford requested.

Cutler combed his fingers through his hair. "Let me think."

Hattie observed Cutler like a raw specimen. She had never been close to a *haole* man before. He was fair, and his beard, if he had one, was so light that she wondered if he shaved. His cheeks showed a blush of sunburn, and at his eyes were the beginnings of crow's-feet. His eyes were so light, Hattie wondered if it hurt him to look at the sun. But his jaw was strong, his neck was thick, and his smile was unabashed.

A boyish grin crept over his face. "I suppose 'The Fairest Woman I Have Met' would be appropriate." He serenaded the ladies with the Irish ballad and then followed it with "When Johnny Comes Marching Home," and both Mrs. Stanford and Miss Benson joined him in the chorus. Then Mrs. Stanford, urged on by Mr. Cutler, sang a solo of "Annie Rooney."

They continued singing as if it were a family reunion. They sang American Civil War songs, French rounds, and childhood ditties. It was during a chorus of "Daisy" that a winter storm blew in. Cascades of rain dashed into the mountains, while the Hawaiian sun shone brightly.

Mr. Akana ran from the buggy with two umbrellas. He handed one to Hattie who held hers over Mrs. Stanford. He gave the other to Miss Benson.

The two men flanked Mrs. Stanford. "On the count of three, we will lift you."

Mrs. Stanford shifted her weight and leaned heavily on her hand. When she did, her bracelet broke. It was a nine-cameo bracelet modeled after Queen Victoria's—a delicate sculpture of rose gold that linked each cameo portrait to the next with etched gold vines.

Hattie bent over to get it. The umbrella tilted and Mrs. Stanford was exposed to the rain.

"Foolish girl." Miss Benson got to the bracelet first and dropped it in her purse.

By the time Mrs. Stanford was helped to the buggy, and the food and plates stashed in their baskets, the rain had subsided.

Mr. Akana coaxed his horses down the switch-backs. The carriage swayed, the horses snorted, and the wind whirled petals across the road. Hattie stared at the surrey's braided fringe, twisting and spinning in a haphazard frenzy.

Halfway down the mountain, the wind shifted and a gust blasted Mrs. Stanford; she shivered. Benson handed Hattie a blanket to cover Mrs. Stanford's lap. Akana reached into his jacket and offered Mrs. Stanford his flask. She refused with an appreciative politeness, so Cutler accepted his offer.

When they reached the foot of the mountain, the rain subsided, sky cleared, and the sun shone unobstructed.

Akana decided to cut through Chinatown. "Beretania Street too much traffic." He turned onto Vineyard, then Maunakea Street—then all movement stopped.

"Trolley accident," a boy yelled from the street.

Mr. Akana looked behind him. He was already stuck in a jam of noodle carts, laundry wagons, and a Hackfield's Department Store delivery truck.

Hattie knew they would be there for a long time. Trolley accidents were common in Chinatown. Mrs. Stanford began to fidget; she cooled herself with a sandalwood fan.

Heat radiated off the macadam streets; the air smelled of charred pork, fried dough, incense, horse manure, and the sweetness of the *lei* shops.

"I'll be right back." Hattie jumped out of the buggy. She headed straight for the Phoenix Bakery. On the sidewalk, two men with wisps of white beards sat on orange crates playing dominoes. Hattie swung open the door; a rusted bell clanged. Within minutes, she left carrying a box of pastries.

"Red bean cookies, salted seeds, peanut candy, and warm wedding cakes." Hattie handed the box to Akana, who offered Mrs. Stanford the first choice. Mrs. Stanford took a wedding cake; on the second go-around, she took three peanut candies.

Benson said, "You had several sweets today, Mrs. Stanford. Probably more than I'm aware of."

"I'll take some medicine tonight."

"Some people should not presume to bring you sweets." Benson cocked her head toward Hattie.

Hattie chose to ignore Benson's remarks. She had become more confident knowing that Benson said nothing to Mrs. Stanford about the night before.

Mrs. Stanford passed the box to Cutler, but he declined. "Do you not eat sweets?"

"I have no taste for them," he said.

"How unfortunate. It's a habit worth acquiring."

"It's a habit that affects some people badly," Benson rebuked.

In the midst of the already jammed traffic, an ambulance wagon tried to get down the street. The driver clanged his brass bell and yelled to the drivers to make way. Carriages inched right and left, men cursed, towers of piled wooden crates toppled and rotten produce was strewn on the sidewalk.

Mrs. Stanford asked Benson if she remembered where the Best Pearls shop was.

Benson turned to Hattie.

"Exotic Pearl on King Street," Hattie answered.

"Is it within walking distance?" Mrs. Stanford asked no one in particular.

"Maybe five or six blocks," Akana said. "But the best pearls are at Fortune Jade." Akana pointed to the next corner. "Just up there, at the open market, then turn left."

Mrs. Stanford decided they would walk to Fortune Jade and Akana would meet them at the shop.

Hattie took the lead with Mrs. Stanford following, tapping her parasol on the cobblestone sidewalk; her pace was determined. Benson followed her, and Cutler was last, scanning the scene.

The motley crew snaked through the crowded sidewalks. They sidled by noodle shop delivery boys with poles balanced across their shoulders and avoided getting hit with the bamboo baskets that swung from their poles. Hattie led them through the open market, past high-pitched hagglers bargaining for hogs' heads and boiled pigs' feet. Mrs. Stanford sniffed anise and cloves and sifted her hands through jasmine rice. Benson walked with her arms crossed over her chest, hugging her drawstring purse.

They turned left and walked under the dragon gate that guarded the entrance to Smith Street. The pearl shop was two doors down.

Sticks of incense smoked the shop with pungent swirls. A smiling Buddha and an altar to the shopkeepers' ancestors were crammed together on a wall shelf. Glass cases lined the booth-sized shop.

Once the four of them were inside, any turning or moving was an orchestrated event. The shop mistress displayed strands of pearls on a black velvet board—one after another, but always one at a time. Each necklace was returned to a locked glass case before the next was brought out. Mrs. Stanford tried on chokers and opera-length necklaces before she spotted the black pearls.

"From the Cook Islands," the shopkeeper explained, bowing and nodding like a listless boat.

"They are exquisite," Benson remarked.

Mrs. Stanford agreed, but she was not enthralled with the clasp, and she selected a carved jade piece to replace the serpentine gold. The clasp was replaced, the pearls were wrapped, and the shopkeeper offered Mrs. Stanford a pair of jade earrings as thanks. Mrs. Stanford accepted them and gave them to Benson as a gift.

After Mrs. Stanford left the shop, Miss Benson stayed behind to arrange the payment for the jewels. Hattie was sure she added her 10 percent commission.

Mrs. Stanford lumbered into the carriage. Her complexion was sallow. Her breathing was labored. Hattie noticed that her hands were swollen and the rings on her fingers dug deep into her skin like the twists of a sausage casing. On the ride back to The Palms, Mrs. Stanford dozed.

When they got back to the hotel, Miss Benson reluctantly reminded Hattie to move some of her clothes into their shared room. "Just enough to see you through the week and don't disturb any of my wardrobe." Then she took her copy of *Jane Eyre* to read on the beach.

Hattie hung her dresses at the back of the closet and slid her basket of toiletries under her bed. Miss Benson's toiletries were scattered across two shelves in the closet.

Hattie picked up Benson's bottle of Miss Lindy's Vanilla Water. She took a sniff and jerked her head back. "A cake gone sour"—that's how Mae described Benson. She was unpacking her undergarments when she heard Mrs. Stanford scream. "Hattie!"

Hattie ran into her room. Mrs. Stanford was lying on her bed fully clothed.

"Get Miss Benson!" Mrs. Stanford's breathing was quick. "Hurry!"

"Should I get a doctor?" Hattie could see this was more serious than one of the matron's nightmares.

"Get Benson! Tell her it's the sugar."

❧ Chapter Seven ❧

Hattie ran through the lobby, the reading room, and the front verandah looking for Miss Benson. She asked the *lānai* hostess if she had seen Miss Benson.

"She's at the beach," she answered.

Hattie ran down to the sand and spotted her. "Miss Benson," she yelled.

Benson didn't turn around.

"Miss Benson." Hattie ran faster. Sand seeped into her shoes. "It's Mrs. Stanford."

Benson put her book down.

"She's ill. She said it's the sugar." Hattie was panting.

"Did you give her any medicine?"

"No."

"Did she ask for any?" Benson was on her feet.

"No. She told me to get you."

Benson headed to the hotel. "Bring hard-boiled eggs to the room." She picked up her already fast pace. "And beef and water for tea." She pushed Hattie. "Go!"

Hattie got a tray of beef and eggs and two pots of water; she told a kitchen boy to report to Mrs. Martin that Mrs. Stanford was ill. "Make sure you tell her that she doesn't want a doctor."

When Hattie got to Mrs. Stanford's room, Miss Benson was leaning over her mistress. She had one arm cradled around her shoulders, lifting her forward as the matron sipped a glass of water.

Hattie parked the tea caddy next to the bed.

Miss Benson reached for the plate of eggs. She crumbled the yolk in her hand and put it to Mrs. Stanford's mouth. "You need to get these down." Mrs. Stanford's mouth gaped open like a baby bird's, and Benson sprinkled the yolk on her tongue.

Miss Benson spoke in lulled whispers. She fed Mrs. Stanford, then she asked Hattie to get the medicine basket from the closet and take out the Garfield tea.

Hattie steeped the tea, and Miss Benson served it to Mrs. Stanford in a hand-painted china cup.

Mrs. Stanford's hands trembled; the teacup clattered. "Never leave me, Gertrude." Mrs. Stanford began to cry, and Miss Benson steadied her mistress's hand.

Hattie's opinion of Miss Benson softened—perhaps her gruffness was only a fierce protection of the matron. She felt like an intruder as she watched them and asked Benson if she were still needed.

Benson dismissed her, and Hattie went down to her office. When Hattie opened the door, she was surprised to see Mae McCauley primping herself in front of the mirror.

"What are you doing in the hotel?" Hattie closed the door quickly.

Mae spun around and grinned.

"Look at you!" Hattie exclaimed.

Mae turned back to the mirror. She poked at her sunburned skin, leaving a ghost of a white pad on her face. "I'd say I had a bit too much sun."

Hattie was more concerned about Mae being

found in the hotel than any sunburn. "You're not supposed to be here."

"What could they do to me?" Mae plopped down on the leather chair under the schoolhouse clock.

Hattie locked her office door. What if Mrs. Martin saw Mae? Or Mr. St. Clair? Mae McCauley thinks only of herself, she thought.

"I have a message from Koa. We've been celebrating his new job. He's a waiter at the Alexander Hotel."

She began to wonder if maybe Miss Benson was a victim of Mae's gossip.

"He's living with his cousin Makana. She has a brood of children and doesn't notice him around." Mae twirled ringlets of her hair as she spoke. "He said to tell you she has a room to rent if you know anyone who needs one. It's four dollars a month."

"I don't."

"He took me surfboat riding this morning." Mae beamed.

"Koa's quite the gentleman." Hattie knew she shouldn't have worried about Koa.

"And then we went to the Seaside Inn for lunch." Mae's red hair looked orange under the office light.

Hattie rolled her chair in front of the file cabinet. "Where he probably knew one of the waiters and lunch was free?"

"But he left a generous tip." Mae smiled. "He said to tell you that Dr. Townsend is having lunch with Mrs. Stanford at the Alexander Hotel tomorrow and that Charles Dole will be there. He also said to remind you that he saved your job. He must have said that three times."

Hattie slammed the file drawer shut.

———•••••———

That evening, before readying Mrs. Stanford for bed, Hattie picked a basket of Tahitian gardenia, jasmine, and white ginger and carried it to Mrs. Stanford's room.

Mrs. Stanford was in her robe, writing a letter to Mrs. Perkins.

My dearest Dora,
  My life today is all one could wish. This afternoon, my driver spotted frolicking whales off the coast, and I was reminded of evenings sitting by the fire when young Leland Jr. first read Moby Dick.
  The grandeur of God is evident in this ocean and sky. I am blessed with long memories as I watch each setting of this mild sun. It brings a close to my day and I welcome the night. Last night, my dear Dora, I slept unfettered. A dear child has taught me to welcome Leland Jr. to my dreams. I know that he seeks his mother's comfort and I have nothing to fear . . .

Hattie greeted Mrs. Stanford then went to the bathroom and set the basket down next to the claw-foot tub.

She drew Mrs. Stanford's bath and watched the hot water steam the room and make the bead board sweat. When it was half-filled, she dumped the blossoms in the tub. A cloud of perfume scented the air.

"What have we here?" Mrs. Stanford stood at the bathroom door. "Is this a hotel custom?"

"No, ma'am. I thought it would remind you of your summer with your Uncle Ira and Aunt Maude." Hattie suddenly felt foolish.

"This was most sweet of you, my dear." Mrs. Stanford approached her and put her hand on Hattie's shoulder. Her touch was firm.

"Are you feeling well?" Hattie was unsure if she was supposed to ask Mrs. Stanford such a direct question, but after seeing her so ill just hours before, she wanted to know.

"Much better, thanks to Miss Benson."

There was a quick knock on the door followed by Miss Benson's entrance. She barged into the bathroom. "What is this?"

The blossoms floated in the tub.

"They're flowers for my bath," Mrs. Stanford answered.

A vein in Benson's forehead protruded; her stare was unbroken.

"To remind me of my Aunt Maude."

Benson asked Mrs. Stanford to allow her a few minutes to finish readying the tub. She shut the door and turned to Hattie. "How dare you be so familiar with Mrs. Stanford."

Benson sieved the flowers out of the water and dumped the blossoms in the toilet. "You are an ignorant who goes beyond her place." Her actions were frenetic. "Someone of your station!"

"I'm sorry." Hattie backed away from her.

"You're no better than a scullery maid. If I had my way, you'd be washing floors." Benson stood and wiped her hand on the towel. "Get out there. Turn on the ceiling fan, open the window, and crank the transom."

Hattie flushed with anger.

"You and I will be in Mrs. Martin's office in the morning."

"Yes, ma'am." But this time Hattie took Benson's words as empty threats, and after she did as she was told, she went back to her office to work on her accounts. Hattie sought refuge in her work. She felt safe in the balance of it—the debits and credits, the accounts payable and receivable. They had a symmetry that was predictable and fair.

By ten o'clock she was caught up on all her accounting. She polished her desk and swept the floor. She didn't want to go up to Miss Benson's room to sleep. She considered staying at the cottage, but she didn't want to give Benson any cause to find fault with her.

She stood outside the door of room 122 and heard Benson snoring. Hattie went in, readied for bed, and slithered under the covers. She rested her head on the goose down pillow. Hattie brushed her hand over the freshly laundered sheets—sheets pressed with steam irons and scented with rose water.

In the morning she was up and out of the room before Benson woke. At eight o'clock she returned with Mrs. Stanford's breakfast. She put her ear to the door and heard Mrs. Stanford moving. Balancing the tray on her knee, she knocked lightly. "It's me, Hattie," she said.

"Enter." Mrs. Stanford was sitting at the window.

Hattie set the tray on the side table. On the tray were two porcelain cups of soft-boiled eggs, a plate of French toast, a bowl of sliced mango, a pot of English Breakfast tea, and a copy of the *Pacific Commercial Advertiser,* steamed and ironed flat.

"Thank you for my bath last evening, Hattie." Mrs. Stanford picked up the newspaper. She didn't look at Hattie.

"There was an accident in Chinatown yesterday." Mrs. Stanford commented on the headlines as she sipped her tea. "A boy was killed." Mrs. Stanford folded over the paper. "A Chinese boy riding the cattle catcher of the trolley was pinned beneath it and dragged ninety feet." She sounded perturbed. "How sad to die with so few memories."

Hattie waited for Mrs. Stanford to realize that was the same accident that had caused their traffic jam. But Mrs. Stanford continued to comment, more to herself than Hattie. "General MacArthur and Captain Pershing are on their way to Manchuria."

Hattie began straightening the room.

Mrs. Stanford set the paper aside and ate her toast. "Hattie, Miss Benson and I will be going to Makee Island this morning, then I will be having lunch at the Alexander Hotel."

Koa was right, Hattie thought. She is meeting with Townsend and Dole.

"I'll have no need of your service today."

"I would be happy to accompany you." Hattie knew the importance of her being at the luncheon.

Mrs. Stanford didn't answer.

"Mrs. Martin told me I was to accompany today." It was a lie Hattie was sure she'd never get caught telling.

"Mrs. Martin is mistaken."

Hattie changed the water in the vase of roses. "Mrs. Stanford, have you seen the botanical gardens? They're near the Alexander Hotel." She tried not to sound too anxious.

"Perhaps next week."

"There's an orchid terrace there. Few tourists know where it is."

"I'm sure it's lovely."

Hattie knew by Mrs. Stanford's tone that she shouldn't suggest anything else. "If you have no more need of me . . ." Hattie's voice faded to silence.

"None," Mrs. Stanford said.

Hattie needed to talk to Koa. She couldn't call him from her office, because Mrs. Martin was in there so often. She decided to use the lobby phone. If she were caught, she could say she was helping a guest. Hattie called the Alexander. The operator didn't answer. She clicked the receiver repeatedly to no avail. Then she paced, following the pattern of the Oriental runners. She tried again—still no answer. She walked outside on the front verandah. That's when she spied Cutler across the street, at the trolley stop. He was talking to the man with the Brownie camera who had been outside Marshall's the day Mrs. Stanford ordered her gown. She saw Cutler count out money into the other man's palm. She thought the exchange curious but didn't want to be spotted, so she retreated into the hotel so as to stay out of it. She called the Alexander again. Still no answer.

That day only Miss Benson traveled with Mrs. Stanford, not even Ted Cutler went with them. When the two ladies were at Makee Island, Miss Benson hired a man to row a boat through the waterways.

Mrs. Stanford delighted in the ride. She reached up for the hanging roots of the banyan tree and tossed feed pellets to the ducks.

When their boat floated under a footbridge, joining Makee Island with Kapi'olani Park, Mrs. Stanford reminisced about her last trip to Venice with Senator Stanford. "It was my birthday," she began, retelling the story that the secretary had heard dozens of times. "And the senator arranged for every gondolier within sight to sing 'Happy Birthday' to me. Even passengers in other boats sang in their fragmented English." As Mrs. Stanford recounted every detail, Benson gazed out toward the bank of the island. It was dotted with picnicking families and courting couples. Among them was a young man with a Brownie camera.

At the end of the ride, Mrs. Stanford stood on the dock. From there, a vista of Diamond Head framed by silhouetted coconut trees could be seen. "This place proves God's love of beauty."

"Mrs. Stanford," someone called.

She turned.

"Mrs. Stanford."

Miss Benson pointed to picnickers reclining on *lau hala* mats. "It's Judge Upton. He's heading straight for us."

The picnickers were a party of native men in loosely formed jackets and women in calico *mu'umu'u*. Upton was wearing a vested suit, winged-collar shirt, and a Windsor knotted tie. "What an unexpected pleasure to see you."

"The pleasure is mine," Mrs. Stanford replied.

"I must apologize. I intended to join you at the Alexander for lunch, but I had the opportunity to meet with the Kamaka family." He gestured back to his group. "And one does not take their invitations lightly."

"My meeting was to be with Dr. Townsend alone." Mrs. Stanford turned herself away from the sun. Her vision was impaired by age and she was sensitive to light. "It's merely to review the details of the dinner."

"Details." The judge smiled. "Invitation lists, flowers, music, and the like. Thank God, Lallah is adept at entertaining. I have no taste for it." Upton's lips were so thin that his mouth disappeared under his moustache when he spoke.

"Lallah has always been social," Mrs. Stanford commented.

The judge noticed Benson looking back at the Kamaka gathering. "Let me introduce you to them," he offered. "They are quite delightful." He leaned over, as if to share a confidence. "And they wield significant political weight in both white and native circles—influence I'll need if I am to defeat Prince Kūhiō."

"The Supreme Court appointment?" Mrs. Stanford asked.

"He is the governor's choice," Upton said.

Miss Benson declined Upton's offer by referring to Mrs. Stanford's luncheon.

"Perhaps before you leave I can arrange an evening with them," Upton suggested.

"Perhaps," Mrs. Stanford answered.

Upton extended his hand to each lady. Miss Benson held his hand for the briefest time she could without being considered rude. Then both women boarded the Thompson carriage.

Once on their way, Benson affected a shiver. "He reached for my hand after slurping *poi* with his fingers. He sucks his hand dry then extends it to me . . . and his native friends . . . he's quite proud of his affiliation."

"He's politically shrewd."

"He wears their friendship like medals."

"As I'm sure he does mine," Mrs. Stanford said.

Mrs. Stanford and Miss Benson arrived at the Alexander Hotel five minutes late. The Alexander was a city hotel. There was neither portico nor *lānai*. From the hotel's oak door entrance to the street was a maroon and tan striped canvas awning.

Where The Palms Hotel was elegant, the Alexander was formal. The Alexander was a men's hotel with private dining rooms of dark paneled wood, where powerful men gathered to make decisions that history would misinterpret as destiny. There were no hostesses in long mauve skirts. Only men served meals—waiters in black trousers and white cutaway frocks. The only time a woman was allowed in the dining room was at lunch, and only as a guest of a man.

It was the manager, Mr. Theodore Hollis, himself who escorted Mrs. Stanford and Miss Benson through the lobby. The lobby was furnished with leather club chairs and marquetry tables. On them were ebony boxes, inlaid with ivory and stocked with Cuban cigars.

Mr. Hollis led the women to the Kamehameha Room, where Dr. Townsend was waiting.

The doctor updated Mrs. Stanford on the sequence of events for the dinner.

"Charles Dole will present you with a calabash on behalf of all the alumni. It will have enameled seals of the United States, the Territory of Hawaii, and Stanford University affixed to it." Townsend added, "Charles sends his regrets. He had planned to join us."

Mr. Hollis showed Mrs. Stanford the deckled vellum menu. "We shall begin with a glass of crimson claret, an appetizer of oyster cocktails followed by consommé, Roquefort cheese, green olives, and salted almonds." He glanced up at Mrs. Stanford before continuing. "An English sole for the fish plate, a main course of rack of lamb, sliced cucumber, and pommes dauphine. For dessert there is pineapple ice." The ice was to be served in a pineapple cut in half, and a cardinal red paper flag would be inserted in the ice. Each flag would have "Stanford" calligraphed in white ink.

Mrs. Stanford walked down the row of Queen Anne cherry chairs. The table was set for twenty-eight. Four sterling candelabras were evenly placed among red carnation centerpieces. "These must be lower, not to inhibit conversation across the table." Mrs. Stanford broke off a piece of fern.

Mr. Hollis made a note of it.

Miss Benson picked up a dinner program and handed it to Mrs. Stanford.

"I prefer scrolls." Mrs. Stanford rolled the tented program and showed Mr. Hollis her example. "To be tied with a cardinal red ribbon and tucked with a white Tahitian gardenia. Don't you agree, Isaiah?"

"It's your pleasure, Mrs. Stanford." He brought over a copy of the souvenir booklet that each guest would take away. The booklet contained photographs of all the buildings on the university campus. On the cover was a pen and ink sketch of the recently completed Memorial Church.

Mrs. Stanford was proud of her building program and Memorial Church marked the halfway point. The campus was her vision, hers and Senator

Stanford's, and she didn't tolerate the slightest deviation from it—not the sequence of building, not the arrangement of furniture in the rooms, not the purpose of each room.

When President Ambrose scheduled a visiting scholar to meet with students in the parlor of one of the girls' dormitories, Mrs. Stanford dictated a memo to him. "Dormitory parlors are not meant for lectures. See me in the morning."

President Ambrose's criticisms of Stanford's "Stone Age" became bolder. During a faculty meeting, Ambrose let slip a disparaging remark that seeped back to Mrs. Stanford. She responded with vitriolic tongue-lashing, calling Ambrose's vision "stale" and one that would have to be adjusted. From that day forth, the president met with Mrs. Stanford daily.

President Ambrose retaliated in August of 1904 when he wrote a memo to the board of trustees to be read at their meeting. "If the university starts the excavating for one more sandstone and tile memorial, the faculty will mutiny and the university will attract professors worthy of the pittance we offer."

It was at that meeting that Mrs. Stanford ordered the ground breaking of Memorial Church.

Mrs. Stanford held the cover of the booklet closer. "It's a fine likeness of Memorial Church."

"The Ellis Orchestra will be in this corner." Mr. Hollis gestured toward the south end of the room where a platform had been built for the musicians.

"I prefer not to see the musicians," Mrs. Stanford said.

"Can you put them in the hallway?" Benson asked.

"It would affect food service," Mr. Hollis said.

Mrs. Stanford walked to the platformed area. "We shall use this area for photographs. I want standing urns filled with red and white carnations." She made a swooping arch with her parasol. "And a comfortable chair here." She tapped the floor. "Where I may be seated and each student may pose for a portrait with me."

Mr. Hollis said, "We could put the musicians behind a three-paneled Oriental screen in the north corner of the room."

He sketched out a floor plan for Mrs. Stanford, annotating his drawing. While he did, Miss Benson wiped her gloved fingers over the candelabras and examined the table settings. She turned over the china plates—Lenox bone china, rimmed in gold. Despite her scrutiny, she failed to find any flaws.

Mrs. Stanford perused the invitation list. Messrs. Roth, Wilson, and Vin Dine, members of the charter class, confirmed they would attend, as would Joy Cartwright, who claimed to be a distant Stanford cousin. Only Mr. Boulware and Miss Woodward regretted. While Mrs. Stanford read over the list, Mr. Hollis described the floral arrangement to be placed in the foyer of the hotel. He had ordered a grand topiary "S" made of twenty-two dozen red carnations.

After all the details of the reception were approved, Mr. Hollis took his leave and Miss Benson announced her departure as well. "I will call for you at seven," Benson reminded Mrs. Stanford, and she left to enjoy a free afternoon.

Dr. Townsend leafed through the souvenir booklet. He looked up at his old friend. "After

Leland died, I thought the university would fail. But you have done well, Jane."

"*We* have done well, Isaiah." Mrs. Stanford referred to Townsend accompanying her to speak to President Cleveland in March of 1894. It was that visit that led to the Supreme Court rejecting the federal government's claim against the senator's estate.

"Although I was surprised to read that you're not building the library."

"I stopped the building of the gymnasium, not the library," Mrs. Stanford corrected.

Townsend stroked his moustache. "The *Advertiser* quoted Ambrose about a moratorium on all building until you returned from the Orient. He specifically referred to the library."

"He defies me in my absence, like a child!" Immediately her breathing was labored. "I'm through with him! He doesn't even have the courage to confront me in person! This is his final act."

She pointed to Townsend. "Arrange a meeting within hours of his arrival in Honolulu. I want Noah Upton there as a witness. I shall dismiss him before he can utter a word."

"Jane, you can't do that. Not without the board of trustees."

"No one will tamper with my university!"

Townsend pulled a chair out for her.

"If there are legal challenges," she added, "let Noah deal with them."

Townsend took her hand. "Let me speak with Ambrose first, Jane. It's not in your best interest to proceed this way." He sat next to her.

"Simon Ambrose will not prevail."

"Trust me, Jane. I shall always stand by your

side." His voice was soothing.

"I want your loyalty to be with the university, Isaiah, not with me." Her head quivered. "Never abandon the university."

"I promise you."

"The university must be foremost." She was nearly panting.

"You have my word." Townsend stroked her hand.

❧ Chapter Eight ❧

That evening Mrs. Stanford and Miss Benson were first to arrive at their dinner table. Mrs. Stanford was gaily dressed in a cornflower blue dress, and it was Benson who wore somber gray. While they were waiting for Dr. Lowell, Mrs. Stanford asked, "How do I look?" But before her companion could answer, Mrs. Stanford boasted, "I believe we both look wonderfully."

"You're in fine spirits," Benson remarked.

"I had a visit from Mr. Cutler this afternoon. The Morse Detective Agency concluded the poison attempt on my life was a ruse."

Before she could continue, Dr. Lowell approached the table and greeted each lady.

"What a marvelous evening," Lowell remarked.

The surf was strong and the trade winds rocked the frosted globe lights.

"It is a most wonderful evening," Mrs. Stanford replied.

Lowell took his place, noting that Cutler had not yet arrived.

"Mr. Cutler will not be joining us," Mrs. Stanford said. Then to Benson's apparent shock, Mrs. Stanford frankly revealed that Cutler was her bodyguard and the reason for her protection. "It is a matter of time before the press will expose the fraud perpetuated. However, it ends well."

"Mrs. Stanford, if you don't mind my asking, you said the chemist's report indicated strychnine. Was he, too, involved in the charade?" Lowell asked.

"The Morse detectives believe that the poison was placed in the bottle on the way to the pharmacy." Mrs. Stanford then addressed Benson. "Miss Dobbs is suspected of foul play, but she is not suspected of murder."

"A twist of Munchausen by proxy," Lowell noted.

"But the ordeal has passed."

"Then I say a celebration is in order." He ordered a bottle of Mumm's champagne and raised his glass in a toast. "To a grand lady, the Mother of Stanford University."

Mrs. Stanford took a sip. "A bit of indigestion," she explained.

Dr. Lowell offered her his medical service if she needed it.

"I appreciate the gesture, doctor, but I'm certain that I am suffering from a bout of overeating."

"Agreed." Benson nodded.

Lowell recited his credentials anyway, as if to reassure her. He was trained in Edinburgh, London, and Dublin. He had been on the faculty of Columbia University Medical School and currently was chief of surgery at Queen's Hospital.

"Thank you, doctor. But this condition is one my secretary can easily manage."

"And often has," Benson added.

For dinner Mrs. Stanford ordered plain broth and steamed asparagus. Despite her restraint, however, her abdominal discomfort increased. Early in the evening, she excused herself to retire.

Benson was on her feet and positioned to assist Mrs. Stanford.

"Stay," she told Benson.

"Nonsense."

"I insist, Miss Benson. Enjoy the evening, listen to the doctor's stories, and in the morning you can recount his adventures to me."

Benson was about to interrupt.

"Miss Benson, Hattie can tend to me."

Hattie was becoming more comfortable with Mrs. Stanford. She laid out Mrs. Stanford's nightwear and poured her a glass of water.

Mrs. Stanford sat at her dressing table. "You're a bookkeeper, is that correct?"

"I am." Hattie brushed Mrs. Stanford's hair in slow, deliberate strokes. Then she began loosely braiding it for bed.

"Miss Benson was a bookkeeper when she first came to me. Is that your aspiration in life? To be a bookkeeper?"

Hattie's dream was to own her own hotel. It would have a broad *lānai* that faced the ocean. On weekend nights a Hawaiian trio would play music, and on Sunday she would serve a dessert of *kūlolo*.

"I'm uncertain of my future," she answered Mrs. Stanford.

"A good Christian woman gives dignity to her work. No matter what her work is."

"Yes, ma'am." Hattie tied a pale blue ribbon to the end of Mrs. Stanford's braid, and Mrs. Stanford settled in bed. Hattie handed her her Bible.

"Will you pray with me, Hattie?"

Hattie nodded, uncertain.

Mrs. Stanford closed her eyes and clasped the Bible to her chest. "Lord, keep my soul this night, and if death comes to me, Lord, bring me an angel to calm my fears. Let him take me by the hand and walk me to the Refuge Land and stand Judgment with me at your heavenly gate. Amen."

Hattie echoed, "Amen."

Mrs. Stanford opened her eyes. "Now get my medicine basket, dear."

While Hattie went to the dressing closet for the medicine, Mrs. Stanford inscribed the frontispiece of her Bible.

Mrs. Stanford directed Hattie to dole out a cascara capsule and pour a glass of water then set a spoonful of bicarbonate of soda next to it. The bicarbonate was in an octagonal cobalt blue bottle with an embossed silver leaf label from Charles Wells & Co., Chemists, King Williams Street, Adelaide.

Mrs. Stanford noticed Hattie admiring the bottle. "I've kept the bottle for its color," she said. "I've had it since my last trip to Australia."

Hattie tipped the bottle and poured out one spoonful of soda then set the spoon and bottle on the nightstand.

"I'll take it later." Mrs. Stanford told Hattie she wanted to drink some water first before taking the soda.

Mrs. Stanford handed the Bible to Hattie.

"What would you like me to read?" Hattie sat on the chair next to the bed.

"Please read the inscription at the front."

Hattie peeled back the onionskin leaf. In her

jagged handwriting, Mrs. Stanford had written, "February 28, 1905. For Miss Hattie Lehua, in thanks for your service. When you pray, pray for me, Mrs. Jane L. Stanford."

Hattie was shocked. "I can't accept this." She ran her fingers across the letters. "This is too dear."

"It's my custom to give Bibles," Mrs. Stanford said. "Though not usually my own," she added.

"I can't, Mrs. Stanford." The leather cover was soft to the touch.

"It's a gift."

Hattie had nothing to match it. All she could offer was her thanks. "I will treasure it."

"Don't treasure it, child, read it."

Hattie thanked her again and was about to say something when Mrs. Stanford said, "You've given me peace, Hattie. It's a peace I haven't known for years."

In all of Hattie's life no one had expressed such gratitude to her. "What would you like me to read?" Hattie opened the Bible.

"Just leave me tonight," Mrs. Stanford said.

"I'd gladly sit until you're asleep," Hattie offered.

Mrs. Stanford said she preferred to be alone.

Hattie retired to her room next door. She sat at the chair next to the window and reread the inscription in the Bible. "When you pray, pray for me."

There was a knock on the door.

"Hattie." Mrs. Martin stepped in. "Miss Benson told me I'd find you here. I've just come from a meeting with Mr. St. Clair."

Hattie was sure Benson had lodged a complaint against her. Mrs. Martin sat on the bed. "Mrs.

Stanford asked Mr. St. Clair if The Palms would release you so you could accompany her to Japan."

"To Japan? For how long?"

"A month, maybe two."

"What about the assistant position?"

"Hattie, after traveling to the Orient, you'll be sought after by every hotel in Hawai'i—even San Francisco. Being my assistant would be something you'd be above."

Hattie knew she should be grateful, but all she felt was fear. The assistant position was what she wanted. But Japan? With Mrs. Stanford? And then there was Benson.

"Think about it, Hattie."

That night Hattie lay in bed weighing her decision. She knew this was an opportunity offered only once. She would see and do things beyond anything she could imagine—travel to the Orient, sail in first-class cabins, wear tailor-made clothes, dine in elegant hotels—but, there was Benson. Hattie looked over at Benson's empty bed. She knew one word from Benson, a suspicion or accusation, true or imagined, and she would fall from grace with Mrs. Stanford. Hattie remembered Mae's words the first day she was in service: "Take my warning, my dear, if Mrs. Stanford shows a liking for you, she'll make your life a living hell."

Hattie fell asleep, confused.

She woke to Mrs. Stanford's scream. "Gertrude! I am sick!"

Benson switched on the lamp. She checked the time. "Eleven o'clock," she said aloud. "You go to her," she told Hattie.

Hattie rushed out of the room. Mrs. Stanford was

standing in her open doorway, leaning on the door-frame. Hattie put her arm around her waist. Mrs. Stanford's breath smelled like vomit. Her nightdress was drenched. "I've been poisoned," she gasped.

Hattie helped the matron to a chair in her room and ran back to Benson. "She's sick."

"It's a nightmare." Benson rolled over in her bed.

"She said she's been poisoned!"

Benson threw off her blanket and pushed Hattie out of the way. When she saw Mrs. Stanford, she yelled, "Get Dr. Lowell!"

Hattie ran to the elevator. Hiram was sitting on his stool, reading. "What's all the commotion?"

"Hiram, get Dr. Lowell. Tell him Mrs. Stanford needs him. Go! Now!"

"What's wrong with her?"

Hattie pulled back the gate herself. "Hurry!"

Hattie raced to her office and fumbled at the door. "Keys!" The lock jammed. "Work!" She shoved the keys in again, threw the door open, and called Mrs. Martin.

In the meantime, Gertrude Benson toweled the sweat from Mrs. Stanford's face.

"Gertrude, my neck," Mrs. Stanford moaned.

When Benson lightly massaged her, Mrs. Stanford's face contorted and her body stiffened. She clamped onto Benson's arms. Then her body relaxed. "Gertrude, I am so afraid."

Benson held her. "I'm here," she said. "I'm here."

"Water," Mrs. Stanford begged.

Benson went to the bathroom to pour a glass of warm water.

She held the glass to her matron's lips. Mrs. Stanford took a sip. Benson stroked Mrs. Stanford's shoulder—her arm shot out in a reflex, then she slumped forward. She looked up at Benson. "I have no control."

Upstairs, the elevator boy was banging on Dr. Lowell's door. The doctor was already awake. He slipped on his trousers and was buttoning his shirt as he opened the door.

"Mrs. Stanford is sick." It was all Hiram knew.

Dr. Lowell tucked his medical bag under his arm and finished dressing in the elevator.

Hiram slid open the elevator gate and pointed to the last room on the right. "Room 120."

There was no need for his announcement. A cluster of guests congregated outside Mrs. Stanford's room.

When Dr. Lowell entered the room, Mrs. Stanford was still sitting on the chair. Her back was stiff, her head thrown back, her fingers spread, and her thumbs pressed into her palms. She opened her mouth to speak but a spasm took over. She clutched at Benson. When the spasm subsided, she told the doctor, "I've been poisoned—the soda."

Dr. Lowell went to the nightstand. He dipped his finger into the bicarbonate of soda and tasted it. "Bitter." He asked Benson if she had given Mrs. Stanford anything to drink.

"Just water," Benson said.

"How much?"

"Less than a glass."

"Has she thrown anything up?"

"No, but she did before she called me." The ceramic basin was splattered with vomit.

Mrs. Stanford's lip curled into a snarl. Her back arched high.

"She needs ipecac," Benson said.

"Not ipecac," said the doctor.

Mrs. Stanford's convulsion subsided, but she still gripped the arms of the chair.

Dr. Lowell shuffled through his bag. "Ipecac might affect her heart." Whatever it was he was looking for, he didn't find. He stood and took Mrs. Stanford's hands in his. "I will get you through this, madam," he reassured her. "I will get you through."

Then he took her chin firmly in one hand, tilting it to the ceiling. He told her he was going to remove her dentures, which he did as gently as possible.

Tears flowed down Mrs. Stanford's cheeks. Her eyes had the wide look of panic.

The doctor set the dentures aside then dug in his bag again, this time coming out with a mustard emetic and handed it to Miss Benson. "Mix it with water and get her to drink as much as you can. I need a stomach pump." He left to call Dr. Knight, who lived only two blocks from The Palms.

Miss Benson held the glass to Mrs. Stanford's lips.

"I cannot." Mrs. Stanford shook her head. "My jaws are set."

Miss Benson rubbed her mistress's cheeks and coaxed her to drink.

"No more." Mrs. Stanford pulled away.

When Hattie returned to the room, Benson told her to fill a basin with hot water, and place it at Mrs. Stanford's feet.

Dr. Lowell was in his suite, telephoning Dr. Knight. He told him to bring a stomach pump with utmost haste. "Mrs. Stanford has been poisoned."

When Lowell returned to Mrs. Stanford's

room, the scene was calmer. Mrs. Stanford was sitting upright with her feet in the basin of water. Hattie was kneeling in front of her, massaging her feet, while Benson rubbed her arms and hands with alcohol.

Mrs. Stanford appeared more comfortable, although her mouth was still drawn, her knees were apart, and the soles of her feet were curled into each other.

The doctor prepared a syringe and injected her with a chloral hydrate. Mrs. Stanford didn't wince but looked at him with a mute pleading.

Hattie stared at Mrs. Stanford's face as she massaged her feet. She thought she saw an edge of a smile, or at least a lessening of fear in her eyes.

"Work more firmly," Dr. Lowell said.

Although she wanted to be gentle with her touch, Hattie pressed harder and slower, careful not to startle when Mrs. Stanford moaned. Tears filled Hattie's eyes.

Without her dentures, Mrs. Stanford's mouth was puckered. Her hair was disheveled; vomit was caught in its strands.

Hattie wished she could fill a tub with flowers and sluice water over Mrs. Stanford's back. She wished she could console her and comfort her, but all she could do was pray.

Hattie thought Mrs. Stanford smiled at her. She forced herself to smile back.

"Sweet Hattie," she heard Mrs. Stanford say. "Dear Hattie."

Then Mrs. Stanford flailed. Her back arched, lifting her hips off the chair, then her feet jerked, the basin tipped, and water drenched the carpet.

"God forgive my sins!" Mrs. Stanford cried. Miss Benson supported her back.

"Where is he?" Dr. Lowell yelled. "He's only two blocks away." He looked toward the closed door as if he could conjure Dr. Knight to appear.

Ted Cutler opened the door. "Dr. Knight's right behind me with the pump." Cutler set Knight's medical bag down—when Cutler saw Mrs. Stanford, he gasped.

"Help me carry her," Dr. Lowell said.

The two men lifted her into bed.

"Mr. St. Clair and Mrs. Martin are on the way," Cutler said.

Mrs. Stanford prayed, "Lord, prepare me to meet my dear ones."

Dr. Lowell took a bottle of chloroform anesthesia from Dr. Knight's bag.

Mrs. Stanford's body rose in an arc—only her head and feet touched the mattress. Her body cramped. She screamed, "This is a horrible way to die!"

Dr. Knight arrived, pump under his arm, panting.

Mrs. Stanford convulsed. There was a violent tremor, then her body dropped. She was still and her jaw was locked in a silent scream.

At 11:40 p.m. on February 28, 1905, Mrs. Jane Lathrop Stanford died in room 120 of The Palms Hotel.

Dr. Lowell closed over her eyes and asked for a handkerchief to tie up her jaw. As he wrapped the cloth around her face, no one moved. The only sound was the whirl of the ceiling fan.

The clang of the elevator door sounded in the hallway. The voices of Mr. St. Clair and Mrs. Martin became louder as they approached. Still, no one moved. When the two entered the room, it was as if a tableau had been destroyed and the sanctity of Mrs. Stanford's death had been invaded.

Then, without a word between them, the two doctors collected the medical evidence in the room. Knight took a clean towel from the bathroom and bundled up the ceramic basin with Mrs. Stanford's vomit. He picked up a pale blue ribbon off the floor and tied the towel with it. Lowell gathered the bicarbonate of soda, the spoon, and glass of water from Mrs. Stanford's night stand.

"Was the bicarbonate the only thing you gave her tonight?" Lowell asked Hattie.

"No," she answered and retrieved the cascara capsules from the medicine basket.

He took the vial.

When the physicians were satisfied, Dr. Lowell said he and Dr. Knight would be in his suite.

Before he left, Dr. Lowell leaned over Mrs. Stanford's body and whispered.

Mr. Cutler approached Mr. St. Clair. "There are some facts you should be aware of. It might be best to talk in your office." Cutler and St. Clair walked down the hall; Mrs. Martin followed.

From St. Clair's office, Ted Cutler wired a message to President Ambrose aboard the SS *Mariposa*. It read: "Mrs. Stanford has died suddenly."

He sent the same cable to the Stanford University Board of Trustees, Inspector Whelan of the Morse Detective Agency, and Mrs. Stanford's brother, Harrison Lathrop in San Francisco, not knowing that Lathrop was also aboard the *Mariposa*.

The news of Mrs. Stanford's death rippled over the phone lines from The Palms Hotel to Sheriff

Dillon's house, from the police station to the attorney general.

Sheriff Dillon was first to arrive at the hotel to collect the evidence. Within an hour of Mrs. Stanford's death, he was in Dr. Lowell's suite questioning the physicians.

Sheriff Robert Dillon was a clean-shaven man who still carried himself with the bearing of his West Point training. He wore wire-rimmed glasses that were planted firmly on his nose, and the part in his graying hair looked as if it were cut with a straight edge. The sheriff was asking the doctors about the cascara when Cutler arrived. He introduced himself to the sheriff as a detective with the Morse Detective Agency of San Francisco.

Only Miss Benson and Hattie were left.

Benson was perched over Mrs. Stanford, removing her pearl earrings, when she noticed Hattie staring at her. "I don't want any jewels to be stolen at the mortuary." Her tone suggested that only the ignorant would do otherwise.

Miss Benson removed Mrs. Stanford's diamond ring, then the aquamarine, and shoved them in her pocket. Mrs. Stanford's mourning bracelet wouldn't budge. She tugged at it but the old woman's arm had grown too fat. Benson unclasped the chain of her locket then turned to Hattie. "See if you can get the rest of it off—except for her wedding band," and she left.

Hattie wanted no part of it. She stood over Mrs. Stanford's body and lightly touched her shoulder. Her body was still warm. Hattie put her hand on Mrs. Stanford's chest, half expecting to feel her breathe.

Hattie had never seen anyone die before. She

saw her uncle's body carried home by fishermen, but he was long dead and bloated by the sea. Mrs. Stanford was just alive, she had just spoken to her—she was alive, then she was not.

"God, give me courage," Hattie whispered. She imagined Mrs. Stanford's soul floating from her body.

Hattie tried to pry off the remaining rings. She twisted them as gently as she could, as if Mrs. Stanford could still feel pain. She took off the emerald, then the topaz. Some of Mrs. Stanford's skin scraped off, and Hattie found it strange that her finger bled. Mrs. Stanford's bracelet wouldn't give way—the mourning bracelet for her husband would follow her to her grave.

Mrs. Stanford's face was contorted. The handkerchief that clamped her jaw was knotted at her head. Its points fell over her hair like a grotesque masquerade of a rabbit.

For all the commotion of an hour ago, Hattie sat vigil alone—from midnight on—just she and the corpse and the soul departing.

It was Mr. Pai from Williams' Mortuary who came for her body. He was a kind-looking man with gentle eyes. Sheriff Dillon followed him. The sheriff, acting as coroner, viewed the body and released it to Mr. Pai.

In the darkness of 4:00 a.m., Mr. St. Clair called six men to act as jurors for the coroner's inquest. He selected himself; Mr. Pembroke, the owner of The Palms; Thomas Albert Belknap, Jared Berry, and William James Crowe, who were guests at the hotel; and his friend Edward Santos Cunha, who lived nearby.

Before the jurors viewed the body, Mr. Pai

cleaned it and moved it to a private dining room where, at 4:45 a.m., all six men attested to her death. It was Wednesday, March 1.

When Mrs. Stanford's body was carried to the hearse, it wasn't yet dawn. The moon hadn't set, the sun hadn't risen. Under cover of gray, before most people were awake, her corpse was taken to Queen's Hospital without the intrusion of reporters.

Hattie stood on the front verandah as the hearse rumbled away. The horses reared, the carriage master snapped his whip, and the peacocks of 'Āinahau screeched their mourning call.

Hattie walked down the steps, onto Waikiki Road. By then the sun had risen, the first trolley rolled by, and a few curious spectators congregated on the front verandah.

She crossed the street, turned down Kukui Street, and went back to her cottage, where she sat until seven o'clock, when Mae McCauley opened the screen door.

Hattie was abrupt. "Mrs. Stanford is dead." She told Mae what happened.

"Benson killed her" was Mae's response.

❧ CHAPTER NINE ❧

On Wednesday morning, March 1, 1905, seven men assembled at Queen's Hospital for the autopsy. Dr. Adolf Henrik, the hospital's chief pathologist, convened the autopsy and functioned as the prosector. As was his habit, Henrik arrived an hour early. He set his leather tool bag on the soapstone counter, examined the autopsy table, and inventoried the supplies. Then he drew his bread knife out of its leather sheath and sharpened it methodically. He checked its edge with his thumb, angling it and pivoting it to the overhead light until there was a uniform gleam; then he moved on to his hammer with hook, his skull chisel, bore and bit, and handsaw.

Dr. Henrik was a graceless man. When the mortician, Mr. Williams, and his assistant, Mr. Pai, rolled the gurney with Mrs. Stanford's body into the room, Dr. Henrik didn't even raise his head.

"Good morning, doctor," Mr. Pai said as he and Mr. Williams lifted the body onto the autopsy table.

Henrik did not reply.

"Shall I sign in?" Pai asked.

The pathologist grunted.

Pai listed himself as the *diener*, the autopsy assistant.

Mr. Pai wedged his shoulder under Mrs. Stanford's body. He placed a wooden pillow under her shoulder blades, causing her chest to protrude and her head and neck to fall back. Next he tried to fix her arms close to her body, but her arms were stiff from rigor mortis, and he forcibly shoved them inside the rim of the table. The table, more like a trough, was rigged with drain plugs. Pai set a dissecting tray of instruments over the legs of the corpse; he covered the entire tray with a towel and covered only the genitals of the corpse.

Dr. Henrik lined up his rib cutters, scissors, and forceps—all exactly an inch and a half apart. He was so absorbed in his ritual that he didn't respond to Dr. Tyler Flynn's "Good morning." Dr. Flynn was the territory's toxicologist.

"Good morning, Dr. Flynn," Pai said as he hooked a metal tray to the white enamel scale. The tray bounced and the red arrow flickered on the dial.

Dr. Tyler Flynn looked like a dull-witted man. His head was so bald it looked waxed and his moustache was as broad as the tail of a dog. Despite his looks, he was a sharp fellow. Unfortunately, most eligible ladies couldn't ignore his looks or his annoying habit of coughing whenever he got nervous. Flynn seemed doomed to life as a bachelor.

Flynn took off his jacket and put on a butcher's apron. As he dressed, Dr. Clifford Solomon, the chief sanitation officer for the territory, entered the room with Drs. Lowell and Knight. They were discussing different breeds of dogs. Dr. Henrik ignored their prattle.

"I've heard you purchased a Highland terrier," Lowell said to Flynn.

"Yes." He randomly arranged the bone saw, hammer, and sail maker's needle on his surgical tray.

"He makes for a good companion."

Dr. Solomon said his wife, Dorothea, wanted a spaniel, but his sons wanted a bulldog.

"Gentlemen, these things are better discussed elsewhere," Dr. Henrik scolded. "We're physicians, not tea matrons."

The doctors exchanged glances and snickered like reprimanded schoolboys.

Dr. Adolf Henrik was an eminent pathologist. He was widely published and his body of work was recognized in America and Europe, but as a social creature he was a clod of a man—expressionless and perpetually serious. His most distinguishing characteristic was his ears. They were sugar bowl handle ears, protruding so far that they forced an observer to consciously not stare at them, but rather to fixate on his flat green eyes instead.

"I'm considering getting an English bulldog," Dr. Knight announced, as if to challenge Henrik's rebuke.

"A marvelous breed, Peter. If The Palms allowed pets, a bulldog would be my choice." Dr. Lowell stepped back for Mr. Pai to pass.

Pai dragged a water hose to the autopsy table and slipped the hose under Mrs. Stanford's raised body. Then he retrieved four brown ceramic crocks filled with formaldehyde. Each was stenciled with yellow block letters: "Queen's Hospital Specimen Jars."

Henrik cleared his throat then announced he was ready to begin; Mr. Pai wiped the blackboard clean of a previous autopsy's weights and measures.

Dr. Solomon recorded, "Wednesday, March 1, 1905, 9:30 a.m." The nib of his pen dragged the smallest of hairs behind it, smudging the words he wrote.

"Those in attendance," Dr. Solomon called out.

"Adolf Henrik, prosector."

"Tyler Flynn, chief toxicologist of the Territory of Hawaii, assistant."

"Ian Lowell, attending physician at death, observer."

"Peter Knight, attending physician at death, observer."

"Edward Williams, mortician, observer."

"Kalani Pai, *diener*."

Dr. Solomon spoke last. "Clifford Solomon, chief sanitation officer, recorder."

Dr. Henrik asked Lowell and Knight to identify the corpse as Mrs. Stanford's.

"It is," they answered.

Dr. Henrik lifted the cardboard tag on the great right toe of the corpse and read, "Jane Lathrop Stanford." Then he described the deceased as a well-nourished Caucasian woman, seventy-six years old. "The body of the deceased is marked by extensive postmortem staining. There is greater than expected violet purple spreading over the face, extending to the ears and lower part of the cheeks. The feet are in the same condition of lividity."

Henrik leaned over the body. He was inches from her skin. The only thing separating him from the corpse was a magnifying glass. The observing doctors leaned slightly forward. The room was silent. The smell of bleach pervaded. The prosector examined each arm.

Then the autopsy room's door crashed open, and all eyes turned to a burly, white-bearded man in a caped jacket. There was a young man at his side.

"I apologize for my lateness, Adolf. It was unavoidable," the older man said.

"Dr. Armstrong." Henrik nodded in recognition.

Dr. Archibald Armstrong had taken a shortcut to medical fame. His celebrity was the result of one accident of fate that occurred forty years prior. By default, as a young resident, Archibald Armstrong assisted Dr. Chase Simpson of Massachusetts General Hospital in the first use of chloroform during surgery on humans. Every medical journal in the world recorded his name as being a member of that team. In truth, Dr. Armstrong's singular contribution was handing the surgeons their implements. But his name was forever linked with that milestone and it catapulted his career. By the age of twenty-eight, the Australian Royal Medical Society appointed him to the faculty of Sydney University Medical College, where he remained until his retirement to Hawai'i in 1903.

"I hope you don't mind, Adolf, but I've brought a first-year medical student from Sydney." He presented Jerrold MacSween, a towheaded young man with a ruddy complexion. "I was telling Jerrold how fortuitous it is for him to see the corpse of a strychnine death." Armstrong lifted his arms and MacSween removed his cape.

"Dr. Armstrong, we are here to determine a cause of death, not to confirm any speculation about strychnine." Henrik's voice was devoid of emotion.

Archibald Armstrong bullied his way past Mr. Pai, clearing a place for himself and MacSween next to the body. He nudged MacSween and pointed to Mrs. Stanford's arms and legs. "Classic strychnine," he said. "The rigidity is beyond rigor mortis."

Dr. Henrik glared at Armstrong. "There is marked rigidity of muscles. The feet are adducted and flexed. The toes are in the state of tension."

Armstrong pointed to Mrs. Stanford's hands. "Take a look at her thumbs." They were pressed into her palms.

Dr. Henrik glided a magnifying glass over the corpse. Twice he paused, spread the skin with his index finger and thumb, and leaned in closer.

Armstrong explained to MacSween, "He's looking for punctures to rule out tetanus. It's the only other explanation for the spasms at death."

Henrik stood at Mrs. Stanford's head as Flynn opened her mouth and prodded her cheeks, tongue, and gums with his fingers. He, too, examined the skin, sometimes stretching it and bringing the magnifying glass closer. But each time, he shook his head and said, "For the record, there is an absence of cutaneous or mucous membrane wounds."

"It's not tetanus." Dr. Armstrong gloated. "I knew it."

Henrik rested his hand below Mrs. Stanford's sternum. He inserted the point of his scalpel at her right shoulder and drew it down to the sternum. Then he made a second cut from the left shoulder to the sternum and continued to the pubis in a perfect Y. Mr. Pai peeled back the skin and muscles of the chest, and Dr. Flynn sawed the ribs and removed the sternum. The smell of raw meat rushed through the room.

Flynn extracted the lungs and plunked them on the scale. Blood splattered on the tile wall. "2096 grams."

Dr. Solomon recorded the weight for the territory, and Pai wrote it on the blackboard. Then Flynn transferred the lungs to the dissecting tray. His apron was splotched crimson.

With steady, long strokes, Dr. Henrik bread-loafed the lungs into one-centimeter slices. The lungs were ashen in color, but showed no gross abnormalities. Henrik asked Solomon to read back his notes, while Pai deposited the lungs into a specimen jar.

With bloodied hands, Dr. Henrik reached for his scissors. He opened the pericardial sac and snipped the pulmonary artery of the heart. Then he thrust his finger into the artery repeatedly. "No thromboembolus," he said.

Dr. Flynn concurred. "There is no evidence of a clot."

Jerrold MacSween looked to Dr. Armstrong as if waiting for an explanation, but Armstrong was engrossed in the procedure.

Dr. Henrik said, "All the valves and vessels of the heart are competent. The blood vessels are full. There is a small quantity of dark liquid blood found in the left chamber."

"There is no clotting?" Dr. Solomon asked.

"There is no postmortem clotting of blood, and the blood is fluid and dark." Henrik's voice was certain.

"Is there an enlargement of the heart?" Dr. Lowell asked.

Henrik turned to Dr. Lowell and said, "Shall we wait for the measurements, doctor? Then perhaps your question will be answered."

"Yes, sir," Lowell deferred.

Henrik stated, "There is thickness of the walls."

Knight elbowed his friend and whispered, "Why did you ask?"

"Miss Benson told me that Mrs. Stanford had an enlarged heart."

Dr. Henrik tossed his scissors in the enamel pan. There was the ping of metal on metal.

Mr. Pai weighed Mrs. Stanford's heart. "281 grams." He posted the weight on the board.

From the back, Dr. Armstrong remarked on the exceptional light weight of her heart. "Obviously not enlarged."

"The liver appears nutmeg in color." Dr. Henrik tugged it out, cut the attachments, and tied off the colon.

Jerrold MacSween gagged.

Armstrong patted the student on the back. "Learn to stomach it, boy. It's the sweet smell of money."

Dr. Henrik shook his head. His fee was $150.

Dr. Solomon recorded as Henrik dictated. "Chest, liver, and kidneys in normal condition. There are a few gallstones. The ovaries are atrophied, but normal for a woman this age."

When Pai slit the intestines in the sink, the room reeked of feces and vomitus. MacSween blanched and reached for the chair behind him. He sat with his head between his legs.

Lowell tapped the young man's shoulder and handed him a pinch of snuff. "It's an old-timer's trick." Then he inhaled a pinch himself. "Despite what the Lord Armstrong says, some of us never get used to the smell."

Pai drained the contents of the intestines and saved them in one of the crocks. As he poured, they looked like muddied pea soup. Next were the gall-bladder, bladder, heart, and blood—each in separate jars with cardboard labels.

Dr. Flynn handed the stomach to Pai. The stomach contained a liter of fluid, but no solid matter except for a few floating particles that were taken out and sealed in a separate jar.

MacSween retched.

"It's the gastric acid," Lowell said.

"Shall we wager on the young man fainting?" Dr. Knight mocked.

Dr. Solomon raised his hand. "One dollar on the boy's skull meeting the floor."

"If you please, gentlemen," Henrik reprimanded.

Pai edged the wood pillow under Mrs. Stanford's shoulders higher up her spine toward her neck. This forced her skull into a desirable angle for Dr. Flynn to make the skull incision. With agility, Flynn sawed off the top of her head and used the chisel to pry the skull.

MacSween looked away as Dr. Flynn pried off the skullcap. There was a tearing sound. Then there was the thud of the hammer hook on the cranium, the chipping of bone with the chisel.

"I've got it," Mr. Pai said.

There was a splash. The brain floated in a glass jar. It was suspended from a string tied to the base of the brain and hooked on the lid.

Dr. Henrik stepped back from the body. He read the weights on the blackboard. "Did you get the urine?"

Solomon replied, "50 milliliters."

Henrik asked, "Dr. Solomon, are you confident of all your measures?"

"I am."

"Mr. Pai, are you certain of all your measures?" Henrik asked.

"I am, sir."

Then, in an unusual gesture, Dr. Henrik asked, "Are there any questions or concerns from the observers?"

There were none.

Henrik then asked, "Dr. Flynn, as assistant, are you satisfied?" The question was a formality.

Flynn said he was satisfied, and Henrik declared the autopsy completed and invited each gentleman to come forward and witness the report.

Dr. Flynn was first to sign, then each man added his name.

When Ian Lowell came forward, he stopped at the head of the deceased. Mrs. Stanford's face was contorted into a garish smile. He put his hands on her cheeks and manipulated her face until it looked more at rest. When he let go, her face returned to its twisted smile.

"*Risus sardonicus*," Dr. Knight said. "I'm sure Mr. Williams can make her presentable." He looked up at the mortician, who simply nodded.

"More proof that it was strychnine," Armstrong interjected. "As is this." He pried open her fingers and as soon as he let go, the fingers recoiled.

As the physicians mulled about, Adolf Henrik sluiced water over his instruments and Clifford Solomon placed the specimen crocks into wooden boxes.

After all observers signed, Dr. Henrik called Police Officer Benitez to escort Dr. Solomon and Mr. Williams to the territory's laboratory. Solomon and Williams each took a wooden crate of specimen jars and followed Benitez down the hall.

Officer Benitez was a surly-looking man who just

cleared the height of the door. His uniform strained at the buttons. When the three men reached the front door of the hospital, Benitez put his back to the door and held it open. Reporters rushed at them. They shouted questions. Cameras flashed.

Benitez yelled, "Step back."

"Is it true Mrs. Stanford was poisoned by her secretary? Were there any knife wounds on her body?" The press had already written its story of Mrs. Stanford's death.

The three men retreated to the autopsy room.

"It's a madhouse out there," Solomon said, pushing the door closed behind him. "These reporters are worse than vultures."

Young Jerrold MacSween climbed up on the counter and looked out the transom window. "I can't see anyone."

"You're looking at the employees' entrance," Lowell said.

Officer Benitez left to call his captain, who dispatched over twenty men to the hospital. Within half an hour, a gauntlet of police officers lined the sidewalk from the hospital's front entrance to the doctors' waiting carriages. The police stood with locked arms while the doctors fled to their buggies.

The news of Mrs. Stanford's death spread through Honolulu. A special edition of the *Pacific Commercial Advertiser* was printed. The headlines were three inches high: "Mrs. Stanford Dead. Poison Suggested." A sketch of Mrs. Stanford drawn twenty years earlier took up a quarter of the front page.

At the rear of Queen's Hospital, a phalanx of police cordoned off the driveway. Hospital orderlies overlapped white-curtain screens normally placed between patients to make a solid wall so Mrs. Stanford's body could be rolled into the hearse without being seen. And while the press was occupied with the physicians at the front entrance, or with the corpse at the rear, Dr. Solomon, Mr. Williams, and Police Officer Benitez slipped out the employees' entrance disguised as workmen. In their toolboxes, they carried the crocks containing Mrs. Stanford's organs.

The scene at The Palms was more controlled. Mr. St. Clair ordered the staff to maintain the privacy of the guests and keep publicity to a minimum. Bellboys and waiters were posted on the sidewalk. Only bona fide guests, police, and authorized press were allowed in the hotel. But the authorized press numbered almost thirty, all men and almost all *haole*.

Six bellboys stood guard at the foot of the stairway in the lobby. Two more guards stood in front of the birdcage elevator with their arms crossed. And if a reporter wandered toward the staff stairway, there were maintenance men and gardeners assigned to guard each door.

Most reporters converged in the bar while they waited for the inquest to begin. A few mulled about asking questions.

An additional desk clerk was called in just to answer the phone. Requests for rooms were overwhelming. The Palms had a waiting list of thirty names. And as for the registered guests, only an elderly couple from Germany moved from The Palms to the Alexander Hotel—paid for by The Palms.

Gertrude Benson pulled her black jumper from the closet. She held it to herself, still on the hanger, then hung it back up. Next she pulled out a rose batiste dress. She stood in front of the mirror, then rejected it, too. She chose a white dress to wear to the inquest—a modest dress of good-quality linen with a high collar and soft, long sleeves. She wore no crinoline and removed the needlepoint sash.

She wore her hair softer that day, loosening her Gibson pompadour to a relaxed wave. At her neck, she wore a cameo of angels in flight tied with a blue velvet ribbon.

She took off her rings, save the four she never removed, and made a slow turn in front of the mirror. Standing tall, with her chin up, she smiled. Then she cast her eyes down demurely; she tilted her head and practiced the movement again before she proceeded to leave the room. At the door, she stopped, turned back, and pulled a lace handkerchief from her drawer to carry in one hand.

The inquest took place in adjoining private dining rooms on the uppermost floor of The Palms Hotel. The white paneled doors that divided the rooms were retracted. One room was arranged in a makeshift court-like style. The second was reserved for the reporters. Between the two rooms were sliding doors that were pulled back to make one large space. Two banquet tables, covered with linen, served as a desk for the press. The reporters dragged the table closer to the first room, completely blocking off passage from one room to the other. They took their seats—all of them hunched over, all sporting moustaches, most of them smoking, lighting cigarettes, sharing matches. They tapped their pencils and checked their pocket watches. One red-haired man sketched as he chewed on his cigar.

Sheriff Dillon, as coroner, sat facing the witness table. To the left of him were two stenographers bent over their machines. The older one, with a protruding Adam's apple, inserted a roll of paper in his Bartholomew machine. He pulled the tape three inches out of the machine and filed the striking keys.

When Attorney General Upton entered and looked over the room, the jurors, witnesses, and spectators were interspersed. Upton suggested to the sheriff that the jurors sit together next to the witness chair. The sheriff, in turn, instructed Deputy Kanahele to rearrange the room.

Hattie and Mae delayed their entrance, waiting in the hall. It was more of a narrow passageway than a hall, with the dining room on one side and a bay window facing the ocean on the other. The windows were latched closed; the trade winds were strong that day, gusting to thirty miles per hour.

Mae's face was bloated from crying.

Hattie didn't offer Mae consolation. She was distracted by Mr. Cutler approaching down the hall. She recognized the man with Cutler but couldn't place him. The discussion between the two men was animated. Cutler counted on his fingers then pointed to the dining room.

It was when the other man took a notepad out of his jacket pocket that Hattie remembered where she had seen him—he was the man loitering in front of Williams' Mortuary the day Mrs. Stanford was at Marshall's Dress Shop, the same man with the Brownie camera who Cutler gave money to at the trolley stop.

"Good morning, ladies." Mr. Cutler ran his finger across the rim of his derby. "I'd like you to meet a friend, Charlie Banks."

"Good morning," Hattie said.

Mae nodded, averting her face.

"Charlie is a reporter." Mr. Cutler slid open the dining room door. A snake of smoke curled out of the room.

When Hattie and Mae stepped inside, all conversation hushed. Hattie walked slowly, conscious of all eyes being on her. She sidled down the last row of chairs and took the second available chair. Mae sat next to her. Charlie Banks and Cutler sat in the row directly in front of them. Slowly the hum of conversation returned to the room.

Sheriff Dillon convened the inquest and swore in the jury. Each man took a separate oath; each signed his oath and a request to be paid for jury service. Deputy Kanahele filled in an attendance sheet and read the duties and responsibilities of the jurors.

Hattie tried not to make eye contact with anyone in the room. She kept her eyes on the wall behind the sheriff. She noticed a rectangle of brighter white paint on the wall. There must have been a painting or a mirror there at one time, she thought, and she noted it to tell Mrs. Martin that the wall needed a fresh coat of paint.

Deputy Kanahele announced, "The first witness is Miss Gertrude Benson."

Benson was not in the room. Attorney General Upton stood and walked out. Heads swiveled. Questions buzzed. After a few minutes, he returned, escorting Miss Benson on his arm.

When they walked in, the men in the room spontaneously stood. Benson made a grand entrance. She walked slowly, with the utmost conservation of movement. As she approached the witness chair, her eyes focused on one juror, then the next, and the next. When she sat, she cast her eyes down on her lap until she was sworn in.

Sheriff Dillon began, "Miss Benson, we appreciate your attendance." He offered sympathetic words but delivered them in an indifferent tone. "Please state your name, your place of birth, and your occupation." He pulled a yellow legal pad closer to himself.

"My name is Gertrude Benson. I have been in service as the private secretary of Mrs. Jane Lathrop Stanford since 1884." She stopped and looked up at the sheriff as if to signal the completion of her answer.

"Continuous service?" the sheriff asked.

"There were a few occasions when I asked permission of Mr. Harrison Lathrop, Mrs. Stanford's brother, for extended leaves."

Hattie remembered Mae's stories about Benson frequently threatening to quit and Mr. Lathrop bribing her with bonuses and doubling her salary without Mrs. Stanford ever knowing it.

"But those leaves were denied," Benson added.

"What were the purposes for those leaves?"

"To nurse my ailing father," she replied softly.

Mae turned to Hattie. "And to save all the starving babies in China," she remarked.

The court reporter leaned over to the sheriff and said something.

"Miss Benson, will you state your place of birth?"

"Harlan, Kentucky."

Mae smirked. "The Royal Princess of Moonshine."

A man, two seats down from Mae, told her to hush.

"Miss Benson, can you make plain the purpose of Mrs. Stanford's trip to Hawai'i?"

Benson lightly bit her lip. "We were here on the advice of Mr. Harrison Lathrop and Dr. Simon Ambrose, the president of Stanford University."

"Louder," one of the jurors said.

"Could you speak up, Miss Benson?" the sheriff requested.

"Of course." She smiled.

"What an insipid face," Mae muttered.

"What prompted these men to offer such advice?"

"There was an occurrence at the Nob Hill mansion." Miss Benson paused and looked directly at Mae McCauley. "On the fourteenth of January, Mrs. Stanford drank some Poland water that tasted bitter to her. I cannot say it was her favorite water at the time, but she was taking it with regularity. A chemist examined the water and determined it contained strychnine." She paused. "After that incident, Mrs. Stanford and I spent three days at the Hotel Vendome in San Jose." The pitch of her voice elevated slightly. "Upon returning to San Francisco, Mr. Lathrop suggested to Mrs. Stanford that she not return to the Nob Hill mansion. We stayed at the St. Francis Hotel until our departure for Hawai'i."

"Was there an investigation of this matter?" the sheriff asked.

"The Morse Detective Agency was contracted. And recently Inspector Whelan sent us word that there was no poisoning." She glanced at Ted Cutler.

"It appears his conclusion was in error."

Mr. Cutler raised his hand. "Sir, I have a question."

Deputy Kanahele reprimanded, "You cannot address the witness."

Cutler scribbled a note and handed it to the deputy. "For the sheriff," he said, and the deputy passed it on.

The sheriff clipped his spectacles on his nose and read the note, then he crumpled it and tossed it in the trash. "Miss Benson, you know Mrs. Stanford well. One may say, you know her better than any other living soul."

She nodded.

"What are your impressions of Mrs. Stanford's spirits during her last days?"

Before each answer, Miss Benson paused, as if collecting her thoughts. "During our trip on the steamer, she became reclusive and spoke little. She was sad and seemed troubled in spirit. She talked about the poisoning often. But after we arrived in Honolulu, she brightened for a short time. We took day trips, but nothing brought her lasting pleasure." Miss Benson addressed the panel of jurors. "She enjoyed her drive to Mount Tantalus, in fact we sang all the way home. And her visits with Mrs. Upton enlivened her. But the evening of her death, her depression was dire."

"Could you explain this to me?" The sheriff leaned back in his chair and crossed his legs.

"That evening she spoke of her son, Leland Jr. He had come to her in a dream. He called her name, and he wanted her to join him."

Mae leaned over and whispered to Hattie, "She's

trying to pin suicide on the mistress."

Benson continued, "Mrs. Stanford was fearful of being alone and begged me to sit with her. She cried and said, 'Gertrude, please don't die before me. I could not bear to live without you to care for me.'" Benson twisted her handkerchief into a cord. "I comforted her, as it is my nature, and assured her that I am in good health, and that she mustn't think of her death. Her response was that she had no fear of death." Benson dabbed her eyes. "She longed to be with her loved ones."

Judge Upton signaled Sheriff Dillon with a crooked finger. He handed him a note.

The sheriff asked Miss Benson, "Has Mrs. Stanford ever spoken like this before?"

"She has spoken of welcoming death before, but never so clearly."

"Can you tell us the specific events of the night she died?"

"She left the dining room early that evening. Dr. Lowell shared our table, and although she appeared gay, I could tell her spirits were low. She asked to be excused. I rose to join her, but she suggested that I continue my conversation with Dr. Lowell. Upon checking in on her later that evening, I noted that she appeared to have been crying. She was often struck with these bouts of melancholia and remedied herself with patent medicines."

"That's not true," Hattie said under her breath.

Benson continued, "I noticed the bicarbonate of soda bottle and the capsules on her nightstand and asked if she felt well. She informed me that the hotel maid had dispensed the medicines." Benson's eye caught Hattie's.

Hattie swore she saw the slightest smirk on Benson's face when she referred to her as the hotel maid.

"Mrs. Stanford then talked to me about the jeweled gates of heaven and how she was anxious to enter the Refuge Land."

Sheriff Dillon flipped over to a clean sheet of his yellow legal pad and continued making notes. "Were these medicines you mentioned purchased in Honolulu?"

"The cascara was a prescription prepared at Wakelee's Drug Store in San Francisco. They were actually prepared for me, but I share them with Mrs. Stanford. And the bicarbonate was purchased quite a while ago. I don't remember when."

"Do you know if the bicarbonate of soda was purchased in California?" the sheriff asked.

"Yes, certainly it was. I simply can't recall from which pharmacy."

The sheriff wrote, "California—pharmacy unknown." Then he drew a five-pointed star next to it and poked the paper with his pencil. "Was this medicine with you at the St. Francis Hotel?"

She shook her head.

Both court stenographers looked up.

"Are you indicating that it was not?" the sheriff asked.

"It was not at the St. Francis Hotel."

"Was it with you in San Jose?" the sheriff asked.

"No. When Mrs. Stanford was in San Jose, she saw a Dr. Vickers. He dispensed all her medicine. In fact, he treated her the day we arrived."

"Was Mrs. Stanford ill?"

"Quite ill. She suffered from a case of the

grippe. Dr. Vickers suspected tonsillitis. Her condition was quite frail."

"So the medicine basket remained in the San Francisco house during all that time?"

"Yes. In the kitchen pantry in the San Francisco house—in the medicine closet with all the rest of the curatives."

"Who had access to this medicine closet?" the sheriff asked.

"Most of the household staff. It was in an open alcove in the pantry."

"Is this medicine closet locked?"

Miss Benson patted light perspiration from her brow. "The cabinet contains burn remedies for the kitchen staff, so it is always unlocked."

"To be clear, Miss Benson, the medicines remained in the kitchen pantry in the San Francisco house until they were taken to the steamer?"

"Yes."

"Was it taken to the steamer by you or by an express company?"

"An express company."

While Miss Benson was testifying, Hattie looked over Charlie Banks's shoulder to see what he was writing: "This well-groomed older woman was most controlled. She listened quietly until her questioner finished every word of the interrogation put to her. She answered nothing without thinking first. She volunteered nothing. She is a frank individual, if anything a bit too engagingly frank. She displays the mannerisms of a woman who feels that every word she says is being weighed. And she carefully weighs each before she utters it."

The sheriff asked, "Miss Benson, while on the

steamship *Korea*, you occupied one stateroom and Mrs. Stanford occupied another, is that correct?"

"No. Mrs. Stanford had a suite. She occupied one of the staterooms, and I shared a room with Miss McCauley, a domestic from Vina Ranch."

"Just a ragamuffin street urchin," Mae muttered.

"During the voyage, where was the medicine basket? In the hold with the luggage or in the suite?"

"In the suite, accessible to me and to Miss McCauley."

"That's a lie," Mae said a bit too loudly. "It was in the hold."

Heads swiveled.

The deputy warned Mae against any more outbursts.

Mae groused to herself, "The blooming liar has gone too far. The basket was in the ship's hold. She wants them to think I did in the old woman."

Banks turned around and smiled at Mae; she shot him a look of disgust.

"Did Mrs. Stanford have occasion to take some of this bicarbonate on the trip?"

"Yes, and so did I."

"From the same jar?"

"Yes."

News reporters wrote furiously.

One of the reporters drew a box around his words: "Mrs. Stanford's companion took the same bicarbonate."

"Did you take any of the bicarbonate the evening of February 28, 1905?"

"I had no need of it."

"Please continue with your account."

"Mrs. Stanford called out, 'Gertrude! I am sick!' I

immediately grabbed for my robe and ran to her, while the hotel maid remained in her bed."

Mae looked over at Hattie.

"Mrs. Stanford whimpered, 'Help me, Gertrude, please.' I ran back to my room and yelled at the maid to get Dr. Lowell. It took me yelling at her twice before she moved."

Hattie felt her pulse throb in her neck. But she sat motionless, while people turned to look at her.

"When I went back to the door, Mrs. Stanford put all her weight on my shoulder, and I assisted her to the chair."

Hattie's breathing quickened. "She is wicked."

Mae reached for her hand. Hattie stared at the ceiling to keep tears from flowing down her cheeks.

While Benson continued her account, Charlie Banks wrote, "During her testimony, it was plain to even the dullest person in the room that Miss Benson was deflecting any suspicion of guilt away from herself and aiming it at anyone else."

❧ CHAPTER TEN ❧

After three hours of questioning, the sheriff and all jurors were satisfied with Miss Benson and the sheriff dismissed her and announced a break for lunch.

Hattie and Mae left the dining room, sidestepping their way through the crowd, one step ahead of Cutler and Charlie Banks.

Banks caught up with them. "Miss McCauley, may I have a word with you?"

Mae ignored him.

He maneuvered himself to get ahead of the ladies. He walked backwards facing them in the crush of the crowd. "Miss McCauley, you seem to have strong opinions regarding Miss Benson." He checked behind himself as he shuffled.

"I have strong opinions about reporters, too. Best not spoken in mixed company," Mae answered.

"Miss McCauley, I would like to hear what you have to say."

Hattie pushed Mae toward the service stairway door, guarded by two hotel maintenance workers.

"If you believe she killed Mrs. Stanford, I could help you prove it." Charlie Banks had the face of a child.

Hattie and Mae scooted down the steps; the guards halted Banks.

The women fled to Hattie's office.

"It's no wonder Mrs. Stanford hated reporters so much." Mae sat on the Windsor chair under the schoolhouse clock. "They feed off the wounded and dead."

Hattie poured two glasses of water and handed one to Mae.

"Hattie, do you remember when I told you that Benson would threaten Mr. Lathrop with quitting?"

Hattie nodded.

"Just before we left, she did it again. Right after Miss Dobbs was fired, Miss Benson told Mr. Lathrop she refused to travel with the mistress anymore." Mae sipped some water. "On my first day in service at the St. Francis, I had to sit with the mistress in the hotel while Benson rode out to Vina Ranch to meet Mr. Lathrop—that's where my mother heard them squabble."

Mae continued, "My mother overheard Benson tell Mr. Lathrop that Mrs. Stanford had gone mad. She said his sister needed an alienist—that she was delusional and prone to fits of hysteria. Mr. Lathrop begged Benson not to quit. My mother said he pleaded with her to accompany her on just one more trip. She said Mr. Lathrop assured her it would be her last. When that didn't work, Mr. Lathrop bribed Benson with a three-month paid holiday—that's when she gave in.

"On that very night, Miss Benson shared a pint with my father. She had no friends at Vina Ranch and Da was already three sheets to the wind with stout. When Miss Benson went in the kitchen, she lifted a few brews with Da, and he—being the gregarious gentleman he is with women not in his family—listened to her woes and sympathized with her plight.

"Miss Benson was taken by Da's charm. They drank together late into the night, and she confided to Da that she was going to renege on her deal and that she couldn't be dragged to Hawai'i with the old woman—not for her weight in gold.

"That's when my Da said, 'Why don't you just off her? You'd get your freedom and a tidy inheritance, to boot.' My mother overheard Da's lame spewing and was afraid he'd be accused of the Nob Hill poisoning. Then Da suggested that Benson should 'off her in Japan,' where no one would ever find out."

Mae looked directly at Hattie. "I think my father gave her the idea. It was the next day that one of the houseboys spotted her in the herb shop in Chinatown."

———

It seemed that everyone in Honolulu was talking about Mrs. Stanford's death.

Those in society bemoaned the unfortunate disgrace brought upon the family. In grillrooms and private clubs, bartenders took wagers on who did her in. The heavy favorite was Gertrude Benson. Their logic was that since Mrs. Stanford had no living children, she probably had bequeathed the bulk of her estate to Miss Benson. It was an ignorant speculation to anyone who knew the matron, and her zealous devotion to the university. Their argument was that even if a pittance of her estate went to Benson, she'd never have to work another day in her life.

For some, Harrison Lathrop was a contender for

the title of murderer. "Blood is never thicker than money" was heard in the plushest bars. The same sentiment was echoed in wharf saloons. And on Maunakea Street in Chinatown, at the White Swan Ale House, there was one lone bet that Mrs. Stanford committed suicide. No one wagered on death by natural causes.

Honolulu physicians waited for the pathologist's report. Attorneys anticipated the reading of the will. And women at quilting bees told stories about caring for mothers-in-law and admitted their thoughts of murder.

Governor Nichols ordered that all flags in the territory be flown half-staff. The legislative session deferred its business for the day, and the courts cleared their dockets.

Mr. Ralph Van Dine, of Stanford's class of 1901, lunched at the Alexander Hotel with fellow alumni and businessmen of Honolulu. They decided to go on with the Stanford dinner as scheduled, not as a social gathering, but as a meeting to discuss a memorial to the Mother of Stanford University. Van Dine proposed that an invitation be extended to all Californians. By the end of the meeting, a memorial committee was formed; W. H. Hoogs was the chair and E. W. Quinn Jr. was designated to select twenty men to escort Mrs. Stanford's body from the Central Union Church to the awaiting steamship. Nathan Lee would arrange the dinner.

Similar meetings were taking place in San Francisco and at Stanford University in Palo Alto. In California the state flags were lowered, banks closed, Union and Pacific Railroad stations were draped in black bunting, and the university cancelled its classes.

The Catholic house servants of Vina Ranch lit candles, and at Nob Hill the household staff openly accused Benson of murder.

In Honolulu, Mayor Kane was quick to point out that the murderer, whoever he was—and he distinctly said "he"—had committed his crime of poisoning in California. Therefore, Honolulu remained a safe city and the murderer roamed free in the streets of San Francisco.

———•◦•◦•———

Sheriff Dillon opened the afternoon session by calling on Mrs. Upton as the next witness. Lallah Upton promenaded to the stand as if she were hosting an afternoon tea.

"Look at her, dressed like a Buckingham duchess," Mae scoffed.

Mrs. Upton wore a lilac silk dress layered with spotted chiffon. She carried a long-handled parasol trimmed with lace. A wide-brimmed chiffon bonnet trimmed in ostrich feathers completed her ensemble.

"The rich have no common sense," Mae clucked.

Hattie kept her eyes on the witness, but a smile crept across her face.

"Kindly state your full name." Sheriff Dillon checked his pocket watch for the time.

"My name is Mrs. Noah Upton or Lallah Upton."

Hattie looked around for Judge Upton. He was conspicuously absent.

"I should say my name was Lallah Hartford before I was married. Lallah S. Hartford, that is. The 'S' is for Symington, not Stanford, in case you might think Mrs. Stanford and I were related."

The sheriff interrupted her. "Where do you reside?"

"In Nu'uanu. But for the record, Symington is my mother's maiden name."

Sheriff Dillon turned to the recorders.

"It is so noted," one of the stenographers said.

"Mrs. Upton, how long have you been acquainted with Mrs. Stanford?" the sheriff asked.

"Our mothers were friends. We knew each other from girlhood in Albany." She turned to the jury. "That's in New York State," she educated them.

Sheriff Dillon leaned back, crossed his legs, and rested the yellow pad on his knee. "Would you say that you knew Mrs. Stanford intimately all this time?"

"I would not say that I knew her intimately all this time. No. When Mrs. Stanford moved to Sacramento to join her husband, we corresponded by mail. Later when we both lived in Washington, D.C., of course we socialized, but for the last twenty years, it was only when fortune allowed us to meet. However, when we did meet, we would speak of private matters. Matters of the heart, that is."

"Did you visit Mrs. Stanford while she was in Hawai'i?"

"Yes, I saw her in 1902 at the university alumni dinner, even though I am not an alumna."

"What about this visit, Mrs. Upton?"

Mrs. Upton tugged at her gloves. "Mrs. Stanford telephoned me upon her arrival and asked me to meet her at The Palms that afternoon. I had sent her a box of Lowney & Huyler Chocolates." She turned to the jury. "They were her favorites. I order them through Hackfield's Department Store."

The sheriff cut her off. "Can you tell us about your visit?"

"That afternoon I met her on the ocean-side verandah. When I arrived, she was asleep in the chair. She looked tired and her complexion was pale. But I suppose some of that must be attributed to the sunless San Francisco winters." She paused. "It does rain so in San Francisco during January."

The sheriff nodded.

Mrs. Upton continued, "Mrs. Stanford and I chatted about our mutual friends. Mrs. Greenbaum's daughter just had a baby, and Mrs. Gloss wished her a bon voyage the morning she sailed from San Francisco."

"Did Mrs. Stanford display any concern for her safety?"

"She did tell me about the attempt on her life, if that's what you mean. Although I didn't believe it at first." Mrs. Upton looked down at her lap. "I heard news that Mrs. Stanford had become overly nervous and was subject to fits of melancholia, so I thought she might have imagined the poison attempt. She asked me not to mention it to anyone, but of course, I shared my concern with my husband, Attorney General Upton. And I was compelled to cable Mr. Claus Huber, who is in San Francisco now since his daughter, Lilly, is to be married to Thomas Vanderbilt this Saturday."

One of the reporters doodled a caricature of an elegantly dressed woman with an ostrich-feathered bonnet and a face totally taken up by her mouth.

"I didn't want to burden Mr. Huber, but, at the same time, I didn't want him to rely on gossip." Mrs. Upton turned to the jurors. "Mrs. Stanford was supposed to give a bridal luncheon for Lilly this week and I wasn't sure her staff notified the Hubers . . .

Mrs. Stanford's leaving was so, well, so quick."

Sheriff Dillon tapped the end of his pencil on the yellow paper. "Mrs. Upton, was there anyone else you shared your concern with?"

"Well . . . I," she stuttered. "I cabled her brother, Mr. Harrison Lathrop, and President Ambrose in California. At the time I didn't know they were sailing on the *Mariposa*. So I sent cables to their homes."

Sheriff Dillon stood up and paced in front of Mrs. Upton. "Why did you cable them?"

Mrs. Upton leaned back in her chair. "Mrs. Stanford had many friends who were concerned over her health."

"Other than the persons you listed, was there anyone else you shared your feelings with?" The sheriff stood within a foot of Mrs. Upton.

"I did not broadcast her condition if that's what you are implying," she answered indignantly. "Mrs. Stanford was a very private person."

There was a chorus of snickers in the room.

Sheriff Dillon jiggled the pencil between his fingers. "Mrs. Upton, how would you describe Mrs. Stanford's spirits the day of your visit?"

"At the beginning of our visit, she seemed fearful of her life being taken—by what means, I don't know. But I do believe she came to Honolulu to get away from her enemies. We talked for a while, then I engaged her in a walk toward the aquarium. I believe fresh air and a good walk can cure melancholia." She punctuated her opinion with a firm nod. "I even recited some verses to cheer her. It was on our walk that she discussed her plans for the university and the spiritualist center."

"What spiritualist center?" the sheriff asked.

Mrs. Upton's back straightened. "The psychic center. Mrs. Stanford believed that all good Christians could contact souls in heaven, and she wanted to establish a Center for the Investigation of Psychic Phenomena at the university. But President Ambrose would have none of it. He's very strong willed, you know." She squared her shoulders. "But Mrs. Stanford believed in these things. She claimed to speak to the senator daily."

"Has this been a recent practice?"

"When we lived in Washington, she and the senator attended séances all the time. Even President and Mrs. Grant hosted séances at the White House. But Attorney General Upton and I never attended. We are Methodists."

"Did you see Mrs. Stanford after that day?"

"No. We were to see each other at the Stanford Alumni Dinner, but it was never to be."

"While Mrs. Stanford was in your company, did you see her take any medications?" Sheriff Dillon asked.

Mrs. Upton gazed at the ceiling as if to recall a scene from her memory. "I did not, although she may have. I did see her use a powder in her tea. She was plagued by headaches, even as a girl. She always carried packets of Orangeine with her."

"Did Mrs. Stanford take many patent medicines?"

"She did." Mrs. Upton smiled. "Even when we were girls, we sneaked off to medicine shows so she could buy Dr. Lyle's Liver Tonic or Seven Sutherland Sisters Hair Grower. We had a carefree youth." Her expression saddened. "But after Leland Jr. died, she never recovered; she was inclined to hypochondria and lethargy." She paused. "I know she took mineral waters, bicarbonates, and Chinese herbs." Mrs. Upton lowered her voice as if to share a secret. "She had a Chinese doctor tend to her at the Nob Hill mansion. She confided that fact to very few. Mrs. Stanford always had a soft spot for Orientals." Mrs. Upton patted the sweat forming on her upper lip.

The dining room was hot. Two ceiling fans spun, but the afternoon sun rays were angled directly into the room. Hattie felt a headache coming on. The still heat, the crowded room, the lack of sleep, and the stench of cigar smoke added to her discomfort. A few times during Mrs. Upton's testimony, Hattie closed her eyes and took slow, deep breaths, trying to ease the pain.

Mae nudged her. "Are you well?"

"Fine."

Mrs. Upton concluded her testimony, and Sheriff Dillon declared the inquest recessed for the day.

Hattie felt faint when she stood to leave.

"Sit," Mae ordered. They waited until the room cleared out and the hallway was free to walk before making their exit.

Mae walked Hattie back to the employee cottages. She tucked Hattie in bed and scolded her as if she were Hattie's older sister. "Do not get out of bed. I'll have food delivered to you."

Hattie tried to sleep but couldn't. Each time she closed her eyes, she saw Mrs. Stanford dying—her arms flailing, her legs jerking, then her body lifting, as if by a marionette's string, then dropping into a crumple.

Hattie recited prayers she had learned as a child, rote and rapid, but the prayers couldn't quiet Mrs. Stanford's screams.

"Our Father," she recited over and over. "Our Father" and no more.

It took hours for her to fall asleep—at first just small slices of peace, merciful pockets, then longer stretches that turned into dreams and dreams into a nightmare about Mrs. Stanford. In it, Mrs. Stanford's body was sewn in a seaman's canvas bag and pitched into the sea. Hattie watched from the shore as the bag sank and sharks circled. Mrs. Stanford called to Hattie, she struggled to get free, but the bag was tangled in seaweed and was swallowed in foam.

———•••◦•———

The sky was black that night. Clouds masked the moon, and the trade winds carried the scent of ginger.

The Central Union Church bells struck eight o'clock and Hattie woke from her nap. From her bed, she could hear Koa's voice on the porch. He was recounting his genealogy to Mae. He was just short of chanting a Kamehameha bloodline when Hattie went out to the porch.

Immediately Koa began asking Hattie questions, not waiting for her response but asking his next question over it.

"Dr. Townsend was asking about you," he told Hattie. "I heard him talking to the manager of the Alexander." Koa was still in the black trousers and white shirt he wore at the hotel restaurant.

"What was he asking?" Mae seemed more curious than Hattie.

"He found out that Hattie gave Mrs. Stanford the strychnine."

"I didn't give her any poison! I gave her bicarbonate!" Hattie couldn't believe her cousin would repeat such accusations.

"I'm telling you what I heard."

"Nobody even knows if she was poisoned." Hattie was already tired of all the talk.

"All the doctors say so. Mae says so, too." He jutted his chin in her direction. "Tell her." Koa jabbed Mae's arm. "Tell her the old lady died of strychnine."

"It's all over the papers," Mae said.

"Wonderful! And everybody thinks I'm the one who gave it to her."

"According to the papers, I'm more suspect than you are," Mae told her.

"I don't even know what strychnine looks like!" Hattie said.

"It's a powder," Mae said.

"What color powder?" Koa asked.

"The Morse detectives told us it's an off-white powder or crystals, like sugar."

"Like the powder that spilled out of Miss Benson's box?" Koa looked at Hattie, wide eyed.

"Hattie, you didn't say anything about any powder," Mae said.

"There was a powder in her box. It spilled on the rug, and Koa and I cleaned it up. But it wasn't white. It was cream, almost pink."

"Did you taste it?" Mae asked.

"Why would I do that?"

"By accident, picking it up?"

Both Koa and Hattie said they hadn't.

"But it wasn't white," Hattie repeated.

"Was there anything else in the box?"

"A paper with some Chinese writing," Koa said.

"It's the strychnine," Mae said it as if she were talking to herself. "Is the powder still in her room?" she asked Hattie.

"I suppose so."

"We've got to get it." Mae instantly drew a plan. "Hattie, you've still got your clothes in there. That's all we need to get in. You could say you have to get them."

"Well, if you're going to get in her room, you'd better do it fast," Koa warned. "She's moving to the Alexander soon."

"Why would she do that?" Mae asked.

"Ted told me there was a cable from the *Mariposa*. Mr. Lathrop and President Ambrose are to stay at the Alexander, and they want her moved there, too."

Ted? Hattie was suspicious of Koa's familiarity. "Why would Cutler tell you that?" Hattie knew Koa told half-truths.

"He's been at the hotel asking a lot of questions. He asked me about when Mrs. Stanford was at the Alexander and who she had lunch with. So, I tell him what I hear and he pays me a dollar."

Hattie wondered what else Koa had told him.

"We can get in Benson's room tomorrow," Mae said.

Hattie wasn't sure that Benson had poisoned Mrs. Stanford. Despite all that Benson did, Hattie couldn't dismiss the care Benson showed the matron. She recalled how she gently held her after she had eaten too much sugar. She remembered how she massaged Mrs. Stanford's arms while she was dying.

The next morning's newspaper headlines were two inches tall: "Secretary Hints Suicide! Confidante Reveals Mrs. Stanford a Spiritualist."

Hattie sat cross-legged on her bed, curled over the *Pacific Commercial Advertiser*. She read aloud, "Someone close to Mrs. Stanford states that it was an open secret that she was anxious to take her place between her departed son and her husband."

"And how much would you like to wager that 'someone close to Mrs. Stanford' was Benson?" Mae sat on her bed with the pillows propped against the headboard.

Hattie continued, "Perhaps Mrs. Stanford was overcome with this feeling to be with them, and in one impulsive moment she took poison to flee this earth?"

"Listen to this one." Mae read from the front page of the *Honolulu Star*. "Miss Benson told this reporter that with her advanced age, Mrs. Stanford's illusions multiplied and the grip of spiritualism tightened on her. During her last days, Mrs. Stanford often cried out in frustration from the vague communion she shared with her son and husband. She claimed during their daily visits, she craved to be with them even more. She said it was unbearable to be separated from them and longed to join them in heaven." Mae slammed the paper on her lap. "She almost comes out and calls the mistress daft."

Mae continued, "Was her secretary discreetly trying to announce to the world that Mrs. Stanford committed suicide?" Mae turned to Hattie. "Discreetly?"

"There's something here." Hattie spotted an article on the second page of the *Advertiser*. "It says that Judge Upton reported Mrs. Stanford took mediums with her on her travels."

Mae scoffed. "Not unless they could haul bags."

Hattie read on. "Attorney General Upton confirms that Mrs. Stanford consulted with her late husband daily on matters of business and the university. Everyone close to her knew that it was her brother, Harrison Lathrop, and president Simon Ambrose who actually governed Stanford University. It was an act of kindness to protect Mrs. Stanford from being exposed as the senile character she was and continue the illusion of her having control."

"Benson must be grinning in her morning mirror."

Hattie ran her finger over an article at the bottom of the page. "There's a cable from the *San Francisco Chronicle* about the Nob Hill mansion. It says, 'Floods of light poured from upper rooms. Silhouettes of motionless figures peered through curtains. None of the Stanford domestic servants are allowed to leave. No word was allowed to escape. The servants are held hostage. The Morse Detective Agency, once more on the job, denied that the servants are under a virtual house arrest. Inspector Whelan claims they are there of their own free will and can leave anytime. But this reporter called the mansion. He heard the telephone jingle, but there was no answer.'"

"It's the same as it was in January," Mae said.

"What do you think will happen?"

"They'll search the house, but they won't find anything. We both know the poison is in Benson's drawer." Mae turned to Hattie. "And right after you finish testifying, we're going to get it."

Before Sheriff Dillon called the inquest to order that morning, he set his briefcase on the table, pulled out his cigarettes, and sauntered over to have a smoke with Ted Cutler. Even at a distance, the sheriff cut a handsome figure. Although he was of average height and build, he had an imposing carriage that commanded quick respect. The sheriff and Cutler appeared to be cordial, almost familiar. Both joked and slapped their hands on each other's backs. But Sheriff Dillon held his back straighter; he didn't smile as broadly. And when he walked back to his desk, he took his yellow pad out of his briefcase and jotted down notes.

A few minutes later, Deputy Kanahele signaled the sheriff that the jurors were ready, and Sheriff Dillon convened the proceedings. Deputy Kanahele called Hattie's name.

"Please state your name and occupation." Deputy Kanahele's eyes were the color of smoked topaz.

"My name is Hattie Lehua. I am a bookkeeper at The Palms Hotel." She looked at Mae, who was sitting on the aisle chair in the last row.

"Have you been working as a bookkeeper during this last week?" the sheriff asked.

"No, sir. I have been acting as Mrs. Stanford's personal maid since her arrival."

"Miss Lehua, what were your duties during that time?"

"I took care of her clothes and tended to her personally." Hattie needed to see Mae's face. It was the only face in the room she trusted.

"Did you accompany her on day trips?" The sheriff's voice was mellow.

"I did." Hattie nodded. "Mrs. Stanford requested that I act as a guide. I did the best I could." Hattie watched as the stenographers banged on keys that struck a ribbon, leaving unintelligible marks that recorded her words.

"Miss Lehua, were you with Mrs. Stanford on the day of February 28?"

"I was."

"How would you describe her spirits that day?" The sheriff lit another cigarette.

"She seemed kind that day."

"Kind?" He put out the match with one sharp flick of his wrist.

"Yes, kind." Hattie heard herself repeat words.

"Would you say she was melancholy in any way?"

"No, she was not."

"Did she speak of suicide, even remotely?"

Hattie sat up straighter. She spoke directly to the jurors. "Mrs. Stanford talked about God that night. She said it was God's will, not hers, as to when she would die. She never alluded to taking her own life, not even remotely."

Sheriff Dillon took notes. "Please tell us what happened the night Mrs. Stanford died."

"I was in bed when I heard Mrs. Stanford call. She said, 'Gertrude. I am sick!' Then I woke up Miss Benson and told her that Mrs. Stanford was calling, and Miss Benson told me to go to her."

The sheriff looked up. "You are stating that you were the first to Mrs. Stanford's room?"

"Yes." Hattie glanced at Mae.

The sheriff made a note on his yellow pad: "Both Benson and Lehua say they were first in room."

"I went back to tell Miss Benson that Mrs. Stanford said she was poisoned, and Miss Benson ordered me to get Dr. Lowell."

The French doors to the inquest room slid open. Dr. Isaiah Townsend entered, causing heads to turn and a buzz to ripple through the room. He walked to the front row. His cane marked his stride with a rhythmic tap. He assumed a chair next to Sheriff Dillon's.

"Dr. Townsend." The sheriff acknowledged the doctor and returned to his questioning. "Miss Lehua, what happened then?"

"I told Hiram, the elevator boy, to get Dr. Lowell, then I went downstairs to call Mrs. Martin."

The sheriff asked Hattie to tell the jurors what happened next. She repeated every detail she could remember about Mrs. Stanford's death. During her explanation, she stopped only once to keep herself from crying.

The sheriff scribbled on his notepad: "Hattie Lehua's account of death consistent with Gertrude Benson's."

Dr. Townsend crooked his finger at the sheriff and Sheriff Dillon leaned over. Townsend whispered in his ear. Then the sheriff asked, "Did Dr. Lowell tell you to massage Mrs. Stanford's feet?"

"I don't remember. Miss Benson poured a bottle of rubbing alcohol into a small basin, and the two of us worked on Mrs. Stanford. Miss Benson massaged her arms, and I massaged her feet." Hattie forced away a vision of Mrs. Stanford's face. "I don't remember if anyone told me to do it. I remember I was kneeling in front of Mrs. Stanford and her feet were in the basin and I was massaging them." She looked at the sheriff. "That's all I remember."

"Did Mrs. Stanford appear to be in pain?"

"Yes. Most definitely."

Dr. Townsend reached over and wrote a note on the sheriff's legal pad. With the pad lifted slightly, the sheriff asked, "Specifically, did the massage create more pain?"

"I can't remember more or less pain. Mrs. Stanford was dying."

While Hattie was testifying, Charlie Banks was composing his report—a report he'd try to sell to any paper that would have it. He wrote, "The young bookkeeper from The Palms Hotel who was assigned to care for Mrs. Stanford was deeply distressed. Several times in describing the death scene, she broke down. When Sheriff Dillon asked Miss Lehua what happened after Mrs. Stanford died, she answered poignantly, 'There was an emptiness,' and she cried." Bank's account had Hattie sobbing through most of her testimony.

Sheriff Dillon brought the tips of his fingers together. "Miss Lehua, it was you who dispensed the bicarbonate of soda and the cascara capsule to Mrs. Stanford. Is that correct?"

"Yes." She wanted to explain that she did only what she was told.

"Did Mrs. Stanford specifically ask for the bicarbonate of soda and the cascara capsule?" The sheriff's voice sounded more like that of a minister's than an inquisitor's.

"Yes." Hattie looked up at the sheriff. "She told me to get them from her medicine basket in the wardrobe room. When I returned to the bedroom, she said, 'I will take a teaspoonful of soda.' And she instructed me how to place it on her nightstand."

"Miss Lehua, did Mrs. Stanford take the bicarbonate of soda or the cascara capsule in your presence?"

Hattie shook her head.

"Excuse me, Miss Lehua, by shaking your head, are you indicating that Mrs. Stanford did not take the soda or capsule in your presence?"

"Yes. I mean no." Hattie was flustered. "What I am saying is that Mrs. Stanford did not take any soda or capsule while I was there. She said she wanted to drink some water first and give it time to get out of her stomach before she took her medicines, so I placed the bottle of soda and the spoon with the soda on it and the capsule on the nightstand."

"And the glass of water?"

"Maybe the water was already there. I don't remember."

"Miss Lehua, how much soda would you say was in the bottle?"

She looked at him, puzzled. "I don't know, sir. It was filled to about two inches from the top." She held up her thumb and index finger, demonstrating what she thought was two inches.

"Could you describe the bottle, please?"

"It was an octagonal glass bottle—a cobalt blue, with a silver seal on it. Mrs. Stanford said she carried it with her from Australia." Hattie wondered why the bottle was so important.

The sheriff summoned an aide who placed a spoon and a clear glass octagonal bottle in front of Hattie. The glass was filled with white crystals.

"Was the bottle shape similar to this?"

"Yes, sir."

"Miss Lehua, please take a spoonful of soda from the bottle."

Hattie looked up at Mae. Mae shrugged her shoulders. Hattie took the bottle in her hand and tilted it. With her other hand, she dipped the spoon into the bottle and took out the soda.

"Miss Lehua, the night of February 28, did you tilt the bottle of soda?"

"I don't remember, sir."

The sheriff's questions came quicker. "Do you remember if you dipped the spoon into the soda at the same depth as you did now?"

"I don't remember."

"Did you tip the bottle?"

"I don't think I tipped the bottle. I don't know."

"Did you pour the soda out?"

"I don't know."

"Did you take it from the top?"

"Probably from the top, but I am not sure." She wondered why he was so concerned about the spoon and the bottle. Who cared about the angle of the bottle? Mrs. Stanford was dead.

The sheriff paused. "Miss Lehua, if you don't object, I would like you to perform the same act again. This time blindfolded."

Heads swiveled and jurors scooted their chairs a bit closer to the table.

Hattie looked at Mae. Mae looked so far away.

Hattie closed her eyes and Deputy Kanahele blindfolded her. The deputy placed a spoon in her right hand, then he put the bottle in her left.

The sheriff said, "Please take out a teaspoon of soda from the bottle, Miss Lehua."

Hattie tipped the jar slightly and poked at the jar

until she felt the resistance of the glass, then she dug the spoon down no more than an inch and withdrew the soda.

"Thank you, Miss Lehua."

Kanahele untied the blindfold and Hattie smoothed her hair.

The sheriff dismissed Hattie.

"Is that all?" Hattie was puzzled.

"For now."

After Hattie signed her statement, the sheriff declared a recess. Hattie and Mae got up to leave. Hattie expected a rush of curiosity seekers to ask her questions, but instead, the men and women stepped aside deferentially, allowing her and Mae to exit.

In the hotel lobby, Hattie spotted Miss Benson with Dr. Townsend. Benson was dressed in black from head to toe.

"Look at her," Mae said. "The Patron Saint of Grief." Then she grabbed Hattie's arm. "Now's our chance. We can get in her room while she's at lunch."

Hattie was unsure. And when she saw Thomas Mahoe at the reception desk, she was certain he would not give her Benson's room key.

"Excuse me." A deliveryman wheeled a dolly stacked with boxes in front of Hattie. She stepped aside, noticing that the boxes were from Marshall's.

"Deliveries in the back," Thomas told the man, and he aimed his pen toward the ocean.

"The guys in back sent me up here. These are for Miss Benson." He pointed to the labels on the boxes.

Hattie stepped forward. "Thomas, I can accept them for Miss Benson." She turned to the delivery boy. "Room 122. Follow me." She asked Thomas for the room key.

"I need Miss Benson's permission to give you her key."

"She's having lunch with Dr. Townsend." Hattie tried to sound officious.

"I need her permission first." His smile had a curve of contempt.

"I doubt if she wants to be disturbed." Hattie reminded Thomas that she and Miss Benson share a room.

"You shared a room," he corrected.

"If you must call someone, call Mrs. Martin." She was hoping to call his bluff.

It worked. Thomas slid the key to room 122 out of its cubby and handed it to Hattie with a warning. "*He* is not allowed upstairs." He shifted his eyes to the deliveryman.

"Miss McCauley and I will manage the boxes," she said.

The deliveryman transferred the boxes from his dolly to a hotel luggage carrier. He tapped the top box. "Tell Miss Benson that Mrs. Marshall put her mourning clothes in this box."

Hattie signed for the boxes while Mae rolled the cart into the birdcage elevator.

"Well, wasn't he the Lord of Arrogance?" Mae said.

"He's descended from royal blood." Hattie smirked.

Mae looked over the boxes. "I bet the spinster ordered five petticoats to go with her black crepe."

The elevator opened to Mrs. Stanford's floor.

"I'll wager she didn't order any mourning clothes for me," Mae said as they rolled the cart to the door. "Now I'll have to go begging to drape myself in black."

Hattie slid the brass key in the lock. A click. When they opened the door, they saw Benson's trunks locked and belted and lined up against the wall.

Hattie opened the dresser drawer where the box had been. The drawer was empty. So was the rest of the dresser.

Hattie checked the wardrobe room. "There's still some unpacked stuff in here."

Several dresses hung in the closet. Valises, hat-boxes, wicker hampers, and paper boxes were scattered over the floor.

Hattie started with the hampers; there were only clothes in them. Mae went through the paper boxes. They were stuffed with postcards and travel ephemera.

Mae moved on to the hatboxes. One by one, she opened them—each contained only a hat.

"Are you sure no one is coming?" Hattie stopped, listening for sounds.

"I'm sure." Mae went to the bedroom and began sliding the Marshall's boxes off the luggage carrier.

Hattie opened a wide embroidered satin valise. In one sleeve was Mrs. Stanford's broken cameo bracelet from the Mount Tantalus picnic, in another were the black pearls that Mrs. Stanford had just purchased. More commissions? Hattie wondered. Perhaps Benson just forgot to return them to the safe-deposit box. She asked Mae if she was listening for anyone in the hall.

"I'm listening!" Mae said.

Hattie unsnapped each pocket of the satin valise. There was the cobalt blue papier-mâché box. Hattie edged the lid off. There was still powder inside.

"I found it!" Hattie pulled out the paper from under the powder. It read: "William Y. S. Lee, Herbalist, 20-141A Grant Street, San Francisco, California." Below were the unfamiliar Chinese characters.

"Someone's coming!" Mae shouted as she hid behind a trunk.

Hattie stood in front of the wardrobe room, frozen.

The lock clicked. The doorknob turned.

God, let it be a maid, Hattie prayed.

The door opened. It was Koa.

"What are you doing here?" Hattie hissed.

"Thomas told me you were up here. And I know where to get the keys."

Mae came out from behind the trunk.

"Did you find it?" Koa asked.

Hattie showed him the box. Koa tucked it in his pocket. "Let's go." Koa checked down the hall. It was empty. He moved the last box off the carrier and rolled it down the corridor into the birdcage elevator. Hattie and Mae followed, casually discussing housekeeping matters in case anyone appeared. Hattie's heart was pounding.

Koa rolled the carrier through the lobby and to the desk. Hattie and Mae returned the key and headed out the lobby, toward the cottage, with Koa not far behind.

The three of them huddled on the bed. Hattie opened the box. She was first to taste the powder. "It's chalky." She passed it to Mae.

Mae refused it. "You don't suppose I'm going to put poison in my mouth, do you?"

"I'll do it." Koa tried it. "It tastes like dirt."

"Dr. Lowell said strychnine tastes bitter," Hattie said.

"Maybe that's what he calls bitter," Mae offered.

"What do we do now?" Hattie asked.

"We find a chemist," Mae told her. "Do you know one we can trust?"

Hattie shook her head.

"What about a pharmacist—some friend or an uncle?"

Both Koa and Hattie answered no.

"Maybe we should give the powder to the sheriff," Hattie said.

Koa refused to trust him. "Haven't you seen the way Townsend maneuvers him? What about Ted Cutler?"

"It's a bit of a problem for me," Mae said. "The man thinks I'm a murderer."

"No he doesn't. I asked him," Koa said. "And when I asked him who he thought killed Mrs. Stanford, he said it would be dangerous to tell me."

"I don't trust him," Hattie said.

"There's no other choice," Koa answered.

❧ Chapter Eleven ❧

Mae McCauley was scheduled as the first witness of the afternoon. It was five minutes before one and Cutler had yet to show up.

Hattie leaned out the ocean-side window to see if Cutler was on the *lānai*. There was no sign of him. The two women agreed they would find Cutler after the proceedings and talk to him together. When Deputy Kanahele called Mae's name, they both took their seats.

The deputy asked Mae to state her full name.

"Mae Elizabeth McCauley."

The sheriff began his questioning. "Where do you reside Miss McCauley?"

"Most of the time, I live at Vina Ranch, the Stanfords' vineyard, but if I am called into service to one of the other houses, I live in that house."

"Miss McCauley, when did you enter Mrs. Stanford's service?"

"I was born at Vina Ranch. My mother, Rebecca McCauley, is a cook. My father, Colin McCauley, handles horses. So you might say, I was always under Mrs. Stanford's care."

As Hattie listened to Mae, she pulled out the box and fingered the painting on its lid—noticing how the hunter, hidden behind brilliant orange flowers, stalked his prey, and the deer leaped, unaware.

"Miss McCauley, have you traveled with Mrs. Stanford before this occasion?"

"I've been to Boston, Washington, D.C., and St. Louis, but never overseas."

The French doors slid open. Judge Upton arrived; he took a seat next to Dr. Townsend.

The sheriff continued, "Miss McCauley, when were you hired for this trip?"

"On February 9, right after Miss Dobbs was fired—after the poison attempt."

"How were you made aware of the attempted poisoning?" the sheriff asked.

Mae snickered. "Sheriff, the entire Nob Hill staff was under house arrest. It wasn't much of a secret."

"Please continue, Miss McCauley."

"When the Morse detectives got to the house, they searched everyone's room—man or woman, it didn't matter. Everybody's but Ah Nee's."

As Mae testified, Hattie wondered if the powder was strychnine. What if it wasn't? The powder wasn't white, and it didn't taste bitter. No matter what the chemist concluded, she was accusing Miss Benson of murder. What if it were an innocent herb?

"Who is Ah Nee?" the sheriff asked.

"Ah Nee is a Chinese. He's been with Mrs. Stanford for as long as I can remember—I think before Leland Jr. died."

The doors of the dining room opened again. Charlie Banks and Ted Cutler arrived together. They sat near the reporters' table.

Mae continued, "Whenever the mistress went away, she always appointed Ah Nee as the caretaker, even if she were gone for a year."

Sheriff Dillon took off his glasses and wiped the

lenses with his handkerchief. "Miss McCauley, how would you describe the relationship among the staff at the Nob Hill mansion?"

"The domestic staff got along well—those of us who knew we were in service." Mae cocked her head. "But she who thought she was above us was ignored."

"And this 'she' you mention, who is she?"

"Miss Benson, of course."

The reporters scribbled furiously.

"Miss Benson always thought she was better than the rest of us, and the way she treated the mistress . . ." Mae rolled her eyes. "Like she was a child. One minute she coddled her against drafts and the next she took her candy away."

Attorney General Upton tapped the sheriff on the shoulder. The sheriff leaned in and Upton whispered in his ear.

Sheriff Dillon asked Mae, "Did Mrs. Stanford object to such treatment?"

"Mrs. Stanford was an old woman. She was afraid and Miss Benson had her under her control. During the last year, the mistress couldn't spend a day without Benson. And after the poison attempt, it got worse."

Cutler and Banks whispered to each other. Hattie scrutinized Cutler as if by examining him she could assess if he were trustworthy.

"Miss McCauley, could you give us an example of this dependence?" Sheriff Dillon asked.

Hattie stood up and edged her way down the aisle. As she passed, the men stood and pushed their dining chairs back for her to pass more easily.

Mae watched Hattie. "The day the expressmen

came to the mansion to pack our goods, Miss Benson was supposed to supervise them."

Hattie made her way toward Cutler. Mae coughed.

"But Mrs. Stanford wouldn't allow her to leave the St. Francis Hotel. So Mrs. Stanford sent President Ambrose to supervise the move instead."

Hattie tapped Cutler's shoulder. Mae coughed again.

"Do you need some water, Miss McCauley?"

"Perhaps," she answered.

Deputy Kanahele poured Mae a glass of water. She stared directly at Hattie, but Hattie didn't turn around; she was speaking to Cutler.

"Miss McCauley, you were saying that Dr. Ambrose supervised the shipment?"

"Supervised like a layabout. The good doctor headed straight for the kitchen and made himself a cup of tea. The place was a mess." Mae watched Cutler and Hattie leave the proceedings. "When I went in the kitchen to get the medicine basket, he startled and fumbled. I gave him a look I learned from my mother, and he put his cup in the sink and wiped the sugar off the table like it was the grandest act of Christian charity." The jurors laughed and Mae appeared pleased by her receptive audience. "Then he brushed off his tweed jacket with his hands, tugged on the lapels, and walked out like he was the Prince of Wales."

While Mae continued her testimony, Hattie and Cutler were in Hattie's office. She explained her suspicion about Miss Benson and showed him the powder.

He dipped his finger in and touched the powder

to his tongue. "Sour." His lips puckered.

"Do you think it's strychnine?" she asked.

"I won't know until I get it tested." He took an envelope from her desk and slid the powder in it, then put the envelope in his jacket pocket. "I know a few people in Honolulu who could take care of it for me. I'll have the answer for you tonight."

Hattie sketched out a crude map to the employees' cottage compound. "We'll wait for you there."

Cutler assured her he would be there before eight.

After Cutler left Hattie's office, she locked the door and sank back in her chair.

Mae continued to testify. The room was sweltering. Pipe and cigar smoke clouded the ceiling. Sweat dripped from Mae's hair. Her collar was darkened with perspiration and her pale complexion was flushed.

"Miss McCauley, Miss Benson testified that the medicine basket was in the stateroom of the *Korea* for the duration of your crossing. Is that your memory, also?" He was poised with his pencil on the legal pad.

"Miss Benson has her facts corked to the moon. The medicine basket was in the hold of the ship. We never took it out during the trip. Not once."

"You are certain?"

"I am."

"Miss McCauley, during the voyage did you ever hear Mrs. Stanford make any statement in regard to suicide?"

"With all due respect, sheriff, Mrs. Stanford doesn't speak much to domestics. I heard her talking to Miss Benson once, if you want to know that."

"Please go on."

"Mrs. Stanford told Miss Benson that it would be dreadful if she died in January—after the poisoning—because some people might think she had taken her own life." Mae addressed the jurors. "She was too tough a woman to kill herself. She buried her husband and her son. If she could outlive that, she could withstand the devil himself."

The sheriff asked the stenographer to see the transcript of the previous day's testimony. As he read it over, he stroked his eyebrow, then announced a ten-minute recess.

Mae hurried to Hattie's office. She knocked at the door. There was no answer.

Inside, Hattie sat with her head resting on her chair. She closed her eyes.

"Hattie?" She knocked again. Mae jiggled the doorknob. The door was locked. "Hattie?" After a third try, Mae left.

Mae asked the *lānai* hostess if she had seen Hattie, but she hadn't. Then she tried the front porch and the reception desk before returning to the inquest to take her place in the witness chair.

The sheriff began. "Miss McCauley, what were your duties while in Hawai'i?"

"I was taken out of service, sir."

Dr. Townsend crossed his arms over his chest as he listened.

"Why was that?" Sheriff Dillon asked.

"Because Miss Benson accused me of threatening her life. It made a fine fantasy, but it wasn't true."

The sheriff jotted "servant squabbling" then asked, "Why would Miss Benson think that?"

"Because I threatened to tell the mistress about all her skimming. I could, you know. She and the butler, Mr. Emerson. They robbed the woman at every step."

"What do you mean?"

"Mr. Emerson and Miss Benson padded 10 percent to any purchase the mistress made. It didn't matter if she bought a pound of liver or an Italian painting. When they paid the bills, they added their commission then split the profits."

Reporters licked their pencil tips and wrote with frenetic speed.

"Was Mrs. Stanford aware of this?"

"Ah Nee told her, but she wouldn't believe him about Miss Benson. She fired Mr. Emerson instead."

"What was the relationship between Ah Nee and Miss Benson?"

"Cats and dogs. A few months ago when Miss Benson and Miss Dobbs were getting along, Miss Benson ordered a Chinese boy to serve them afternoon tea in their rooms. When Ah Nee found out, he went looking for Benson. He told her that she was a servant just like the rest of us and she should get her own tea. Miss Benson said no Chinaman could speak to her like that. So Ah Nee went directly to Mrs. Stanford, and Mrs. Stanford made Miss Benson apologize to Ah Nee in front of the entire household staff. After that, Miss Benson threatened to send him back to China, and Ah Nee threatened to put rats in her bed."

Sheriff Dillon amended his notes. He drew arrows from one paragraph to another.

Dr. Townsend slid a note to the sheriff.

"Miss McCauley, did you ever witness Miss Benson cause harm to or threaten to harm Mrs. Stanford?"

"No, sir, not physical harm."

"Lastly, Miss McCauley, were you present at Mrs. Stanford's death?"

"No."

"That is all, Miss McCauley."

The sheriff thanked Mae and declared the inquest concluded for the day. The court stenographers sealed their paper rolls in manila envelopes and stuffed them in portfolios.

Mae went down to Hattie's office. But there was still no answer, so she sauntered back to the cottages.

It was six o'clock by the time Hattie got home. Koa and Mae were on the porch. Mae was fanning away mosquitoes with a section of the newspaper; Koa was sitting on the top step, next to a bag of boiled peanuts and two empty bottles of beer.

The three of them waited for Cutler. There was little conversation among them except for a few barbs from Mae about Hattie giving the powder to Cutler without her being there.

By eight o'clock it was dark. The constellation *Na-hiku* pointed its dipper to the North Star. Tree snails trilled and moss floated from the limbs. At nine o'clock the Central Union Church bells tolled.

"Maybe he's not coming." Koa angled the cap of his beer bottle against the porch step and banged it open with the heel of his hand.

"He's coming," Mae said.

"Maybe we should have left it alone." Koa said, peering down the alley. "Besides, why would Benson want to kill her? She lived like a queen." Koa took a slug of his Primo Ale.

"She was desperate to leave," Mae said.

"No one gives up that kind of money."

"If you've taken care of her all your life, maybe you would," Mae said.

"I don't know," Koa argued.

Mae put out her hand for Koa to pass her the peanuts. "The butler said that when Benson was in Egypt, she begged an antique dealer to find a replacement to take care of Mrs. Stanford. She even booked herself passage back to New York—paid for it herself."

"It's hard to believe anyone would kill Mrs. Stanford—even Benson. She may be a thief . . ." Hattie didn't finish her sentence.

"Maybe somebody put her up to it," Koa suggested.

"She's too clever for that," Mae said.

"What if they made her feel important?" Hattie wondered out loud.

"It would take a lot of money for me to do something like that." Koa spit peanut shells.

Hattie was first to spot Cutler turning down the alley. He was too far away for her to read his face. He walked briskly. Hattie noticed he had changed his clothes. He had on a loose-fitting suit. His collar was fresh and his tie was a dark paisley. He rested his foot on the porch step, right next to the bag of peanuts.

"Well?" Koa said.

"It's face powder."

Koa slapped his knee. "I knew it. I knew Benson wouldn't give up the money."

"It doesn't prove she didn't do it," Mae fought back.

Cutler reached in his jacket pocket and took out a pack of cigarettes and laid them on the porch railing. "The problem is, even if you did catch her with strychnine, you would have handed Benson her freedom." He tapped the end of the cigarette against the back of his hand.

Koa put two fingers to his lips, signaling Cutler he wanted a cigarette.

He handed Koa the pack. "A prosecutor could never prove you didn't plant the powder in her room. You should have called me or the sheriff."

"She's guilty as sin," Mae insisted.

"You need proof, Miss McCauley."

Koa took a drag of his cigarette and coughed. He held it out to the moonlight. "It's black," he said. "And strong."

"They're Egyptian. Dr. Lowell gave them to me."

The inscriptions on the pack were thick curves of writing, and the logo was a camel sitting in front of a sphinx.

"Was Dr. Lowell in Egypt the same time as Mrs. Stanford?" Mae asked.

"Within a few weeks," Cutler said.

"Then Dr. Lowell may know the antique dealer who Benson talked to—that should put the nail in her coffin."

Mae repeated her story. Whenever Cutler asked her for details, Mae provided them. There wasn't a question she didn't answer. Hattie wondered how many facts Mae was making up.

"She was willing to pay her own way, cross land and ocean," Mae emphasized.

"But she actually never left Mrs. Stanford. The antique dealer could be passing on a good story," Cutler challenged.

"Why would he lie?" Mae said.

"Notoriety?" Cutler speculated.

"You need to find out," Mae said.

The next morning, Hattie picked the newspaper off the porch. Photos of Mrs. Stanford took up the top half of the first page. She read the headline as she walked back to her bed: "Maid Calls Secretary a Liar."

Mae dragged the mosquito netting from around her bed. "Last night's *Star* called my testimony amusing," Mae said. "What does the *Advertiser* say?"

"I'm reading about the will." Hattie sat on her bed. "It says that according to the Stanford University Board of Trustees, Mrs. Stanford's will is to be made public in San Francisco today."

"What time?"

"Let me finish." Hattie put her feet up. "The editorial says, 'Could it be that someone will profit by Mrs. Stanford's death? Perhaps her closest heirs were in a hurry to taste their money? Was it not clue enough that on January 14, 1905, this poor woman suffered from a poison attempt?'"

"Poor Mr. Lathrop, he'll cry his eyes blind when he reads that."

Hattie read more. "The report from San Francisco says a team from the Morse Detective Agency and the San Francisco Police Department stated they have narrowed their suspects to three persons, but refused to name them." Hattie turned to Mae. "Who do you think they are?"

"Benson, Dobbs, and I don't know. Maybe it's me."

By the third day of the inquest, a routine was established: the jurors signed in and Deputy

Kanahele read their duties and responsibilities. Few people arrived on time. Even Hattie went to her office and made daily entries before going up to the dining room. Mae decided to sleep in an extra hour.

Dr. Lowell was the first witness of the day. He arrived in a pin-striped double-breasted suit. He wore a sling over his right arm as the result of injuries sustained in a car accident he had been in the evening before. Lowell was riding in Dr. Armstrong's motorcar. The two were on their way to the Isenberg estate for dinner. Armstrong drove too close to the gate, and the passenger's side fender hit the lava rock wall. He steered to the left and applied his brake, causing the car to swerve and hit the wall broadside. It impacted at the passenger door. Lowell was in the front seat, riding with his arm hanging over the side. He yanked it in before his arm was jammed, but smashed it against the windshield pillar.

The two physicians spent the evening at Queen's Hospital, where Dr. Lowell was treated for a five-inch gash.

Judge Upton chatted with Lowell before he testified. "I hear there were no broken bones."

Lowell held up his sling. "Thankfully, no tendons were severed. It could have been the end of my career."

"Fortuitous," Upton remarked.

Dr. Lowell took the witness chair. The deputy swore him in and asked his name and occupation.

"Dr. Ian Lowell. I am a physician."

"Please state your titles and diplomas and where you are in practice."

Lowell handed the sheriff his curriculum

vitae. "I entered the profession in October of 1881, over twenty-three years ago. I am a Doctor of Medicine, a Doctor of Surgery, Fellow of the Royal College of Physicians of Edinburgh, Member of the Royal College of Surgeons of England, Licentiate of the Royal College of Physicians of London, and I served with the 5th Dragoon Guard in India for six years before immigrating to Hawai'i. I am the current president of the Honolulu Medical Society. I could go on, sheriff, but there's a full listing on my vitae."

Sheriff Dillon skimmed the two pages provided by the doctor. "This will suffice, doctor. How long have you practiced in Hawai'i?"

"Seven years on the fifteenth of this month." Dr. Lowell adjusted his sling.

"Where do you reside, doctor?"

"I reside, with my wife, at The Palms Hotel."

"Doctor, on the evening of February 28, 1905, did you have occasion to visit the room of Mrs. Jane Lathrop Stanford?"

"I did."

"Why were you called there?"

"I went to bed about a quarter past eleven, and I was called up very shortly afterwards."

"Who called you?"

"The elevator boy. But before he arrived, I heard a commotion. When he knocked on my door, I put on my trousers, and he told me Mrs. Stanford was in need of a doctor. I grabbed my medical bag and shirt and finished dressing in the elevator."

"Who was in the room when you entered?"

"Mrs. Stanford and Miss Benson."

"Doctor, please tell us what happened then."

And once more, the details of Mrs. Stanford's death were repeated; this time described in dispassionate clinical terms.

Dr. Townsend twisted the end of his moustache as he listened to Lowell testify. Townsend coughed. The sheriff turned around and after a brief exchange, the sheriff asked Dr. Lowell, "You say the maid massaged Mrs. Stanford's feet. Did she do this of her own accord?"

"I did not direct her to massage Mrs. Stanford's feet. When I saw what she was doing, I directed her to apply stronger pressure."

Townsend raised his walking cane and tapped the table in front of Sheriff Dillon. He rapped on a journal article.

The sheriff lifted the article. "So you were aware that Miss Hattie Lehua was massaging Mrs. Stanford's feet and you allowed it to continue?"

"Mrs. Stanford appeared to take some comfort in it, and it did no harm. In fact, it was then that she thanked the maid for massaging her or at least called her name."

"Could she have been calling her name in pain? Signaling her to stop?"

"No, it was clearly a tone of endearment. She may even have called her 'my sweet.'"

Hattie stared ahead, expressionless. It's true, she thought, she did call my name, and Dr. Lowell said it was in a tone of endearment. Hattie recalled the vision of Mrs. Stanford's face, the slight smile, and the pleading eyes. When Hattie returned her attention to the sheriff's questioning, he was asking the doctor about Mrs. Stanford's spasm.

"Yes, she died in a spasm," Lowell stated.

"Could you tell what caused the spasm?"

"At the time, I suspected strychnine."

"Do you say that because Mrs. Stanford told you she was poisoned with strychnine the month before?" the sheriff asked.

"First of all, Mrs. Stanford told me that the January attempt on her life was a ruse. But certainly, it was natural for me to suspect strychnine given this information and the fact that when I arrived in her room, she told me she was poisoned. However, I based my medical opinion on the manner in which Mrs. Stanford died." Dr. Lowell turned to the jurors as if instructing them. "While I was in the army, I saw soldiers die of strychnine. It's a horrid death— a death once seen, it's never forgotten. Strychnine causes a distinct and eccentric rigidity of the body. There is a unique condition of hands and feet, and Mrs. Stanford displayed classic conditions."

"Doctor, for the record, do you clearly state that in your opinion Mrs. Stanford came to her death from strychnine poisoning?"

"I will state that the condition of her body clearly exemplified death by strychnine, and I expect that the chemists' report will confirm such. Whether there was any felonious intent in the ingestion of the strychnine is not for me to say. However, I will testify that if I had been called to the scene of death without anyone informing me of anything but the fact that the victim was sick for twenty minutes before, I would have strongly suspected strychnine."

Again Townsend whispered to the sheriff. A reporter drew a cartoon of Sheriff Dillon as a hand puppet at the end of Dr. Townsend's arm.

"Dr. Lowell, since you were the physician in

attendance upon Mrs. Stanford's death, why did you not perform the autopsy?"

Lowell adjusted his sling before he spoke. "Since I had formed such a strong opinion about the cause of death, I thought if I performed the autopsy, the autopsy might be called into question. Critics might contend that I suspected strychnine and therefore I looked for it. Rather than raise any questions regarding the veracity of the procedure, I asked Dr. Adolf Henrik to act as prosector."

"Why Dr. Henrik?"

"I wanted someone who had nothing to do with the case and a professional whose reputation was beyond reproach. I was aware of the notoriety of the deceased and acted with exceptional caution in choosing a competent and impartial physician."

The sheriff crossed out his questions as he asked them. "Doctor, are you familiar with the drug strychnia?

"Thoroughly."

"How would you distinguish its symptoms from a case of acute indigestion?"

Lowell chuckled. "Well, in all my years of medical practice, I have never seen a death certificate signed 'acute indigestion.' Unless there is a physician present who can recall such a case, I think that it is a universal statement." Lowell directed his comment at Townsend.

Most spectators laughed. Then Sheriff Dillon questioned the doctor about the items he removed from Mrs. Stanford's room and the procedure he used to collect them. Nothing Lowell said was challenged and when he was completed with his testimony, the sheriff thanked him, and the doctor signed the required papers and left.

As was the routine, the sheriff called a recess, and Hattie went down to her office. Mae was waiting outside her door.

"I thought I would see you at the inquest," Hattie said.

They both stepped inside.

"I was on my way upstairs when I heard a bit of hubbub. I asked what was going on." Mae primped her hair in the mirror. "I found out Mrs. Stanford's trunks are to be moved to Dr. Townsend's house and the jewels are going to the bank." She turned to Hattie. "We should check the mistress's belongings before they're packed away. Maybe that's where Benson hid the poison."

Mae's use of the word "we" annoyed Hattie.

"It's our last chance," Mae said.

Hattie was having more doubts that Mae wanted to find out the truth about Mrs. Stanford's death. Because of Mae's obsession, Hattie had broken into Benson's room and falsely accused her of hiding poison. She felt lucky that Cutler had said nothing to the sheriff or Mr. St. Clair. Hattie had no intention of taking another risk. She would not break into Mrs. Stanford's room, nor would she allow Mae to.

Mrs. Martin knocked on the open door and entered Hattie's office. She told Hattie she had to speak to her in private as she turned toward Mae, who left without comment.

Mrs. Martin shut the door. She took off her glasses and rubbed the bridge of her nose. The pinch marks from her eyeglasses were a reddish purple. "Mrs. Stanford's belongings are being transferred tomorrow. Mr. Hackfield is acting on behalf of the family. He's arranged for the trunks to be held at Dr. Townsend's home and her jewelry to be deposited at the First National Bank. So I'll need the inventory the bank clerk witnessed when Mrs. Stanford checked in."

It was the first time Hattie had thought about the inventory since Mrs. Martin asked her to do it. Somehow, with being pressed into service and Mae moving into her cottage, she forgot about contacting the bank and never took care of the inventory.

"I have to look for it. With the inquest, my filing has suffered a bit." Hattie tried to sound calm.

"When you find it, put it on my desk. It's just a formality—I'm sure there won't be any discrepancies. But I need it before tomorrow."

After Mrs. Martin left, Hattie leafed through the Stanford file as if an inventory would magically appear. She clearly recalled Mrs. Martin's words, "Schedule a clerk from First National Bank to witness a match." It seemed impossible that she had forgotten. She hoped that between dealing with Miss Benson, the inquest, and the press, Mrs. Martin would forget about the inventory and the transfer would be made without notice.

In the lobby of The Palms, Ted Cutler approached Dr. Lowell as he exited the elevator. Cutler commented on the taste of the Egyptian cigarettes that the doctor had given him. Lowell leaned forward from his waist and slipped his hand under his sling as if reaching for his cigarettes.

"No." Cutler waved his hand. "I'm not interested in the cigarettes, doctor. It has to do with your time in Egypt. There may be a link with Mrs. Stanford's death."

With that, Lowell invited Cutler into his suite. Lowell's suite overlooked the Pacific Ocean. On the foyer table was a gallery of framed family photos. Cutler picked up the Lowells' wedding photo. Lowell was posed in white tie and tails standing next to his seated bride, who held a bouquet of cascading roses.

"Gin?" Dr. Lowell asked.

Cutler nodded.

Lowell motioned for his guest to sit.

"I'll be direct, doctor. I heard a rumor that Mrs. Stanford was difficult during her time in Egypt, and when the Stanford party was in Assouan that Miss Benson sought escape."

Lowell handed Cutler his drink. "There are always rumors." Lowell seemed hesitant.

"But some are based on fact."

"And some not."

"Dr. Lowell, you know I have Mrs. Stanford's interest at heart. And of course, anything you say would be held in the utmost confidence."

"Agreed." Lowell nodded. "As you know from our dinner conversations, Mrs. Stanford and I were not in Assouan at the same time. She left six weeks before I arrived, but there was still gossip." The doctor sat down on the couch across from Cutler. He was drinking water. "The manager of the Cataract Hotel told me Mrs. Stanford was terrified of leaving her room. Her mail was delivered, her meals were taken in the room, and she had all gifts from the Egyptian elite inspected before she accepted them." Dr. Lowell reached for his cigarette case with his left hand. "In fact, the manager told me Mrs. Stanford's butler slept in a chair outside her room. But I'm not sure if that's true."

Cutler lit the cigarette for the doctor.

"The manager told me that Miss Benson had asked him to arrange a tourist's companion for Mrs. Stanford. She told him she had to return home—something about her father being in poor health." Dr. Lowell put the cigarette to his mouth using his left hand. "According to him, Miss Benson was desperate. She offered him one hundred dollars to make the deal. Of course, he refused."

"There's another story circulating that it was an antique dealer," Cutler said, "not the hotel manager, who was asked the same thing."

"Yes, that would be Mr. Clayton Adams. Mrs. Stanford and I both used him while we were in Egypt. He told me a similar story, but I didn't believe him. Adams is quite a theatrical type who enjoys building up intrigue to increase the price of his antiques.

"Mr. Adams told me that Miss Benson offered him money to book her passage to New York. As I recall there was nothing about tendering a replacement for herself. His portrayal of Miss Benson was most unkind, as it is of most women. He refused her offer, not wanting to offend Mrs. Stanford. She was, as you might expect, an excellent customer. When Mr. Adams declined, Miss Benson threatened that she would see to it that Mrs. Stanford would never use his services again. Adams knew it was an empty threat. He's the only dealer in Egypt who can guarantee authentic artifacts. He told me then she accused him of gouging Mrs. Stanford." The doctor smiled. "Considering the source, he was quite amused."

"How so?" Cutler asked.

"The 10 percent commission. It is de rigueur."

"Is Mr. Adams a credible man?"

"That depends on your question. I have been doing business with him for twenty years, and he has always been straight with me. But I never ask him how he obtains the art he sells." Dr. Lowell took a long drag on his cigarette.

"Do you know how it ended with him and Miss Benson?" Cutler finished his gin.

"Mr. Adams traveled with the Stanford party to Cairo. He claimed she was more relaxed there, but the scuttlebutt I heard among British officers was that she cut short her tour of the pyramids because she had a premonition of being kidnapped."

"Did her fears have merit?"

"To some extent." The doctor put out his cigarette with one twirling motion. "A short time before Mrs. Stanford arrived in Egypt, a copper mine heiress, Miss Ellen Stone, had been kidnapped and carried into the mountains of Bulgaria. She was held for ransom and after it was paid, her body was delivered in pieces in a sack. For weeks before Mrs. Stanford arrived in Egypt, the newspapers heralded her as one of the richest women in the world. So, yes. I think it was reasonable for her to be fearful. She was a tempting prize."

"Did you fear for your own life?"

"My entire assets are worth less than Mrs. Stanford's luncheon jewels," Lowell said. "But when I first arrived in Assouan, the hotel manager warned me about bands of Egyptian Raisuli who were targeting Europeans—theft mostly. He insisted I never travel alone, and was adamant that I not venture out of the city without a bodyguard. Nothing out of the ordinary for travel in that region of the world. There's always a rebellion or tribal war." Lowell asked Cutler if he wanted another drink; Cutler refused.

"Doctor, is there any way for me to contact Mr. Adams in Egypt?"

"In Egypt?" Lowell went to his desk and presented Cutler with a business card. "His office is in San Francisco. Most of California society uses him."

❧ CHAPTER TWELVE ❧

The transfer of Mrs. Stanford's goods began. Miss Benson, dressed in black, stood with a clipboard resting on her hip. Mr. Hackfield strolled through Mrs. Stanford's room, tugging at trunk locks and attempting to lift the covers of valises.

Zachary Hackfield was an aristocratic gentleman. He stood six feet tall. His moustache was waxed to a curling spiral, and his beard was trimmed in a perfect spade. After he checked every inventoried bag, he confirmed all was secure.

It was a humid day. The temperature was a stagnant eighty-five degrees and despite the ceiling fan being on and the door and windows flung open, little air was circulating through Mrs. Stanford's room. Miss Benson patted the perspiration from her brow. The heel of her hand was smudged with ink.

Mr. Hackfield signed the drayer's inventory sheet and told Miss Benson he was retiring to the bar, leaving her to direct the laborers.

The talk in the bar was about Mrs. Stanford's will. A Maui attorney hypothesized that Mr. Lathrop arranged the murder of his sister. Then he went on to complain about his own brother, whom he suspected of tampering with the family estate.

Judge Upton proclaimed his opinion of the

Chinese. "They are an inscrutable lot. If the Chinaman, Ah Nee, received one red cent, obviously he killed her." Miss Benson was never mentioned as a suspect.

Hattie entered the bar to deliver a message to Hackfield from Mrs. Martin. The message informed Hackfield that the First National armored truck would arrive at 3:30. Hackfield folded the note, creased it with his fingernails, and said, "Assure Mrs. Martin that I shall be prompt."

On the way back to her office, Hattie walked through the front lobby. The sunlight streamed through the entrance of the hotel. Hattie had never seen the doors of The Palms closed. But at 3:15 they would be locked and Wells Fargo guards would be posted at every entrance during the transfer of Mrs. Stanford's goods.

The impact of Mrs. Stanford's death was far reaching. The judiciary, anticipating a trial, petitioned the legislature for money to hire additional personnel. Newspapers doubled their circulation. Hotel owners hoped the publicity given to Waikīkī would boost tourism in the islands. And every politician savored the national limelight as if it shone only on him.

The day before Mrs. Stanford died, the *Honolulu Star* editor had criticized the sheriff's office for invading a Mormon plantation in Lāʻie to track down a clan of polygamists. The *Pacific Commercial Advertiser*'s political cartoon had lambasted Dr. Gear for his decision to support the watering down of milk, and the worst controversy on the sports page was the schedule of prep school sports. But Mrs. Stanford's death turned Honolulu upside down. People who had the slightest acquaintance of her, or even an imagined acquaintance, enjoyed instant celebrity and freely gave interviews to the press.

The Chinese, Japanese and Portuguese papers all devoted their front pages to the news. The neighbor island newspapers sent reporters to Honolulu. The Catholic, Mormon, Anglican and Congregationalists newsletters all commented on her death. The royalist, anarchist and constitutional monarchist tabloids ran articles linking her death to their political causes.

In the midst of all this frenzy, Mrs. Stanford's body rested at the Williams' Mortuary while junior reporters perched over Teletype machines ready to receive the text of her will.

Sheriff Dillon deferred the start of the inquest at the request of a juror, but at 9:30 he refused to procrastinate any longer and called the inquest to order.

The first witness of the day was Dr. Knight. The sheriff asked Dr. Knight almost the exact questions he had asked Dr. Lowell. Knight corroborated Lowell's account of Mrs. Stanford's death, and he affirmed the testimony given regarding the autopsy.

Then the sheriff asked, "Doctor, from what you observed while attending Mrs. Stanford's death and the autopsy of her corpse, what is your opinion as to the cause of death?"

"Strychnine. I have no doubt," he answered. "I have witnessed only one strychnine death before Mrs. Stanford's and, God willing, I shall never see another. It is a ghastly death. And in Mrs. Stanford's case, the spasms were textbook. The only other cause of death I suspected was tetanus, but that was ruled out during the autopsy."

Knight's testimony was suddenly drowned out by newspaper boys hawking their special edition. "Secretary Gets Twenty-Five Thousand Dollars! Doctor Says It Was Strychnine!"

Reporters rushed from the room.

Hattie heard the newsboys from inside her office, then she heard the clicking of heels down the hall. She knew it was Mae.

Mae burst into the room reading the paper. "Twenty-five thousand dollars! Look at her." Mae tossed the paper on Hattie's desk. "A face like a pound of tripe." There was a sketch of Benson on the front page. It was an unflattering penned profile. "Thirty-one million dollars to the university," Mae recited. "And two and a half million to her brother, Harrison. Like he needs it. The man spits gold."

Hattie picked up the paper. "I see Ah Nee was given five thousand dollars."

"Well deserved." Mae granted her approval.

Hattie spread the paper out on her desk. "And Mrs. Stanford remembered your parents."

"One thousand dollars for a lifetime of service. She gave the gardener five hundred."

Hattie skimmed the list of servants given five hundred dollars: gardeners, valets, and coachmen. The charitable organizations were mentioned next— a full column of them. Five thousand dollars each to the Hospital for Children and Training School of Nurses, California Women's Hospital, and the Roman Catholic Orphan Asylum.

"Ten thousand dollars to the Sisters of the Notre Dame?" Hattie asked.

"The old woman had a taste for Catholics and candles."

"And twenty thousand to the Sisters of the Holy Spirit in Florence, Italy?"

"They were the ones who took care of Leland Jr. when he was dying."

"Listen to this." Hattie read out loud. "Mrs. Stanford bequeathed the wardrobes of her dear son, Leland Stanford Jr., and her beloved husband, Leland Stanford, to her brother, Harrison Lathrop." Hattie lowered the paper. "Has she kept their clothes all this time?"

"Down to their socks."

"Did you read the last paragraph?" Hattie asked Mae.

"The legal stuff? No."

"It says, 'I have no doubt about a future life beyond this mortal world; a fair land where no more tears will be shed and there will be no more partings. To this, my last will and testament, I have sworn on this 10th day of February, AD 1905, in the city and county of San Francisco, set my hand and seal in triplicate and is witnessed by John Saunders and Gertrude Benson.'" Hattie turned to Mae. "She changed her will right before she sailed, and Benson was a witness."

Mae snickered. "You choose to be blind, my dear. Benson probably dictated the will."

———◆◆◆———

After the newspapers hit the streets, The Palms was inundated with phone calls for Miss Benson. She refused all calls and all visitors—including Dr. Townsend. Her only communication was a message she left for Mr. Hackfield. She wrote, "In light of the circumstances, I will not be able to oversee the transfer of Mrs. Stanford's goods."

As a result, Hackfield asked Mr. St. Clair to witness the transfer. Both men reconciled the inventory, and two First National guards witnessed the reconciliation.

Hattie stayed in her office, trying to stay out of sight of Mrs. Martin. She was terrified that Mrs. Martin would remember the neglected witnessed inventory. With every footfall past her door, she was sure it was she. When a knock on her door turned out to be Mae once again, Hattie was relieved.

Mae was in grand spirits. She had convinced herself that the disclosure of the sum bequeathed to Benson would result in her being named as the murderess. She was almost giddy. "It's a closed case!" Mae grabbed the back of Hattie's chair and swiveled it around. "And we are off to celebrate!"

She took Hattie's skimmer off the hat rack and handed it to her. "Lock up your files, missy, we're off to the Elite Parlor Emporium."

Hattie agreed, not because she thought celebrating was in order but because it was a chance to leave the hotel—beyond Mrs. Martin's questioning.

The two women took a carriage to the Emporium. As they rode down Waikiki Road, Mae waved to pedestrians with her cupped hand. "For ten cents, I'm the bloody Queen of England."

Her exuberance was uncomfortable for Hattie.

The waitress at the Emporium seated the women at a round marble table next to the window. The ice cream parlor had a black and white checked tile floor and white bead board walls. A polished brass soda machine glinted in the sun, and stained-glass lamp-shades hung over the marble counter.

"It reminds me of Ghiradelli's in San Francisco," Mae remarked.

Hattie glanced out the window toward the Spanish-style customs house and the neoclassic design of the Hawaii Theatre. "Does Honolulu look like San Francisco?" she asked.

"Honolulu looks more like Boston to me," she said. "Every one of those houses on the trolley line looks like some Yankee picked up his family home-stead and slapped it down on that street—right down to the wilted geraniums."

Hattie wanted to tell Mae that most of Hawai'i didn't look like that.

"My parents lived in Boston when they first came from Ireland." Mae read over the menu as she spoke. "Da says when they lived there, all my moth-er did was pray the rosary and walk to daily mass with all the other Irish women. At Vina Ranch she's forced to go to church with Portuguese women and the one English Catholic." She closed her menu and placed it at the edge of the table. "But she's still mourning the old sod."

The waitress came to take their order.

"Two seltzer waters and two ice cream sundaes. My treat." Mae slid the jar of maraschino cherries from the center of the table. "Have you ever thought about moving to San Francisco?" Mae asked Hattie.

"I don't think I'd feel comfortable there." Working at The Palms was enough exposure to *haole* for Hattie.

"Feeling comfortable is reserved for the rich."

For Hattie, it was a matter of skin color, not money.

"My mother is saving money so she can be buried in Ireland. But the Ireland she misses is a green pasture where the sun always shines and no one is dying of starvation and the damp."

The waitress set down two sundaes and two glasses of seltzer.

"She yearns for the gray of a sunny Irish day." Mae opened the jar of cherries and topped off their sundaes. "One more for good luck." She plunked a second cherry on each. "She's always bemoaning that she feels like a foreigner in America. But me, I don't care."

Hattie dipped her spoon into the ice cream. "Sometimes I feel like a foreigner in my own country, or what was my country." It was the first time Hattie had ever admitted it.

"It's no wonder you feel like a foreigner, with your queen locked up and a missionary's son running your country." Mae spoke her mind easily.

"Koa thinks we can bring back the queen. He's still hoping for a revolution."

"Men love the poetry of war. And it's the women who have to bury what's left." Mae poked her spoon in the air as she spoke. "They think if they're not warriors they're less than men. It's an Irish disease—we live by the songs of the rebellion."

"It's different in Hawai'i. We were too small to fight," Hattie said.

"And is Ireland vast?" Mae raised her eyebrows. "The British buried our language and teach our young ones a history that has nothing to do with fact. There's the real fight."

Hattie had no idea what went on in Ireland. She only knew about Hawai'i. For her entire life, Hattie had avoided politics. To her it was a fool's game. She accepted the course of history.

The next morning, before the cable office opened, Cutler was sitting on its front stoop smoking a cigarette. He unfolded his message to Inspector Whelan and checked the accuracy of Clayton Adams's phone number against his business card. He cupped his hands to the window of the office. It was ten minutes to eight. In San Francisco it was almost 10:00 a.m. Cutler was certain that by noon a Morse detective would be questioning Adams.

Across the street, two newspaper boys squabbled over the territory of that particular corner. Cutler bought a paper from each of them then tossed them each a penny tip. He leaned against the wall of the office and read the paper. Most of the articles were reprints from the special edition. A few interviews with Honolulu physicians were added. Doctors who had never seen Mrs. Stanford's body offered their opinions of the cause of death.

Both editorials welcomed the arrival of Mr. Harrison Lathrop and President Ambrose that afternoon, and the social page listed a descriptive inventory of Mrs. Stanford's jewelry.

Cutler spotted news from San Francisco. According to police chief Jerrold G. Brown, "The San Francisco Central Precinct has been crammed with cranks confessing to or accusing someone of this heinous crime. I have spiritualists and fortune-tellers camped on my steps, and every social freak is banging on my door pleading guilty. Dozens of people have turned themselves in.

"Of those persons observed in the precinct, most, as expected, came from the ranks of those on the dole or with petty violations of the law. The only exception was a large well-groomed man, one may say obese, in a white linen suit, with an ebony walking stick, and sporting a white felt fedora. He claims not to have committed the crime, but says he knows the identity of the murderer and will divulge the name for one thousand dollars. Police Chief Brown categorized him as a crank."

As soon as the office opened, Cutler sent his cable. He took a carriage back to the hotel and by the time the first witness was being sworn in, he was sitting at the inquest joking with Charlie Banks.

Deputy Kanahele swore in Dr. Henrik.

When the sheriff asked the doctor about his training, Henrik droned on reciting his credentials.

"I'm not sure I'll be able to stay awake," Banks admitted to Cutler.

"He is boring," Cutler agreed.

"It's not the doc," Banks said. "I was at the Seven Seas Saloon until three."

Henrik placed his textbooks, marbled notebooks, and reading glasses on the table in front of him. He began his testimony with the basic facts of the autopsy. "The body was that of a well-nourished Caucasian female. Her weight was estimated between 220 and 240 pounds; the corpse yielded a fluid weight of 160 pounds."

"Try to focus on his ears," Cutler told Banks. "That should keep you awake."

Henrik turned to the jurors. "Purplish red spots were spread on the lower portion of her body.

Postmortem staining was found across her face, cheeks, and ears."

"Picture his ears purple," Cutler whispered, not moving his lips.

Banks stifled a laugh.

"The hands were still clenched in fists with the thumbs pressing against the palms." He demonstrated by placing his own hands into the described position. "And the feet had the soles turned in, the instep strongly arched, and the toes extended." Dr. Henrik leaned back in his chair then lifted his feet in the air so that the soles of his shoes almost touched. "Something like the position of mine now."

"Doctor, what is the significance of these positions?"

"That he can clap like a sea lion?" Cutler continued his joking.

"They are typical of death in a spasm, caused by strychnine or tetanus. However, I thoroughly examined the corpse for external wounds and found none, therefore tetanus was eliminated. During the autopsy, I found no pathological cause of death. I mean by that, that there was no disease in any organs to account for her death."

"Could you be more specific, doctor?" Sheriff Dillon asked.

"May I refer to my notes?" Henrik opened a notebook. "Let's see." He flipped through pages. "I will begin here." He read, "The large intestines were distended with gas. The contents were drained into a jar." Henrik addressed the jury. "The contents were chocolate colored and the consistency of pea soup."

Cutler muttered, "Did you say you were order-ing pea soup for lunch?"

Banks strained to hear the doctor.

"The lungs were normal. Next we examined the heart. The left side contained dark fluid, a black-look-ing blood. There was a certain amount of fat around the heart, but no more than you would expect to find in a woman of her nourishment. There was slight evi-dence of atheroma at the base, but nothing that could begin to cause death."

"Dr. Henrik, was the heart enlarged?"

"No."

The sheriff wrote down the doctor's answer. "Please continue."

"The stomach contained two pints of fluid with a faint odor of mustard. There was no solid matter, save a few particles that were taken out and sealed in a jar."

Sheriff Dillon's questioning of the doctor lasted over two hours. Most of the questions were general; Henrik's responses were detailed and technical— weights and measurements of organs, color and condition of organs, and methods used for their preservation. During his testimony, Henrik often asked to make his points clear to the jury and he passed around diagrams for them to view. When describing what death from strychnine looks like, he unrolled an etching of a male corpse and held it up for both jurors and spectators to see. The corpse was contorted and arched.

Sheriff Dillon asked the doctor about the stomach pump. "There have been comments made in the newspapers by Honolulu physicians that if the pump had arrived earlier, Mrs. Stanford would be alive."

Dr. Henrik folded his hands on the table. "In my

opinion, the stomach pump would have been useless. During the autopsy, I found an absence of food and a clean condition of the stomach. Any liquid taken in prior to death would have been absorbed rapidly. Therefore, a stomach pump would have been no use."

Sheriff Dillon flipped back two pages of his notes. "Dr. Henrik, early in your testimony you stated every organ of the body was healthy?"

"I did not state that."

The sheriff set the pad on his knee. "What did you say?"

"I stated that in the examination of the organs, I discovered no pathological cause of death."

"Dr. Henrik, is it your opinion that Mrs. Stanford came to her death by strychnine poisoning?"

"Mind you, the evidence given to us through autopsy was that the organs were normal. That would not indicate strychnine death, or anything else. It showed there was no natural cause for death. The toxicologist's report will confirm or deny the presence of strychnine in the body."

"Doctor, didn't the postmortem appearance of Mrs. Stanford's body prove death due to strychnine?"

"There are no such absolute markers. However, Mrs. Stanford displayed all appearances generally associated with strychnine poisoning and the autopsy ruled out tetanus."

Dr. Townsend tapped the sheriff on the shoulder.

One of the reporters wisecracked, "Here go Townsend's cross-examinations."

The sheriff asked, "Dr. Henrik, have you seen a case of strychnine poisoning before?"

"Only the corpse of a dog."

There were a few snickers.

"Dr. Henrik, have you discussed this case with anyone?"

"Of course."

Charlie Banks checked his watch. "His testimony is taking longer than the autopsy."

"Doctor, did you hear rumors that Mrs. Stanford was poisoned before you performed the autopsy?"

"Sheriff, I observed the condition of the body without the influence of rumors or yellow journalism."

"Now it's our fault," one of the reporters chided.

"Thank you, doctor. Not only for your testimony but for your effort in explaining complex medical facts to the jurors."

Henrik didn't respond. He gathered his books in a pile and asked if the inquest would pay his carriage fare back to the hospital. Sheriff Dillon reached into his own pocket and handed Henrik some money.

It was expected that Sheriff Dillon would announce a lunch break, but after reading a note handed to him by Deputy Kanahele, he announced, "Gentlemen, I have received word from Dr. Tyler Flynn about the toxicology report. Dr. Flynn is requesting a delay in his appearance." The sheriff put on his glasses as he read the note to the jurors. "Unexpected complications have arisen and the report will not be available for at least one, perhaps two days." The sheriff took his glasses off. "Given that fact, I am suspending the inquest. Gentlemen, enjoy your day of leisure."

Immediately after the recess, Ted Cutler headed to the bar. The Palms bar had become the most popular watering hole in Waikīkī. At lunch it was standing room only. Cutler leaned with his back against the bar and his foot resting on the rail. He was sipping his second glass of Scotch.

A dapper young man in a gray pinstripe suit introduced himself. "Parnell Regan."

Cutler extended his hand. "Ted Cutler. Were you upstairs?"

"I was." Regan was wearing an 'Iolani Club tie. "I found the description of the brain as an under-cooked flan particularly appealing."

"Actually the pea soup was my favorite," Charlie Banks remarked.

"This is Charlie Banks." Cutler introduced him to Regan. "Someday he'll have his own byline."

"But first I need to get a paper to hire me."

"When you scoop this trial, every paper in town will be vying for you." Cutler handed Banks a beer. "He's been staking out everyone from Miss Benson to Mr. St. Clair. Be careful, Mr. Regan, or he'll be watching you."

Banks shook his head. "What business are you in, Mr. Regan?"

"I'm an attorney, contracts mainly."

"Are you here as a spectator?" Banks asked.

"One of the unwashed masses," he said.

Banks pumped Regan for information. "Mr. Regan, in the event of an arrest in this case, where do you think the trial will be held? Here or San Francisco?"

Regan casually rested his elbow on the bar. "If the poison was prepared in San Francisco with the intent it be taken in Honolulu, the jurisdiction could be in either place. You see, when a crime is committed in two different states, the jurisdiction isn't clear. But I suspect the attorney general will rule it should be in California."

"Which attorney general? Hawai'i's or California's?" Cutler asked.

"It'll be Attorney General Upton's call. But my guess is that he would base his ruling on a San Francisco case of seven years ago. Cordelia Beck."

"I'm not familiar with the case," Banks said.

Regan set his drink on the bar and settled into the role of storyteller. "Gentlemen, let me tell you the story of Cordelia Beck." He tugged at his jacket lapels then mockingly cleared his throat. "Miss Beck was a thirty-one-year-old spinster who was known to those who less appreciated her shrewish charm as 'the antique virgin.'" He said it as an aside. "But dear Cordelia had a secret life as the paramour of Jack Dunne. Jack Dunne was a member of the press. No offense to you, Mr. Banks." Regan slightly bowed. "He was a gambling man and a womanizer and a drunk. And it was common knowledge that he lacked skill in each. Dunne was married to a wealthy Delaware farmer's daughter who had followed him out to San Francisco after the wedding."

Cutler raised his glass. "Ah, yes. To farmers' daughters."

"To farmers' daughters," they toasted.

"After a year of living with him in California, she returned to her family, leaving Jack to his drink and his women. One of those women was Cordelia Beck. Sadly, Miss Beck took Jack's affection for her as sincere, and she encouraged him to get a divorce. But Dunne had no intention of it. He told Cordelia that as long as his dear wife, Wanda, was alive, he felt bound to his vows."

"The plot thickens," Cutler said.

"Yes, gentlemen, the plot thickens." Regan grinned. "Dear Cordelia wrote an anonymous letter to Wanda Dunne telling her about her husband's carousing in a detailed, but most sympathetic, manner. She wrote 'woman to woman knowing the sorrow you must bear, I must inform you of his indiscretions.' To soften the blow, Cordelia sent Wanda a box of her homemade bourbon bonbons. Unfortunately, the bonbons were flavored with more arsenic than bourbon and Wanda Dunne died." Regan took a sip of his drink before he continued. "In the Beck case, the ruling was that the jurisdiction was in San Francisco since the poison was baked there. Precedent was set, and Cordelia Beck was tried, convicted, and sentenced to life in prison. She reportedly died at San Quentin of 'softening of the brain due to melancholy.'"

Cutler ordered two cigars from the bartender, giving one to Regan.

"But the problem is, two years later a man standing in Nevada shot a man who was standing in California and that case was tried in California."

Cutler lit Regan's cigar.

"However, if I were a betting man"—the attorney puffed on his cigar—"my money would be on California and that the murderer of such a noted figure will end his days in San Quentin."

"Or her days," Charlie Banks remarked.

"What if the crime were committed in another country, like Japan, for example?" Cutler asked.

Regan pursed his lips. "That depends on the treaties between the countries. From my limited knowledge of Japan's police work, I suspect the murderer would get off scot-free."

———◆•◆◆•◆———

Hattie read over the inventory of jewels in the newspaper. She read the list twice. It was incomplete. The broken cameo bracelet, the black pearl necklace, the diamond ring, and the aquamarine and topaz rings were missing. So were the locket, a brooch, and several other rings.

Hattie put down the paper and went directly upstairs to Benson's room. With an easy smile, she explained to the chambermaid that she needed to pick up a few items of clothes she had left in Benson's closet. Once inside, she headed straight for the closet and the embroidered valise. She set it on the desk and opened every pouch—there they were—all the missing jewelry and more. Hattie shoved the jewels in her pocket, knocking the ink blotter off the desk. When she put it back, she noticed words on the blotter, "ruby ring, portrait brooch, sapphire," in black ink, clearly written.

Benson wrote out a new inventory! Hattie tore off the paper and shoved it in her pocket, too.

The maid asked Hattie if she found everything, and Hattie said that Miss Benson was mistaken. Hattie had left nothing in the room.

Hattie walked down the steps. Perspiration beaded on her face. Her pulse raced. She made it through the lobby, down Waikiki Road, then ran until she got to her cottage.

Mae was hanging her stockings on the clothesline. "There's some fresh papaya inside. Koa brought it."

Hattie was panting.

"He's out back." Mae hung the last of her clothes.

Hattie sat on the bed. She felt like a thief—it wasn't supposed to feel like this.

Mae swung open the door. She had her laundry basket on her hip. "I heard Dr. Henrik's testimony was quite amusing."

Hattie was trembling.

"His pea soup and flan descriptions are all over town."

I shouldn't be afraid, Hattie told herself. But she couldn't stop shaking.

Mae put the wicker basket down. "What's wrong?"

Hattie didn't answer.

"Was it Benson?" Mae sat down next to her.

Hattie reached in her pocket and emptied the jewels on the bed.

"Jesus, Mary, and Joseph. What did you do?"

"I don't know," Hattie said.

"Well, I'd say you've done it quite well."

Hattie showed Mae the crumpled blotter pad. "Benson wrote out an altered inventory."

Mae smoothed out the paper.

"I found the jewels in the closet, I saw the cameo and the pearls, but I thought she just forgot to put them in the safe deposit box, or maybe it was a 'commission.' Then I read the paper."

Koa opened the screen door. "What is that?" He stared at the jewels.

"They're Mrs. Stanford's," Hattie answered.

"You stole them?"

"I didn't steal them. Benson stole them."

"And I suppose you have them out on loan?" Mae put on the aquamarine ring and turned her hand for the stone to catch the light of the sun.

"I didn't steal them," Hattie said.

"That's what we'll tell the police." Koa picked up the pearl earrings.

"She didn't actually steal them." Mae put the black pearl necklace to her neck. "They were already stolen. You can't steal something twice."

Koa grinned at Mae. "You're right. Benson steals from the old lady, and Hattie steals from Benson— there's no proof of the crime." He put the topaz ring on his pinky, then took the pearls from Mae and wrapped them around his head. "How do I look?"

"Like a Hawaiian prince," Mae said.

"Don't you see?" Koa said. "None of this jewelry exists. We can sell it all and split it three ways."

"Koa, don't."

"Don't what?" He wedged the topaz off his finger.

"I'm going to return the jewels to Mr. Lathrop," Hattie said.

"And what will you tell him? Somehow, you found his sister's jewels in your lap?" Koa sat on Mae's bed. "Hattie, if you want to do good with the money, give it all to me."

"Why can't you be serious?" Hattie asked.

"I am. Give it to Ka Leo. With that kind of money, we could send five lawyers to Washington, D.C. We could pay for ads in newspapers. Who knows what we could do?"

"I didn't steal them to give them away, Koa."

"So you admit you stole them," Koa said.

"No, I didn't." Hattie was on the verge of tears. "All I know is that I'm going to the Alexander and talk to Mr. Lathrop," she said.

"I'm sure he'll accept a call from a hotel employee," Mae scoffed.

"I can try."

❧ Chapter Thirteen ❧

On March 10, 1905, the SS *Mariposa* docked at an empty Alakea Wharf. The Royal Hawaiian Band, the *lei* sellers, waiting families, and press were sequestered in warehouse number 201—such was the far-reaching power of Stanford University.

The press was restricted; no cameras were allowed. The street was cordoned off and from the dock to the hotel, Harrison Lathrop and Simon Ambrose were buffered from any contact with the public. At the Alexander Hotel, Mr. Hollis had reserved the Lahaina Suite for the Stanford party. Dr. Isaiah Townsend was in the suite waiting for them.

After a cursory exchange with Dr. Townsend, Harrison Lathrop retired to his bedroom. Since hearing of his sister's death, he had become a recluse. Lathrop sat at his desk and read through the condolences. As he hunched over them, he placed each in one of three piles. When he came to the letter from the Williams' Mortuary, he folded it and put it in his breast pocket.

Harrison Lathrop's resemblance to his sister was marked—the protruding eyes, the rounded nose, even the rectangular shape of his face was evident under his beard. And although he was junior to her by three years, on that day, he appeared to be an aged man.

Lathrop called for a carriage to take him to the mortuary. Townsend offered to accompany him, but Lathrop preferred to go alone. He paced the parlor until his buggy arrived.

On the ride to Williams' Mortuary, twice Mr. Lathrop asked the driver how much longer the trip would take. The entire ride was less than ten minutes.

When he entered the mortuary, Mr. Williams accompanied him to view Mrs. Stanford's body. Mr. Lathrop staggered at the sight of it.

He stood at his sister's casket, then knelt on the velvet kneeler. He reached for her hand and cradled it to his cheek. From the back of the viewing room, he could be heard talking to his sister, praying for her. He asked her to forgive him for not being with her when she died, and he took comfort knowing she was with her husband and son in heaven. After about fifteen minutes, Mr. Williams approached Mr. Lathrop and rested his hand on Lathrop's shoulder.

Mr. Lathrop leaned over and kissed his sister. "She looks peaceful."

Mr. Williams nodded, although even in death Mrs. Stanford looked like a woman in charge.

"I would like a lock of her hair."

Mr. Williams said he would arrange it.

"And I would like a death mask to be made." Lathrop's voice was hoarse.

"I'll take care of it."

"It must be by someone superior, with experience in making masks."

"I'll commission Joseph Rosenstein, a sculptor," Mr. Williams assured him.

"I want her to be wearing her pearl drop earrings

for the mask. They were my present to her this Christmas."

Mr. Williams's voice was soft. "Usually a mask does not extend so far."

"I want the earrings to be part of the impression."

Mrs. Stanford's body was devoid of jewelry except for her wedding band and mourning bracelet.

"I want her surrounded with violets," Mr. Lathrop continued. He motioned to a side stand intended for flowers. "And portraits of her husband and son should be at her side."

Mr. Williams made note of it.

"A Stanford ensign should be displayed."

Williams nodded.

"Do you know any nuns?" Mr. Lathrop inquired.

"Nuns?"

He explained that nuns sat vigil with Mrs. Stanford after Leland Jr. died. "She is never to be alone."

"There are Sisters of St. Joseph here," Mr. Williams said.

"Tell them I shall be generous," he said.

"Sir, I believe their motive is elsewhere."

While Harrison Lathrop was at Williams' Mortuary, Isaiah Townsend and Simon Ambrose discussed the impact of Mrs. Stanford's death on the university.

Townsend broke open a bottle of brandy and poured Ambrose a drink. Townsend made polite inquiries about the ocean crossing. Ambrose's replies were curt. His disinterest in parlor talk was evident; his first question to Townsend was about the proceedings of the inquest.

"Your grief is overwhelming." Townsend handed him the brandy.

Simon Ambrose was a fine-boned weasel of a man. "Of course, I am distraught, but the university is my main concern."

Townsend poured himself a drink.

"Any delay in probate would cause a financial crisis that the university could not survive," Ambrose said.

Townsend sat on the red leather club chair across from Ambrose. "Stanford University exists because Mrs. Stanford saw it *through* its financial crisis."

"With all due respect, doctor, Mrs. Stanford ran the university like a fish monger's wife. She doled out cash on the first of each month—one month's allotment at a time, never two and never a penny more than my projected obligations. And currently, there are no arrangements for me to continue meeting the bills." President Ambrose crossed his legs. "I can depend on the sentiment of the faculty for one, maybe two months, but even academics must eat."

"Had it been left to academics, the university would have failed years ago."

"The pending demise of the university was greatly exaggerated."

"For six years Mrs. Stanford funded the university out of her own money." Townsend was referring to the years the senator's estate was locked in probate.

"Yes, yes, I know." Ambrose waved his hand in the air. "And all the presidents before me had less money, fewer buildings, and no faculty to speak of. Times have changed, doctor." Ambrose swirled the brandy in his snifter. "It's loyal of you to repeat the myth of the federal government being the university's adversary, but I would lay blame with Owen Coswell—if blame can be laid, since the senator *did* use railroad money to fund his university."

"It is an unproven accusation." Townsend bristled. "The charity of the Stanford family is beyond computation—charity from their personal assets."

"True, the university is a fine tribute to the dearly departed boy. But his legacy will be a bankrupt school if the estate is locked in probate." Ambrose lit a cigar and tossed the match in the crystal ashtray.

"I've been aware of that from the beginning," Townsend said.

"The inquest is the only obstacle. All the railroad holdings have been liquidated, and given Owen Coswell's mental frailty, he poses no threat." Ambrose puffed on his cigar. "The university is due thirty-one million dollars. And with Harrison in such a state of morbid grief, it is up to the two of us to ensure it."

"And the issue of justice?" Townsend asked.

"Even if the mourning Miss Benson is a murderess, it must be overlooked for the greater good."

"It is a repugnant alliance."

"But necessary." He exhaled his cigar smoke to form a ring.

"You overlook the fact that both attending physicians have testified that they suspect strychnine poisoning."

"Then we discredit them." Ambrose flicked his cigar in the ashtray.

"They are well respected."

"Then we shall make a spectacle of the inquest.

We'll give the press a carnival barker that can cry foul."

"What are you suggesting?"

"We take our case to the public—get a physician of note to plainly explain that the inquest doctors have been infected with a conspiracy theory." Ambrose unnecessarily flicked the cigar again. "What about Archibald Armstrong? Is he still in the islands?"

"Armstrong wouldn't risk his reputation. Even if he would, his price would be too dear."

"I assume you are unwilling to come forward?"

Dr. Townsend did not respond.

"No, I didn't think so."

"There is someone who may be willing," Townsend said. "He's a young doctor, just out of medical school—a very ambitious fellow."

--•-••-•--

The next morning Ted Cutler ate his breakfast on the banyan tree *lānai*. There was only one other couple up at 6:00 a.m.—an elderly couple sharing a pot of tea.

Cutler sat at a wrought iron table close to the beach. He sipped his coffee as he read the morning paper. The headline of the *Honolulu Star* was "Butler Admits Graft."

Cutler read, "Mrs. Stanford's former butler, Mr. Louis Emerson was questioned by police at his San Mateo ranch. Emerson, forty-five years old, came to the Stanford household ten years ago, after lengthy employment with the celebrated Miss Lillie Langtry.

"Inspector F. X. Whelan of the Morse Detective

Agency, along with San Francisco police detective Bruce Bennett, described Emerson as frank. Thomas said that during the interview, Emerson talked with relaxed freedom while his wife entertained the men with refreshments. The butler appeared light spirited in telling his stories about traveling with Mrs. Stanford. It was only when the topic turned to graft that his disposition darkened.

"Mr. Emerson stated, 'There is a delicate acceptance of those in service that the practice of skimming is to be tacitly ignored. It is more common than not for the head of the household, be it the butler or the secretary, to take a commission, as it is called.' Emerson explained that commissions were seldom taken on small purchases and mainly occurred when Mrs. Stanford desired to acquire some article of art for the university museum or some jewelry. The butler plainly stated that many of these commissions were split with Miss Benson."

Cutler broke off a piece of lemon scone. "When Inspector Whelan asked Mr. Emerson about his relationship with Miss Benson, he stated that he deplored the publicity she must now suffer and that he would not comment on their friendship."

Cutler read on. "Beneath the stairs at the Stanford mansion, servants were more willing to discuss that relationship. According to a Nob Hill chambermaid, 'Miss Benson and Mr. Emerson shared a friendship that was improper, and when Emerson threw her off for the likes of another Lizzie, her heart ran cold and she called the wrath of God down upon him. We all knew his days in service were numbered.' That same sentiment was directly repeated or implied by several domestics at the mansion."

The article continued, "It is believed that the Chinese house manager, Ah Nee, reported Miss Benson's and Mr. Emerson's skimming to Mrs. Stanford. When Mrs. Stanford confronted her, Miss Benson claimed it was not she but Mr. Emerson who was the offender. Mr. Emerson was dismissed that day."

"A woman scorned," Cutler muttered to himself. The article went on, "It is incomprehensible to most San Franciscans that Miss Gertrude Benson, who was so handsomely paid, would seek to exact even more money from her benefactress. It is accepted that Miss Benson, by reason of her twenty-one years as Mrs. Stanford's companion, had more control over her than any living person. She thoroughly understood her whims and idiosyncrasies and catered to them on demand.

"Taking into account her salary and perquisites amounting to between three and four thousand dollars a year, and the grand life and manner in which she lived, most had dismissed Miss Benson as a suspect. But now that the terms of Mrs. Stanford's will have been made public and the fact that Miss Benson sought to be relieved of service has been uncovered, she becomes an active suspect."

Cutler lit his first cigarette of the day and waved his match in the air. A pearl gray dove landed on his table. He swatted it away and returned to reading his paper. "Antique Dealer Questioned. Blah, blah, blah," he mumbled as he skimmed another article.

The dove flew back. He pelted it with a piece of scone.

"Clayton Adams described his first meeting with Mrs. Stanford at the Cataract Hotel in

Assouan. He said, 'I was having a drink at the cafe and was telling a fellow American about the tribal uprisings in Kabul. Prisoners on each side were executed by being tied to the muzzle of a cannon, and then a fellow prisoner was forced to fire the cannon. I didn't realize Mrs. Stanford was within earshot of that conversation, and when I spotted her, I spent time with her reassuring her that those incidents were in remote areas in the desert. But it is my regret that I may have played a part in aggravating her fears.'

"When Mr. Adams was questioned regarding the commissions of Mr. Emerson and Miss Benson, Adams shrugged it off, explaining that it was part of doing business with the rich and that most dealers build the cost into their prices."

"Here it is!" Cutler slammed the paper with his hand. "Mr. Clayton Adams corroborates the fact that Mrs. Stanford would not leave her hotel room in Assouan and that the butler was forced to stand guard outside, including sleeping in a chair outside her door. But he refutes the statement that Miss Benson never left Mrs. Stanford. He claims Miss Benson arranged a meeting with him, and it was then that she told him she must leave the country. At first, she claimed that the climate was too variable for her health, then she changed her story, saying her father was gravely ill. Her pleas became more desperate until she finally confessed that she could not live with Mrs. Stanford anymore and begged him to find a replacement for her. When he refused, she asked him to deliver a letter to the American consulate. She wanted the consulate to send a physician to examine Mrs. Stanford. But Adams declined.

"Miss Benson said she was on the verge of madness. But Adams would not give in, and the next day he left for Ceylon to avoid all complications. Regarding any noticed relationship between Miss Benson and Mr. Emerson, he would not comment and said no further business was ever contracted between him and Mrs. Stanford."

Cutler tossed the paper on the chair next to him. "So did Benson kill the old lady or not?"

———————

When Gertrude Benson read the headlines that morning, she flung the paper on the floor. She pulled back the window curtain to check the commotion on the street and saw a battery of reporters on the sidewalk. She immediately called Mr. St. Clair demanding that The Palms provide her with a bodyguard during her ride to the Alexander.

Mr. St. Clair approached Mr. Cutler on the *lānai*. "I have a sensitive issue I need to discuss with you."

When St. Clair asked Cutler if he would serve as Miss Benson's bodyguard, Cutler accepted.

Cutler shepherded Miss Benson from The Palms through the service exit. Her face was shrouded by a heavy mourning veil, which served only to confirm her identity to roaming reporters. He hustled her into a Thompson carriage and drew the curtains closed and latched the doors.

Miss Benson sat across from him. Her head was down, her hands were folded in her lap, she did not speak. Cutler smiled, as if he were recalling the description of her in the paper as a "self-consumed middle-aged woman."

Upon arrival at the Alexander Hotel, Mr. Hollis escorted Miss Benson to her room. After she was safely secured, he read a prepared statement to the reporters in the lobby: "Given the sad associations with the death of Mrs. Stanford at The Palms Hotel, Mr. Harrison Lathrop has requested Miss Benson move to the Alexander Hotel. We hope her privacy will be respected." Hollis folded his paper, side-stepped the reporters, and proceeded to see Ted Cutler to Mr. Lathrop's suite.

The Lahaina Suite was well appointed with brass electric-light sconces, Persian rugs, Palladian windows, and a crystal chandelier. The small dining table was set with floor-length linen, a compote of fruit, biscuits, and a sterling tea service.

When Cutler entered the room, only Ambrose and Townsend were in the parlor; Lathrop was in his room resting.

"Mr. Cutler, thank you for calling on us during these unfortunate circumstances," Dr. Townsend greeted him.

President Ambrose lowered the newspaper and nodded.

"I don't think the papers are covering any other story." Cutler addressed President Ambrose.

"It's deplorable." Townsend shook his head. "It just feeds to the appetites of the vulgar. At least we can be grateful that the *San Francisco Herald* was sensitive."

Cutler walked over to the table and helped himself to a mountain apple. "I received a cable from San Francisco this morning. The police there are considering Miss Benson as a suspect. It will surely make the afternoon papers here."

Ambrose tossed the newspaper on the side table. "There is no evidence to incriminate Miss Benson, or anyone else. And in due time, I am sure it will be shown that Mrs. Stanford died of natural causes."

"Not from what I hear." Cutler bit into the mountain apple.

In the middle of Cutler's comment, Harrison Lathrop entered the parlor. Lathrop's eyes were rimmed with red. His face was bloated and his step was no more than a shuffle. "Mr. Cutler." He extended his hand. "Thank you for your service."

"I'm afraid I failed in averting the crime," Cutler apologized.

"I've been assured by reputable physicians that Mrs. Stanford died of natural causes," Lathrop eased him.

"I hope you're right, but it's doubtful." Cutler's lip was flecked with bits of apple.

"What do you mean doubtful?" Lathrop sat at the dining table.

"The doctors at the inquest are saying she was poisoned," Cutler reported.

Mr. Lathrop asked him to be specific.

"The autopsy revealed no natural cause of death, and both attending physicians testified that Mrs. Stanford's death had the appearance of strychnine poisoning."

Dr. Townsend interjected, "Harrison, the appearance they describe is also consistent with a heart attack."

"It's all up to the chemists," Cutler said. "If they find strychnine in the body, it's murder."

"I understand they've been delayed another day," Mr. Lathrop commented.

"More tests," Cutler responded casually. He recalled the *Star*'s morning editorial: "Is it that the chemists don't want to reveal their conclusions until they are verified by every possible test? Or are they attempting to manipulate their data until they attain some preferred result? Could it be that persons interested in the estate of Mrs. Stanford are exercising influence in the management of the coroner's inquest to avoid any contest of the will?"

Harrison Lathrop asked Cutler about Gertrude Benson. "I've heard there have been threats on her life."

"None that I'm aware of."

"And Miss McCauley?"

"Miss McCauley can well defend herself." Cutler smirked.

"Your meaning?" Lathrop raised his eyebrows.

Cutler told Lathrop about the events of the last few days, including Mae and Hattie stealing the envelope of face powder from Miss Benson's room. "They both seem a bit overzealous, but well intentioned."

"Does Miss McCauley believe Miss Benson murdered my sister?"

"It appears so, though I don't take Miss McCauley seriously," Cutler said. "In my opinion, Miss McCauley suffers from a severe case of jealousy."

Simon Ambrose interrupted, "Mr. Lathrop, several demented accusations are being tossed about. Not only Miss Benson, but each one of us is accused. I understand that a Maui paper names you as the prime suspect." Ambrose seemed to enjoy saying it.

Lathrop did not dignify the remark. He asked Cutler if he had any evidence to suggest that Benson was disloyal.

"No."

Just as Cutler had predicted, the headlines of the Honolulu papers heralded the news that the San Francisco police considered Miss Benson a prime suspect. With one sweep of the pen, Gertrude Benson was transformed from a sympathetic figure to a conniving shrew. They labeled her a nefarious opportunist; her greed was not to be forgiven.

Mae McCauley rocked on the cottage porch, reading her paper, reveling in Benson's unmasking. She read and reread every accusing passage with delight. She savored every phrase and peppered her reading with exclamations of "God forgive me for wishing her the noose."

But Mae's fantasy was short lived.

Hattie arranged to meet Ted Cutler in her office. She told him about the witnessed inventory she never executed and the incomplete inventory of jewels in the newspaper. Then she unwrapped the towel to expose the jewels. "They were in Miss Benson's luggage."

Cutler fingered the cameo bracelet. "Is this the bracelet that broke at the picnic?"

She nodded. "It's not on the inventory, neither is the rest of this." She handed Cutler the blotter paper. "Miss Benson made a new list. If you match those words to the inventory sheet, I believe you'll find a match."

Cutler smoothed the blotter sheet and held it to the light. "The words overlap."

"The words 'ruby' and 'brooch' are quite clear," Hattie said. "So is 'portrait.'"

"So after I told you to call me or the sheriff if you had any suspicions, you stole the jewels."

"I didn't take them to accuse her. I took them to give them back to Mr. Lathrop."

"You've probably given her another out." Cutler picked up the topaz ring.

"I tried to call Mr. Lathrop, but the Alexander operator wouldn't put through my call."

"You didn't honestly expect them to, did you?" He put the ring down and placed a call to the Lahaina Suite.

Ambrose answered the phone. After a brief exchange, Cutler said he was on his way to the Alexander with Mrs. Stanford's jewels.

Ambrose accepted the news coolly. After he hung up the phone, he turned to Townsend and said, "We have a complication." He repeated his conversation with Cutler. "The jurors will find it a small leap from Benson's stealing from her dead mistress to murder."

Townsend called Attorney General Upton.

———•◦•◦•———

Sheriff Robert Dillon's staff was already stretched thin. The police maintained a two-man watch over the autopsy specimens stored at the Territory Dispensary Laboratory. An officer was assigned to guard Dr. Flynn and one to Dr. Henrik, after his office was vandalized the night of the autopsy.

Then, a few hours after Harrison Lathrop's visit to Williams' Mortuary, there was an attempt to steal Mrs. Stanford's body. Two police officers were assigned post at the mortuary.

The precinct phones required full-time manning, crowd control consumed at least twenty men, and then there was the security of the citizenry of

Honolulu and the investigation of routine crime. The latter not getting its due.

The sheriff petitioned the legislature for funds to deputize additional personnel. But given that the budget was crippled by the embezzlement of the territory housing director and other ineptitudes of the legislature, Dillon assumed request would flounder in a docket that would never be read.

When Attorney General Upton offered to assign his chief inspector, Chester Shannon, to the sheriff's office, Upton was surprised that the sheriff declined. Dillon based his refusal on the possible conflict of interest that would arise if the attorney general's chief investigator were on a case in which the attorney general was a witness. It was a decision based on conscience, not any forewarning or information about deals being made.

In his memorandum to the attorney general, Sheriff Dillon wrote that he wanted to "preserve the integrity of the proceedings."

The next day a meeting took place in the gazebo of Dr. Townsend's home. President Simon Ambrose, Attorney General Noah Upton, and Dr. Townsend each made his position clear.

Dr. Ambrose was emphatic that he needed immediate and unencumbered access to the funds from the estate or "the university will die with its mother." All men agreed that there must be no delay in settling the Stanford estate.

At first Isaiah Townsend tendered spurious sentiments of preserving Mrs. Stanford from a legacy of being murdered. Then he spoke in a slow rhythm as he moved to the core. "We must sustain her utmost desire—the continuation of the university as a memorial to Leland Jr. The conclusion of the inquest must be that Mrs. Stanford died from natural causes. The testimony of the physicians must be discredited. I will see to it."

In exchange for Dr. Townsend's actions, President Ambrose was to support the annexation of Hawai'i as a county of California. Townsend handed Ambrose a list of prominent politicians that Ambrose was "to deliver." Townsend continued his proposals at a measured pace. President Ambrose was to staff the Honolulu Aquarium with professors from the university and fund a marine research lab.

"Are these proposals or demands?" Ambrose was indignant.

"There is leeway in the number of professors." Townsend was patronizing. He had negotiated the annexation of Hawai'i and faced presidents and queens. Ambrose was a feeble opponent.

"And you, Judge Upton, what extortion do you propose?" Ambrose sniped.

Upton presented his demands like a union negotiator. "If this case comes to court, I will relinquish jurisdiction to the State of California, citing the Beck case as precedent. Attorney General Kent is deeply indebted to me. I've looked away on several occasions for him."

"This is not an ordinary case," President Ambrose reminded the judge.

"Making my services worth even more."

"And if you are inflating your influence on the attorney general?"

"Kent knows I have evidence that would result in his disbarment, but more than that, I can supply witnesses to his wife that would cause him to fall from her grace and deny him access to her fortune."

Ambrose conceded with a tilt of his head.

Upton continued, "In exchange for my services, you will appoint me as dean of the Stanford University Law School—a generously paid but not exacting position."

Ambrose asked, "Why should I give in to your piracy?"

"In exchange for your cooperation, you will remain president." Dr. Townsend sipped his tea.

"Gentlemen, that's not much of a prize. There's not a major university in America, and perhaps some abroad, that wouldn't court me."

"Perhaps." Dr. Townsend set down his tumbler. "But you see, while she was here, Mrs. Stanford asked Judge Upton and me to begin a search for a new university president."

"Given the track record of the university, I'd say I am an institution!"

"Admittedly not a damaging fact, but there was that threatened vote of no confidence by your faculty and those indiscretions with Stanford coeds, again nothing irreparable. But it's those damning little toads you allow to slip out of your mouth that may do you in."

"To what toads do you refer?" His tone was sharp.

"Were you not quoted in an interview stating the senator had the ethics of a London whore?" Upton unclipped his glasses from his nose. "The spite of a peanut vendor was your phrase, was it not? One I understand you took pride in."

"Sentiment felt by hundreds." Ambrose reached for an orange.

Upton went on, "And then there are your statements that Mrs. Stanford suffered from dementia. I believe you are quoted as saying the old woman needed to be committed to an asylum. That, President Ambrose, is libel."

"That's foolishness." He dug his knife into the orange skin.

"But a good lawyer can cause fools to be hanged. You see, Ambrose, I can cast you as the arrogant ferret that you are—a man who may not be trusted, a gossip, and a womanizer of coeds whose fathers donate handsomely to their daughters' school. And then, there are the ledgers that prove you've embezzled."

"I have never stolen a cent from the university!"

"I never said you did," Upton said casually.

"President Ambrose, I believe that cooperation is in your best interest," Dr. Townsend stated flatly. "It is all in the spirit of preserving the Stanford legacy."

"Do we have a deal?" Upton asked the president.

Ambrose peeled his orange in one long stroke. He nodded.

Dr. Townsend addressed Ambrose. "I've arranged for you to meet with a young doctor by the name of Speckerd. You will deliver a medical report I've drafted. The report thoroughly refutes the attending physicians' observations. Speckerd will claim the report as his own and gain professional esteem as well as receiving a gift of thanks from me."

"Thirty pieces of silver?" Ambrose sniffed.

"You'll meet Dr. Speckerd at the Temperance Society Tea Room today," Townsend instructed.

"And the issue of The Palms Hotel maid and the jewelry?" Ambrose said.

"Easily handled with a phone call to a Royalist newspaper," Judge Upton said. "They're always eager to print *haole* scandal and rarely check their facts."

———◦•◦•◦———

The Temperance Society Tea Room was a genteel establishment frequented by women who wore organza hats and brought their poodles to lunch.

Dr. Speckerd sashayed in, doffing his cap to every fine-featured beauty, no matter what her age. President Ambrose eyed him as he made his way to their table—a seating for two next to a potted palm.

Charlie Banks had followed Ambrose from the Alexander Hotel. He ordered a rose hip tea and made idle chatter with his waitress, a gray-haired temperance volunteer. As he spoke, he faced Ambrose's table and watched the president slide an envelope across the table to Speckerd. Speckerd opened it, exposing the greenback bills, and counted them. Then Ambrose handed Speckerd a black leather folder and left.

CHAPTER FOURTEEN

Hattie was standing in the corridor outside the inquest room waiting for Ted Cutler when Charlie Banks arrived. "Have they started?"

"Just starting now," Hattie told him.

Banks went in. Hattie stayed outside waiting for Cutler. She wanted to know what happened when he returned Mrs. Stanford's jewels to Mr. Lathrop, but Cutler never showed up.

When Hattie heard Deputy Kanahele call the inquest to order, she went inside. The deputy announced a change in the schedule of witnesses. He called Miss Gertrude Benson to the stand.

Benson was cloaked in black. She approached the witness chair solemnly. She wore a black straw hat; her face was veiled. She lifted the netting. The black of her dress deepened the dark circles under her eyes.

Sheriff Dillon was direct. There were no pleasantries exchanged, nor did he offer her any thanks for returning to the stand. "Miss Benson, would you care to comment on the statements of Mr. Emerson and Mr. Adams regarding commissions you received during your service with Mrs. Stanford?" The sheriff handed her copies of the *Honolulu Star* and the *Pacific Commercial Advertiser*.

Miss Benson set the newspapers on the table in

front of her and took out a prepared statement from her black drawstring purse. She turned to the jurors.

"Gentlemen, it is true that I received commissions. Mrs. Stanford knew I received them. The first time I received money was during the trip to Australia in 1898. Mr. Emerson gave the commissions to me." She read her statement in a slow monotone. "I immediately informed Mrs. Stanford about Mr. Emerson's bribe and urged her to dismiss him. But she said he deserved a second chance and let him off with a reprimand."

Charlie Banks took notes as Benson spoke.

"The next week, in a general store in Hobart, Tasmania, Mrs. Stanford told Mr. Emerson to wait outside until we finished our shopping. But as soon as we were in the store, he walked in and stood right behind her. This annoyed Mrs. Stanford. And again she told him to wait outside; she would call him if she needed him."

Miss Benson strayed from her prepared statement and addressed the jurors. "On returning to the hotel that afternoon, I talked with Mr. Emerson. I told him not to annoy Mrs. Stanford. I told him she was an ailing women and that I absolutely forbade him from making her uncomfortable, since if she became annoyed, I would be the one left to deal with her."

Of course, Hattie said to herself, Miss Benson would never want discomfort to fall upon herself.

"When Mr. Emerson offered me commissions again, I reported it to Mrs. Stanford. But she said, 'Commissions or no commissions, I need Emerson.'"

Benson returned to her written statement. "I thought the commissions had stopped, but during our travels to India in 1901, I discovered that they had not. I confronted Mr. Emerson about it and he immediately bribed me with gifts of meerschaum pipes for my father."

She flipped the page of her text. "It was during that trip Mr. Emerson paid me half his share of commissions. I cannot tell you exactly how much he gave me. My estimate is three thousand dollars. I gave over all of this money to Mrs. Stanford."

"And I'm Abe Lincoln," Charlie Banks snickered.

"When I turned the money over to her, she said, 'Too bad I cannot trust others as I can trust you. Too bad, isn't it, Gertrude?'"

Hattie wondered if anyone believed Benson.

Miss Benson dabbed perspiration from her forehead. Her hankie was white linen, bordered in black satin ribbon. "If Mr. Emerson took commissions after that, I'm not aware of it. And in Egypt, I never received any money at all. Mr. Adams is ill informed."

Mrs. Martin quietly slid open the door. She whispered to Hattie that she needed to speak to her. Charlie Banks watched as Hattie left with Mrs. Martin. When the two women walked down the hall, they passed Mr. St. Clair and Mr. Cutler walking toward the inquest. Cutler averted his eyes.

Mrs. Martin closed the door to her office and motioned for Hattie to sit. There was a seriousness to her behavior that alarmed Hattie.

"Hattie, have you seen today's copy of the *Sovereign?*" she asked.

Hattie wondered why Mrs. Martin would even mention the *Independent and Sovereign*. It was a

Royalist newspaper that was published irregularly, and when it was printed, its circulation was never more than two hundred.

Mrs. Martin held up the paper. Its headline was bold: "Palms Maid Steals Jewels from Mrs. Stanford." Hattie didn't have to read any more.

"Mr. Cutler says this is true." Mrs. Martin paused as if she were waiting for Hattie to explain.

Hattie wondered where she could begin? She wanted to tell Mrs. Martin about the night Mrs. Stanford died, when Benson tugged the rings off her body. Then there was the face powder and the inventory she forgot to have witnessed and the jewels.

The jewels were to be proof—proof of what she wasn't sure. Proof that Miss Benson stole from the mistress? The whole world knew that already.

All Hattie wanted to do was to give the jewels back to Mr. Lathrop, but suddenly, it all seemed like a tale.

"According to Mr. Cutler, this is grand larceny." Mrs. Martin sounded sympathetic. "Hattie?"

Hattie had no answer.

Hattie was dismissed from The Palms, and that evening she moved into Koa's cousin's house. It was a two-story clapboard structure down a dirt alley on the outskirts of Iwilei. The second floor was rented to bachelors. Rows of men's trousers hung over the balcony rail. Two bare-chested men stood and watched as she and Koa walked to the porch and Koa introduced Hattie to his cousin, Makana.

Makana was only two years older than Hattie, but she looked at least thirty. Her hair was piled in a loose bun. Her eyes were round. Her lips were full and her skin was the color of wet sand. Clamped to her legs were twin girls about six years old. She shooed the twins off and welcomed Hattie with a hug. "Jacob." She called her elder son. "Come put auntie's bags in her room." A dark-skinned boy shyly picked up Hattie's bags, opened the screen door, and carried the bags down the hall.

Makana sat on the *pūne'e*. She patted her hand next to her, motioning for Hattie to sit. Hattie noticed Makana's bulging *mu'umu'u*. Not even its flowing fabric could hide the fact she was *hāpai*.

Makana patted her belly. "The new baby is coming in May. My husband wants another girl."

Hattie looked around the room—a tattered *pūne'e*, two cats, and children in all manner of dress.

Makana explained the house rules to Hattie. The bachelors, including Koa, lived upstairs, where no women were allowed. Hattie would have a room downstairs, and she would share in family meals. Then she showed Hattie to her room. "Pay me when you can—these are bad times for Hawaiians."

A week ago Hattie would have pitied Makana. Now, Hattie considered herself lucky to share what little Makana had.

Hattie's room was as wide as the mattress of her iron bed was long. Outside she heard the bachelors upstairs arguing, women scolding children, children crying, and dogs barking. There was the smell of food frying, untended dog manure, and the sweetness of plumeria. She unpacked her bags and crawled into bed. The mattress was thin, the sheets were threadbare, and the smell of previous boarders lingered. She closed her eyes, let the tears drip down her cheek, and fell asleep.

The next morning the roosters woke her—the roosters and the heavy footfalls of the bachelors readying for work. The bed's crossbar had dug into her ribs through the night. She rubbed the blossoming bruise.

"Everything is useless." It was her new morning prayer. She lay there, unwilling to face the day.

Makana's children ran up and down the hall. They were scrambling outside her door. There was a thud, then more stumbling. Makana yelled. One of the twins yelled back and Hattie heard Makana order her into the kitchen.

Hattie sat up. Mrs. Stanford's Bible was on the orange crate bedstand. She thought of the inscription, "When you pray, pray for me." Hattie wondered who was praying for her.

"Hattie?" Makana knocked before she came in and handed Hattie the *Advertiser*. The headlines asked: "Where Is The Palms Hotel Maid?"

Hattie read silently, "Is Hattie Lehua a thief, or was it Miss Benson's hands that were caught in the till? Could it be that the missing maid knows more than she told at the inquest? Did she flee for her life? Does she have information that put her in danger?"

Hattie skimmed the paper, catching phrases as she read. "When questioned, Mr. St. Clair refused to comment about the theft from a guest's room, and as to the whereabouts of Miss Lehua, he said he didn't know. Mrs. Martin, Miss Lehua's immediate supervisor, said she had no information, but corrected this reporter's referring to Miss Lehua as a maid. 'She is a bookkeeper.'"

"There's more." Makana turned the paper to

page eighteen. It was a notice for a reward in bold black letters.

"Mr. Harrison Lathrop puts out a plea for Hattie Lehua to contact him. If anyone knows the where-abouts of Hattie Lehua, Mr. Lathrop will pay him $250."

———•••••———

All over Honolulu, citizens devoured details of the case. They repeated information freely, fabricating any facts that were missing. The ghoulish and macabre became instantly in vogue. Ouija boards sold out, works of Poe were read in parlors, and pigtailed girls jumped rope to "Lizzie Borden had an ax."

"The key to the case is the toxicologist's report." It was a phrase repeated at kitchen tables and pool hall bars. All of Honolulu waited. So, the day Dr. Flynn rode up to the front steps of The Palms, it caused an immediate stir. The inquest room was standing room only—even women were among the spectators, sitting side by side in hats so wide their brims brushed together when they gossiped.

Among the spectators was Dr. Bernard Speckerd; he was dressed to the nines in a gray brocade vest and double-breasted suit.

Dr. Flynn took his seat. He placed a notepad, a wooden box, and two bottles on the table. Flynn's curious look—his bald head and exaggerated moustache—gave him the appearance of an eccentric scientist. He coughed and cleared his throat as he recited his name and credentials. "In addition to being a medical doctor, I have a doctorate in chem-

istry from the University of California and am currently the food commissioner of the territory and
the territory's toxicologist."

As Sheriff Dillon spoke, a reporter sketched the
doctor's face. "Were you present at the autopsy performed on the body of Mrs. Jane Lathrop Stanford?"

"I was."

"Did you receive any of the organs taken from
the body?"

"Yes, sir, I did. May I refer to my notes?" Flynn
cleared his throat.

The sheriff nodded. "These notes were made at
the time, were they?"

"No, sir." He flipped open the notebook. "They
were made from memory. The originals were lost,
perhaps stolen." He fumbled to the page. "Yes, here it
is—the list of materials. Besides the organs, I received
urine, stomach contents, two kidneys, and contents
of the intestinal tract. All these were delivered to the
laboratory by Dr. Solomon, Mr. Williams, and Police
Officer Benitez."

"Did you receive any other items?" the sheriff
asked.

"The cascara capsules, a bottle of bicarbonate, a
glass with bicarbonate mixed with water, and a basin
of body fluids." He cleared his throat.

"Will you please tell us about the examination of
these items."

"My staff and I,"—he turned to the jurors—"I
was assisted by my colleague, Dr. York. We began
our test with the bicarbonate of soda." He lifted a
bottle to the jury. "This one is from Mrs. Stanford's
room. It still contained bicarbonate at the time."

He unscrewed the top of a second full bottle of

bicarbonate. "I will demonstrate with this newly purchased bicarbonate." Then he opened the wooden box and took out two cups, a scale, and a spoon. "We scooped out some soda and divided it into three piles. Each pile weighed ten grams. Like I'm doing with this." The doctor spooned out some bicarbonate into a cup, measured it, and passed it to the jury. "This is what ten grams looks like." It appeared to be not much more than a teaspoonful.

The jurors passed it around.

"In the first ten grams, the examination yielded fourteen one-hundredths of a grain of strychnine."

"Strychnine." The word rippled through the room.

"The test of the next ten grams yielded eleven-hundredths of a grain of strychnine, and the third yielded seven-hundredths of a grain of strychnine."

Juror Cunha raised his hand and was recognized by the sheriff. "Dr. Flynn, are you saying a grain or a gram?"

"A grain."

"How big is a grain?" Cunha asked.

Flynn looked at the ceiling and took a deep breath. "One ounce would contain approximately four hundred grains."

Another murmur rippled through the room.

"Dr. Flynn, can you state whether strychnine is an ingredient of bicarbonate of soda?" the sheriff asked.

Flynn wiped a stream of sweat from his forehead. "It is a foreign substance. Most definitely, it is a foreign substance."

"Please continue, doctor."

"Next we examined the urine and one kidney

with negative results. However, the intestinal fluid gave the color reaction indicating strychnine was present. Although the test was positive, no crystallized strychnine was evident under the microscope."

"Doctor, could you explain this color test?"

"Of course." Dr. Flynn ran his finger around his shirt collar. "It is commonly known as the 'fading purple test' because a color reaction occurs when sulfuric acid and potassium bichromate are added to the test material. If the material changes from cobalt blue to royal purple then fades to orange, we know that strychnine is present."

Disregarding protocol, Dr. Speckerd yelled from the back of the room, "But there are other chemicals that produce positive results. Are there not?"

Heads turned. Deputy Kanahele sprung to his feet. "Silence."

"I am a doctor," Speckerd announced.

"Sir, you will sit down." Kanahele's voice boomed.

Dr. Townsend never turned toward the commotion. Instead he and Judge Upton exchanged glances.

"I would like to respond," Flynn said.

"I should be heard," Speckerd objected.

"You will be ejected," Kanahele warned.

Speckerd flipped the back of his jacket toward the ceiling and sat with indignant flourish.

Dr. Flynn turned toward the jury. "It is true, there are other bodies that will give the chemical reaction resembling that of strychnine, but we took all precautions against it." Flynn then addressed Speckerd directly. "Doctor, my staff combined all we had of Mrs. Stanford's remains. We minced it into a slurry that was simmered, washed, and evaporated.

Then we processed it and tested the extraction. We found a color reaction indicating strychnine, but the residue was too minute to weigh."

Dr. Townsend passed the sheriff the first note of the day. "Dr. Flynn, is it true that strychnine is a common ingredient in patent medicines?"

"I will not comment on patent medicines."

The sheriff twirled his pencil. "Doctor, did you analyze the contents of the capsules on Mrs. Stanford's nightstand?"

"Yes."

"Was there any strychnine detected?"

"Sheriff, strychnine is not necessarily foreign to patent medicines," he answered. "We did find nux vomica, and in each capsule there was one-fifteenth of a grain of strychnine and one-fifteenth of a grain of brucine."

A few of the jurors shook their heads. Mr. Cunha asked, "What is brucine?"

"It is a poison, an alkaloid poison, but much weaker than strychnine. Brucine and strychnine come from the same seed. It is the *Strychnos nux vomica* plant."

The jurors nodded their heads as if they understood.

The sheriff asked, "Dr. Flynn, to be clear, are you stating that there was strychnine in the capsules?"

"Yes."

"Doctor, could the amount of strychnine in the capsules alone have caused the death of Mrs. Stanford?"

"It's uncertain."

"Could that amount alone have caused a color reaction?"

"Yes. But I would like to repeat that the presence of strychnine in the bicarbonate of soda is a foreign substance."

"Could a pharmacist have accidentally added strychnine to the mix?" the sheriff asked.

"It's improbable since all bottles containing poison are labeled with red ink and marked with a skull and crossbones, and they are kept in locked cabinets." His answer was emphatic.

The sheriff turned around to Dr. Townsend, as if asking if he had any more questions. Dr. Townsend shook his head.

The sheriff excused Dr. Flynn. He thanked him and advised him that he may be called back to testify.

"Certainly," Flynn said.

As Sheriff Dillon announced the lunch break, Dr. Speckerd rose again. "For those of you who are interested in an education of this fading purple test, I invite you to lunch in the library." And like a Pied Piper, the doctor left with most of the spectators trailing behind him. Dr. Lowell and Sheriff Dillon were among them.

Dr. Speckerd stood behind a long library table. He took off his jacket. He adjusted his sleeve garters and tugged the points of his gray brocade vest. On the table in front of him were objects covered with white linen napkins. The event had the feel of a magician's show.

Dr. Speckerd gave a slight bow. "Gentlemen, I come before you to correct an impression that the fading purple test is a definitive test to prove the presence of poison. Certainly, it does react with strychnine, as Dr. Flynn said, but the good doctor neglected to explain the strength of this test."

Speckerd removed the linen cover and unveiled a white porcelain dish. "To illustrate my point, I will place this strychnine crystal in the dish." He held up the crystal with tweezers. "It is so small as to be almost invisible to the naked eye." He extended his arm so those in the front row could see. "Not larger than the tip of the finest needle, wouldn't you say?"

Those in the front rows agreed. The doctor placed the crystal in the dish. Next he held up a pipette. "In this pipette is sulfuric acid." He released one drop on the strychnine then placed bichromate of potash on top of them.

"Now gentlemen, observe." With a small glass tube, he drew the two colorless liquids together. The liquid turned from colorless to rich blue. "From an Orleans plum." Speckerd almost sang his words. Then the color went to a darker purple. "To mulberry." It turned a bright, clear red. Then it faded to a tangerine yellow.

"Like a sweet orange." Speckerd looked pleased with himself. "This is your fading purple test," he announced.

All that was missing was a décolletage tart of an assistant to exclaim, "Voila!"

"The amount of strychnine I used in this demonstration is the same amount used in most patent medicines."

"Like liver tonic?" one man shouted from the back.

"Precisely."

"And Women's Helper?" asked another.

Speckerd nodded. "One one-thousandth of a grain of strychnine will result in a positive test." He gestured to the man who had asked the question.

"What does this mean to you?" He walked to the back of the room and put his arm on the man's shoulder. "It means, if your wife were to die after taking a fatigue tonic she bought at the pharmacy, the fading purple test would indicate she ingested strychnine."

Sheriff Dillon whispered to Dr. Lowell, "Is that true?"

He nodded.

Speckerd returned to the table in front of the room. He took a sip of water before he continued. "But let us suppose that a full grain of strychnine was scattered on top of Mrs. Stanford's bicarbonate of soda. First of all, you should know that a full grain of strychnine will not always produce death—the lethal dosage is almost twice that."

Again the sheriff turned to Dr. Lowell as if to confirm Speckerd's claim.

Dr. Lowell explained, "The amount varies. A trace could cause death in someone her age."

Speckerd continued, "But, for the sake of argument, let's say that Mrs. Stanford ingested one grain. And here is the rub, good friends. Strychnine is one of the most stable poisons known to man. Dissolve it in hot sulfuric acid and we can still recover it! Dilute it, age it, bottle it with fine brandy, if you will—it would still have shown up in her organs!"

"He's playing a shell game," Dr. Lowell muttered.

"There should have been crystals heavy enough to be weighed!"

There was a silence among the spectators. Then Speckerd lowered his voice as if he were confiding some trusted secret to them. "So, gentlemen, when you are considering this case, remember, if your wife died after taking Women's Helper, you could be accused of murder."

———

When Dr. Speckerd walked into the afternoon session of the inquest, Dr. York, a chemist for the territory, was at his side. The two gentlemen chatted easily.

Sheriff Dillon made a note to himself: "Speckerd and York—cordial."

The sheriff asked Dr. York to state his professional background.

"I am Dr. Braden York. I have an advanced degree in analytical chemistry from Queen's University in Ontario, Canada. Currently I am the chemist for the United States Agricultural Station and an adjunct chemist at the Territory Dispensary Laboratory."

The sheriff repeated the same questions he had asked Dr. Flynn. Then he veered off. "Dr. York, how were the tested samples of bicarbonate taken?"

"I don't understand."

"I mean, when you took the samples from the bottle, did you pour all of it out and mix it, then measure it out? Or did you take it from the top of the bottle?"

"We scooped it from the bottle using a spoon."

"So, doctor, the first sample yielded fourteen one-hundredths of a grain, and the last sample yielded half this amount. Is this correct?"

"It is our result."

"Doctor, can you speculate as to why there is

such a discrepancy between the top and the bottom layers?"

"It was not a top and bottom layer, sir. It was the first and third samples."

"Then, doctor, can you speculate as to why there was a discrepancy between the first and third samples?"

"I will not."

"Doctor, if strychnine were poured on the top of the bicarbonate of soda without it being mixed, what pattern of distribution would you expect to find?"

"I refuse to speculate." Dr. York looked over at Dr. Speckerd.

"I am asking you as a chemist, doctor, if a foreign substance were poured into a material and that substance were not mixed, what would the pattern of distribution be?"

"It depends on the weight and the volume of the foreign substance." York folded his arms over his chest.

"Doctor, do you know the weight and volume of both the strychnine and the bicarbonate in this case?"

"I do."

"Mr. York . . ."

"Dr. York," the chemist corrected.

"Yes, Dr. York, if the strychnine had been poured on the top of the bicarbonate and not mixed, could there have been a higher concentration at the top of the soda?"

The chemist sighed. "Sheriff, these questions call for speculation. I refuse to speculate."

"Dr. York, would you compare sugar crystals to strychnine?"

"What do you mean?"

"Are they approximately the same weight and volume as those crystals you found in the evidence of this case?"

"Yes, they are similar in weight and volume." York crossed his legs, affecting annoyance.

"And are the weight and volume of commercial bicarbonate of sodas all approximately the same?"

"Yes."

The sheriff motioned to Deputy Kanahele to set a tray on the witness table. The tray was covered with a linen napkin.

The sheriff looked directly at Dr. Lowell and instructed Deputy Kanahele to lift the napkin, revealing two jars of crystals—one white and one deep crimson.

"Dr. York, in this jar is bicarbonate of soda." The sheriff lifted the jar of white crystals for the jurors to see. "In this jar"—he lifted the second—"is colored sugar used by the pastry chef of this hotel."

The sheriff took a teaspoon of the sugar and sprinkled it on top of the bicarbonate. Then he lifted the jar. Most of the crimson sugar remained at the top of the jar.

"I object to this display," Dr. York said.

The sheriff shook the jar—most of the colored sugar remained on top.

"This is a carnival show!" York objected.

"Perhaps it is the day for carnival shows." The sheriff passed the jar to Mr. Pembroke, the head juror.

The jurors examined the bottle; some tilted it. One juror shook it vigorously, but most of the colored sugar still remained in the top third of the jar.

The sheriff asked, "Doctor, is it possible that there may have been a higher concentration of strychnine at the top of the bicarbonate of soda?"

"I refuse to answer."

"But is it possible?"

"I will not be drawn into this debacle."

"Then we shall move on to the autopsy." The sheriff referred to his notes. "Will you corroborate the fact that strychnine was found in Mrs. Stanford's intestinal tract?"

"I will not."

The jurors turned to each other. Mr. Pembroke raised his hand. The sheriff asked Mr. Pembroke to please wait.

"I will not say we found strychnine." York looked directly at Dr. Speckerd. "The only conclusive evidence of strychnine would be the recovery of a weighable quantity. All other results are scientific inference."

"Doctor, are you stating that there was no strychnine in Mrs. Stanford's body?"

"I state for the record that I do not believe there was as much as one one-thousandth in the entire organs."

"Doctor, is that a scientific fact, or is it your personal speculation?"

"It is my opinion as a chemist."

"Then it is speculation." The two men glared at each other.

Dr. York broke the silence. "It is my opinion as a man of science."

The sheriff cocked his head and directed his remark to the jurors. "It is his opinion." The sheriff smiled. "Dr. York, as a man of science, will you state for us if strychnine is a foreign substance in bicarbonate of soda?"

"It is."

"How do you store your strychnine?"

"In both laboratories it is in a locked cabinet with all the other poisonous materials."

"Is it labeled as a poison?"

"Yes, in red ink and with a skull and cross-bones."

"So it is unlikely that a pharmacist could have accidentally mixed strychnine with the bicarbonate?"

"I repeat, sheriff, I will not speculate. Such speculations are left to the police."

"Forgive me, doctor," the sheriff said. "You do not speculate, you have opinions."

Dr. Tyler Flynn raised his hand. "Sheriff."

The sheriff recognized Dr. Flynn.

"May I make a statement?"

"Of course."

Dr. Flynn stood in the aisle. "I would like to explain some facts to the jurors." He looked over at them. "The human body is two-thirds fluid. Mrs. Stanford's fluid weight was recorded at 160 pounds. It would be easy for the small amount of strychnine needed to kill a person to have been dispersed throughout her body. If such were the case, there would be no visible or weighable trace of the poison left. To get all the particles of strychnine, we would have had to test the entire body. And that's never done." Dr. Flynn paced in front of the jurors. "Because Mrs. Stanford drank four or five glasses of water before she died, that could have disseminated the poison and dispersed it throughout the system." He looked at each juror. "Do you understand what I'm trying to tell you?"

Mr. Pembroke asked, "Do you mean the strychnine could have been someplace else?"

"Precisely, and to test her entire body we would have had to turn 160 pounds into slurry."

"Is there anything else you would like to add, doctor?" the sheriff asked Flynn.

"I would like to repeat that strychnine is a foreign substance in bicarbonate."

CHAPTER FIFTEEN

After the session, Speckerd held court in the lobby of The Palms Hotel. A semicircle of reporters huddled around him as he regaled them with his opinions. Unknown to him, Dr. Lowell was exiting the birdcage elevator behind him.

Speckerd pontificated, "Dr. Lowell's very treatment of Mrs. Stanford on the ill-fated night could have caused her death. He may be a fine army doctor, adept at handling dying soldiers, but not patients who might survive."

Dr. Lowell appeared amused. "I am interested, doctor. Proceed."

Speckerd willingly did. "If Mrs. Stanford had ingested strychnine, massaging her limbs would have caused excruciating pain and triggered the lethal spasms." He cocked his head, like a punctuation mark.

"Dr. Speckerd, you are comfortable with the title 'doctor'? I believe you graduated from Columbia last year?" Dr. Lowell folded his arms across his chest. "Dr. Speckerd, if my knowledge of strychnine were limited to a fourth-year medical textbook, I would agree. But research refutes you." Lowell paused. "How odd that you, a graduate of Columbia, haven't read Dr. Papayoanou's work in toxicology." Lowell addressed the reporters cordially. "Gentlemen, Dr.

Papayoanou is a professor at Columbia, a medical school of which I myself was once on faculty. He found that patients poisoned with strychnine often experience a sense of relief when massaged and that a firm touch does not trigger spasms. In fact, it calms the patient and relieves anxiety. I will be happy to loan you the text, Dr. Speckerd—unless you're too busy finding rich widows to invest in your rubber plantation. That is your current scheme, isn't it?"

"It is a poor debater who attacks the man," Speckerd countered.

"Even if the man debates poorly?" Dr. Lowell smiled.

Dr. Speckerd regrouped. "I believe my demonstration of the fading purple test far exceeds any comments made about foot massage."

"Quite," Dr. Lowell agreed. "It was a performance worthy of a stage at the Orpheum."

Hattie had hoped the arrival of a new day would change her life, as if the setting of the moon or the rising of the sun could make her ordinary again—a hotel bookkeeper with no reward for her whereabouts. She refused to feel desperate; she knew she would find another job; she knew all of this would pass. She wouldn't dwell on her worry. Move forward, she told herself. But she spent most of her day in bed trying to quell a throbbing headache, nausea, and creeping despair.

When Koa came home from work, he knocked on her door. He had arranged a job for her at the Alexander. He showed her the uniform. It was a long-sleeved gray dress with a detachable white collar and cuffs.

"This is for the laundry room?" Hattie asked.

"No, your job is to collect shoes and clothes. You pick up and deliver the clean stuff."

It was a better job than she thought she could get.

"You start tonight."

"Do they know who I am?" she asked.

"I told the boss you're my cousin from Maui. Besides, nobody cares who delivers the laundry."

"What if Benson sees me?"

"She never leaves her room."

"And Cutler? I don't need him to get me fired from another job."

"Hattie, you work from midnight to eight. Who's going to see you?"

Hattie put on her uniform and walked to the trolley stop. Everyone she saw was in a uniform—bellmen, waiters, streetcar conductors, or drayers.

She boarded the trolley, not raising her face to anyone, staring out the window into the dark Honolulu night. She got off at the Alexander Hotel and headed to the laundry room not knowing what to expect.

Mrs. Sumida was the clothing service directress. She was an older Japanese woman with skin the color of a thrice-used tea bag. She pointed to the wall and told Hattie to wait there. The skin on Mrs. Sumida's hands was split and cracked.

Hattie stood with her back to the wall, afraid of getting in the way. In front of her was a bank of steam iron presses worked by women with sweat-soaked towels wrapped around their necks. One woman ironed the daily newspapers.

Sweat dripped from Hattie's forehead, her hair, eyebrows, her neck and spine. She breathed in the smell of carbolic acid and steamed wool.

The women shouted orders to each other over the hiss of the steam. Mrs. Sumida pointed to the door and led Hattie into a long room jammed with rows of rolling canvas bins. At the far end of the room were polished brass clothing racks. On the bottom of the racks were men's shoes, and on the top shelf, over the clothes, were the women's shoes.

Mrs. Sumida wagged her finger at an Asian girl who was sorting shoes.

"This is the new girl Hattie," Mrs. Sumida said. "This is Lydia."

Lydia looked like she was sixteen.

"Lydia will take you around tonight. If you learn, you keep the job." Mrs. Sumida handed Hattie a ruffled white pinafore apron that matched Lydia's, then she left the two young women alone. Lydia spoke in half phrases, explaining the job by doing. There was no chatting between them. She took Hattie to the sorting room, where clothes to be laundered were put in canvas bins, shoes were put in wooden cubbyholes, and clothes to be pressed were left on the cart.

Lydia took a man's suit off the cart. She pulled the sateen lining from the pockets. "You empty the pockets and turn them inside out. If not, the pressers holler," Lydia said. "You try." Then she stepped back for Hattie to work. As Hattie walked in front of her, Lydia said, "I know who you are." Her voice had a flat, casual tone armed with threat.

I've been discovered already, Hattie thought. But she made no apology. She didn't owe a laundry worker an explanation. She also knew how fast news traveled among the housekeeping staff. It was a matter of time before the hotel manager would know her identity.

"My name is Hattie Lehua," she told Lydia, and she emptied the pockets of the next jacket.

The two women worked without further comment. Hattie followed Lydia as she rolled the brass cart down the cement corridor to the service elevator and up to the fourth floor. The guest corridors of the Alexander Hotel were painted burgundy and lighted by brass torchieres. And unlike The Palms, the halls were dark and smelled more of cigar smoke than lavender.

Lydia unlocked the door of an unoccupied room and rolled the cart in. The dressers in the room were mahogany, trimmed with brass pulls; the bedspread was satin, and the lamp on the nightstand had a stained-glass shade.

"Come." Lydia motioned Hattie to come around to the back of the door. She shut the door. "This is how we do." Lydia's English was awkward, but the manner in which she addressed Hattie made it clear that she was the superior.

On the back of the door was a long boxed panel that protruded into the room. Lydia unlocked the panel exposing a narrow closet with clothes hangers and a shelf for shoes. It was the same system The Palms used for guests to have their garments cleaned.

"They put their clothes in here. Then we take them out from the front." Lydia led Hattie back out to the hall.

Hattie deferentially nodded.

Lydia closed the guest door. Then from the hall-way, she showed Hattie how to unlock the panel to pick up the clothes. Lydia held up the brass key that had been dangling from her pinafore. "One key for each floor. If you lose the keys, you get fired."

Lydia lifted the clipboard from the cart and explained the process to Hattie. The room numbers and guests' names were checked against the work sheet. The work sheets were pinned to clothes. For shoes, the work sheets were shoved inside.

Lydia's final instructions to Hattie were not to sleep on the job or steal towels.

The morning's *Pacific Commercial Advertiser* headlines read: "Expert Toxicologist Says No Strychnine in Stomach." The *Advertiser*'s editor wrote, "Rather than providing a definite answer regarding the cause of Mrs. Stanford's death, the conflicting reports of the chemist and toxicologist cause even more controversy."

The paper reported allegations of collusion among the autopsy physicians, and a Mr. Gregory Stott wrote a letter to the editor accusing Dr. Lowell of being drunk the night of Mrs. Stanford's death.

In truth, it was the press more than the public who was interested in the intrigue of the story. Most citizens had become impatient and wanted a fast verdict, and the testimonies of Police Officer Benitez and Hiram Loa, the elevator operator, held no sus-pense.

Officer Benitez's testimony was short. He reiterat-ed the events of the case without contradicting any previous witness. After the deputy dismissed the officer, the sheriff surprisingly called for a ten-minute recess. Few spectators left their valued seats, but when ten minutes turned to fifteen and fifteen to twenty, some spectators crossed and recrossed their legs, they jigged their feet. Reporters tapped pencils on their thighs. Pocket watches were drawn out of vest pockets, and one or two sighs turned into a loud chorus. Speculation as to the cause of the delay swelled through the room.

Finally, Sheriff Dillon returned. He questioned Hiram, the elevator operator, for less than five minutes, then Deputy Kanahele announced an end to all testimony. "As all information pertinent to the case of Jane Lathrop Stanford has been recovered and reported, we shall clear the room for the jury to deliberate."

A jam of people clogged the hallway. There was a bottleneck in front of the elevator. Ted Cutler and Charlie Banks opted for the stairs—equally jammed, but at least the crowd was moving. When they made the final curve down to the lobby, Cutler spotted Parnell Regan across the lobby and waved to him. The two men inched and wedged their way through the crowd.

"It'll take us ten minutes just to get to him," Cutler said.

When they got to the bar, Regan ordered a round of beer. "Did anything happen in the morning session?" He handed Cutler a beer. Cutler passed the mug to Charlie Banks, but as he did, Banks was shoved, spilling some beer on Regan.

Regan shrugged it off, brushing the beer from his lapel.

Cutler answered Regan, "We had to listen to a cop and the elevator operator."

Banks took a swig of his beer. "How long do you think the jurors will deliberate?" Banks asked Regan.

"Five hours minimum."

Once again, the crowd pressed forward. This time it was Cutler who was bumped and he, too, spilled beer on Regan.

Regan suggested they wait on the banyan tree *lānai*, where it was less crowded. Cutler seconded the idea, but Charlie Banks wanted to stay put.

"Are you afraid you're going to miss a scoop?" Cutler scoffed.

Banks still refused.

"Come on," Regan said. "They won't be back for hours. I'll put money on it." As Regan was making his wager, Deputy Kanahele emerged from the elevator and announced, "The verdict is in."

Cutler checked his pocket watch. "Less than fifteen minutes. So, Mr. Attorney, what's your call?"

"They came back with natural causes."

It took longer for the spectators to reassemble in the dining room than it had for the jurors to reach their verdict. Once order was established, the sheriff formally asked the jurors if they had arrived at a verdict.

"We have," Mr. Pembroke responded.

"Is it in writing?" the deputy asked.

"It is." Pembroke placed a folded piece of paper in the center of the sheriff's table.

The sheriff read it and handed it to Kanahele; the time was five minutes to eleven. Kanahele cleared his throat.

"The jurors of the inquest into the death of Jane

Lathrop Stanford, who being sworn to inquire when, how, and by what means death came to her, do say that Jane Lathrop Stanford came to her death at Honolulu, Island of Oahu, Territory of Hawaii, on the 28th day of February, in the year of the Lord, 1905, from strychnine poisoning."

There was an outburst of clapping. Sheriff Dillon raised his hands. The spectators quieted. "Continue with the verdict, please," the sheriff said.

Kanahele continued, "Said strychnine having been introduced into a bottle of bicarbonate of soda with felonious intent by a person, or persons, unknown to this jury."

"Poisoned!" The word surged through the room. Reporters ran out before the sheriff could order them to return to their seats. Within the hour of the verdict, newsboys were hawking papers with three-inch headlines: "Mrs. Stanford Murdered."

Sheriff Dillon himself called Mr. Lathrop to inform him of the verdict.

"I see," Mr. Lathrop said. As he spoke, Lathrop reached for the arm of the chair. His body sagged. "Yes." His voice was level. "I appreciate it." He nodded into the phone. "Thank you, sheriff."

"The verdict?" Ambrose asked.

"She was poisoned." A sick dread showed on Lathrop's face.

"Why should I be surprised? A horde of fools led by Lowell." Ambrose's voice was as pinched as his sentiment.

Lathrop appeared sapped of spirit.

"We should present the evidence to a jury in San Francisco—let rational men review the case." Ambrose's words were as quick as they were sharp.

"This is a farce. The only truth is that we shall have years of entanglements in probate."

Harrison Lathrop raised his head. "How can you be this cold?"

<hr />

That afternoon Rev. William Kincaid drafted his homily for Mrs. Stanford's service. The Central Union Church choir practiced funeral hymns with their organist, Dr. Jan Rensel. He chose "Lead, Kindly Light," "Mighty Fortress Is Our God," the doxology, and "Jesu, Joy of Man's Desire." The choir members were to wear black robes for the service, the clergy would be in hooded black vestments, and black bunting would swirl around the church's front columns.

At the Thompson carriage barn, groomsmen hauled out black plumes for their horses and carriage boys waxed the hearse and fitted it with black fringe. City workers nailed signs to telephone poles to alert drivers to the diverted traffic patterns during the procession. At Alakea Wharf, carpenters built scaffolds for bunting and street vendors set up folding tables for selling mourning bands and buttons.

At four o'clock that afternoon, Attorney General Upton announced his decision to give up jurisdiction over the Stanford case to the State of California. Surrounded by the governor, the mayor, and fourteen Republican legislators, Judge Upton cited the Beck case as precedent.

Legislator Dennis Packard stepped forward to support Upton. "The legislature welcomes the attorney general's ruling." Packard faced the photographers as he spoke. "The territory was not eager to expend $20,000 on a criminal trial, or in demonstrating that no criminal trial is necessary. This is California's business, not ours. The criminal inquiry shall be made in and at the expense of that state." He puffed out his chest like a victorious general.

The press displayed minimal interest in their announcements. The legal mechanics of the case had been played out in the dailies for at least a week. The reporters wanted more drama, so they turned their pens to their own speculations and reported them as news. Their questions were somewhat the same: "Does it seem possible that Mrs. Stanford would have swallowed a bicarbonate that had the same bitter taste of the water that made her ill just six weeks before? Is it possible that Mrs. Stanford's hysteria could have caused her symptoms? Did the autopsy reveal any sign of dementia?"

The *Star* interviewed Dr. Eliot Rand—a retired general practitioner. Rand opined that Mrs. Stanford died of fright. He used death after a rabid bite as the foundation of his conclusion. He stated, "A majority of people who die from rabies die from their own power of imagination and not the disease itself. Because death by rabies is so dreaded and its symptoms are familiar to most, patients actually elicit the fatal spasms much like the spasms that caused Mrs. Stanford's death."

The *Advertiser* resurrected a story about a young sailor who was forced to drink from a bottle by his shipmates. The bottle was clearly marked with a skull and crossbones. According to the reporter, the old salts told the boy he had drunk poison. The shipmates described the taste of the poison as a "burning fire." The sailor died within hours. In fact, the young man drank nothing more dangerous than whiskey. The article ended, "But, alas, the poor boy died from a clear case of lethal imagination."

The society page editors moved to the limelight, digging for details of the pomp of Mrs. Stanford's memorial. There hadn't been a death of note in Honolulu since Princess Ka'iulani died six years before. While Ka'iulani's cortege was a procession of royals, Mrs. Stanford's would be a pageant of *haole* power. Governor Nichols, Mr. Zachary Hackfield, Representative Carl Smith, Mr. C. M. Cooke, Mr. Van Dine, Mr. William Castle, and Mr. Charles Dole were pallbearers. President Ambrose was the lead pallbearer.

During Attorney General Upton's address, Ambrose was at the Honolulu Aquarium attending a reception in honor of Ichiro Kosaki of Japan, the president of Todai University.

Dr. D'Angelo, the director of the Honolulu Aquarium, was a man about seventy years old. He had a substantial black handlebar moustache that whisked over his deep olive skin. He was a light-spirited man, almost playful, and he brought a child-like enthusiasm to everything he did.

Dr. D'Angelo had invited aquarium trustees, benefactors, staff, and university students to the reception. He had tanks of specimens set up on the lawn under a canvas awning, and a collection of Australian shells was displayed in glass cases. Royal blue linen draped sixteen round tables, and a string quartet played.

The Castle and Cooke families were well represented, including a herd of their grandchildren, who ran around the lawn led by chief instigator, Sophie Cooke.

Mrs. Aaron Bird, Mrs. Gardner Wilder, and Miss Lillian Bacon served tea under a green and white striped tent. And young girls, wearing organza hair bows as wide as swans, passed confections and punch.

Dr. D'Angelo escorted President Ambrose over to Mrs. William Castle.

"Mrs. Castle, it is my pleasure to see you again." President Ambrose smiled. It was a smile that an objective observer might describe as the smirk of a self-serving sycophant.

Mrs. Castle shaded herself from the sun with her parasol. She expressed her condolences to Ambrose on the death of Mrs. Stanford and thanked him for attending the reception during such a mournful time.

"It is my way to honor Mrs. Stanford's legacy." The words glided out of his mouth.

"What is your opinion of our burgeoning aquarium?" Mrs. Castle asked him.

"This is one of the finest collections of fish in the world. It rivals that of the Naples Aquarium." Ambrose turned to D'Angelo and lifted his glass, referring to the fact that the Honolulu Aquarium had lured D'Angelo away from that prestigious institution. "Nowhere can one see such a marvelous variety of tropical specimens."

"We were fortunate to get him," Mrs. Castle remarked, knowing it was her husband who was instrumental in the negotiation.

A young man approached and whispered in D'Angelo's ear, and D'Angelo informed Mrs. Castle that the program would begin.

D'Angelo began his speech with his condolences to President Ambrose and all of Stanford University upon the tragic death of its founder. He enumerated Mrs. Stanford's contributions to the academic world, noted her charitable works, and applauded her as a woman of strength, ethics, and dignity. Then he lightened his manner and entertained his audience with a story about Mrs. Stanford and President Ambrose squabbling over a card game—each of them keeping separate score and both claiming victory. The story may or may not have been true.

Ambrose's smile appeared strained.

Dr. D'Angelo followed with a joke about Ambrose discovering an entirely new variety of fish on his last trip to the islands. "New to him at least, and one that pleased him," D'Angelo said. "But, it wasn't much of a fish." He pursed his lips and shrugged his shoulders. "It was a little, pudgy, ugly-looking beast, with a blunt round head and a beaked mouth with fascinating teeth. It looks like the kind of fish that boys in Naples caught in creeks and then pounded its head because it stole their bait. The Hawaiians call this fish *uhu*."

The audience laughed and Dr. D'Angelo translated for President Ambrose. "*Uhu* is a common parrotfish."

"And an exceptional specimen it was," Ambrose recovered.

Then D'Angelo adjusted his stance and modulated his voice. His tone became formal. "Today we are privileged to have more than one university president with us." He extended his hand in the direction of a distinguished man in his seventies clad in a gray silk kimono. "President Ichiro Kosaki of Todai University has traveled to visit our institution."

Kosaki bowed to D'Angelo, who returned an even deeper bow.

"This is a fortuitous turn of fate, since both Presidents Kosaki and Ambrose are interested in the development of the Honolulu Aquarium for research. Now, due to this blessing of a face-to-face meeting, these men are announcing a joint research project to study the medicinal benefits of sea plants at our aquarium."

The announcement brought cheers from the typically reserved trustees.

"This project will be funded by their respective universities, and a combined and most distinguished faculty will reside in our islands."

A second burst of applause broke out, and each president made brief remarks. President Kosaki's remarks were translated from Japanese. President Ambrose began, "My only regret is that Mrs. Stanford is not with us to share in this momentous occasion. The Honolulu Aquarium and the potential for world-renowned marine research were a priority in her vision for the expansion of Stanford University. I am sure she looks upon us today and blesses us all." Then he concluded by thanking the people of Honolulu for their sympathy.

That evening Attorney General Upton, President Ambrose, and Dr. Townsend dined in a private meeting room at the Alexander.

President Ambrose was direct. "Gentlemen, do we have an assessment of the situation?"

"It's not good news." Upton continued hesitantly, "It seems Prince Kūhiō is intent on using this case to further his bid for the Supreme Court."

"Can he have the case moved back to Hawai'i?" Ambrose asked.

Upton shook his head. "No, but he can cause damage in California."

"Ah, yes, but you have the California attorney general in your pocket." Ambrose mocked Upton.

"It does us no good to squabble," Dr. Townsend scolded them. "Sometimes destiny interferes with the best of plans."

"And what do you propose we do about that interference?" Ambrose asked.

"It's obvious that the second autopsy must conclude that Mrs. Stanford died of natural causes," Townsend said. "And the only man for the job is Archibald Armstrong."

"I thought you said he would never risk it?" Ambrose said.

Upton said, "He wasn't as tough a negotiator as I expected."

"Wasn't?" The corners of Ambrose's mouth drew down. "The deal is done?"

"I have met with Armstrong," Upton admitted.

"So I'm informed after the fact?" Ambrose's eyes widened. "A formality at best?"

"We are informing you now," Dr. Townsend said.

"What was Armstrong's price?"

"In its own way, more than expected," Townsend said.

"Are we to buy him all of Australia?" Ambrose huffed.

"It's not money." Upton took a sip of Madeira, as if to defer Ambrose's rage, then cautiously set down his drink. "He wants Stanford University to confer him with an honorary degree for his contributions in medicine."

"The man is a buffoon. This is an insult to my integrity," Ambrose said.

"Don't act so wounded," Townsend admonished. "You can suspend your integrity for what it's worth."

"This must be undone," Ambrose insisted.

"It's a small price to pay," Townsend said.

Upton told Ambrose, "He wants an honorary degree to recognize his contributions to the field of medicine. It is to be conferred upon him at commencement and we all must attend."

"He's a cat playing with a mouse!"

"He is," Dr. Townsend agreed.

"There is more, gentlemen." Judge Upton lifted a bulging portfolio. "This afternoon Harrison asked me to draw up terms for a reward. If Armstrong's autopsy is the least bit ambiguous, I am to release the terms immediately. It is an offer of two-thousand five-hundred dollars for anyone with information leading to the unmasking of his sister's murderer."

"We are trapped," Ambrose remarked. "Does Armstrong know about the reward?"

Upton shook his head.

"Perhaps we could find another doctor to take his place," Ambrose suggested.

"Simon," Dr. Townsend started, "now that Armstrong knows our plan, how much do you think he would extort if we were to change our minds now?"

"Fine. Cast me in your charade," Ambrose huffed. "Once more I have no choice."

———•◦•◦•———

After dinner that night, Hattie took the laundry in for Makana. As she unpinned the clothes from the line, she watched Makana's twins sit on their father's lap—one daughter on each leg. Nehoa pointed out the constellations, teaching his daughters their names and how to read their signs. Each girl vied for Nehoa's attention. Each curled her arm around her father's neck; each pulled him closer to herself.

Hattie brought the clothes in the kitchen and folded them on the kitchen table while Makana dried the dishes. "What's it like working for rich *haole*?" Makana asked.

"My boss was nice." Hattie wanted to believe that Mrs. Martin would help her get a job after the publicity about Mrs. Stanford died down.

"Koa wanted to get Nehoa a job at the hotel—a waiter—but Nehoa likes security. And night work pays good."

In the middle of their conversation, Makana paused to kiss Moses's bruised finger.

"Koa likes getting jobs for people," Hattie said.

"He said he's bringing your friend from California tonight—the maid."

It was Mae's last night in Honolulu. Hattie hoped to see her again.

While Hattie and Makana were talking, Koa and Mae were riding the trolley through Honolulu. Mae asked Koa about each building they passed. The first was the Opera House; the next was 'Iolani Palace. Koa left the details of its history unsaid. He was more enthusiastic pointing out Queen Lili'uokalani's house. Mae thought it looked like a Boston sea captain's house. The house was a three-story white clapboard with square columns, a wide wraparound porch, and a widow's walk that capped the roof. All around the yard were torches placed in red ginger.

"Her husband was a *haole* sea merchant," Koa said. "But he died in China trying to make money to finish the house."

"He sounds like an Irish husband."

"He was Italian," Koa said. Then he pointed to a church on the ocean side of the street. "That's the Catholic cathedral."

Mae blessed herself.

Mae was so taken with Koa's stories about the green-painted firehouse and the Buddhist temple that was haunted by forty-four spirits that neither of them noticed a carriage following the trolley.

When Koa and Mae got off the trolley to transfer to the King Street Line, the carriage pulled over and stopped. When the couple boarded the King Street trolley, the carriage followed them until Koa and Mae got off at the Iwilei stop, where a *haole* man got out of the carriage.

Koa and Mae walked down the alley to Makana's house. The *haole* man was half a block behind them.

Hattie welcomed Mae at the door. "I brought these for the children." Mae handed the basket to Makana. The basket was filled with pastries from The Palms and the Alexander.

304 ❧ Dorothea N. Buckingham ❧

Makana set the basket on the floor. The room was crowded with Makana, Hattie, Koa, Mae, two young boys, and a cat. They all found places on the *pūne'e*, the floor, and a stool.

Mae prattled nervously, curling her hair around her finger as she spoke. "Mrs. Martin sends her regards. She is quite concerned about you. She asked Mr. St. Clair if you could come back, just as a clerk, but he said no. Then she tried again. And Thomas, the desk clerk, took relish in telling me that St. Clair had refused her."

Makana caught sight of the twins peeking into the front room. "Back to bed," she told them, but Mae was taken with them and asked if it was all right if they had some cakes. Both girls trailed into the room.

Mae continued, "Mr. St. Clair wants you branded as a thief. He told Mrs. Martin if anyone called for a reference she was to say that The Palms regrets any association with you."

Until that moment, Hattie believed she could recover her job. She had convinced herself that her time of shame would pass and all attention would fade.

As Mae spoke, Lana pressed on Mae's face. "*Luluā'ina*," Lana said.

"Is that her name?" Mae asked.

Koa laughed. "No, it should be yours. It means freckles."

Then Makana introduced the girls. "My mother-in-law named Pua. It means flower. And I named her rascal twin Lana. It means calm as still waters—not a good match."

"Koa means the warrior," Koa offered unsolicited.

"Most fitting." Mae winked at Hattie. "And Hattie . . . well, I need no translation for that."

"Her Hawaiian name is Malu Lani," Koa said. "Protected by heaven."

"These days I'm not so sure," Hattie said.

The *haole* man approached the house. He knocked on the front door.

Koa answered it. "It's Charlie Banks." Koa opened the door.

As soon as Banks stepped in, Mae attacked. "What are you doing here?"

"He's a reporter," Koa explained to Makana. "He was at the hotel a lot."

"Looking for a story?" Mae kept on.

"He's a good man," Koa defended.

"Says who?" Mae wouldn't give up.

Hattie wanted Mae to stop.

"You probably sold that pack of lies to the paper, just for . . ."

"Stop!" Hattie said. "Can we just listen to what he says?"

Banks approached Hattie. "I want to give you a chance to tell your side of the story."

"There is no my side," she said. "Besides, my side doesn't matter."

"It should," Makana said.

"It'll only make things worse," Hattie said.

"He's the one who will make it worse, just twist the truth to his own liking," Mae said.

"It's not that I don't trust him," Hattie said apologetically. "It's that I have nothing to say." Hattie could sense that Mae was angered by her answer.

"In case you change your mind . . ." Banks

reached in his pocket for his notebook. He wrote something down and handed it to Hattie. "That's the phone number for the Seven Seas Saloon. I'm there every night. And if I'm not there, they can always find me."

"She won't," Mae snapped.

Hattie put the paper in her uniform pocket, and Charlie Banks left.

"He wants something," Mae said.

Hattie wanted to believe Charlie Banks. She couldn't give up trusting everyone. She also knew it was the last time she would see Mae and she didn't want it to end badly.

Mae fumbled through her purse. She took out an envelope and handed it to Hattie. "It's from Koa and me."

Inside was $120.

"It's enough for a round-trip passage to San Francisco," Koa said.

"But you can cash in the return if you decide to stay in San Francisco," Mae added.

Hattie looked at the cash. "This is a lot of money."

"I've been saving," Koa said. "Besides, most of it is Mae's."

"You could start a new life," Mae said. "I can get you a job."

Hattie didn't wrestle with her answer. Her answer was certain. "I can't."

"You may change your mind," Mae said. "Why not keep it for a little while?"

Hattie handed the money back to Mae. "If I come to San Francisco, I'll pay my own way."

"With the wages from the Alexander?" Mae asked.

"With the wages from where I go next," Hattie answered.

CHAPTER SIXTEEN

That night at work, Mrs. Sumida handed Hattie a clipboard. "Sixth and seventh floors, Diamond Head." Then she walked away.

Hattie hung the clipboard on her cart, and rolled it down the hall. Lydia was right behind her. While they waited for the service elevator, neither spoke. Lydia took Hattie's clipboard off the cart and exchanged it with her own. "Now you have eight and nine. They're all suites." Hattie had no idea if Lydia was doing her a favor or not.

Hattie pressed the elevator button for the eighth floor. Suite after suite, she checked the guests' names against the register on her clipboard. She pinned work orders on jacket lapels and stuffed them in shoes. It took her three hours to complete the floor, then she went back to the sorting room with a full cart.

It was 3:00 a.m. The shoeshine boy pointed to the loading dock and told her she was allowed a break.

On the dock, produce vendors made their deliveries in the pitch of night. They heaved and stacked crates of persimmon, guava, and wild strawberries, and kitchen boys in paper cone hats lugged the crates inside. Each time the kitchen doors swung open, Hattie could hear the chefs hollering.

Hattie watched them. She was tired, thoughtless,

at peace. Work until exhaustion, she told herself. Don't think—not about Mae, about Mr. St. Clair, and if you have to think, think about the clothes that need to be cleaned, pressed, or mended.

But she wondered if she should move to San Francisco. Mae said she could get her a job. Maybe she should move to Maui. She had family there. But do what? Work on the plantations?

"Don't think," she said out loud.

"You." One of the laundry women yelled to Hattie. "Sumida-san say back to work." Hattie went in, wiped down her brass cart, rolled it down the hall, and took the service elevator to the ninth floor.

One suite after another, Hattie removed and tagged clothes. The next suite was the Lahaina Suite. She unlatched the door. Two mourning suits hung in the closet. The order said "To be pressed only." One of the suits was exceptionally small. She hung the suits on her cart and read the names of the guests off her register: Harrison Lathrop and Simon Ambrose. She gripped her pencil and formed each letter. She wrote Harrison Lathrop's name.

Did she dare leave him a note?

Hattie knew the day after next, the Stanford party would sail for California. Harrison Lathrop would be gone forever. Leaving a note that night might be her only chance to contact him.

As she worked down the hall from suite to suite, she composed her letter—changing her words and phrases, trying somehow to explain her actions. But each time she did, she thought she sounded more and more foolish. She decided it would be better to wait. She could take a day to gather her thoughts and leave the note the next night.

When her shift was over, Hattie was still trying to find the right words. She stepped outside into the morning's light. The street vendors were already hawking their wares, trolleys were running, and bicycles lined the street. But the traffic seemed exceptionally heavy, and rows of buggies were double-parked in front of the Alexander. When Hattie walked by the entrance, she saw that the front doors were open and a bevy of reporters were crowded in a semicircle. Charlie Banks was at the rear of a group of men. He turned his head, caught her eyes; she skirted off to the trolley.

In the lobby of the Alexander, Noah Upton delivered a statement on behalf of Harrison Lathrop. "It is with the encouragement of friends, both new and long-standing, who support me in my quest to seek out a resolution to the question of my sister's death that I am acting to end this ambiguity. It is with the support of the medical community of Honolulu that I have agreed to their suggestion to conduct a second autopsy of her body. It will be an autopsy of the heart only."

Charlie Banks edged his way toward Ted Cutler. Cutler was scanning the crowd.

"Ted," Banks said.

Cutler barely acknowledged him.

Upton continued, "Dr. Archibald Armstrong, a senior statesman of the medical world, will preside as prosector of the autopsy. Dr. Armstrong has had a distinguished career and was a faculty member at Sydney University Medical College for most of that time. Since his retirement, he has been active in the Honolulu Medical Society and was elected its president twice. His work in the field of surgery, particularly of the heart, is recognized worldwide. Dr. Armstrong will be assisted by Dr. Bernard Speckerd." Upton folded his paper and put it in his vest pocket. "Dr. Armstrong assures me that his preliminary finds will be delivered this afternoon. These will be initial conclusions only."

A few reporters began asking questions.

Upton said, "We will present the results as soon as they are delivered. A full disclosure of the autopsy will be available at a later date."

"Ted, why the second autopsy?" Charlie Banks asked.

Cutler ignored him.

"Didn't the first one give them the answer they wanted?"

Cutler moved toward Upton.

"You heard him. They just want to get to the truth." Cutler followed Upton into the elevator.

No spectators were allowed at the second autopsy. The procedure took place at Queen's Hospital. It began at 7:00 a.m., and by early afternoon, Drs. Armstrong and Speckerd were in the lobby of the Alexander Hotel standing shoulder to shoulder with Harrison Lathrop, Simon Ambrose, and Isaiah Townsend. Ted Cutler was at their side.

President Ambrose stepped forward to the podium. "Gentlemen." He called the reporters to order. "Gentlemen." He stretched out his chin and cleared his throat. "If I may have your attention."

Ambrose looked over his audience. "I am certain you are all familiar with Mr. Harrison Lathrop, Dr.

Townsend, and Dr. Armstrong. But for those of you who may not recognize him, may I ask Dr. Bernard Speckerd to step forward."

"More like Dr. Beau Brummell," the reporter standing next to Charlie Banks quipped.

Banks smiled. The reporter continued, "Patent leather shoes and an ascot. The doc looks like he woke up in a Chinatown whorehouse."

Dr. Speckerd stepped forward.

The reporter turned to Banks. "You ever heard of this guy Speckerd?" The reporter wore a crumpled bowler; his breath smelled of tobacco and coffee.

Banks shook his head.

Dr. Ambrose continued, "Gentlemen, Mr. Lathrop and I want to thank all those physicians who labored so diligently to determine the cause of Mrs. Stanford's death. We are aware that many lights burned long into the night. We do not come to disparage these physicians, neither are we here to discredit them."

"We do not come to praise the physicians," the reporter mumbled as he took notes, "we come to bury them."

Ambrose added, "This second autopsy was not a contest of setting doctor against doctor."

"Then what was it?" The reporter said it loud enough to cause heads to turn.

"It was a journey toward truth." Ambrose's voice was stern.

Banks moved closer to the podium.

"Afraid of sticking too close to me?" the reporter asked Banks. Then he stuck out his hand. "Patrick McNally."

Charlie Banks shook his hand. "Patrick McNally of the Associated Press?"

"One and the same."

McNally was one of the reporters who had sailed from San Francisco to cover the story. He was known as a bulldog of an investigator, and his capacity for Scotch was legendary.

President Ambrose relinquished the podium to Dr. Armstrong.

Armstrong affected a bow. "Gentlemen." He cleared his throat. "I have agreed to give a preliminary report of my findings so this grieving party can depart with a sense of closure. These are my initial impressions. A complete transcript of the autopsy, which will present the detailed body of evidence that led me to my conclusion, will be forthcoming." He projected his words as if they were to be inscribed in gold.

Banks noticed McNally's rumpled jacket.

Armstrong leaned on the podium. "Dr. Henrik is correct in his statement that Mrs. Stanford's heart was not enlarged. And, as he noted during the autopsy, there was some fat surrounding her heart. When I saw this condition during the procedure, I was suspect why his examination of the heart was cursory. His only inspection consisted of a small cut made to get blood for analysis. Upon my examination of the heart, I observed that the walls were thinned, the heart itself was flabby, and the muscle tissue was a deep crimson."

He removed his spectacles and clasped the podium with both hands. "During the first autopsy, Dr. Henrik probed an artery with his finger. I believe I witnessed some resistance at that time, and questioned to myself why Dr. Henrik did not investigate any further. In my more thorough examination of the

heart, I found the arteries to be occluded. In fact"—
Armstrong turned to Speckerd—"Dr. Speckerd will
confirm that the deposits were so hard and gritty
that I lost the edge on the blade of my scalpel."

"Of course, he'll confirm it," McNally opined.
"The little parasite tied his future to the old codger."

McNally's remarks went unchecked, though the
surrounding reporters appeared quite amused.

"I would describe the consistency of the deposits
to be that of ceiling plaster," Armstrong stated. "I am
prepared to testify under oath that when I examined
the exterior of the heart, ruptures were visible to
me." He paused dramatically and stood erect.
"Gentlemen, it is my conclusion that Mrs. Jane
Lathrop Stanford died of acute neuralgia, akin to
angina pectoris—a natural cause."

McNally raised his hand. "Doctor," he called
from the back. "A question."

"I will not answer any questions until the full
report has been written."

"But Dr. Armstrong . . ." McNally wouldn't quit.

"I have no further remarks to make."

"Doctor . . ." McNally turned to Banks. "I do it
just to annoy them."

President Ambrose stepped forward.
"Gentlemen, in our judgment, and I speak for Mr.
Harrison Lathrop, after careful consideration of all
facts brought to us, we are satisfied that Mrs.
Stanford's death was not due to strychnine poisoning, nor to any wrongdoing. In studying the statements of those who were with her in her last
moments, we find no evidence that any of the characteristic symptoms of strychnine poisoning
occurred. We think it is probable that her death was

caused by a combination of circumstances. Among these, her advanced age, her unaccustomed exertion during strenuous day trips, the unsuitable food, and the exposure to inclement weather. And these conditions were perhaps somewhat aggravated by the presence of strychnine and other drugs in the cascara capsule and possibly by the small amount of strychnine contained in the bicarbonate of soda."

McNally scribbled shorthand in his spiral notepad. Periodically he poked the brim of his bowler.

Ambrose stated, "The fact is, the strychnine found in the body was not in excess of the usual patent medicine proportions. We recognize how the attending physicians may have concluded that Mrs. Stanford died of poisoning under the extraordinary circumstances. We regard it, however, as without medical foundation and wholly incompatible with the evidence in our possession." He lowered his voice. "On behalf of Mr. Harrison Lathrop, may I express our appreciation to all."

"This guy is arrogant enough to think we believe them." McNally walked away and gave his bowler one last poke.

———

Immediately following his statement, Ambrose informed Townsend that he would be at the aquarium if he were needed. When Ambrose arrived at the aquarium, Dr. D'Angelo was in the seaweed laboratory.

"Dr. Ambrose. Look!" D'Angelo held up a reddish seaweed in his gloved hand. "The Hawaiians call it *limu make o Hāna*." He gestured to the wall where a line of white laboratory coats hung.

Ambrose put on a coat and approached the tank; D'Angelo halted him. "Gloves. You must glove."

Ambrose put on a pair of thick yellow latex gloves.

"Two pairs," D'Angelo advised.

Ambrose struggled, stretching the second pair over the first.

"It's the deadliest of poisons," D'Angelo warned as he rotated the seaweed to catch the afternoon sun. "And yet so beautiful. Don't you think?"

The seaweed looked more like a coral limpet than a plant.

President Ambrose took the specimen in his hand and angled it to the light. "What does the Hawaiian name mean?"

"Hāna's seaweed of death. The natives on Maui have a myth about tentacled seaweed that hated to be disturbed. When it was touched, it shriveled up and a moan could be heard throughout the sea. Then, in revenge for the invasion, it killed its intruder. We suspect it may have truth."

It glistened like a gelled star. Ambrose held it closer to his face. "It looks like a simple sea anemone."

"But one puncture of your skin and your muscles will cramp, the tongue swells, and death is certain—an asphyxiation."

"Has a lethal dosage been measured?" Ambrose asked.

"All we know is that less than one one-thousandth of a grain can kill a fifty-pound dog. The notes are gruesome." Dr. D'Angelo clucked his tongue. "The eyes protrude and the body succumbs in violent tremors."

Ambrose set the *limu make o Hāna* back in the tank, not dropping it, but setting it down on the bottom, getting the sleeve of his tweed jacket wet. Then he carefully removed his gloves.

"Put the gloves in here, doctor." D'Angelo pointed to a galvanized tub having a red skull and crossbones painted on it. "We wash them separately."

"Who is doing the research on it?" Ambrose said.

"Dr. Etsuo Sato in Naha. He's trying to prove that it will shrink deadly tumors." D'Angelo walked to the bookshelves and pulled out summaries of Dr. Sato's work.

Ambrose took off his lab coat. The wet sleeve of his jacket smelled like seaweed.

"This same seaweed is present in the Ryukyu Islands. They call it red death in Japan." D'Angelo showed Ambrose one of Dr. Sato's sketches of a victim—a young woman pearl diver. "Sato works under the auspices of Todai University. And now, with its collaboration with Stanford, who knows? Perhaps we can isolate the curative."

President Ambrose returned the book to the shelf and strolled down the aisle of tanks. He read the identification cards as he examined each specimen. "*Microcoleus lyngbyaceus*. This is quite lovely." Strands of teal floated through the water.

"Stinging *limu*," D'Angelo stated. "Not poisonous, but it can burn."

"Is everything in here noxious?" Ambrose lifted a towel hanging next to the sink and wet it.

"So it seems." D'Angelo smiled.

Ambrose wiped his jacket sleeve with water, but the rancid smell was trapped in the wool. He reached into his jacket pocket; inside was a pharmacy envelope, which he crumpled up and tossed into the trash can, then he washed his hands.

"Perhaps we should adjourn to my office." D'Angelo invited Ambrose in and put a pot of tea water on to boil.

During their conversation, Simon Ambrose repeatedly sniffed at his sleeve and commented on the stench. Upon his return to the hotel, he immediately took off his jacket and placed it in the laundry service compartment to be cleaned.

CHAPTER SEVENTEEN

That night when Hattie unlocked the door of the Lahaina Suite, a short tweed jacket was hanging inside. The attached note read, "For immediate attention." The jacket smelled of fish.

Hattie wrote President Ambrose's name on the work sheet and pinned it to the jacket. Then she took the two mourning coats off her cart. She hung them in the door; she fingered the note she had written to Mr. Lathrop in her uniform pocket, then she moved on to the next suite without leaving the note.

She couldn't, not now, she thought. She would leave the note in the morning when she returned President Ambrose's jacket. Hattie continued her debate all the way down the hall, in the elevator, and while she bundled shirts in the sorting room. It was then that she decided it was best not to contact Mr. Lathrop at all. She should let Mrs. Stanford rest in peace. She moved on to the men's jackets, pulling out the pocket linings and turning their collars up. There was no need to cause Mr. Lathrop any more sorrow.

When she lifted Ambrose's jacket off the hanger and pulled out the pocket lining, a white powder sprinkled on the floor. It flecked the cement and dusted her uniform.

Not again, she said to herself. It would be easier not to notice.

She pulled the lining out of Ambrose's other pocket. Nothing spilled out. She went on to the next jacket, but she was distracted.

She brushed the powder off the folds of her skirt. They were more like crystals than powder. Hattie remembered Mae's description of strychnine looking like sugar. She patted some of the crystals and licked her finger. It was bitter—beyond bitter.

Hattie crouched down, hovering over the small patch of crystals on the floor. There weren't enough to pick up—they were lost in swirls of cement.

The shoeshine boy came in to collect the shoes and saw Hattie hunched over. "You sick?"

"I'm fine," she said and pretended to button her shoe while the boy collected the bins of shoes.

Hattie stared at the crystals. They're nothing, she told herself, and she blew them away with one short breath, then she stood up and moved on to the next jacket. She emptied the pockets of the next four jackets, then went back to Ambrose's. She cupped her hand under the lining and pulled it out, separating the seams. A few clumps of lint mixed with crystals were stuck in the folds. She let them drop into her hand, then slid them onto a work sheet and folded the paper in fourths.

What am I doing? she said to herself. I am at the bottom of my life. Why make things worse?

She rolled her cart toward the loading dock. A produce vendor took off his cap and wiped the sweat from his brow. He gave Hattie a lopsided grin. She stopped her cart and waited for him to go back to his truck, then she took Ambrose's jacket, rolled it

under her arm, and ran down the alley, down
Merchant Street, into Chinatown, into a noodle shop,
where she put her money on the bar and called the
Seven Seas Saloon.

Within minutes, Charlie Banks was there.

<hr />

At 7:00 a.m. the next morning, the Stanford party
was assembled in the Lahaina Suite. Attorney
General Upton was pinning a diagonal black sash
from Dr. Townsend's left shoulder to his right hip.

Mae McCauley sat directly across from Miss
Benson. Mae kept her eyes cast down during
President Ambrose's tantrum about his jacket not
being returned from the laundry.

"The expressmen will be here to pick up our luggage and I still have no jacket." He lit his fourth cigarette of the morning.

"Do you want me to go downstairs to get it?"
Cutler asked. He was wearing a black suit, black tie,
and a mourning armband.

"I need you here when the drayers arrive. Which
may be tomorrow if we have any indication of how
things get done on this godforsaken island." Ambrose
pounded his cigarette out after only three puffs.

"If it doesn't come on time, I can ship it to you,"
Townsend offered.

"How can these people be so incompetent?
Cleaning a jacket is not a monumental challenge. I
wait to return to San Francisco!" Ambrose said.

"There are others who share that sentiment,"
Upton muttered.

Through it all, Harrison Lathrop sat silent.

There was a knock at the door. "Laundry service."

"Finally." Ambrose opened the door. There stood Hattie and Charlie Banks.

Miss Benson gasped.

Cutler told Lathrop that Hattie was The Palms maid.

Hattie stepped forward. "My name is Hattie Lehua." She approached Mr. Lathrop. The president's jacket was folded under her arm. "I have some information for you, sir. Last night, in the laundry, white crystals fell out of Dr. Ambrose's jacket." She hesitated, and looked at Cutler. "They tasted bitter."

"She's a demented servant who will do anything for notoriety." Ambrose yanked the jacket from her.

Hattie reached into her pocket and handed Lathrop an envelope. "The crystals are in there."

Lathrop had yet to speak.

"First she accuses Miss Benson of murder, now it is I who am the target of her hysteria," Ambrose said.

Lathrop tapped the envelope on the table. "Miss Lehua, why are you doing this?"

She wanted to tell him it was because Mrs. Stanford gave her her Bible; because she asked her if she would go to Japan; because when she was dying, she called her name. But she answered, "I don't know."

Lathrop handed the envelope to Cutler; he tasted the contents. "Bitter." His face cringed.

Upton stated, "Even if it were strychnine, there's no proof it was in Ambrose's jacket."

"May I have your jacket?" Lathrop asked.

"I should say not," Ambrose protested.

"Why not?" Lathrop asked.

"You are encouraging madness, that's why!"

Upton defended Ambrose. "This is legal folly. The girl could have placed it in there herself. No judge in the world would allow this in his court."

"I'm not doing this for any court." Lathrop turned to Cutler. "Can the substance be tested before we sail?"

Cutler answered that he wasn't sure.

Dr. Townsend advised against testing the substance. "If you do this, the university will suffer, no matter what the outcome."

Lathrop directed Cutler to get the substance tested.

Cutler proceeded to leave immediately.

"I'm going with you," Banks said.

Cutler stopped. "Don't you trust me?"

"I just want to make sure." Banks shut the suite door behind them.

"I have never endured such a grave insult," Ambrose said. "I am an innocent in this charade."

"I pray that's the truth," Lathrop responded. Then he addressed Hattie directly, saying he would inform her of the results but nothing more.

Hattie thanked him. She stood there, not knowing if she should leave or not. Then Mr. Lathrop stood, as if signaling the party to depart for the service. Judge Upton, Dr. Townsend, President Ambrose, and Miss Benson fell in line. Mae was last; as she walked by Hattie, she took her arm and the two women walked the hall together.

At the sidewalk, Hattie and Mae embraced, then Mae boarded the carriage. Hattie stood at the curb and watched as the cortege rode away. When she could see them no more, she walked to the Alakea Wharf.

As Hattie was making her way to the dock, Cutler and Banks were speeding to Queen's Hospital.

At the Central Union Church, the Episcopal bishop Henry Bond Restarck and Rev. William Kincaid accepted the body of Mrs. Stanford at the door. Both clerics were vested in black hooded robes. The casket was draped in the ensign of the university. The pallbearers escorted the casket down the aisle led by President Ambrose.

The interior of the church was devoid of excess. The church held seven hundred guests that day—five hundred in the main body, and two hundred in the balcony. As the casket was rolled down the aisle, the congregation stood.

Lallah Upton was at the end of a pew. When her husband passed, she held her head even higher and turned to those next to her, smiling condescendingly.

The choir sang "Lead, Kindly Light," then Rev. Kincaid preached from the text of St. Paul's Second Epistle to Timothy. "I have fought a good fight, I have finished my course. I have kept the faith. Henceforth, there is laid upon me a crown of righteousness."

As he preached, Dr. Flynn was analyzing the crystals at a Queen's Hospital laboratory.

Miss Benson sat in the second pew. She was heavily veiled and her shoulders convulsed when she sobbed.

Bishop Restarck addressed Mr. Lathrop. "In such grief we must seek the Lord. In such pain we must submit to his love. The consolation of joys, earthbound, are fleeting, but they sustain us, until we are rejoined with the Lord."

Then the bishop blessed the casket, using a ti leaf to sprinkle the holy water. After the casket was blessed by each cleric, the recession began.

The casket was loaded into the hearse. Mr. Lathrop and President Ambrose rode in the first carriage. Miss Benson was in the second with Mae McCauley.

Few onlookers lined the route; most were crammed at the dock. Hattie stood on Alakea Street. She was wedged behind two women wearing wide-brimmed straw hats banded with braided 'ilima.

It was late morning. The air was scented with unfallen rain and the sun shone through a gray sky. A black patch of nuns congregated on the pier, standing in a stiff and dignified formation. Newspaper photographers ducked and bent and aimed their cameras down the street.

"They're coming!" It rippled through the crowd.

Young fathers held toddlers on their shoulders, mothers leaned over to point to the oncoming cortege, and the Royal Hawaiian Band played Handel's "Dead March"—even they sounded still and gray.

Hattie stood on her tiptoes. She was bumped from behind and stumbled onto the woman in front of her. The woman gave her a threatening look.

"Sorry." Hattie stepped back. She weaved back and forth to see the oncoming parade.

"I'm too short," one of the women complained to her friend, and they elbowed through the crowd moving closer to the street. Hattie stuck behind them.

"I still can't see," the woman complained.

From where Hattie stood, she caught sight of the

black bunting draped at the foot of the gangway and officers of the SS *Alameda* standing at attention on deck.

"You can't see because you need glasses!" Her friend had no patience with her.

Hattie sighted the hearse, the horses with tall black plumes, the black surrey of the carriage, and then a man lifted his child on his shoulders and blocked her view.

"Excuse me, can you see what's going on?" Hattie asked the women in front of her.

They ignored Hattie.

"Look, there are violets on the casket," one said. "I wonder why they draped it in red?"

"It's the Stanford flag," Hattie said.

The woman turned. "And the violets?"

Small bouquets of fresh violets were pinned to the Stanford ensign. "They're her favorite flower."

"How would you know?"

"I was her maid," Hattie said. "When Mrs. Stanford was here, I was her maid."

"The Palms maid?" The women exchanged glances.

Hattie nodded.

The woman with the spectacles thrust Hattie in front of herself. "And what else can you tell us?"

Hattie identified Harrison Lathrop, Simon Ambrose, and Isaiah Townsend. She recited her facts while straining to find Cutler or Banks in the crowd.

There was no sign of either. Her heart sank. A curtain of mist descended. It was as if shadowy gauze were being pulled on the final act of a badly acted play. A soloist from the Royal Hawaiian Band sang "Aloha 'Oe."

From her angle of vision, Hattie could see Captain Dowdell accept Mrs. Stanford's casket at the foot of the gangway. The casket would be placed in the forward part of the ship, in a black-draped partition of the mail room.

"Who's that woman?"

"Miss Benson, Mrs. Stanford's secretary."

"So *she's* the one." The woman's opinion rang through her words.

Benson was being escorted up the gangway by an *Alameda* officer wearing a high-choker white uniform.

"And behind her is Miss Mae McCauley." Hattie wanted Mae to turn around. She wanted Mae to find her so she could wave a final good-bye. But Mae didn't turn—and there was no sign of Cutler. Surely, they can't sail without knowing, Hattie thought.

Simon Ambrose was walking up the gangway.

Hattie watched in defeat as Dr. Townsend bade farewell to Mr. Lathrop.

"And them?" The woman pointed to two men running on the wharf.

It was Cutler and Banks.

"The young one is a reporter. The other was Mrs. Stanford's bodyguard."

"Not a very good one," one of the women cracked.

Cutler handed Lathrop a note. Lathrop read the note, expressionless, and handed it back. Then he reached into his jacket pocket and gave Cutler an envelope and pointed to Mr. Hackfield on the dock.

"What's going on?" the woman asked.

"I don't know," Hattie said.

Mr. Lathrop walked up the gangway, heavily leaning on his cane. Charlie Banks followed him and the two spoke. Their backs were to the crowd. Mr. Lathrop shook Charlie Banks's hand.

"What is he doing up there?" the woman's friend asked.

Banks turned. He cupped his hands over his eyes. Hattie waved. He didn't seem to see her. She stepped out into the street.

"He's coming this way," the woman said.

Banks ran straight toward Hattie. He handed her the note.

What was she hoping for? The blackest fact she could know?

She unfolded the paper. It was a note on Queen's Hospital stationery: "The chemical analysis of the tested substance yielded a confirmation of pure strychnine." It was signed by Dr. Tyler Flynn.

Hattie caught sight of Mr. Lathrop at the ship's rail. She lifted the note in the air.

Lathrop nodded.

❧ EPILOGUE ❧

Six weeks after Mrs. Stanford's funeral, Simon Ambrose was removed from office as president of the university. Dr. D'Angelo invited Ambrose to be the research director for the Honolulu Aquarium. During his first week at the aquarium, Ambrose was accidentally stung by the *lima make o Hāna* and died an excruciatingly painful death.

Upon returning to San Francisco, Miss Gertrude Benson made a generous donation of five thousand dollars to the university. She died alone on April 12, 1929, without even a cat to mourn her.

Mr. Harrison Lathrop died on November 24, 1912. He was buried at Stanford University in a secluded grove between the mausoleum and the arboretum. Sadly, his monument has been given over to indifference. It's overgrown with weeds, its gate is rusted, its tiles cracked, and the angel of grief has become a nest for squirrels.

Charlie Banks became a reporter for the *Pacific Commercial Advertiser*.

Mae McCauley married an Irishman who longs to return to the old sod.

Koa Lyons never married. He continued to be active in Ka Leo until his death at age sixty-two. He died one week before the attack on Pearl Harbor.

Mr. Ted Cutler stayed on as a detective with the Morse Detective Agency. His career was unremarkable.

In the envelope Mr. Lathrop gave to Mr. Hackfield was an authorization to transfer the twenty-five-hundred-dollar reward to Hattie Lehua. Along with the authorization was a letter from Mr. Lathrop to the manager of the Mid-Pacific Shipping Lines directing him to hire Hattie as head bookkeeper.

Hattie donated half of her reward to Ka Leo to finance John Nahulu's trip to Washington, D.C. As a result of that trip, the president sent Congressman Blount to investigate the overthrow of the queen.

Congressman Blount determined that the overthrow of Queen Lili'uokalani was illegal. Based on his report, President Bill Clinton signed the Apology to the Hawaiian People in November of 1993.

Hattie Lehua worked for Mid-Pacific Shipping Lines for three years. It was there she met Jack Ka'ai, a harbor pilot. The couple courted, were married, and had three children—two sons and one daughter.

Hattie named her daughter Makana Jane.

❈ FACTS OF THE CASE ❈

On February 28, 1905, Mrs. Jane Lathrop Stanford, wife of senator Leland Stanford, cofounder of Leland Stanford Junior University, died in room 120 of the Moana Hotel in Honolulu, Hawai'i.

Mrs. Stanford's death was attended by Bertha Berner, her secretary and companion of twenty-one years; Dr. Francis Howard Humphris; Dr. Harry Vicars Murray; and Mrs. Stanford's personal maid, Mae Hunt.

A cable was immediately sent to Mr. Charles G. Lathrop, Mrs. Stanford's brother, informing him, "Mrs. Stanford died unexpectedly."

Dr. Humphris informed deputy sheriff William T. Rawlins of Mrs. Stanford's death. At that time, he told the sheriff he suspected the cause of death to be strychnine.

On the night of her death, Mrs. Stanford made Dr. Humphris aware of the January 14, 1905, strychnine poison attempt on her life.

That attempt took place at the Stanford's Nob Hill San Francisco mansion, on the corner of California and Powell streets. On January 15, Mrs. Stanford and Miss Berner fled to the Hotel Vendome in San Jose. While Mrs. Stanford was in San Jose, the Morse Detective Agency conducted an investigation at the mansion. The results of that investigation were destroyed in the 1906 San Francisco earthquake fire.

Early newspaper accounts of the crime quoted chemist Louis Falkenau stating he found strychnine in the bottle of Poland water delivered to him on the evening of January 14, 1905.

The strychnine found by chemist Falkenau was of an agricultural grade—common rat poisoning—and the quantity was sufficient to kill twenty men. There is a controversy as to whether the poison was present in the water when Mrs. Stanford drank it, or whether Miss Richmond, a maid, placed it in the bottle on her way to the pharmacist to have it analyzed. Two rumors circulated about Miss Richmond. One was that she had a history of endangering her mistresses then saving them from the brink of danger. The second rumor was that she wanted to incriminate Miss Berner for attempted murder. Among the domestic staff, Miss Berner was not well thought of. She treated the staff as subordinates, which caused much ill will in the household.

Upon coming back to San Francisco from San Jose, Mrs. Stanford did not return to her home. Her brother suggested she stay at the St. Francis Hotel for her own safety. She remained at the hotel until February 14, when she sailed on the SS *Korea* for Honolulu. Her plans were to continue on to Japan for an extended holiday.

This trip was at the urging of her brother, her attorney, and Dr. David Starr Jordan, president of Stanford University. Upon her sailing, Dr. Jordan issued a statement that Mrs. Stanford would take up leisurely travel "for the purpose of recuperation from tonsillitis."

Mrs. Stanford, Miss Berner, and Miss Mae Hunt

departed San Francisco on February 14, 1905, and arrived in Honolulu on the morning of February 21.

During the stressful years after Senator Stanford died in 1893, Mrs. Stanford's mental and physical health were the speculation of many. Board of trustee members and railroad associates of the senator advised Mrs. Stanford to close the university. The United States was experiencing a depression, and the Stanford estate was tied up in probate for years.

There are conspiracy theories that imply former Central Pacific Railroad associates of Senator Stanford caused his estate to be inaccessible to his widow, and that they also arranged for the federal government to call in fifteen million dollars of construction loans, leaving Mrs. Stanford in dire financial straits.

Mrs. Stanford financed the university out of her own funds during the "six pretty long years." She used the payment on Senator Stanford's ten-thousand-dollar life insurance policy and the ten-thousand-dollar monthly allowance the probate court allotted her to keep the school afloat. And while there is no record of Mrs. Stanford taking a cable car through San Francisco during that time, there are several accounts of her walking Nob Hill, rather than hiring a cab, to make her calls on the social elite.

In the spring of 1894, Mrs. Stanford visited President Cleveland asking for his assistance in reviewing the government's case against the Stanford estate. Two years later, on March 2, 1896, the estate of Senator Stanford was released. Mrs. Stanford subsequently sold her stock in the Central Pacific Railroad and turned over eleven million dollars to the university trustees.

It was nine years later that the alleged attempts were made on her life.

On the morning of her death, February 28, 1905, Mrs. Stanford and Miss Berner hired a carriage to take a day trip to the Pali Lookout. Upon return, Mrs. Stanford rested. She ate a light dinner that evening, complained of stomach pains, and returned to her room early. At around 10:00 p.m. she called out to Miss Berner and Miss Hunt. Miss Berner, seeing Mrs. Stanford's condition, ordered the maid to get medical attention.

Upon his arrival in her room, Mrs. Stanford informed Dr. Francis Howard Humphris that she had been poisoned, and Miss Berner supplied the details of the January Nob Hill attempt. Dr. Humphris called Dr. Francis Root Day, requesting that he bring a stomach pump to the Moana and not to "spare the horses" in coming. Dr. Day arrived minutes before Mrs. Stanford died.

Although Dr. Humphris was the attending physician at her death, he requested that Dr. Clifford Brown Wood perform the autopsy so that there would be no question as to the objectivity of the results.

The autopsy was conducted at Queen's Hospital on March 1. Dr. Wood served as the prosecutor. Other physicians present were: Dr. Francis Howard Humprhis, Dr. Harry Vicars Murray, Dr. Francis Root Day, Dr. John S. B. Pratt, Dr. Frank E. Sawyer, and Dr. William E. Taylor. Also present were Robert Duncan, chemist and toxicologist; Mr. Williams, the mortician; and the morgue assistant.

The autopsy uncovered no natural cause for death, and the possibility of tetanus was ruled out.

A coroner's inquest was held in the dining room of the Moana Hotel.

The toxicology report presented at the inquest confirmed the presence of strychnine in the bottle of bicarbonate of soda that was next to Mrs. Stanford's bed and in the intestinal tract of the deceased. Controversy over the amount and source of strychnine in Mrs. Stanford's body was played out in the press. The debate as to whether or not the amount present was sufficient to be fatal continues to this day.

Pharmacist W. E. Jackson of the Stanford Pharmacy of Palo Alto stated that he sold Mrs. Stanford and Miss Berner bicarbonate of soda on February 6, and it did not contain strychnine.

On March 9, the coroner's inquest jurors delivered their verdict after deliberating less than ten minutes: "Jane Lathrop Stanford came to her death in Honolulu, Island of Oahu, Territory of Hawaii, on the twenty-eighth day of February, A.D. 1905 from strychnine poisoning, said strychnine having been introduced into a bottle of bicarbonate of soda with felonious intent by a person, or persons to this jury unknown and of the contents of which bottle Jane Lathrop Stanford had partaken."

Dr. Jordan sailed from California to Honolulu to escort the body of Mrs. Stanford back to California. He was accompanied by Timothy Hopkins, lifelong friend of Mrs. Stanford.

David Starr Jordan was appointed the first president of Stanford University in March 1891. His tenure lasted until 1913, when he became chancellor. Mrs. Stanford considered Jordan a confidante during the years when the senator's estate was in probate.

Once the funds were released, President Jordan

was eager to develop the academic program of the university, while Mrs. Stanford was determined to execute the building plan. This led Jordan to refer to this period as the "Stone Age."

Jordan rejected the theory of murder and held that position until his death. He denounced the Honolulu physicians and at one point accused Dr. Humphris of putting strychnine in Mrs. Stanford's bicarbonate himself.

On March 15, 1905, President Jordan's statement appeared in the *Evening Bulletin:* "In our judgment, after careful consideration of all of the facts brought to our knowledge, we are now fully convinced that the death of Mrs. Stanford was not due to strychnine poisoning nor to intentional wrongdoing on the part of anyone. We find in the statements of those who were with Mrs. Stanford in her last moments no evidence that any of the characteristic symptoms of strychnine poisoning were present. We think that death was due to a combination of conditions and circumstances. Among these we may note, in connection with her advanced age, the unaccustomed exertion, the surfeit of unsuitable food, and the unusual exposure during the picnic to which she went on the day of her death."

Jordan and Hopkins consulted Dr. E. C. Waterhouse for his opinion regarding Mrs. Stanford's death. According to the Honolulu newspapers, Dr. Waterhouse reviewed the testimony of the attending physicians and the autopsy report, and from these documents he opined that death was due to natural causes.

Waterhouse declined to make any public statement. And it was soon disclosed that he had never seen the deceased's body, a fact Waterhouse admitted. He stated that the lack of opportunity of direct observation seriously affected the value of his opinion. The text of his report was never released.

Jordan and Hopkins left Honolulu without any physician publicly backing their theory of death by natural causes.

Just as the SS *Alameda* was to leave Honolulu, Dr. Jordan gave a dockside interview stating that Dr. Humphris knew little or nothing about strychnine poisoning. He accused the other Honolulu physicians of accepting Humphris's statement without critically examining the evidence. Jordan's criticism went unchecked. A reporter quoted Dr. Jordan saying plainly, "Dr. Humphris and his associates don't know what they were talking about."

Two days later, on March 17, the *Pacific Commercial Advertiser* released the rebuttal of the Honolulu physicians. They stated, "She [Mrs. Stanford] did not die of angina pectoris because neither the symptoms of the attack nor the condition of the heart confirms that diagnosis. It is imbecile to think that a woman of Mrs. Stanford's age and known mentality might have died of an hysterical seizure in half an hour. . . . 'Her advanced age, the unaccustomed exertion, surfeit of unsuitable food and the unusual exposure,' either separately or combined could not cause death as Mrs. Stanford died. No Board of Health in existence could allow a certificate based on such a cause of death to go unchallenged."

The heart and brain of Mrs. Stanford were preserved and underwent an autopsy by Dr. Ophuls of Cooper Medical School in California. This report was never released nor is it in the collection of the Stanford University Archives. Dr. Jordan states that Dr. Ophuls found the cause of death to be "rupture of the coronary artery."

The bad blood between Jordan and the Honolulu physicians continued over years. Not only were the professional reputations of the Honolulu doctors impugned, but Jordan also accused them of collusion with the police to fabricate a crime and later added extortion to his accusations. Controversies regarding payment of fees owed to the physicians were followed in newspapers in both Honolulu and San Francisco. Dr. Wood and Dr. Day charged $150 each for their autopsy services—a fee Jordan found exorbitant.

The cause of Mrs. Stanford's death is still argued today. Support can be made for every theory—natural causes, suicide, an accidental overdose of strychnine, strychnine poisoning.

It is true that there were rumors that Mrs. Stanford suffered from dementia. There was gossip that her death was a suicide. And there was the scuttlebutt among the Nob Hill servants that Bertha Berner murdered her mistress.

There was conjecture that Dr. Jordan wanted control over the university and that he had heard unconfirmed reports that Mrs. Stanford was planning to replace him. There was a theory that he arranged her murder. There was hearsay about a Chinese houseboy who threatened Mrs. Stanford's life; and there was a report of an English maid who had a history of saving her master's life after a poisoning attempt. Periodically, one or all of these theories emerge as popular.

There are two unreputed facts in the case. First, that strychnine was found in Mrs. Stanford's bottle of bicarbonate of soda, and second, that strychnine is a foreign substance in bicarbonate of soda.

The events of *Poisoned Palms: The Murder of Mrs. Jane Lathrop Stanford* are fictitious. Much of the chronicle of her last days in Hawai'i is true. Some press coverage of her death was taken from the original text; inquest testimony has been both embellished and skewed to support the story line.

Just as the events of Mrs. Stanford's death are fictitious, so are those regarding the politics in Hawai'i in 1905. The braiding of fact and fiction is wound so tightly, that those who know the history of the times may begin to believe the manufactured events.

It is true that the Republic of Hawai'i was annexed by the United States in 1898, and in 1905 there were attempts to return Queen Lili'uokalani to the throne. And, in fact, there was a short-lived scheme to annex Hawai'i to San Francisco County. But none of this is related to Mrs. Stanford's death. The only uncovered association between President Jordan of Stanford University and the scheme to annex Hawai'i to California was a casual remark he made supporting the idea after his delivery of the 1902 commencement speech at Kamehameha School.

The overthrow is a fact of history. On November 23, 1993, President Bill Clinton signed Public Law 103-150, the "Apology Resolution," in which the Senate and House of Representatives of the United States of America apologizes to Native Hawaiians on behalf of the people of the United States for the overthrow of the kingdom on January 17, 1893.

The Waikiki Aquarium was established in March of 1904. It was operated by the directors of the Honolulu Rapid Transit Authority. Jordan did visit the aquarium, then known as the Honolulu Aquarium, several times, and he praised its fine collection. But no contractual or implied relationship between the university and the aquarium was uncovered in research. Both the Castle and the Cooke families contributed to the aquarium. In 1919 it came under the auspices of the University of Hawai'i. The site of the present aquarium is on property adjacent to the original site.

While the Moana Hotel was the site of Mrs. Stanford's death, the fictitious Palms Hotel is not intended to reflect any events that occurred at the hotel during Mrs. Stanford's stay in Honolulu, neither are the characters representations of any Moana Hotel staff. The Moana Hotel has no affiliation with this work of fiction.

Poisoned Palms: The Murder of Mrs. Jane Lathrop Stanford manipulates and twists historical fact to support the plot and create a sense of intrigue. The definitive nonfiction work on Mrs. Stanford's death is *The Mysterious Death of Jane Stanford* by Robert W. P. Cutler, MD (Stanford University Press, 2003).

There are many theories about the cause of Mrs. Stanford's death, but since all records of both autopsies and final reports of the Morse Detective Agency, the San Francisco Police Department, Hawaii Sheriff's Office, and Stanford University are lost, no firsthand documents exist. There is only a copy of the Honolulu's Coroner's Inquest in the Stanford University Archives.

❧ ACKNOWLEDGMENTS ❧

The research for this book was possible because of the free and public access to library and archive collections. My thanks to the archivists of Stanford University Archives, particularly Tim Noakes. To the staff of the University of Hawai'i's Hamilton Library Pacific Collection and the Microfilm Collection, to the librarians of Hawaii State Public Library System, particularly to Patrick McNally, my thanks. To the staff of the Hawaii State Archives, the Hawaiian Children's Society Library, the Mission Houses Museum Library, *The Honolulu Advertiser*, *Honolulu Star-Bulletin*, *San Francisco Examiner*, and the *San Francisco Chronicle*, thank you.

Thanks to Susan Shaner, Hawaii State Archivist, for introducing me to the late Robert W. P. Cutler, MD, retired senior associate dean of Stanford University Medical School and a fellow researcher of the Stanford case. Working with Robert was never boring or uncomplicated. He is the real force behind *Poisoned Palms*.

Mahalo to Caroline Spencer; no matter what scheme I presented, her answer was always the same—"Go for it, kid."

My thanks to my critique partner, Trisha Nelson. To Dr. and Mrs. Braden A. Shoupe, Dr. and Mrs. James Papayoanou, and Dr. Mary Flynn, ME, who provided me with those marvelous autopsy sounds and smells, thanks. For less gruesome medical information, my thanks go to Norma Meyer, RN, Kim Kiakona, RN, Jean Williams, RN, and John Haddock, DVD. For editorial assistance, my thanks to Eileen Townsend, Nicole Dumas Buckingham, Ian MacSween, Cindy Chow, Melode Reinker, Kirsten Whatley, and Rhonda Saki's 6th grade at Nanaiakapono Elementary School.

Special thanks to Dale Madden for sticking with me on this project. It wasn't a straight road to the finish line. For this and for *My Name is Loa*, thanks for believing in me and taking the risk.

I send thanks to the late Virginia Wageman, my first editor, who demanded, inspired, nurtured, and mentored me as well as so many others.

To my husband, Jack, who gave me a copy of Watty Piper's *The Little Engine That Could* after an exceptional I-should-quit-writing-and-get-a-real-job rant. Shantih. We are wonderfully foolish grandparents!

To all who remain unnamed, to those who called me, e-mailed me, and bought me emergency cups of coffee, thank you. I promise you all the next book will be easier.

❧ BIBLIOGRAPHY ❧

Berner, Bertha. *Incidents in the Life of Mrs. Leland Stanford, by her Private Secretary, Bertha Berner.* Ann Arbor, MI: Edward's Brothers, Inc., 1934.

―――. *Mrs. Leland Stanford: An Intimate Account.* Stanford, CA: Stanford University Press, 1935.

Casabona, H. "Jane Stanford's Suspicious Death in Hawaii." *Stanford Daily,* November, 1981.

Catts, A. B. "Medical Society in the Early 1900's." *Hawaii Medical Journal* 54: 1955.

Cooke, S. J. *Sincerely Sophie.* Honolulu: Tongg Publishing Co., 1964.

Coover, John Edgar. *Experiments in Psychical Research at Leland Stanford University.* Stanford, CA: Stanford University Press, 1917.

Cutler, Robert W. P. *The Mysterious Death of Jane Stanford.* Stanford, CA: Stanford University Press, 2003.

Elliot, O. L. *Stanford University: The First Twenty-Five Years.* Stanford, CA: Stanford University Press, 1937.

Hawaii Supreme Court Records: Vol. 36: 793–795.

Hawaii Supreme Court Records: Vol. 43: 430–432.

Honolulu Star. March 1902–July 1902. January 1905–December 1906.

Humphris, F. H. "Feasting In Hawaii." *Paradise of the Pacific* Vol. 19: 12.

Jordan, D. S. *The Story of a Good Woman: Jane Lathrop Stanford.* Yonkers-on-the-Hudson, NY: World Book Co., 1922.

Katsuki, "Medical Men Who Helped Shape Hawaii." *Hawaii Medical Journal* 40: 1981.

McDonald, "Sam" Emanuel B. *Sam McDonald's Farm: Stanford Reminiscences.* Stanford, CA: Stanford University Press, 1934.

Nagel, G. W. *Iron Will: The Life and Letters of Jane Stanford.* Stanford, CA: Stanford Alumni Association, 1940.

———. *Jane Stanford: Her Life and Letters.* Stanford, CA: Stanford Alumni Association, 1975.

Ogle, G. "The Mysterious Death of Mrs. Leland Stanford." *The Pacific Historian* 25: 1981.

Pacific Commercial Advertiser. Honolulu, Hawaii: June–August 1902, 1905–1906.

Pratt, J. S. B., Jr. *The Hawaii I Remember*. Honolulu: Tongg Publishing Co., 1965.

San Francisco Chronicle. January 1905–August 1905.

San Francisco Examiner. January 1905–August 1905.

Siddal, J. W. ed. *Men of Hawaii: A Biographical Reference Library, Complete and Authentic, of Men of Note and Substantial Achievement in the Hawaiian Islands*. Territory of Hawaii: Honolulu Star-Bulletin, Ltd., 1921.

Stanford University, *Stanford: A Man, A Woman . . . and a University*. Stanford, CA: Stanford University Publication Services, 1966.

Territory of Hawaii. *Coroner's Inquest: Jane Lathrop Stanford*. Honolulu, Hawaii, 1905.

Tutorow, N. E. *Leland Stanford: Man of Many Careers*. Menlo Park, CA: Pacific Coast Publishers, 1971.

Wilson, G. *With All Her Might: The Life of Gertrude Harding Militant Suffragette*. Fredrickton, NB: Goose Lane Editions, 1996.

❧ ABOUT THE AUTHOR ❧

Dorothea "Dee" Buckingham is a graduate of University of Hawai'i Library School. She first became aware of the story of Mrs. Stanford's death as a librarian at Hawaii Tokai University. Glen Grant, a faculty member at the time, showed her a 1905 newspaper clipping about the case. Intrigued by the unsolved mystery, Dee researched the case for three years and in doing so uncovered interrelated events about the politics of the newly formed Territory of Hawaii. After reading countless pages, interviewing scholars, and sitting and "listening" to Mrs. Stanford speak to her, when asked if Mrs. Stanford was murdered, her response is long, circuitous, and changes each time.

Dee lives in Kailua, O'ahu, with her husband, Jack, where she is now a full-time writer. She is the author of *My Name is Loa*, a historical novel set in 1898 at the Leprosy Settlement on Moloka'i, and a contemporary young adult novel, *Staring Down the Dragon*.